The PASSAGES of HERMAN MELVILLE

Also by Jay Parini

The PASSAGES of HERMAN MELVILLE

A NOVEL

JAY PARINI

CANONGATE

Edinburgh · London · New York · Melbourne

Published by Canongate Books in 2011

1

Copyright © Jay Parini, 2010

The moral right of the author has been asserted

First published in the United States of America in 2010 by Doubleday,
a division of Random House, Inc.

First published in Great Britain in 2011 by
Canongate Books Ltd, 14 High Street, Edinburgh EH1 1TE

www.meetatthegate.com

'Herman Melville', by W. H. Auden, copyright © 1976, 1991,
The Estate of W. H. Auden

Book design by Maria Carella

British Library Cataloguing-in-Publication Data
A catalogue record for this book is available on
request from the British Library

ISBN 978 1 84767 979 6

Printed and bound in Great Britain by CPI Mackays, Chatham ME5 8TD

This book is printed on FSC certified paper

For Devon, always with every word

The
PASSAGES
of
HERMAN
MELVILLE

Deep, deep, and still deep and deeper must we go, if we would find out the heart of a man; descending into which is as descending a spiral stair in a shaft, without any end, and where that endlessness is only concealed by the spiralness of the stair, and the blackness of the shaft.

H.M., *Pierre*

LIZZIE

1.

I had become, in middle age in the midst of marriage to Herman Melville, a captive. And I wanted my freedom.

But it's the rare bride who says "I do" and doesn't. I *did*. Even at the worst of times, I believed in the power of love—a bit of naïveté, perhaps. It carried me, however. To the end, it carried me.

H.M. (as we called him) was, to put it kindly, a volatile man, with improbable highs and lows. One had to avoid him at all cost in the valley of his shadows, where darkness was his name. Yet part of my faith was to know he would climb, looking out at times from glittering heights. That once in a while I shared his view was my consolation over the days—months, even years—when I bided my time, unsure I would make it. Or that he would.

Word of my misery spread to my family in Boston, and urgent letters from my brothers arrived, one of them from Lemuel, who understood my plight. "You must act, Lizzie," he said. "Herman is a madman, plain and simple. Have I not said as much before? You didn't listen to me!"

The other was from Samuel, who failed to register the gravity of my situation. "One can never be sure about the consequences of one's actions in life," he wrote in his lawyerly way. "In other words, act with caution, dear sister. Tread carefully!"

Tread, tread, tread . . .

I had been treading long enough.

Two decades had passed since August 4, 1847, when I stood there as a bride in my white gown and feathery veil of tulle in the sunlit living room of our house on Mount Vernon Street among a crowd of well-wishing relatives and close friends. I was almost drunk with joy, believing I had found my very own Charles Dickens—a robust and blossoming man of letters, who would lift us to fame and good fortune.

The pocket doors had been opened between the front parlors, and there were flowers everywhere in tall Oriental vases: stephanotis, gardenia, lilies, and cascades of yellow, pink, and red roses from the back garden—my stepmother's brilliant handiwork. Through open windows I could hear the clatter of hooves on the cobbles outside.

Herman stood before me in a handsome blue suit (purchased with a loan from his brother Allan and made to measure by one of the finest tailors in Manhattan). Young Thomas, his teenaged brother, looked suddenly mature, almost a man, having grown a beard for the occasion—if the raspy shadow on his chin could be described as such. I was dreaming, in a whirl; but I noticed the rustling dresses of the women, the rows of polished boots. The air was humid, almost unbearably so, and yet the porcine Reverend

Mr. Young stood before us in full canonicals, sweating indiscriminately, eliciting the solemn words: "I do, I do." Afterward, we signed our names boldly in the gilt-edged Bible that Aunt Lucy had provided, her gift for the wedding, with our initials engraved on the leather covers: H.M. and E.S.M.

I had become, at a stroke, Elizabeth Shaw Melville.

"You have taken a massive step, my dear," said his mother, whispering in my ear. "I will expect you to take good care of him. He deserves that much." Her round red face was impassive, and she stared at me through the narrow slits of her eyes like a sea turtle. I saw that she hated me, and did not respond. One should *not* respond in these situations.

This marriage was "an unlikely match," as my stepmother put in less than delicately a few weeks before the ceremony. "He has no stable profession," she said, "and there is a touch of insanity among the Melvilles. You need only ask your father. He will tell you the truth if you insist." As I knew, my father had once nearly married H.M.'s aunt, Nancy. In a strange way I considered Herman more of a brother than a husband. To marry him seemed only to extend an arc already begun before my birth.

I did ask my father about this fabled "touch of insanity," but he refused to say anything about the madness that had gripped Herman's unfortunate father at the end, reducing the poor man to raging incoherence while tenderhearted Herman, an innocent boy of twelve, stood to one side, helpless and defeated. I think Herman spent the whole of his life trying to comfort that child, to convince him that all would be well.

Allan Melvill (the "e" was added later, as it seemed more familiar to American eyes) left his family destitute, thus forcing them upon the frowning mercy of Maria's wealthy relatives in Albany. (My father, always loyal to old friends, also supplied a good deal of money in the form of loans he knew would never be repaid.) "It was a failure of nerve in Allan, and nothing more," my father mused, lighting his pipe with exaggerated slowness behind the burl desk in his study, shifting uneasily in a cracked red leather chair that had belonged to his father. The scales of justice—fitting for a judge—stood on the fireplace mantel behind him, a reminder of the balancing acts he performed daily as chief justice of the Massachusetts Supreme Court.

"Allan glanced at his noble ancestry, then shrank in fear," my father said, fingering his long white locks, which touched the shoulders of his jacket. His belly ballooned from his starched shirt, nearly popping the buttons. "Greatness was not in the cards, not for him, alas," he continued. "I felt sorry for the boys, especially young Herman, who seemed quite lost."

My dear and wonderfully supportive father died in the spring of 1861, leaving me adrift. My family could do nothing for me. I was a Melville—hardly a Shaw at all—trapped in this sad house in Manhattan. Somehow I had to get away from Herman. I didn't really want to leave him, but there seemed no choice. Sometimes we think by feeling. We go where we must, as the path turns, taking us willy-nilly where it will.

Anyone who actually read his novels—*Mardi* or *Moby-Dick* or that repulsive *Pierre*—could guess at the truth, that my husband was not balanced. He walked the edges of life, peering into the abyss, taking his readers with him. He sought everything or nothing, quarreling with God, accusing Him of indifference, even hatred of the human race. This instability disfigured his novels and stories, which one critic called "the unhappy products of an overheated imagination."

Readers (myself included) much preferred his first books, *Typee* and *Omoo*—and for good reason. One could peruse them without strain, although their morality remained in question. (My husband never cared what anyone thought of him—especially a critic! That would have been pandering, and H.M. did not pander.)

Having resettled unhappily in New York in the fall of 1863, Herman grew restive. He realized, I think, that a mere change of scenery could not solve his problems or heal old wounds. Now fits of temper interrupted his more usual silence, especially at meals, when he would shout at me and the children. (Nothing we did seemed to please or comfort him.) After dinner he would sulk in the parlor, consuming large quantities of whiskey while laboring over books of philosophy composed by wordy Germans with names one could neither spell nor pronounce. "My eyes, my poor eyes," he complained, as darkness fell and the lamps flickered. "I shall be blind soon, and you will have to read to me."

He was not modest and often compared himself to the English poet John Milton, who went blind in old age, relying on his wife to read to him, to write down his thunderous interminable lines.

"I will never read to you," I told him.

"You hate my work," he said. "You hate whatever I do."

How could he say such a hurtful thing? Had I not copied and recopied several of his novels while sitting in the cold north parlor at Arrowhead, our farmhouse in the Berkshires, shuddering because he failed to cut and stack enough logs for the fire? Had I not recited countless passages by the light of many candles, reading them aloud in the wee hours of night, making little and large alterations at his request? His handwriting revealed the waywardness of his character, its uncertainty and awkwardness. His inconsistent spelling suggested an inconsistency in his soul. I told him as much one night, sending him into one of those rages where he shattered glasses against the wall and frightened Maria, his mother, and his obsequious sisters. Our children cowered upstairs, terrified by their father's ill temper.

"You must not arouse him so, my dear," said Maria, repeatedly.

"Oh, do you think so?" I would say.

"I do indeed, and you should mend your ways. This will never do. Not for me, not for my son."

Maria had been a not-so-silent partner in this marriage from the beginning, a constant companion, presiding over meals, knitting in the parlor wherever we lived, snoring in the bedroom next door, eavesdropping, offering "gentle" suggestions, defending her son. She glowered at me, as if I could never do the appropriate wifely thing to make her precious Herman comfortable, happy, proud, self-confident, and successful. I could never, in her view, get it right. "My son requires a delicacy of approach," she said one day, in a dark hallway at Arrowhead after I had scolded him about leaving open the barn door, prompting our elderly horse, Waldo, to wander off by himself down Lenox Road.

"He is not so fragile as you think," I explained.

She glared at me as though I were a shrew, then walked away in her usual huff. One could hear doors slamming throughout the echo chamber of that icy house.

I should have listened to Lemuel, who understood from the outset that Herman Melville would make a poor match. "Johnny Harrison is the one for you, Lizzie," he told me. Johnny was Lemuel's best friend, a Harvard man, and a lawyer in Boston. He was nicely dressed, polite, almost decorous in manner.

But I did not like decorous and polite men, not in those days. I had lived my life among the decorous and polite.

For better or worse, I found H.M. appealing, even irresistible. I had heard of his exploits and adventures from his older sister, Helen, a dear friend. He had sailed around the globe, gone whaling, lived among cannibals in the South Seas, and walked the streets of Liverpool and London. In New York City, he dined frequently in the best literary company. He had huge ambitions for himself, although his temper made his life (as well as ours) difficult, frustrating and offending those who might otherwise have championed his cause.

I didn't mind the short temper, not at first. I certainly admired the alertness in his eyes, their penetration—he could look through a wall of stone. I also liked his maturity. He was twenty-eight, and he understood the ways of the world. I believed I could tame the beast that lay within his breast, and to a certain extent I did. But it was intricate work, the work of a lifetime.

He had burst into our house one evening after dinner, unannounced, fresh from his adventures at sea. Full of improbable tales, he sat with my father in his study, where they drank sour mash and debated the great issues of the day. Although Herman had no formal education, having been forced to leave school early, he managed to work his way steadily through eons of Greek and Roman history, modern English and American literature, as well as some of the great European philosophers. He later borrowed thick volumes bound in buckram from my father's library, which he proceeded to underline as if they were his own!

"This young man has an inquisitive mind," my father told me, purring with approval. "You needn't worry about him."

But I did nothing but worry for twenty years, and then the situation became impossible for me, or so it seemed. I could not imagine myself living for another two or more decades in the House of Melville. Ways of escape crowded my thoughts.

Each evening he came home from his work as inspector at the New York Custom House covered in grime, his white collar soiled, hands filthy. He carried the smell of the city about him, its reek and plunder, the red dust. He made very little money—the salary was an insult to a man of his station—but that wasn't the problem. The money didn't matter as much as he thought it did—not since we had left the Berkshires and moved back to Manhattan. I had a sizable legacy now from an aunt in New Hampshire, and my father had advanced us plenty of funds over the years, paying off old debts that Herman had incurred behind my back. Father's death had made our economic lives more than a little easier.

But the fluctuating moods of H.M. troubled me. Gloom surrounded him for weeks and months, driving him beyond what was tolerable. I could feel despair coming upon him as we lay in bed, a storm blowing up in his body. Yet he was a survivor, a man who clung to his daily habits as if for dear life.

In New York, he followed a routine that, perhaps, saved him from mental shipwreck. He rose at dawn, reading ponderously at his desk or taking notes, drinking coffee in the front parlor, with hot bacon rolls followed by a fat cigar. He left home promptly at eight, taking with him his badge of office, Number 75. He often jumped a horse car down Broadway, walking slowly westward to the Custom House office at 207 West Street, off Gansevoort—a street named for his illustrious maternal grandfather. After doing paperwork for an hour or two, he set off on his rounds—the part of the job he adored.

God knows where he went in the course of a day. An acquaintance of mine had seen him as far north as Central Park, a landlocked oasis where he would have found no ships to inspect. He often lingered in Battery Park to watch the vessels coming and going. Mainly he trudged along the Hudson, calling on foreign vessels, checking cargoes, absorbing tales of the sea. I often imagined him sitting on a bench, his face to the sky, listening to voices that called from the past, from the wharves themselves, from black openings between red-brick buildings that overhung the docks and the dark passages of his mind. As he said almost nothing about his work, I had to guess what it was like for him, that he strolled the wharves obsessively, visiting ships, checking lists of imported goods. In the late afternoon, he sat alone in one tavern or another and listened intently to stories of sailors long at sea. I dare say, he wished he could, like them, begin another passage. He was always hoping for another passage.

But he had already gone to sea many times, and he knew the world like few men know it, having been around Cape Horn and back. He had seen, and done, any number of odd, unspeakable things. Once in a while he divulged secrets, usually when full of whiskey, though I begged him to spare me the lubricious details. I had no wish to know about his carnal exploits or impossible desires. It was not my duty to wade through the muck and molder of his fantasies. He had lived a thousand lives thus far, in a short space. In a way, he was already posthumous, ghosting the streets, watching and listening. Ever seeming to wait—but for what?

The children adored him, and feared him. They hovered in his wake, especially the boys, Malcolm and Stannie. Poor stuttering Malcolm tried so hard to please his father. *Oh, Daddy Daddy,* he would cry, pushing over the consonants with difficulty. *Daddy Daddy Daddy.* Do you want me to get you something? Would you like to hear a song? (He sang in a fluting voice, so beautifully it could break your heart.) But it drove me to distraction, this fetching and fiddling. H.M. paid little mind. He would never grant his sons the attentions they sought and surely deserved, although this was not for lack of love. He was simply incapable of expressing certain emotions—except in his writing. Feelings seemed to lodge and fester somewhere out of sight, restive, shy of the light.

In the evenings he tormented Malcolm. One night he actually whacked him on the cheek with the back of his hand, raising a red welt. The boy—my God, a young man of nineteen—had merely come home late for dinner. He had been out with his friends, as boys of that age will do. But Malcolm was neither drunk nor horribly late, and he had a right to friends, as I told Herman when Malcolm had retired quivering to bed. You can't hope to control a young man trying to find his place in the world.

"It's not your business," H.M. said.

"It's entirely my business," I replied. "I am his mother!"

We stood face-to-face at the top of the stairs.

"Stay out of this," Herman said, as the boy lay sobbing in his bedroom behind a door, pathetic.

I could hear the crying and could hardly stand the sound of it, so painful and unmanly.

"Stop it!" Herman shouted to his son through the door.

I put a hand on his wrist. "Malcolm is an adult," I said. "He may do as he wishes."

"He may not!" Herman said. The rank odor of whiskey on his breath disgusted me.

"I tell you, let the boy alone."

"And I tell *you* to mind your business!"

"I shall do as I please," I replied. "He is my son as much as yours."

With that, Herman lashed out, striking the side of my head. I felt a trickle and, touching icy fingers to my ear, saw the blood: a scarlet daub that glistened and shocked me.

"You have drawn blood," I said, quietly.

Herman glistened with horror. He seemed to lurch toward me, and I stepped back. I did not want him to touch me.

"Lizzie!" he cried, reaching toward my arm as I stepped backward and away from him, losing my balance, falling down the stairwell. The movement was beyond my control. I fell a whole flight to the landing at the bottom, where I hit the back of my head on the floor.

I remember little of what followed. When I tried to stand, the hallway spun, a blur of walls and pictures. The blood-bright roses in the copper vase seemed to explode. There was a high thin whine,

a trilling, in the air, a wavering sound like a jungle bird. Was it Stannie? He stood there in the hallway above. It was his voice, I was sure
it was. And then Maria came from the swirl, stood arms akimbo, a
heavy shadow. I could see her ankles, bare and swollen, and the mottled veins that rose to her calves.

"He did this," I explained to Maria, rising from the floor, showing her the blood on my fingers.

"What have you done to your wife, Herman?" she asked, as he
stood in the middle of the stairs.

"I tried to reach her . . . reach for her."

"He hit me," I said.

I could hear Maria gasp, the air rushing through her wide-
spaced yellow teeth.

Was Malcolm beside me now? Someone had certainly appeared
at my elbow. I staggered into the side parlor, noticing the painting
of the Bay of Naples, its blue flag of a sky, the white sails, the little
boats coming and going in this fantasy world of brightness. My
knees weakened, and I found myself stretched on the plump green
sofa and staring at the white pillar behind it, the one crowned by
the bust of Antinous. Who was this man, and why did we have his
bust in the parlor? I called to my husband: *Herman, Herman . . .*

"Yes, my love?"

"Can you hear me, Herman?"

He was sobbing, on his knees, beside the sofa. "I love you
dearly," he whispered.

His hand was thick on my thigh, the blunt, hairy fingers. His
beard grizzled against me, and his face was wet with sorrow, the eyes
misty globes, hot and drizzly. He smelled of old sweat and
whiskey—a putrid combination.

Oh my love, he muttered.

Or was that Malcolm who spoke? His face was white, the beautiful boy in the doorway, a shining face on the pillar of his young

slender body, a terrified and livid boy-man with a fluting voice, who sang like an angel to calm us.

"I meant nothing, my darling. I didn't mean to hurt you. Forgive me. I beg you. I would never hurt you," Herman said, blubbering.

I could not imagine a way to go now, where or how.

Particularly, I remembered standing with my father on the wharf when a large ship was getting under way, and rounding the head of the pier. I remembered the yo heave ho! of the sailors, as they just showed their woolen caps above the high bulwarks. I remembered how I thought of their crossing the great ocean; and that that very ship, and those very sailors, so near to me then, would after a time be actually in Europe . . .

As I grew older my thoughts took a larger flight, and I frequently fell into long reveries about distant voyages and travels, and thought how fine it would be, to be able to talk about remote and barbarous countries; with what reverence and wonder people would regard me, if I had just returned from the coast of Africa or New Zealand; how dark and romantic my sunburnt cheeks would look; how I would bring home with me foreign clothes of a rich fabric and princely make, and wear them up and down the streets, and how grocers' boys would turn back their heads to look at me, as I went by.

H.M., *Redburn*

THE GREEN BOY

2.

What Herman *really* wanted was a whaler, its promise of expansive Pacific skies and infinitely unfolding green seas; but his practical older brother Gansevoort explained impatiently that one would have to go all the way to Sag Harbor or New Bedford to find such a berth.

"Another day," said Gans, with a swagger that rankled Herman, who nevertheless agreed to settle for a dull packet ship, of which the Manhattan wharves offered many choices.

They went down to the familiar docks at South Street. Herman had often walked these streets, eyeing the forest of tall ships, their blackened strakes handsomely curved, masts like crosses, empty of sails. He had dreamed of going to sea for many years, since he first read an account by the English sailor William Strachey of his shipwreck in the Bermudas—an array of islands that had always seemed a magical place to him. The main island was perhaps the original setting that Shakespeare had in mind when summoning Prospero's cell in *The Tempest*. One day, Herman told himself, he would visit the Bermudas.

Oliver P. Brown was captain of the *St. Lawrence,* and he welcomed the Melville boys into his smoky, oak-paneled cabin. A Swede of fifty, his mother had married an English sailor who later died at sea, as he told anyone who cared to listen. He had a curly orange beard and massive head, seemed gruff but not unfriendly, and spoke in heavily accented irregular English. His large desk, littered with papers and charts, was nailed to the floor. A cut-glass decanter filled with an amber liquid glittered on a sideboard.

Herman's eyes fastened on a brass sextant and other instruments of navigation occupying a wooden box on a shelf below a small porthole. He also noticed a row of books that told of adventures on the high seas: the Indian Ocean, the Galápagos and Sandwich islands—such romantic names! He made a mental note of a large tome about the Dutch admiral Jacob Roggeveen and his search for the elusive continent called *Terra Australis,* a land of wonders in distant Pacific waters. That voyage of 1722 had led to the discovery of Easter Island.

Herman felt his brother tugging at his elbow, trying to recapture his attention—not the easiest task.

"What am I doing for you?" the captain asked, offering the boys a seat at the table.

"My brother seeks a position on your ship," said Gansevoort, falling into officious English. "He is an able-bodied seaman, as you will see."

"And how old the brother, he is?"

"Almost twenty," Gans said. "He has been a schoolmaster recently, near Albany, and a surveyor. He seeks adventure."

"Seeks, yah! Adventure, this is good for him. Young man they like it; older man, not so much. She is killing me, adventure. I am not so happy to this idea, not so much, no longer. But young man, yes."

It frustrated Herman to hear Gansevoort speak on his behalf, yet he felt strangely tongue-tied this morning, unwilling to unveil himself. He wished he had come alone, as it would have made things easier. On his own, he rarely felt at a loss for words.

Captain Brown stared at Herman, sizing him up. H.M. met his gaze steadily, noticing that Brown had eyes like chips of blue ice that shone eerily in their sockets. His curly orange beard and mustache drew attention away from a cleft palate. The overall effect—taking into account the broken English—was highly disconcerting.

Gans continued in a blithe fashion, unaffected by Brown's oddity: "My brother, you must know, had a recent opportunity to see the world as a gentleman should, with a tutor. Our mother, bless her, offered to back him on such a trip. But Herman, you will understand, has a mind of his own, an independent streak."

"A mind is good, yah."

"My brother has a very good mind."

"I am liking your brother," Brown said. He smiled at Herman as if he were a side of beef in a butcher's shop, all set for carving.

Gansevoort overrode the captain, continuing in his rambling public mode: "Our father, sadly, passed some years ago. He was a merchant who traveled abroad on business. He brought back the most wonderful tales of Liverpool, Paris, and London."

H.M. glared at his brother.

"You have wealthy father, you tell me?" Captain Brown asked.

"Yes, we did. But he is gone."

"And where he is going?"

"Passed, you see. He has died."

"I'm sorry for him."

Gansevoort shifted in his seat. "He died quite a number of years ago," he added. "Eight years ago, to be exact."

"What does your brother say, Hermia?"

"Herman," Gansevoort said. "Hermia, I believe, is reserved for young ladies."

Herman reddened as the captain swung the square lantern of his big head toward him, ignoring Gansevoort's brief note on gender.

"Tell me the truth now. Do you want to work on my ship, Hermia?"

"Yes, sir. Very much so."

"We have only boy position."

"Cabin boy?"

"Too old for the cabin! Sailor boy."

"Whatever is required," H.M. said. "I want to be a sailor."

"This is good, yah," Brown said. "You help with ship, what is needed, in the riggings, cleaning decks, this kind of work is good for you. We are needing so."

"I will be glad for such a position."

Captain Brown smiled broadly. "We sign the papers, eh? I will do this. Just waiting."

The captain pulled a contract from his desk, and the terms were put before Herman and Gansevoort.

"Only twelve dollars? Am I reading this correctly?" Herman asked.

Gansevoort whispered, "It's not about the money, not now."

Herman understood what his brother meant. He was out for experience, not money—at least at this point in his life. Money would follow, in due course. Of that he felt quite certain.

Within minutes, H.M. found himself signing up for a journey aboard the *St. Lawrence* that would last for some four months, to

Liverpool and back on a packet ship, its length nearly 120 feet, displacing 356 tons. He would sleep in the forecastle, sharing a bunk with two other men, sleeping in rotation, doing whatever sailors did during their waking hours. He was not quite sure what that was, but he would learn.

Lately his prospects had dwindled—his time as a teacher had been nothing short of horrific—and few options presented themselves; so this was a good moment to take to the sea, as any number of young men in his family had done before him. "No young man ever regretted going to sea," an uncle in Albany had said, and he believed that.

He signed in a bold hand.

"I am glad for this gentleman on board," said the captain, blowing on the signature so the ink would dry. "We have good ship, Hermia. A fast ship."

"Thank you, sir. Thank you."

He was told to report for duty in just two days, and he fully believed this experience would change his life forever—he felt quite sure of it.

Gans came into the bedroom with a package for Herman. "Something for the journey," he said.

H.M. took the small gift in brown paper, tied with blue string and sealed with wax. He shook it gently.

"Open it, eh?"

"A book, I will suppose."

"Not quite."

Herman unwrapped a leather-bound diary, with blank pages. The letters "H.M." had been pressed into the cover.

"Write down what you see, what you think. It may come in

handy one day. The memory plays foul. There is no trusting what we recall. It's good training for the mind and enforces a kind of discipline."

"A discipline of seeing."

"That's it. Capital phrase, that." Gansevoort drew himself up to his full height, lording it over his younger sibling. "I shall want to read this when you return, so be careful what you say."

"Oh, I shall say what I please."

Gansevoort sighed, aware that his brother had not lied to him. He never did, although his expansive nature was such that truth took many forms, and his fond embellishments soon hardened into fact.

Herman's excitement could hardly be exaggerated as he stood on the quarterdeck during first watch, late at night. They had passed Governors Island, off Manhattan, in the early afternoon, slipping through the narrows, heading into the broad Atlantic. It was cloudy at the outset, but the atmosphere cleared at last, and one by one the stars emerged. One could count them, if one had the time, Herman thought, gazing upward. A half-moon showed the outline of its missing part, burning on the waters, while a steady breeze drew across the bow, rather warm for early June at sea, he reckoned. The sleek ship cut through the waves easily, parsing them slantwise—like a sled going downhill easily—as the sails puffed and the ship tilted. The loudness of the swish beneath the hull surprised him, as did the raw wet edge of the air.

For the first time in his life, he was at sea. The fact itself delighted him, and he wondered if he could ever happily return to his old life as a groundling.

The chief mate strolled the deck, smoking a long-nine cigar. The red tip was all Herman could see until the man stood in his face, squinting as if to inquire about something, questioning without questions. His jaw seemed to move without words emerging.

"I'm all right, sir," said Herman.

The officer smiled faintly, aware that Herman Melville was a green boy. This was not unusual on such a voyage, as many young men signed on for a variety of reasons. Some sought an interlude of adventure in their otherwise routine lives on land, while others imagined a career at sea for themselves. Still others reckoned a job was a job, and ships provided room and board for a period of months—not unlike jail but without the social taint. A few misguided youths harbored fantasies of making money, although anyone with the slightest experience of such voyages would know better. There was no money to be made as a merchant seaman in the lower ranks. One was lucky to make even a little money on a whaler. Experience itself was the coin of this watery realm.

"What am I to do, sir?" asked Herman.

"Whatever I say."

"Yes, sir."

The officer disappeared, leaving Herman alone at the rail until a fine-boned, smooth-skinned boy of eighteen stood beside him, materializing from below. This was William Hamilton, also from Manhattan, in a blue Havre frock and black hobnailed boots.

"I am Billy," he said. His sandy hair was pushed under a black wool cap. His eyes shone. His light beard was almost invisible, drawing a ghostly shadow on his chin and cheeks.

Herman felt somewhat weighted down by his own name, which seemed by contrast heavy, even ornate. But he introduced himself after an awkward pause.

"Are you happy?" Billy asked, gripping the rail to steady himself as the ship heeled.

It was the most peculiar question Herman had yet encountered in two decades on this planet. How could one answer such an inquiry without dissembling? And what right had anyone, especially a stranger, to ask such a question? How could one possibly vouchsafe the truth of one's answer?

Herman nevertheless ventured a reply. "Happy enough, I should hope. It's my first time at sea."

"Mine, too."

"Perhaps we should hold on to our judgment for a piece?"

"I hold on to nothing but this rail."

Herman soon learned the astonishing truth of this. Billy apparently held no grudges: an unusual thing aboard ship, which is a container of grudges. It was not easy to refrain from bitterness or avoid aggravation, as men on a ship grate against one another in close quarters, chafing and rubbing, sometimes clashing. More usually they test and taunt. There is a good deal of boasting as well, especially at night on long watches, when the old dogs gather about the windlass and the stories begin. The green boys stand apart and try to listen, although at ten or fifteen paces from the speaker the voice is absorbed by the winds, the ship's slicing motion, the snap of sails and low perpetual whine of the rigging.

Life at sea is stories. That was the first lesson that Herman Melville learned on this crossing to Liverpool. And he made sure to record these tales, as soon as he could, in the journal that Gansevoort had given him—its white pages like snowy fields devoid of footsteps. He propped himself on one elbow in his bunk, in the snug glow of a whale-oil lantern, making observations, trying to recall what he had seen and heard. He would include snippets of tales, hoping that these fragments would jog his memory in later years.

"I lived a dream most of the time," he wrote one night. "And when I could erase the ship and its pressing atmosphere, almost believed I was in some fairy world, and I half expected to hear myself called to, out of the clear blue, or from the depths of the sea.

But I did not have much leisure to indulge in such thoughts; for the men were now getting stun'-sails ready to hoist aloft, as the wind was getting fairer and fairer for us; and these stun'-sails are light canvas which are spread at such times, away out beyond the ends of the yards, where they overhang the wide water, like the wings of a great bird." He read this passage again, nodding to himself, grunting with satisfaction. It was good, he thought. Excellent, in fact!

The stories of the older men held him fast, as they talked of distant ports in Gibraltar, Bombay, Rio, Valparaíso. They spoke of the haunted isles of the South Seas, where lithe young women with nut-colored skin swarmed the ships as soon as they dropped anchor. They would climb aboard, eagerly offering their bodies to hungry sailors who had not been with a woman for months, even years. The conventional boundaries broke in these circumstances. All the normal rules of social intercourse no longer applied.

Herman sensed a strange but agreeable attraction between himself and Billy Hamilton. An invisible wire drew them together, as one night on watch when their conversation took a sudden turn in the most intimate and surprising direction.

"Have you made love to a girl?" Billy asked.

The manner of the inquiry seemed thoroughly innocent, and yet it was a most shocking thing to ask on short acquaintance, even aboard a ship of men.

Herman thought carefully about his response. It was frankness that empowered his friendship with Billy, and he would not sacrifice this. "I have not yet had much occasion for relations of this kind," he said. "So the answer would be no. I have not yet had this opportunity."

"My sister had a friend at school, a lovely black-eyed girl," Billy said, more to himself than to Herman. "Her name was indeed Susan. I called her my black-eyed Susan."

"A good name, Susan," Herman said, relieved to feel the lamp of attention move away. "And you enjoyed physical relations with this young flower?"

"I did not," said Billy. "It was much on my mind at one point. I think of her still. The opportunity, as you say, arose, but it faded as quickly. I do wonder at my hesitance."

And so the friendship began, with revelations and frank conversation, in a spirit of inquiry. Herman realized that with a friend like Billy life at sea was infinitely more acceptable: you did not feel quite so alone. He sought the company of Billy Hamilton each day, and his presence lightened any occasion. They had nearly adjacent bunks in the forecastle, and sometimes he woke early to watch his new friend as he slept, his pale lips pursed in a peculiar way, his eyelids fluttering.

Another New Yorker aboard the *St. Lawrence* was Robert Jackson, a man of thirty-one, with a pockmarked face and yellow-green eyes. He blazed with the fever of a life ill spent in foreign parts, and he had been everywhere: to remote islands east of India, to the African coast and the lusty ports of South America. He praised the rank debauchery of brothels in the Far East, where women had—as he put it—"no sensible restraints." They were, he said, "wide open country." He suffered from bodily ailments resulting from his behavior, or so it seemed. Large tracts of skin had fallen from his back and neck, coming away in patches. He had running sores on his hands and feet. He coughed throughout the night, often disgorging blood into a handkerchief that had become permanently stained, a disgusting piece of cloth that lay on the floor beneath his bunk and stank.

Jackson had been at sea for much of his adult life, circling the globe countless times, although this depth of experience brought no similar depth of wisdom. He was bad-tempered, violent, and petty. Whenever and wherever he could, he made those beneath him feel uncomfortable, though in the company of any officer he remained polite, even obsequious. And the captain looked well upon him. "Jackson, come to my cabin for a word," he would say.

What sort of word might this be?

The captain of a ship rarely invited anyone except another officer into his cabin. He dined alone most nights, served by Moses Walker, a tall black steward (who spoke to no one aboard ship but slipped from shadow to shadow). Once in a while, the captain dined with the first officer, Mr. Shaw, a tiny man whose clenched face and needling eyes frightened the crew, had no sense of humor, and disliked drinking aboard ship, although he did nothing to restrain the men in this regard. Herman would see him sitting alone at the desk and reading his Bible while he moved his lips.

"You are reading the Gospel of St. John, sir," Herman said one day, risking interaction of a kind rare aboard a merchant ship.

The officer looked up in surprise. "You have some knowledge of the Good Book, son?"

"I have read the Gospels."

"And which is your favorite?"

"St. Matthew, sir. There is more of Jesus among his men in those pages. It is gentler than St. Mark or, certainly, St. John."

A conversation unfolded, and several of the crew looked on in wonderment that a green boy should engage an officer in learned conversation. Rumors of this conversation spread, and they soon created a distance that could not easily be closed between Herman and nearly everyone else aboard the ship. It was rumored, falsely, that H.M. was "the son of a preacher."

Billy heard about this conversation, and he queried Herman on the matter. "You are not afraid of these officers," he noted. "It is unusual."

"I have officers in my own family."

Billy explained that he was shy in the presence of officers. He

was afraid of many things, he said, including Robert Jackson—who
tormented him, attempting to give him a kiss on the ear one night
when they stood alone on larboard watch. He'd called Billy a "fine
sweet girl," telling him to meet him another time in a secret place
"where nobody would find them." Jackson's eyes had rolled like
low little moons, marbled with veins, thick with translucent slime.
He had as many black as white teeth, and several gaps among them.
His body reeked of Stockholm pine tar, the sort that mingled with
old hemp to make oakum.

Billy, of course, refused this meeting.

"He stinks of death," Billy said. "I know that smell."

"You must ignore him," said Herman.

The fact that Billy felt terror in the company of Robert Jackson struck Herman forcefully, and he determined to protect his
friend. H.M. was not weak, or slight, or especially timid. He had
been in fistfights and knew how to defend himself.

Once, near the yardarm, he playfully taunted Billy, hoping to
teach his new friend a defensive move or two. He balled his fist,
jabbed at the boy's chin, grazing his jawline. When Billy cowered,
Herman decided to cease, though he suggested that his companion
would be wise to learn a cross-hook. "Just catch Jackson squarely
in the jaw," he said. "Plug him once like that, and he'll give no further trouble. He's a coward at heart."

This was not a good thing to have said to gullible Billy Hamilton. The next night, on second watch, Jackson sidled behind him,
drawing close to the boy, who stood at the rails under a bright moon
that opened a sequined pathway on the sea. The ship ran downwind, lunging over whitecaps.

"You're a darling girl," said Jackson, in a louche whisper, coming too close for comfort. An oakum-gummed hand rested on Billy's
shoulder.

Billy tensed, livid. His fist formed a wrecking ball, and—

surprising himself as much as anyone who later heard the story—
he caught Jackson perfectly on the bridge of his nose. Jackson collapsed like a man of cards, fluttering to the deck, writhing and
squirming. Blood sputtered from his nostrils, and he groaned: a dull
animal sound that brought half a dozen onlookers, including Herman. Billy just stood above the fallen man, amazed by his own ferocity. He had not realized he possessed such strength and felt oddly
pleased by his performance, though horror competed with pleasure
for pride of place. A few other hands swarmed, in aid of Jackson,
helping him to sit.

"The bloody fool," Jackson cried, glaring up at Billy. "I'll have
you in chains. You have no right!"

The captain got wind of the incident, and he called Billy on the
carpet in his cabin. Herman could not persuade his friend to reveal
what the captain said, yet it was evident that Billy had been devas-
tated by the conversation, as he seemed crestfallen. Herman guessed
that his friend had not dared to explain to the captain exactly why
he had taken a vicious swing at Jackson, although it was hardly
uncommon for men aboard ship to get into fights.

Herman took it upon himself to call on the captain one afternoon, when he should have been sleeping in forecastle, catching up
after a long morning watch.

"What you be wanting, Hermia?" Captain Brown asked, opening the door to his cabin only a foot, leaning forward. His face was
inexpressive, immovable. A narrow slant of light fired his beard with
a reddish tint.

"I would like to have a word about Billy Hamilton, sir . . . if I
could."

The captain opened the door wide for Herman and listened as
he launched into an explanation of sorts: Jackson had been tor-
menting young Billy. He confessed that he himself had urged Billy
to take a swing at the man if he approached him in ways that could

not be countenanced. Herman was in the midst of this oration
when, with terrible force, the captain seized his throat with a rough
hand, digging his nails into the skin.

"Do not speak to me so!" he said. "How dare coming to my
cabin, boy, and to say this?"

Herman found himself outside the cabin, the door having been
slammed and bolted. He was trembling, and his neck burned. Had
the captain not understood that he was the son of a gentleman? Was
there not some base level of camaraderie among a certain class in
America, those who ran the engines of commerce and government,
who commanded the military, who presided over the workings of
the nation? Apparently this captain of a lowly packet ship—a Swede
to boot, with the pretension of an English name—had failed to register this important lesson.

It was an otherwise pleasant crossing for Herman, as he had few
expectations. Everything was new and fresh, inviting. Indeed, Liverpool arrived in what seemed a blink, vastly reducing the work-
load of the seamen. The task of unloading bales of cotton stored in
cargo belonged to others, leaving little to do aboard ship. At daylight, all hands appeared on deck, which they duly scrubbed. They
swept out the moldy corn and droppings in the chicken coops,
cleaned the pigpens, patched sails, or worked in the rigging. They
shifted barrels of oakum that were used for caulking. The shockingly slow pace pleased Herman, who worked beside Billy most
days. The officers remained unobtrusive figures who appeared and
disappeared but said almost nothing. At the appointed hour, most
sailors poured ashore, a great wave of men with a little cash in their
pockets to buy a cheap meal, a plug of tobacco, perhaps a whore.
Herman had heard the men whisper about the dark passages of
Booble Alley, where tarts might bare a breast in some shadowy
doorway or call from a high window.

The whole teeming city was theirs to inhabit as best they could.

Billy and H.M. had no money to spare, so they walked the elaborate docks of Liverpool. H.M. had never seen such structures as these, which had recently transformed this city into a major port, a destination for cargo and passenger ships alike. "Surrounded by its broad belt of masonry," wrote Herman in his journal, "each Liverpool dock is a walled town, full of life and commotion; or rather, it is a small archipelago, an epitome of the world, where all the nations of Christendom, and even those of Heathendom, are represented. And here the ships are comfortably housed and provided for— sheltered from all weathers and secured from all calamities."

Here, as he observed, were the Clarence, Waterloo, Trafalgar, and Victoria docks, each of them crammed with ships from around the globe. Most impressive was the Princes Dock, occupying some eleven acres of iron-gray water. There was also the Customs Dock, reminiscent of the one his paternal grandfather—a hero of the Boston Tea Party—had administered in Boston at the behest of a succession of presidents.

One Saturday Herman and Billy joined several of their shipmates to view a curious exhibition of sorts. A whaler in dock, the *Priscilla,* allowed visitors aboard to view a bizarre spectacle: a swordfish had mistaken the ship for a whale, its natural enemy and competitor. It had rammed the hull with such force that its bony blade pierced through successive layers of copper, larch, and oak, coming clean to the other side—a matter of more than eighteen inches of penetration. The primal energies of this creature obsessed Herman for days; he marveled at the wild impulse of this tremendous fish, its compulsion to drive its spirit into the depths of matter.

He had always been a walker, and now he roamed the dank streets of Liverpool with Billy or, much like his father twenty years before, alone. He strolled along the Mersey, observing the river's metallic surface, a sheet of foil torn by the occasional barge. He stalked the Leeds and Liverpool Canal, and thought about his recent (and brief) spell as a surveyor of canals in upstate New York: another attempt at a career that didn't quite pan out. Often he just hovered by the docks to listen idly to preachers who railed against the sins of man to crowds of bored seamen. They conjured terrible images of the forked flames of hell, which awaited all who refused to acknowledge the way, the truth, and the life.

"All we like sheep have gone astray," Herman muttered to himself, recalling a phrase from Isaiah that he had memorized as a child. Guilt coursed through his body, as he rehearsed the wickedness of his thoughts, thanking God that nobody else could listen to the thoughts of another. His dreams, however lurid, remained in the silent depths of his brain, unexposed to the world at large.

He rambled in the oily passages and alleyways of this city with growing revulsion, and one day within the honeycomb of a street called Lancelot's Hey heard a small catlike voice that rose amid the rubble of a former warehouse. At first Herman thought he'd imagined the forlorn cry. But the voice came again, luring him down a set of stone stairs to a pit where in one dismal, reeking corner he found a broken madonna. She suckled two scrawny infants: one hung from each empty breast, and the woman's head was bowed as she wailed, moaned, or wheezed—the sound hardly fit any human description. One of the infants glanced up, as if searching for Herman's gaze, then closed its eyes again. The woman herself made an effort to lift her head, glancing at her appalled visitor briefly, without expression, before lowering her gaze.

"I'll find help," he said.

Returning to the brighter world he accosted a policeman, who merely shrugged. It clearly annoyed him that anyone should seek him out on such a topic. "That is not my street, sir," he said. "Not a bit." Then he questioned the young sailor: "Are you not a Yank, man? I can tell by your talk. Get back to whatever ship is yours, then. Go where you came from."

Herman shook his head. He went in search of food and drink, returning with a pail of milk and a loaf of bread—gifts from a young kitchen maid who worked in a boardinghouse near the docks. He bent to the poor mother, giving a sip or two of milk to one of the infants; the other refused, clenching its jaws as tightly as its eyes. It had obviously given up on the prospects of life. The mother said nothing, although she opened her mouth for a crumb of bread, which Herman laid on her tongue. He tried to give her milk, but she pressed her lips together tightly and refused anything additional. Her fate, it seemed, was sealed. So Herman left the bread and milk beside this sad tableau, aware that nourishment was not the issue here, in this rank cellar hole where hope itself had taken flight.

He recalled a phrase in a poem by Robert Burns, about man's inhumanity to man, with its final stanza emblazoned in his mind:

O Death! the poor man's dearest friend,
The kindest and the best!
Welcome the hour my aged limbs
Are laid with thee at rest!
The great, the wealthy fear thy blow,
From pomp and pleasure torn,
But, oh! a blest relief for those
That weary-laden mourn!

Herman thought about this wretched woman and her infants: these abandoned scraps of human life. If we could actually comprehend the truth of what happened daily in the dark streets of New York or Liverpool, London or Calcutta, we should never sleep again, he decided. It would hurt too much to know about these things.

A few days later, having slept fitfully since his last visit, H.M. returned to the vault, lured by curiosity more than any wish to provide further help. Descending into the cave he found the mother and her infants gone, erased altogether from the picture. Quicklime glistened in the spot where they had knelt, and the air stank of death, though the bodies themselves had been removed by the authorities. They had finally *done* something, being aware you could not leave corpses rotting, not even in this unofficial chamber of torture. Disease could spread rapidly from mounds of decomposing flesh, and modern hygiene required disinfection. This was the nineteenth century, after all, not the Middle Ages.

A while later, H.M. sat in the Peacock, a clamorous and steamy alehouse by the docks, with a glass in hand, attempting to console himself as best he could. He could hear above the crowd a piping English voice belonging to a handsome gentleman, perhaps in his mid-twenties, who spoke loudly of his wish to visit the United States, which he called "a beacon, a fine nation." This assertion met with some resistance, but he would have none of what he called "their grudge against a real democracy." He was a good-looking young man: his hands were milky and soft, the nails clean and clipped. He had no beard or mustache, a pale complexion. His expensively tailored wardrobe included a colorful waistcoat and a high white collar. One did not see many young men of his class or comportment within sight or sound of the docks, with their network of cellars, sinks, and hovels. Most of the fellows in the Peacock wore canvas trousers, had scruffy cheeks, and smelled of months at sea, a ripe odor resulting from a lack of hot water and soap. A fair number spoke no English.

"So you wish to visit my country," H.M. said, appearing at the man's elbow.

"And who might you be?"

"Call me what you please, but the name is Melville."

"I say, Mudville. Are you from New York, then?"

"You're an intuitive fellow," Herman said. He had seen Gansevoort adopt such an outgoing manner in public, but he usually held back. "I'm from Manhattan, yes. As was my father before me— may he rest in peace."

The gentleman introduced himself as Harry Crawford, and before long he and Herman took off together along the quay for a breath of night air, as it was difficult to hear above the din. Crawford had a good deal of capital at his disposal, he explained oddly and without prompting from Herman.

"And what might be the source of this income?" H.M. asked.

"Pater was a clever man," Harry said. "Made his bundle in the wool trade. We lived in fair style in Kent until, alas, a mysterious ailment overtook him, a liverish thing. Died in a matter of weeks. A bit much for old Mater, I must say. She followed him up the old pillar as well, or down the slide. Left me a poor orphaned boy at six-teen. I've been trying, without luck, to exhaust my fortune for the past six or seven years."

It seemed obvious that Crawford had recited these details countless times, perfecting the tone of dismissal, even derision. H.M. found it all quite amusing.

In Harry Crawford's company, over the next day or two, Herman discovered the pleasures of Dale Street, in the center of Liverpool, with its colorful tea shops and brightly lit establishments that sold everything from drapery and linen to fine bone china and silverware. At one point Harry treated his new American friend to a broad English fedora and a tweed jacket "from the Yorkshire dales," as well as a pair of twill trousers and solid English brogues. He would have sprung for a frock coat, but this seemed more than Herman could bear.

"I can't wear these clothes at sea," H.M. explained.

"Not to worry, old man," said Harry, in his lofty manner. "I am whisking you to London for a few days, and you will look the part in Piccadilly. Yes, indeed!"

H.M. noted that Captain Brown was not likely to give permission for him to abandon his post for such an excursion. Even though work on the *St. Lawrence* had almost ceased, he still spent much of the day aboard ship, occupying himself with mundane chores such as weaving rope yarn for lashing or creating hemp collars for shrouds. It astonished him how many arts and crafts an ordinary jack-tar must learn, being part weaver, part carpenter or blacksmith or sailmaker. He had, in fact, learned rather superficially how to use a range of specialized tools, including serving mallets, toggles, prickers, marlin spikes, and heavers: instruments that an experienced sailor kept in a canvas bag, preferring his own tools to those provided by the ship.

"I'm not unfamiliar with the seaman's life," Harry said. "I've reefed a topsail myself, aye," he claimed, without elaboration. "Your captain will not miss you. Trust me, my dear." If worse came to worst, Harry boasted, he would personally escort his new friend back to New York, paying for his passage. He had been planning such a venture in any case, and this might provide the ideal occasion. "You would make an excellent guide. A companion, too, as all gentlemen require one."

"A gentleman's gentleman," H.M. said.

"That's right, old boy."

The offer being too good to refuse, H.M. explained to Billy Hamilton that he would take "French leave," as sailors called it: disappearing for a few days, without telling anyone. "Cover for me, Billy," he said in a low conspiratorial voice. Billy nodded, saying that Herman needn't worry. Half the crew had already lost themselves in the brothels and pubs of Liverpool, and some would never again fetch up aboard ship—any ship.

Herman might never again make the journey to England, and this chance to see the glorious dome of St. Paul's and the enticements of the Strand could not be missed. So he packed a canvas bag and met up with Harry Crawford for a large breakfast of buttery porridge, the eggs of gulls and partridges, and sides of streaky bacon at the Peacock before they took the morning train for London.

From the perspective of a smoke-filled compartment, H.M. witnessed a pageant of rural England: the spreading oak and laurel trees, the copper beeches, the luxurious green meadows that sequestered puff clouds of grazing sheep, villages with thatched cottages, the ubiquitous churches and rectories with adjacent glebes and drooling cows. Moving at a speed that astonished Herman, they passed several Georgian country houses of surpassing elegance, and one or two castles with crenellated towers and impregnable walls. The wheezing engine drew them forward through tunnels, along narrow bridges over flashing rivers, through moorlands, swales, and dense primeval forests. This was, to be sure, the land of Mr. Pickwick, with its Tudor country pubs and village greens, coaches piled high with trunks and cases, with odd travelers afoot on gravel lanes and byways.

Glimpse after glimpse of life arrested Herman's attention, stirred his fantasies. At one point, for instance, he noticed a doctor and a priest in long black coats running across a close-cropped green lawn to the door of a lonely thatched cottage, and he could only imagine what sad scene awaited their attendance. H.M. closed his eyes, leaned back into the horsehair seat, stretched his legs. The cabin reeked of steam and smuts of coal dust, even with the windows shut.

"You're dreaming," said Harry, wistfully. "That's wonderful. Dream on, dear boy."

They arrived, under cover of darkness, at Euston, and spent the night in a tawdry but inexpensive tavern on the edge of the West End, sharing a bed overlooking a mews, where the braying of an old mule below the window kept Herman awake through much of the night, as did the heavy breathing of Harry, who slept with an arm over Herman's chest, a cheek nudging his shoulder.

At dawn, he heard the clattering of hooves over cobble, the shouting maids in the hallway. A Cockney sparrow on the windowsill sang itself out.

Setting off by himself after breakfast, Herman walked among the throngs in Piccadilly and Green Park, where the town houses of the rich amazed him with their self-evident splendor. He followed the rush of Pall Mall into the vast urban pocket of Trafalgar Square, where he paused to admire the National Gallery, completed only a year before. Finely dressed ladies moved about in their sleek cabriolets, and at one point an equipage drew by with a retinue of liveried servants holding on to their hats. Herman could not see its occupant, as the curtains were drawn, and wondered who could afford such opulent transport: perhaps a duke or duchess, even the prime minister himself.

He slipped behind the dark columns of St. Martin-in-the Fields to the Strand, where he found a motley crew of whores and beggars, pickpockets, ruffians, and rakes. The wind spun bits of paper in the street as H.M. stood on the pavement, his arms crossed, deep in meditation.

A light hansom pulled up at the curb, and—to Herman's astonishment—the voice of Harry Crawford called out, "Mudville, ahoy!" He waved his friend into the fly. "Enough of walking," he said, and off they went, skidding around corners, plunging through opulent leafy squares, passing churches and monuments, skirting the edge of the Thames. "And there is your St. Paul's," said Harry, gesturing toward the giant dome, not unlike a wildly overblown robin's egg. John Milton was born nearby, H.M. recalled; indeed, the blind poet had spent his last days in genteel poverty here, in Artillery Walk, the greatest poet of the age in permanent exile within his own country, the lines of *Paradise Lost* or *Samson Agonistes* throbbing in his head.

"You're a dreamy fellow," said Harry.

Herman had grown tired of people calling him dreamy, and grunted.

At Harry's command, the cab skidded to a halt in Carter Lane, where rats the size of small cats picked at scraps—peelings and pigeon bones—dumped at the bottom of a drainpipe. "Here's a decent tavern," he said, as the driver opened a trap for payment. The horse brayed, impatient to get moving again, with or without customers. "I dare say, you'll like the Old Bell."

"A drink would suit me," said Herman, the same man who had signed a temperance pledge only three months ago. Then again, this was another country.

Afternoon deepened into dusk, and soon a vaguely tipsy H.M. followed his friend into a wilderness of West End streets, coming to rest at a private club buried at the end of an obscure alley, where a clatter of raindrops came like a cavalry charging over the rooftop tiles. Herman drew up his collar.

A keeper at the gate recognized Harry Crawford and beamed, saying, "Good evening, sir. How good to see you!" Harry slipped a shilling into his open palm, and H.M. followed his friend into the large front hall, where gentlemen sat in clusters, smoking and drinking, playing cards. The room glowed yellow in gaslight, with oak doors that opened onto gaming tables or corridors that led deeper into the labyrinth. Herman had never seen the likes of this establishment before: the slick tessellated floor, the burnished marble on the walls, red and green velvet couches with elaborately brocaded cushions, a sense of Oriental decadence permeating the scented air. Nothing in the exterior of this establishment would have prepared a passerby for these interior delights.

As they strolled into a cozy antechamber, they were offered glasses of brandy on silver trays. Rouge-cheeked women winked from corners. On the walls were frescoes of a kind that startled H.M., who had thus far acquired no direct experience of the rev-

elry depicted in such an explicit manner. On one panel, for instance,
young boys cavorted with Roman nobility beside a spurting foun-
tain. On another were white breasts and pink buttocks in profusion,
with a variety of young women in various states of undress. Harry
appeared taken by the attentions of a particular woman, whom he
obviously knew, accepting a nibble on the ear, a peck on the back
of the neck. He called her Mizzy or Mitsy: Herman could not quite
hear, as Harry whispered close to her, letting a hand cup her left
breast.

"We shall have a bit of fun," Harry said, turning to Herman
with a knowing glance. "It's all on me, old boy. Enjoy yourself."

Herman was not so innocent as to misunderstand what Crawford meant. This was, he realized, a gaming house and a bawdy
house as well; men came to "play" in every sense.

"I don't like to borrow," said H.M., without conviction.

"There is plenty of money," Harry reassured him.

Suddenly a boy of no more than seventeen entered the room,
his lips a deep red, as if darkened by rouge. He was extremely thin,
and his white silken shirt was unbuttoned to the waist. He had the
blondest and straightest hair Herman had ever seen.

"*He* is a nice one," said Harry.

The young man sat on Harry's knee, and Harry kissed him on
the neck, rested one hand on the young man's thigh.

Herman felt strangely queasy. He had never seen a thing so
deliberate, so unnatural. But it was thrilling as well, he knew that
much.

"My name is Frederic," said the young man, looking at Herman. "I have some friends who would like to meet you."

Harry was beaming. "It's up to you," he said to Herman.

H.M. looked at his boots. His body was on fire and he could
hardly breathe.

As if beckoned, a dark-haired young woman appeared from the

shadows at Herman's elbow. "He's coming with *me*," she said. Her eyelashes curled upward from eyes like moist ivory balls that turned in their sockets.

"She's all yours, dear boy," said Harry to Herman.

"I'm Arabella," she whispered in Herman's ear, leading him down a hallway into the deep chambers of the club.

He looked back over his shoulder at Harry, who seemed delighted as lithe young Frederic nibbled on his earlobe. But Harry paid no attention to his American friend, having other things on his mind. And Herman knew enough about Lot's wife to resist looking over his shoulder again.

As he soon discovered, Arabella was a wonder, with such long legs, such a narrow waist. Her eyes glistened as she examined Herman closely, a swathe of hair cutting across her forehead like a crow's wing. She smiled at him coyly, kissing him on the forehead when they stopped before a door that led to her candlelit room.

"Here we are, Harold," she said.

"Herman," he said. "I'm Herman . . . Morgan."

"A pirate's name," she said, with a sly grin.

As it were, H.M. would never forget what happened that night, nor would he ever divulge this secret to the world. Certain things, he decided, are better left in some obscure corner of memory, packages one never quite unpacks.

H.M. stood on the deck of the *St. Lawrence* and watched as the docks of Liverpool fell away in the damp gunmetal gray of distance. A low mist swirled, and soon nothing could be seen of shore. He said to Billy, who stood beside him, "You would be surprised, I think, if I told you everything about my visit to London."

"Tell me all, dear oracle."

Billy tried as best he could to persuade Herman to reveal the depths of his wicked behavior in London, his utter debasement, but Herman resisted. It was bad enough that Harry Crawford was aboard. It would have been easier to forget everything without his presence on the ship. Fortunately, Harry could not easily mix with his newly discovered American friend: the rules of the sea subtly discouraged connections between the higher class of passengers and ordinary seamen, although Harry did somehow manage to converse a good deal with Billy Hamilton, who charmed him, as he had charmed Herman.

Herman had not been prepared for the trouble in steerage that occupied them on the return voyage, having taken for granted the relative lack of passengers on the voyage out. Before its departure from Liverpool, the ship had been stuffed with impoverished immigrants, mostly Irish, who had been exiled by famine and disease. For some years, they had suffered late blight on their potatoes—the primary food in their culture and one that kept them from starvation in better years. A million or more men and women, with their children and grandchildren, had left home in desperation, and hundreds now crowded below in rude bunks, barely able to stand or move about; they pressed against the cooking fire near the hatch, eager to warm themselves or collect a bowl of soup. Fevers spread easily in such quarters, and they did. The dread word "cholera" could be heard in terrified whispers about the ship.

The journey from Liverpool to New York City might last anywhere from eighteen to fifty days, depending on the strength and direction of winds, the kind of ship, and the luck of the Irish. The *St. Lawrence* was, as H.M. knew, a fast ship, and from the outset he could feel a stiff westerly blow, with high clouds racing against the sky. All signs pointed toward a swift journey.

Curiosity drew Herman into the ill-lit chambers of steerage one day, and the apparition shocked him: faces like strange flowers bobbed on the stems of thin necks, a sickly bouquet. Dirty children

moved about slowly and with strange quietness, begging for crumbs
of bread from bedraggled mothers or random adults. Wizened and
white-haired immigrants leaned against wooden casks, speechless
with sorrow, wondering what trick of fate had pried them loose
from native soil, set them on these perilous seas. Young men huddled on trunks, trading stories and smoking tea leaves; their vaguely
sweet vapors filled the cabin, offering relief from the predominat-
ing stench, the reek of human beings in a state of peril, the fumes
of sweating selves, with the odor of urine always too apparent.
There was a corner where the young wives and eligible maidens
gathered to talk about their futures in low voices, trading rumors
about this promised land of milk and honey that lay before them—
at least in theory.

Many of them stared at Herman like a visitor from a strange
planet. What did he want with them? Was he there to make trouble, or looking for someone in particular? Was he just another one
of those who gawked at scenes of tragedy and despair, seeking reas-
surance that they were not themselves in trouble?

"A piece of bread, sir?" asked a small boy, tugging at Herman's
sweater.

H.M. fished a piece of hard candy from a pocket and placed it
in the boy's palm, then withdrew. He was out of place in steerage,
and he knew it.

The ship had been at sea for barely a week when the dying
began in earnest. The dead were often pulled from the clutches of
their wives and husbands, fathers and mothers: the living could not
let go. Within hours, they rolled the bodies in damp bedding, tossing them overboard into the wake as the ship beat on through dull
seas, indifferent to these scenes of human suffering. It was shocking
how quickly cholera diminished the ranks of the passengers and, in
three cases, the crew. It was impossible to contain the disease, as the
captain noted within earshot of H.M., who felt a sudden heaviness

in his own chest. He swallowed with difficulty, touched his damp forehead, wondering if a fever had taken hold.

One day Herman sat on the windlass with Billy during first morning watch, delighted to have him to himself. They watched the billows, with their avalanching foam. The ship made a crisp cutting sound as the keel parsed the sea. They bantered easily, with Herman teasing Billy about the attentions paid to him by Harry Crawford. Such talk—the lightest of banter—put out of mind the horror of the dying immigrants below.

Suddenly Billy grew serious. "Are you afraid of death?" he asked.

Herman did not have a ready answer.

"I have no faith in God's mercy," said Billy. "He is not a very nice God, I fear."

"What do you mean?"

"Have you looked below? Or seen the bodies dropped into the swill?"

"It is a contagion, beyond control."

"It's in God's control, and He seems quite willing to let them suffer."

"Let *us* suffer," H.M. added.

"We suffer. Yes, we do."

At this, the sound of an organ rose, as if to replace suffering with beauty. It was Carlo, the black-eyed Italian boy, who often wandered about the decks with his instrument, hoping for a penny, a piece of candy, a sympathetic touch on the shoulder. He played a melancholy song, one of his *canzoni di Napoli*.

"He's a good lad, Carlo," said H.M.

"Yes, a sweet boy."

They sat for a long while in silence, listening.

That night, sleepless in his bunk, Herman listened to the writhing of Robert Jackson in the bunk below. One could already hear the rattle of death in his throat, could smell his decomposition. Jackson had refused all work for the past week, saying quite simply to his superiors, "I prefer not to." The phrase etched itself in H.M.'s brain.

It was obvious that Jackson could not work: his eyes were yellow and glutinous. His cheeks burned. Perhaps cholera had added weight to the already heavy stone on his chest. His mouth foamed, and at night he cried wild things, calling out peculiar names: women he had met in the South Seas, in India, and in other foreign ports. He declared the captain of this ship a "stinking sodomite," and railed against this or that sailor. Those trying to sleep lay cringing, afraid to hear their names spoken.

The ravings of Jackson reminded Herman of his dying father, and the weeks of violence and incoherence that had ushered Allan Melvill to his eternal rest. Herman recalled sitting in the ill-lit parlor on Market Street, in Manhattan, reading Sir Walter Scott while his father raved. He understood little of the incoherent snatches of language that his father shouted, perhaps fortunately. His father often seemed like a mad accountant, adding miscellaneous sums in his head, cursing his creditors, hurling abuse equally at God and man. Too often he shrieked the name of Maria, his dutiful if horrified wife—the daughter of a grand Dutch family, the Gansevoorts—who could hardly believe her marriage had come to this.

Allan occasionally called for his children: Gansevoort, Herman, Helen, Augusta, and Thomas. Other times he argued with members of his or Maria's family, who refused him further loans. The business of importing fine dry goods from France had failed miserably, and he still had outstanding accounts that would never be settled in Paris and Toulon. Incongruously, he denounced his own father, Thomas Melvill—a hero of the Boston Tea Party—who loomed large in the family's imagination.

H.M. was only twelve, teetering on the brink of manhood,

when his father died. Gansevoort called him Little Herman, though
a faint mustache grazed his upper lip and his voice had sunk nearly
an octave to an adolescent's husky whisper almost overnight. The
boy had no school to attend now, as the family could not afford to
educate him further, having depleted all "discretionary funds," as his
mother put it. The Melvilles lived, then as before, on borrowed
money, depending on the generosity of relatives and friends
(who deeply resented Allan for his general failure to thrive). Bankruptcy and impoverishment should never have happened to a
descendant of a noble Scottish clan, a man who had been welcomed
at the family manor house in East Neuk of Fife. Allan had failed at
everything he tried. Just two months shy of fifty, he fell apart completely.

H.M. often thought about his grandfather Thomas, who had
boarded the ships of the East India Company in the winter of 1773
after a fiery meeting at the Old North Church. Thomas had raced
beside Samuel Adams and other patriots as they bulled their way
down Milk Street, swelling in number as they approached Griffin's
Wharf, where they hauled crates of precious tea from the holds and
dumped this cargo, unceremoniously, into the icy waters of Boston
Harbor. Now *that* was courage!

That single act defined a life, and the lives of those following in
his steps, the sons and grandsons of Thomas Melvill, who had continued in his revolutionary vein, leading a bold attack on the British
fleets in 1776. By 1778, Thomas had risen to the rank of major, and
George Washington himself appointed him as customs inspector, a
post renewed by successive presidents, including Adams, Jefferson,
and Madison. The latter, in fact, elevated Melvill's status, appoint-
ing him naval officer in charge of Boston Harbor, overseer of the
Custom House. Presidents Monroe and John Quincy Adams had
renewed the appointment. But trouble came when Andrew

Jackson—Old Hickory—refused in 1829, for political reasons, to extend Melvill's tenure as overseer of the Custom House. It was a moment of betrayal engraved in the minds of his sons and grandsons. It surprised everyone that a reputation could evaporate so quickly.

After Allan's death, Maria Melville begged for help from her uncles in Albany, who continued to loan money without warmth or grace, propping up this unhappy branch of the family tree. So Maria and her brood drifted from house to house, with funds never quite sufficient for their aspirations. And Little Herman determined that, whatever else happened in his life, he would remain in firm control of his family and their finances. He would make a life for himself independent of bequests, the evil whims of the marketplace, and the pettiness of uncles, aunts, and cousins. He would know the world as thoroughly as it could be known, examine its rough and beautiful surfaces, meet the races of men, and record the wealth and poverty of human experience. If he could not attend a school, he could read and reason. More important, he could write. He knew he could write, had always known this. It was his great and wonderful secret, a private stash of self-worth. He could put into words things unimaginable except by himself.

"What ho, Mudville?" Harry Crawford asked loudly, shaking Herman from his reveries as he stood on the foredeck and gripped the rail. "A beautiful night at sea, what?"

H.M. nodded, regaining his composure. "You will soon be walking on American soil," he said.

"I look forward to it—the land of the free, as you say." The mockery in his voice irritated Herman, who merely grunted. He would be glad to get rid of Crawford forever.

A few days later, approaching noon, H.M. heard the steward's ecstatic declamation: "Off Cape Cod!" The captain had been scan-

ning the horizon with his quadrant from the quarterdeck, but he
said nothing about the prospects for landfall. Yet the signs were
there: shore-bloom had washed around the ship, with a tangy fra-
grance that recalled for Herman the verbenas planted at home, near
Albany. He could hardly wait for the day when he would thrust his
hands into the soil again, the rich loam. The high seas had their
charms, but he missed the land. He even wondered if this were his
last voyage. The experience had been thrilling but exhausting, and
he was full of mixed feelings and wanted only to sit before the fire
at home and listen to Maria Melville as she told her stories, the same
old stories, which would often center on her father, the hero of Fort
Stanwix, the pride of the Gansevoorts. But they were lovely and
memorable stories, about a better time in history.

Now fresh winds arose, sharp and fragrant, and the captain
ordered full sails. The main topgallant held firm, though as breezes
stiffened in late afternoon the order came to douse the topgallant
and put a reef into all three topsails. As the men worked to settle
away the halyards, hauling out the reef tackle, up from his tomb in
the forecastle emerged Robert Jackson: Lazarus risen. All faces
turned with amazement in his direction.

Before the men had fully secured the reef tackle, Jackson scram-
bled up the rigging in view of everyone on deck, taking a top spot
at the extreme and precarious weather end of the yard. It was as if
he had heard a mighty trumpet, and its blast had aroused him for his
own End Times. He would not die fastened to a bunk, retching and
writhing. He had something more dramatic in mind.

"Haul out," he cried, "to windward, ho!"

As he spoke, blood splattered his chin, and almost at once he
swung out, gripping the yard. The sails bellowed, cracked. And
Jackson, riding the yardarm over the side, was flung—or flung
himself—into midair. He fell sideways, seeming at first to hang in

the wind like a gull with wings spread, then dropped into the sea, which churned about and soon engulfed him.

All onlookers gaped, without a word spoken.

No head bobbed in the water, yet the mate gave no order to haul back the foreyard and man a rescue boat. Everyone understood that Robert Jackson had claimed his fate by taking his own life.

What amazed Herman most was that no mention was made of this spectacle. Even Harry Crawford, who had watched the drama with fascination, said nothing of Jackson's self-destructive dive except to quip: "Those who live by the yardarm, die by the yardarm."

One last thing remained for Herman after the ship docked in New York Harbor: to be paid. But to his dismay and astonishment, the captain (in the seclusion of his private quarters) explained to him calmly that, in fact, he was *not* to be paid—not a penny. He actually *owed* a bit of cash to the company. "And let's see what you owe me," said the captain, "and then we square the yards. Hermia, by running from my ship in Liverpool, you forfeit your wage, which is twelve dollar; and as there is advanced to you, in money, hammers, and scrapers, seven dollars and seventy-five cents, you owe to me in precisely that sum. Now, boy, I will thank you the money, if you please."

Herman shook his head, withdrawing from the cabin, stunned. In monetary terms, the journey had been a pointless exercise.

But it hardly mattered, as within three days he was once again in his mother's house near Albany, fussed over, fed, and clothed. His stories—in severely edited versions suitable for feminine ears—went down well. The family hearth had never seemed warmer than in the weeks after Herman returned from sea.

In the months that followed, he tried his best to forget about the allure of Billy Hamilton and the cynical laugh of Harry Craw-

ford. He sought diligently to banish from his memory the image of
Robert Jackson's fatal dive. As best he could, he erased thoughts of
his adventures in London's dark and seamy quarters, as these things
would only torment him. He wanted badly to begin his life again
on terra firma, though he knew he had first to tame his own wild
nature.

*That matches are made in heaven, may be, but my
wife would have been just the wife for Peter the Great,
or Peter the Piper. How she would have set in order
that huge littered empire of the one, and with
indefatigable painstaking picked the peck of pickled
peppers for the other . . .*

*The truth is, my wife, like all the rest of the world,
cares not a fig for my philosophical jabber. In dearth of
other philosophical companionship, I and my chimney
have to smoke and philosophize together. And sitting
up so late as we do at it, a mighty smoke it is that we
two smoky old philosophers make.*

*But my spouse, who likes the smoke of my tobacco as
little as she does that of the soot, carries on her war
against both. I live in continual dread lest, like the
golden bowl, the pipes of me and my chimney shall yet
be broken . . . She herself is incessantly answering,
incessantly besetting me with her terrible alacrity for
improvement, which is a softer name for destruction.*

H.M., "I and My Chimney"

LIZZIE

3.

My family pulled any number of strings to get Herman a job at the Custom House in 1866. And so by day he wandered the busy docks of Manhattan, surveying all manner of cargo, checking lists against lists, writing reports that nobody would read, listening to stories— he never tired of stories. He worked long days, six days per week, and for these efforts he was paid $4 per day—a mere gesture in the direction of an income. Nevertheless it was a respectable position, appropriate for him. His grandfather had, after all, spent decades in the Custom House at Boston Harbor, and his friend Hawthorne had done the same thing in Salem, so the position had some resonance in the windy attic of his mind.

It relieved me to hear the door close in the morning, the lock turn, and Herman's footsteps on the pavement. I would peek through the gauze curtains to see if, indeed, he had begun his solitary trek, always in dark glasses, a walking stick in hand. While he was gone, I would have a stretch of peace—if I could avoid his beastly mother.

The avoidance of Maria—a robust figure with her round red face and ugly mustache—became a minor occupation; she had a way of looming, and if she managed to corner me, she would offer advice, feigning good intentions. If one agreed with her, as signaled by a nod, all was well. "Quite so, Maria," I would say, as needed. But when I disagreed, she would shake her head gravely, as if to say: *I always knew that my dear son had married an ignorant shrew!*

Often I would steal away to the holy sanctuary of All Souls, where I had begun to have a life of my own, a sense of peace. My husband had no time for religion, not in the usual sense. He held long, rhapsodic disputations with God, I dare say. He raved and ranted, shaking a fist at heaven. But once, when I asked bluntly if he believed in the Almighty, he burst into cackles, as if I had asked the most amusing question. "My poor dear Lizzie," he said, "you already have had *one* almighty father. Do you require another?"

How could he talk this way about my father, a man who wore his greatness lightly? It was on the residue of his funds, of course, that we survived at all.

I could drag H.M. to services now and then: he admired decorous behavior, and churchgoing was suitably decorous. There was a period during our thirteen years in the Berkshires when I could count on him to sit beside me in our family pew in Pittsfield on Sunday mornings, his head bowed, his shoes moderately clean, his hair less tangled and filthy than usual. In the early morning, he often read the Bible with maniacal vengeance, though it was the Old Testament that intrigued him and that he quoted at the breakfast table as if it were the morning news. He preferred a slaughtering and violent-tempered God, the sort who might boom from a burning bush or turn people into pillars of salt, to our gentle Lord and

His sandal-shod followers, who turned the other cheek when struck. H.M. did not turn a cheek.

He was full of resentments, grudges, and ill opinions of various neighbors, literary friends, and relations. My family had not worked quite hard enough to secure him a government appointment, he told me. (He—the least diplomatic of men—had hoped for a consulship in Florence or some such place.) The critics had obviously failed to discover his genius. Even his early admirers had abandoned him in mid-flight after the disaster of *Mardi*—a novel which the New York *Examiner* had called "a tedious fantasy of travel by sea that fails on every count as a narrative. It begins well, but it ends in the mists of confusion and incoherent dreaming. Mr. Melville himself must wonder what he has wrought. Readers will not stay with him long enough to make an informed decision."

Friends cheated him, almost invariably. Even those who loaned him large sums of money behind my back had somehow not lived up to their end of the bargain—in his view. It seemed (to him) that nobody worked to further his interests, and nobody cared what became of him. He sensed, quite rightly, that my family in Boston had lost respect for him. This was certainly true of my brothers, who had never acquired enough respect for Herman to say they had lost it. My father, on the other hand, had found something agreeable in him, though I doubt he read his son-in-law's novels with much attention. Indeed, if Herman referred to something in a book of his, my father would aggressively change the direction of the conversation: a sure sign that he had no rabbit of substance to pull from his hat. My stepmother, whom Herman called "the savage" (her name was Hope Savage Shaw), considered him thoroughly irresponsible. "A man who fails to make a living for his family, fails as a man," she would say.

In his forties, H.M. abandoned fiction altogether, turning to write poetry with a vengeance: strange, awkward poetry that held little fascination for publishers. As one of his former editors at Harper and Brothers told him frankly: "Poetry is not a commercial proposition." Who would have guessed?

Within six or seven years of moving back to New York, my life had become unbearable. The children cowered when their father arrived home at seven, staying in their rooms until called for dinner. Malcolm, in particular (whom we called Mackie or Barney, depending on our mood—the latter term an affectionate leftover from infancy), found him terrifying. He would come into my sewing room after Herman went to the Custom House and fret about what he had said or failed to say in his own defense. He hung on his father's words, as if God lay behind that wiry beard and wild stare. And Herman seemed quite determined to torment the boy, asking awkward questions. Was he playing cards or drinking? Did he understand that life was *difficult,* and that to succeed in America, this "hard and improbable country," as he put it, one must follow a profession or take some risks in business? (This was, after all, the frantic period right after the war that Mr. Twain had called the Gilded Age—although Herman always said he noticed "more age than gild.")

Owing to family circumstances, H.M. had not been able to finish his schooling, never attended a university, nor enjoyed a profession (unless you counted writing). Malcolm—as H.M. explained repeatedly—had more options. We had friends in high places, he said; he would see that Malcolm got a foot on a lower rung of the ladder. "But you must climb yourself, my dear boy," he would say. "Climb! Climb!"

That strange utterance hung in the air, a threat. Herman would say these things vehemently, sometimes pounding a fist on the table for emphasis. This frightened the children and upset me, but he did not really wish to cause harm. He could not have expected Malcolm to push himself forward in the world in any blunt fashion or to climb some invisible ladder to financial or social prominence.

Malcolm did not climb, as I would quietly explain.

He was never meant to climb, as anyone could see. He stammered when he spoke or fell into agonizing chasms of silence. It was good that he had recently acquired one or two friends at the office, and it was encouraging to see that now and then he enjoyed an evening on the town with boys of his own age. Leaving school at seventeen, he assumed a position in the Great Western Marine Insurance Company, run by our friend Mr. Lathers. He worked a solid eight or nine hours when the office grew busy, and Mr. Lathers often treated the young men in his employment to a good lunch at a chophouse. With a salary of $200 per year—an excellent sum of money for a boy of that age—he was a young man who deserved respect, not ridicule and disparagement.

I tried to explain this to my husband, who told me that Malcolm would be a man when he did something to prove himself, as if a job in the insurance business was not worthy of him.

The irony was that Herman had scarcely proven *himself*, at least not consistently. He had attempted, without luck, to make a profession of writing, as his friend Hawthorne had done. He tried to force a place for himself among books and bookmen. At times, he aspired to the literary firmament itself, regarding himself as a star in the Pleiades. "A wandering star, perhaps," my brother Samuel quipped one day, after I had foolishly mentioned my husband's aspirations. "Or falling star."

Since we left the country for New York in 1863, with tails between our legs, I considered H.M. less a star than a cinder, a burned-out fragment of his former self. Even his best friends in the literary world, such as Evert Duyckinck, had turned their backs on him. His *Pierre* had been the last straw: a perverse novel if one ever existed, bristling with Herman's nervous tendencies, revealing sides

of himself one should have taken pains to conceal. "A piece of madness," said one reviewer in Boston. "It is a cry of distress, not a work
of fiction." His most recent work, shorter fictions, were mere pot-
boilers, hardly worthy of notice. He produced them for monthly
journals and collected them hastily in books. Most evenings he
wrote poems in our bedroom by candlelight into the wee hours.

"You are many things, Herman," I said, one evening as we sat
in our bedroom after dinner, "but hardly a poet."

I meant no harm. It was a wife's duty to speak the truth, and
this was the God's truth as I considered it. Poetry is not something
you can force.

Herman took badly to my remark, as I should have anticipated.
He rose from his chair, looking at me coolly and without love.
I watched his face turn into an overripe tomato, red and stretched;
he gasped, horribly, then threw a fat volume of Milton at my head.
The edge of the book caught me in the left eye, though I tried to
avoid it. I knelt on the floor, covering my face. What a man I had
married!

Once again I determined to leave him as soon as I could engineer an escape.

"I did not mean to hurt you, Lizzie," said Herman, standing
over me.

"You threw it," I said.

"I lost my temper, however briefly."

To his credit, he helped me to my feet, putting a wet cloth to
my eye, rubbing the skin in circles. There was almost a touch of
fondness in that motion, though I would certainly have a black eye.
Everybody would ask about it, and I would have to invent a story,
as I'd done before.

"Say nothing about the book," H.M. said, in a stern voice.

"Oh, I shall put an article in the newspapers. The headline will read: Herman Melville has tried to knock out the eye of his long-suffering wife."

"That is hardly amusing," he said.

He withdrew to the wing chair by the window, pale and pathetic. A man who cannot control his feelings is a sorry man, perhaps no man at all. My stepmother had said as much.

"I shall pretend that I walked into a door," I said. "I am always walking into doors. It has become a habit of mine. Or perhaps a pigeon flew into my eye! Would that sound more plausible? The pigeons have become intolerable in Manhattan."

Herman disliked my attempts at irony and looked away.

In the morning, as expected, my eye was a ring of purple, a disk of darkness. The mirror said as much, and there was no way to disguise it: no powder could conceal it, although I tried. My husband had turned me into a monster.

He left earlier than usual, without pausing to inquire after my condition. I had fully expected him to grovel at my bedside with a forced apology, some awkward, insincere peroration. I had become used to this groveling, since there had been any number of embarrassing scenes in the past year or so as Herman had grown less and less able to control his temper. Once he punched a fist into the wall of the dining room, bruising his knuckles, shattering the plaster, shocking the children. That occasion had something to do with Malcolm, who had refused to answer his father's bludgeoning questions with alacrity and due respect.

My sad dear son!

He had grown increasingly frightened of his father yet eager to please him as well. Some days he tried to impress him, announcing that he had read one book or another, submitting to Herman's interrogations and sighs, that sense of not living up. "Malcolm is weak," H.M. would say, far too loudly, after a second or third glass of whiskey. He never uttered such a thing to the boy's face, but one does not have to say a thing directly. A young man knows what his father thinks of him.

Covering my face with a shawl, I went to All Souls to pray, hoping nobody would comment on the black eye. I liked being in church on a weekday, without the pressure of a service. That holy chamber swelled with the presence of God. Kneeling, praying aloud, I began to weep uncontrollably.

"Dear Mrs. Melville," said a voice.

It was sonorous and steady—not God speaking but the next best thing, the Reverend Mr. Henry W. Bellows, our rector, with his halo of white hair.

"Mr. Bellows!"

"You are not well, Mrs. Melville."

I turned toward him to let him see my eye, exposing it.

"My God . . ."

"It is Herman's doing," I said. "He threw a book at my face."

Mr. Bellows seemed quite shaken by this information. At once, he asked me to come to his study in the adjoining rectory for a conversation.

I followed, led by his mastering spirit. One did not easily resist Mr. Bellows. He had made a huge impression on the community of All Souls, especially among the ladies.

"You are so kind," I said, seated beside him.

"You must tell me everything, Mrs. Melville," he said, leaning forward. His large eyes welcomed an explanation. We sat before a coal fire, and an elderly servant brought us both a cup of milky tea and some sesame biscuits on a silver tray. "Help yourself, my dear," he said, waving the biscuits under my nose.

I munched slowly, telling him about Herman's ravings, his hostility to me, his appalling attitude toward the children, his outbursts.

There was much to tell, and I said more than I should have done. I even mentioned that he now fancied himself a poet—a comment that lifted the clergyman's unruly eyebrows.

There was a pause when I finished my catalogue of Herman's ill behavior.

"I fear that your husband is unwell," said Mr. Bellows. It was a kindly way to put this. But Mr. Bellows was kindness itself, a man of compassion. His eyes shimmered like cornflowers by the road-side on a bright Berkshire morning. I had never actually seen such blue eyes or such white teeth—nature had been kind to this man.

"My brothers believe he is mad," I said.

"And what do *you* think?"

"He is quite mad," I said.

Mr. Bellows sighed. The lines in his forehead deepened as I added further stories about H.M. and his dire comportment. Oddly enough, I found myself softening toward my husband as I spoke. He was a difficult man, yes, but he had been loyal to the family for these many years. He adored the children, however much he frightened them. As a man who craved adventure, he had sacrificed a good deal to live as he had lived, among women and children, rarely seek-ing the company of other men. If he drank excessively, as he most certainly did, he did so at home, not often in a seedy tavern among other drinkers. It was not such a horrible fault that he preferred to write poetry than to sit and gossip beside me as I knitted sweaters and socks. I could sense a warmth toward H.M. in my breast, a ris-ing affection.

"But he struck you in the eye," Mr. Bellows said.

I nodded, sucking in a breath.

He looked at me hard. "Mr. Melville has hurt you." He touched my eye rather tenderly.

After a long blush, biting my lower lip, I told him about the

incident on the stairs, when H.M. pushed me to the bottom. I
glossed the remark by saying it was most unlike him. He did not
usually lose his temper, not in that way. He might sulk and storm
about the house, a veritable soot cloud of resentment, or remove
himself for hours upon end to work on his poetry after dinner; he
might take a long midnight walk in the city, returning at three or
four in the morning, wild-eyed, exhausted. But he *rarely* struck or
pushed me.

Mr. Bellows shook his head, asking bluntly if I wished to abandon Mr. Melville.

"How could I leave him?"

"Remove yourself from the marriage," he said. "Most women
would find your position intolerable. A wife should not have to sub-
mit to indignities of the kind you describe."

"Herman would never permit such a thing," I said. The idea of
separation had played in my head before this moment, but I had dismissed it. One did not leave one's husband.

"It should not remain his choice," said Mr. Bellows.

I wondered what he meant by this.

"I have an idea," he said, almost glistening in his chair. The halo
seemed to brighten around his head, radiating goodness.

I sat back to listen, my hands shaking so that I could hardly grip
my cup of tea. The plan he put forward shocked me.

He suggested that my brothers in Boston should organize my
kidnapping. They would hire men to come for me, and these men
would push me into a carriage and bar the door. They would whisk
me to my old house on Mount Vernon Street. The Shaw family
would close ranks, not permitting me to leave. They would issue a
statement to Herman, stating that he must accept the situation as
presented. He was not to attempt any reconciliation, as this was an
irrevocable move. They would explain that in their best judgment

the marriage had become untenable. As for the children, they were old enough to choose between their mother and father. Herman must accept the fact that the union was hence dissolved, as he had failed to behave properly in the role of husband.

Mr. Bellows grew breathless as he painted the scenario, dictating the terms of the separation. It would be a grand gesture, a marvelous one, he said. I would be free of Melville and his madness forever. Herman could not pry me loose from the family fortress on Beacon Hill. That was my haven, and I could live the rest of my life in peace there, surrounded by family.

The prospect of life in Boston—apart from H.M.—had considerable appeal. I thanked Mr. Bellows profusely, taking myself eagerly back to Twenty-sixth Street, where I wrote to explain the plan to Sam, asking him to communicate with Lemuel and Oakes. They must kidnap me, I said!

Alas, the plan struck them as unworkable, perhaps melodramatic. Sam answered by return of post, saying that a kidnapping would only confuse matters. "My Dearest Sister," he wrote:

> You have an exaggerated sense of the world's view of your marriage. The world has no opinion of your marriage. I do believe that is your misconception, and it creates unnecessary difficulties. If you wish to enforce a separation between yourself and Herman, we do believe the best route is simply the most straightforward one. You should come on a visit to our family home in a routine manner, and from there inform your husband that a separation must occur, as you wish for this to happen. What would be the point of pretending that you were not party to the separation? Herman would certainly attract the interest and sympathy of the law on his side. One is not actually permitted to kidnap one's relatives.

If you wish to convince the world that your husband is insane,
it would make sense not to behave as if you were insane.

Your Loving Brother, Sam

Samuel had many good points in that letter. Kidnapping was perhaps out of the question. (I realized that Mr. Bellows was a man of enthusiasms, which can lead one astray.) If anything were to change, I must take matters into my own hands, however difficult. I must resolve, if possible, to act.

In truth, however, I knew more deeply than before that I could do nothing to advance my cause. My fate had been sealed that day on Mount Vernon Street, when I accepted the hand of Herman Melville in marriage. Yet I wondered how I could possibly continue at his side without withering on the vine. I also wondered how my dear sons Malcolm and Stannie could possibly cope with the intrusions and interference of their father. I could see the household collapsing before my eyes, though I remained helpless to put a stop to the process. I had become a spectator of my own most unfortunate life.

*Squeeze! squeeze! squeeze! all the morning long; I
squeezed that sperm till I myself almost melted into it;
I squeezed that sperm till a strange sort of insanity
came over me, and I found myself unwittingly
squeezing my co-laborers' hands in it, mistaking their
hands for the gentle globules. Such an abounding,
affectionate, friendly, loving feeling did this avocation
beget; that at last I was continually squeezing their
hands, and looking up into their eyes sentimentally, as
much as to say, Oh! my dear fellow beings, why should
we longer cherish any social acerbities, or know the
slightest ill-humor or envy! Come; let us squeeze
hands all round; nay, let us all squeeze ourselves into
each other; let us squeeze ourselves universally into the
very milk and sperm of kindness.*

H.M., *Moby-Dick*

THE VOYAGE OUT

4.

At twenty-one, Herman wanted to educate himself in a more systematic fashion. He had been reading a good deal, especially in the afternoons, while he spent his mornings looking for work in Manhattan, urged on by his brother.

It struck him more concretely each day that in some incalculable time to come he would write books—novels or collections of poetry, perhaps even travelogues such as John Lloyd Stephens's magnificent *Incidents of Travel in Egypt, Arabia Petraea, and the Holy Land.* He had known this truth in his heart for years, eagerly reading the volumes that Gansevoort passed along to him with elaborate notes.

Gansevoort was his Harvard and his Yale, and seemed to bask in this role. "Now you must read this one *carefully*," he would say, leaving a tome on his brother's bedside table. "It was meant for *you*, Herman. You will see what I mean."

Novels especially appealed to H.M., and he dissolved whole shelves of Scott, Cooper, Defoe, Smollett, Captain Marryat, and, of course, Charles Dickens, who had taken the world's heart in his palms with the adventures of Mr. Pickwick and his intimates. "A good writer," said Gans, lifting himself a few inches to make a pronouncement, "will not only inform but shape your mind, your character."

But were his mind and character not already formed? H.M. had experienced a fair number of profound thoughts, he decided, and he would set them down eventually in books that would take Gansevoort by surprise. Little did his brother know how deep were the rivers of thought and feeling that coursed through his mind. Yet his present circumstances were hardly conducive to writing or serious reading.

He lived in a bedraggled cedar-shingled boardinghouse on Beach Street, near St. John's Park, in a single room with a double bed he shared with Eli Fly, his dearest friend from boyhood. Both sought work in Manhattan, and they would feel grateful for whatever they could find: 1840 was a foul year for employment, as the economy had caught a very bad cold (some would say a bout of pneumonia—if not the plague). "The old purse is slender," H.M. would say to Gansevoort, who invariably slipped him a few bills, much as a father would do. (Since the death of Allan Melvill, Gansevoort had occupied the chair at the head of the table, and he took this position in the family quite seriously.)

Among the memorable books passed on by Gansevoort to H.M. recently was *Two Years Before the Mast*. That brightly lit memoir had turned Richard Henry Dana, Jr., into a national celebrity. As Herman read it, he recalled his own voyage to Liverpool and back: a vivid waking dream. (The chalk-faced strumpets of Booble Alley often jeered at him lewdly from the corners of dark mental passageways, and he could never quite banish thoughts of Harry Crawford and their London exploits.) And as no suitable occupation seemed to present itself, Herman decided to take himself to sea again. He dreamed of going around the Horn, in Dana's wake, sailing into limitless waters among green islands. He could imagine himself standing at the bowsprit with uplifted chin as the ship bucked the swells, with cracking sails overhead, all of this under a massive gold doubloon of sun that illumined the western sky and scattered its bounty on the ocean in a thousand smaller coins.

Stories about the sea enchanted him. In a recent copy of the *Knickerbocker,* which he found in the library of the Young Men's Association (to which Gansevoort belonged), he learned of Mocha Dick, a huge bull whale, white as a sail, who had smashed several ships in the course of an infamous life. The idea of chasing such a legendary creature through grape-deep Pacific waters stirred a wild feeling of joy in him. He could already see the reeling sky, could feel the dip and sway of the whaleboat. He yearned to see a harpoon flying through the air and plunging into the tough skin. In reveries, he saw old Mocha Dick, with serried irons like battle flags and scars left over from previous hunts, the great animal dragging a trail of broken lines—the remnants of countless victories over his pursuers.

Gansevoort took H.M. and Eli Fly to dinner most evenings at Sweeny's, on Fulton Street. This old tavern occupied a spacious room below street level, with sawdust floors and a pressed-tin ceiling encrusted with the smoke of generations, its long brass oyster bar along the west wall crowded with young men of business, who made full use of the shiny spittoons. Gans taught the boys to eat on the cheap by ordering a plate of "roast beef mixed," which meant the meat came with a heaping side of yellow turnips and potatoes mashed with a bit of milk and swimming in butter. You could get a crusty loaf of day-old bread as well, with a pitcher of water. Once in a while, when Gans felt especially flush, they drank ale in pewter tankards, rarely stopping at one draft each.

Eli quickly found work as a scrivener. His elegant handwriting was his calling card: the neat, clear script made him invaluable, as did his command of spelling and grammar. But it was difficult to think what Herman Melville could offer a prospective employer. He had no obvious skills. His handwriting was illegible, and he looked "too much like a caveman," as Gans put it, referring to his brother's thicket of dark hair and beard, his soiled collar and dirty fingernails. Herman's boots perpetually wanted shining, and the colorful plaid waistcoat he affected most days did not inspire the confidence of prospective employers. Its design masked countless spattered meals, and it did not convey an impression of dignity.

"What you require," said Gans, as if reading his brother's mind, "is a good-sized whaler."

H.M. leaped at this notion. As Gansevoort pointed out, whaling was a form of employment generally open to a young man with a strong back and no wish to remain at home. It would certainly help that he had been on a ship before. Nobody could doubt that he understood what life in the forecastle offered, or failed to offer. Although the prospect of being at sea for years at a time proved daunting for many, Herman had no immediate plans.

"I shall help you to find a good ship," said Gansevoort, in his most avuncular mode.

They set off by coach over narrow dirt roads one Saturday morning, taking leave of Eli Fly (who would no longer have to worry about Herman not paying his share of the rent). It was a two-day journey, but Gansevoort seemed to know the object of his travel. A brand-new ship named after the Acushnet River lay at anchor in New Bedford, Massachusetts. The brothers soon discovered an inexpensive if somewhat crepuscular inn that catered to whaling men in port, and everyone seemed to know of this vessel. The next morning they went aboard to inspect her—more than three hundred and fifty tons of ingenious shipbuilding, a little world made cunningly, with a blacksmith shop, cabins for carpentry and sailmaking, and more; almost anything a man could wish for in several years at sea could be found on the *Acushnet*. It stretched a hundred feet from bowsprit to taffrail and featured a huge boiler, with tryworks for rendering the catch of the day. This was more than a mere ship, thought Herman; it was an industrial site. The ill-fated but magnificent whale—a beast that had inspired dreams and legends over many centuries—gave everything it possessed to its mammalian cousins: flesh, skin, tooth, and bone, its voluminous blubber. Not a bit was wasted, although its oil was the main thing, clean and bright in burning, used throughout the world for lamps.

The innocent aura of a new ship took Herman by surprise. He had unpleasant memories of the filthy, rat-infested, insect-drilled forecastle of the *St. Lawrence,* in whose cave he lay awake for days at sea, pitching and rolling, fending off the strangest dreams. But this was spanking new, oak-sweet, and painted a peculiar color of gray-green, with twenty bunks for ordinary seamen—not one of them yet soiled.

"You will have no complaints, Herman."

"There is no such thing as a sailor without complaints," H.M. replied. "I'll complain vehemently. Just wait for my letters."

In fact, he liked very much what he saw here, signing on without hesitation, eagerly accepting the advance payment of $84, which the first mate provided in crisp bills in a blue envelope. For Maria, the omnipresent motherly spirit in his mind, he peeled off $20, as if to prove he was not an ungrateful son, despite her complaints about his indifference to her welfare and general lack of good manners. He offered another $5 to Gansevoort, "for services rendered."

"You are hopeless," said Gans, refusing the money. "This is pure brotherly love. Brotherly love!" He had always given to H.M. whatever he could afford, expecting nothing in return apart from respect. The Melville family ties needed no further lacing. "I dare say," he added, "you'll find a way to spend the cash. Before long, I shall be scratching about for you once again."

Herman had proved hopeless with money, at once contemptuous of its power in the world and cynical with regard to its scarcity in his life. His plan was, somehow, to summon from thin air large sums that would obliterate the need to think about such things. But this was not a good plan, as it had no basis in the realities of any working life that H.M. could envisage for himself—unless he found authorship profitable, as only Washington Irving had done before him on these shores.

Gansevoort knew something about money, and he understood that a whaling voyage was hardly a lucrative adventure for a lowly seaman, who might consider himself lucky to come home with any surplus whatsoever, no matter what his theoretical cut of the profits. And his brother would be a lowly seaman indeed aboard this ship, a sailor without much experience. As H.M. knew himself, he was going to sea for the adventure, the real pot of gold, setting out with few expectations, aware that improbable events lay before him and that these would shift his life in unlikely ways.

The captain was Valentine Horatio Pease, an oily stout man of forty-three with a face like a block of cheddar and a scraping voice. Fond of scented lotions, he applied them liberally to his hair and face, even to his body; as a result, he had a perfumed quality unusual, if not ridiculous, in a man of the sea. His eyes were slate-gray, impermeable, with lashes so faint they appeared not to exist at all. He entertained a high view of himself, putting his opinionated views forward with blunt ferocity, brooking no opposition.

Pease kept largely to himself in his aft cabin, where yellowing charts were spread on a trestle table nailed to the floor. The first, second, and third mates bunked forward of these quarters, as did other skilled men, such as those who steered the whaling boats, the coopers and carpenters, the harpooners, the steward and cook. One's rank in the hierarchy of the ship was absolute, and the farther aft one slept, the higher one's position. All authority, of course, ended in Pease.

H.M. slept near the bulkhead, deep in the forecastle, with a range of old and young salts around him, including a small band of 'Gees: snugly built, leather-skinned men from the Azores who spoke to each other in a dialect of Portuguese. They knew very little English and kept to themselves, being suspicious of everyone else and determined to create their own little familiar world aboard ship. They fascinated Herman, as did a robust Indian harpooner called Tandoo, from Gay Head; he was splendidly bald, his skin the shade of tannery leather, with silvery hair like clumps of crabgrass on his waxy scalp. Standing well over six feet, he would invariably challenge those who got in his way with a ferocious glare. There was a story there, Herman decided, and he planned to engage Tandoo in conversation in due course.

Quickly the forecastle filled with tobacco smoke and the odors of sweaty, unwashed seamen. These smells seeped into the woodwork, soiling the mattresses and wool blankets. H.M. nevertheless observed a difference between these relatively fresh quarters and those he suffered aboard the *St. Lawrence.* This was in every way a more pleasant affair, with fewer rats and spiders than was usually the case on seagoing vessels. Even the lice lay quiet for some weeks, hatching and multiplying, getting ready for the usual infestation. Herman generally found the whaling crew more professional than those on a packet ship; these men had signed on for a long and difficult voyage, so expectations for a modicum of civility arose.

"She ain't so bad, this ship," said Toby Greene, a wiry (if not especially attractive) young man who occupied a bunk near Herman.

"I quite like her," H.M. said, telling him about his previous ship and its deplorable conditions.

Toby was talkative, and soon Herman learned a good deal of interesting trivia about his boyhood in Rochester, where his father had made a modest fortune in the fur trade, importing "only the best pelts" from Canada. His sister was a schoolmistress, a spinster and bluestocking by nature, a "reader of long and boring books." His older brother surveyed the canals of New York State.

Toby and H.M. had much in common, and it amused them to think that they had recently spent a summer in Albany not a mile apart. Each was twenty-one years of age, slender, and blue-eyed (the eye color being a shared oddity, as each was also dark-haired). It would not have surprised anyone had they claimed brotherhood, though Herman was by nature a more brooding fellow, capable of deep spiritual troughs. For his part, Toby Greene was resolutely cheerful, a model of equanimity, rarely showing the slightest sign of distress.

Another man aboard this ship who caught the attention of H.M. was the second mate, Jack Hall, from a village in Yorkshire. Hall had been at sea for fifteen years, though he was barely thirty. He had a strong intellectual bent, and never tired of saying that he might have gone to Cambridge had his father not lost his money on the gambling tables of London. He kept a volume of poems by Samuel Taylor Coleridge in the pocket of his pilot coat, a habit that appealed to Herman, who admired the fact that Hall could recite long stretches of *The Rime of the Ancient Mariner.* He seemed especially to relish the stanza where the mariner explains that his shipmates despised him for killing a bird that had thus far brought them good fortune:

And I had done a hellish thing,
And it would work 'em woe:
For all averred, I had killed the bird
That made the breeze to blow.

Ah wretch! said they, the bird to slay,
That made the breeze to blow!

Hall immediately took a shine to this bookish young American, someone who had apparently made his way through much of Milton, Dickens, and Defoe. Their literary conversations expanded, often during night watch, when there was ample time for such a luxury.

"You will admire *Robinson Crusoe,* I assume," Hall said, standing at the rail one night under a gibbous moon.

"I have read the story more than once," Herman replied.

He adored this tale of survival by intelligence and craft, set within an exotic tropical setting; but he refused to overstate matters, as his father had done, and as his older brother often did. It was better to retain control over one's enthusiasm. "I quite liked it, yes. Defoe is a straightforward writer."

"Around the Horn, coming up on Chile," Hall explained, "we shall pass the very island where Selkirk was marooned."

Alexander Selkirk, as H.M. knew, was an adventurous Scot, the model for Crusoe, although the novelist had transported his hero to the Caribbean, a more hospitable climate than what he might have found off the west coast of Chile or Peru. Now, for the first time, Herman began to think about the nature of fiction, and how it so often depended upon, even hugged, reality, embracing true stories; but the author's mind was a crucible, a virtual try-pot. It rendered whatever happened into something utterly fresh and strange. At times, it echoed Truth back to itself in sharper, shapelier tones. Herman realized with a shudder of quiet pleasure that what occurred here, aboard the *Acushnet,* might find itself one day in a work of fiction by his own hand. He knew it would, and vowed to listen keenly, to watch and record in his journal whatever transpired, collecting snippets of conversation, images, phrases, ideas for tales,

moods, inklings, omens. Sometimes he just listed unusual words that
caught his fancy: oleaginous, refractory, priapic.

The voyage seemed unremarkable during its first days. The
small city of the crew went about its business in efficient ways, each
man aware of his role and willing to perform in that capacity. A new
ship takes time to acquire its selfhood, to forge a collective spirit.
H.M. found the emotional temperature aboard this ship relatively
cool at first, and this seemed appropriate for a machine dedicated to
killing. But it would be difficult work. On wintry seas, as he
guessed, hands would freeze to the lines, even with gloves. Ears
would quickly grow numb in the translucent cold.

Now a dry snow ticked the deck, and the sails seemed reluctant
to bellow, as though inhaling winds might freeze their white lungs.
The *Acushnet* hardly seemed to move as short northern days and
cold sunlight merged into deep starry night, with the freezing spray
off the sea always a reminder that this ship had chosen to invade a
difficult element. Icicles formed on the bulwarks, gleaming like the
tusks of elephants. The sound of the keel as it plunged ahead formed
a constant backdrop to H.M.'s thoughts, rising and falling. All the
while the vessel moved south, slipping inexorably into warmer
zones.

This astonishing transformation took a while to make itself
apparent, but after a week or two nobody could doubt the shifting
quality of air, which grew softer if not warmer. Every degree of lat-
itude worked to pry loose the grip of winter. And before long the
Acushnet slipped almost imperceptibly into the green and balmy
waters of the Bahamas, just one among the seven hundred or so
whaling ships afloat somewhere in the world and manned, according to Jack Hall, by more than eighteen thousand men. (Hall seemed
endlessly knowledgeable about such things, and rarely tired of showing off what he knew, especially around the younger men.)

Soon enough, the crew found what it had come for: whales.

Their humped, shimmering backs appeared in the middle distance as they blew, showering a fine spray high in the air before they breached the water, their flukes gleaming. The first sight of one thrilled H.M., who had never guessed it would startle him so.

Jack Hall, as ever, stood by his elbow and explained that they slapped the water to remove barnacles and parasites. It was also, he said, a form of communication: they called to other whales in the school, perhaps warning them that trouble approached.

And this was indeed trouble for a whale.

The fat captain, who stood on the quarterdeck by himself, close to the mizzen shroud, raised a fist in the air and bellowed, "We'll get you, aye, we shall!"

"He is mad," Hall said to H.M. in a conspiratorial register. His voice carried in the breeze, and the captain seemed to glower at him. Glowering was, for Pease, a normal state of being, thought Herman. He had never seen much else from this peculiar captain, especially in the presence of Hall. It so happened that the two of them, captain and second mate, had clashed many times in front of the crew, as when the captain had slapped a young sailor from the Azores who had not leaped immediately to a command on the fore-deck, knocking him sideways onto the planking and leaving him in a pool of blood with a broken nose. The 'Gees rushed around their fallen countryman, one of them applying a handkerchief to the bridge of his nose.

Hall, in a fit of anger, followed after Pease and told him bluntly that his action was "uncalled for."

"What is that, sir?"

"The sailor is deaf," Hall said. "He could not hear your command."

Pease stared at Jack Hall, as if unable to calculate the true depth of this offense. The captain of a whaler is God of his ship, and one did not question his behavior, however intemperate or arbitrary.

Even the deaf must obey orders instantly and without question. Those who failed to respond in appropriate ways must be struck down. It was the only way to maintain discipline at sea. All captains worthy of their rank understood this.

Yet Pease was not like most captains. He was a gathering storm of petty resentments and frustrations, and his darkness grew more and more intense with each passing week. He often seemed quite drunk by midday, lurching from rail to rail on deck, and his aggressions multiplied. Once he ordered a badly injured Azorean (the young man had a broken arm) into a whaleboat, which was unthinkably cruel and—for the other men in the boat—dangerous, as Jack Hall told him bluntly. The captain glared as Hall led the frightened seaman back to his bunk below.

Later that day, Hall was summoned to the captain's quarters. What transpired between them was never known, but Hall seemed chastened, angry, and determined to get revenge. All he said to H.M. and Toby Greene was that "Pease will pay a price for this tack."

The tension on the vessel eased as a fairly large school of whales appeared, quite magically, on the horizon. H.M. watched with fascination as these otherworldly creatures, forty to sixty feet in length, were hunted down by small whaleboats, which ventured as far as fifteen miles from the mother vessel.

One heard the cry emerging from a cloud of sails: "Thar she blows!" Once the exact location of the whale was determined, the captain would order, "Stand by and lower." Three boats went off, chasing the beast, which might wisely turn tail, "up flukes," and sink. The whaleboats kept a quarter of a mile between them, scattering to increase their chances; indeed, a cruel system had evolved for trapping a whale, and it usually worked well.

At last H.M. was chosen to go out with them, giving chase on the banks, the boatheader shrieking for the men to pull on the oars, to "follow the birds" that swarmed around the whale, who rose toward the surface again, erupting. There was a roar of waters as this improbable creature churned, revealing its size and weight, its elegant curves and silken sides. The oarsmen hove up, pulled, and the mate at the steering oar would call to the harpooner, "Stand and give it!" The boat pressed forward, and the cold iron flew in the bright air, stuck in the beast's blubbery sides, and the line—wet now, its manila glistening—tightened; a hideous thrashing began again, as water sloshed over the gunwales.

Herman would never forget the wonder of his first encounter with a baleen. This strange beast with the rankest of breath had breached the water not twenty yards off the boat, slapping the surface as if to defy its pursuers, diving again, disappearing. Then it rose suddenly—only yards away! The creature fixed H.M. in its glassy orb, accusatory or questioning, looking right through him with its furious eye. Herman felt an immediate connection to the whale, a weirdly intimate, almost holy sense of kinship with another living and sensible thing. He wanted to reach out, stroke its head, to explain himself, saying, *I'm not like the others. I don't want you to die.*

But didn't he? He had signed on as part of the killing apparatus, and he played his part, another cog in the great wheel. This was, after all, the age of functionality, the machine age. The poor whale was simply another piece in a large and varied scheme.

The whale had been eerily colorless, a pale shimmer of mass, this fifty-foot manifestation of flesh and spirit, weighing perhaps fifty tons. It had vast flippers, mottled but sleek, with a swishing fluke that churned the water in helpless defiance. A smaller dorsal fin rose feathery and stiff. Herman could see any number of deep grooves running along the side of the whale, runnels like streaks of fat in a piece of raw steak. Herman froze now, ceasing to row as commanded, transfixed by the beast, like nothing else in this wild world—the embodiment of some unearthly spirit that would have to die, relinquishing itself to these inferior creatures who seemed to have the greater need for its flesh, and who had the means to acquire it, however violently.

The whale tried to escape, as it must, dragging the boat behind it, spinning in the water. It heaved and spun for a while, hoping to free itself in whatever way it could; then it subsided—more quickly than H.M. thought was decent—as if relaxing into its own demise and aware that nothing could save it, that struggle itself would only compound its agony and terror. Soon the other whaleboats bobbed around, got fast, and more irons were stuck in the sad beast's sides. Then a lance drove into the life of the whale, the massive heart itself. Blood gushed, and the water turned eerily vermillion in a whirlpool that spread in concentric ripples. The boats circled and swayed, taking on water as the men leaned into their oars, pulled with an awareness that their lives depended on the effort. Always the beast fought dearly for its life, spewing blood, gushing as the suds around became what Shakespeare in *Macbeth* called "the multitudinous seas incarnadine." Yes, this is what Shakespeare meant, H.M. decided. It was pleasing to him, the way language and life collapsed at times, inhabiting a gaudy phrase with ease.

After a while the whale subsided fully, gave way to its fate.

Relieved and exhilarated, even triumphant, the men rowed the carcass back to the ship; but a slow and difficult business lay ahead of them, as H.M. learned, leaning into the oars, calling on every ounce of muscle and willpower. The whaleboats hardly seemed to move at times. The *Acushnet* loomed to one side, in the near distance; but the gap between whaleboats and mother ship closed so gradually it was hard to tell that any progress had been made, and often the whalers competed with blood-frenzied sharks, who swarmed and nipped. It was a wonder any flesh remained for cutting.

Eventually the *Acushnet* rose beside them, and the badly mangled beast was hooked, hauled aboard, cut, and tried. In due course, barrel after barrel was filled with its liquid essence.

The cutting at first appalled H.M., who hadn't quite understood the extent of a whale's slobbery gore. Yet he grew accustomed to the butchery, to the boiling in the try-pots. The alchemy that transmogrified a whale into oil took three or four days per whale, depending on its size. And it was a sight to witness: the pots bubbling and steaming, the oil drained into pans, transferred to cisterns and barrels. The hold filled with its valuable store.

When not performing some task above or below, H.M. lay in his bunk in the forecastle, where he slept or scribbled notes in his journal or made his way through another of the English novels that Jack Hall had loaned him. He understood in a visceral way now that the work of whaling, this murder at sea, led directly to the light that glowed in countless parlors and bedrooms, that illumined the flickering pages of a thousand books. In the dark process that involved him so intimately aboard the *Acushnet,* death itself seemed necessary to produce light, even the life of the mind.

From port in Rio de Janeiro, Captain Pease shipped home an impressive one hundred and fifty barrels of sperm oil: just a hint of the bounty to come. He stood rubbing his large hands greedily, directing the men as they worked below decks, shouting orders that most of the crew followed haphazardly: this captain did not have the gift of command. Yet other officers worked to ensure that the task was accomplished, it being in their financial interest to ship as much oil home as possible. H.M. labored beside the others, the entire crew plus a dozen Brazilians hired for the day, easing the precious treasure from one ship to another.

Pease knew that his employers, the craven owners of the *Acushnet,* would smack their lips as this cargo arrived safely in such quantity. His good name, as a whaling captain, would be revived, which was necessary, as his previous two voyages had yielded little profit for anyone, in large part because of what he called "recalcitrant" crews who resisted his direction. One more disappointing venture would probably mean the end of his career in whaling.

After a difficult day's work at the dock, H.M. walked with Toby Greene through the boisterous streets of Rio. He had never seen such colors, life in such bounty and profusion. He bought a fair number of silver and bead trinkets from eager brown children and ate an array of sweets and grilled meats purchased from street vendors. Whores of every shape and age caught his eye, beckoning from the shadows of doorways, baring tawny breasts, cooing.

"These girls should have more respect," said Toby, a devout Methodist.

Recalling his episode in the London brothel, Herman flushed, smiling to himself. He pretended that he, too, found such behavior in women reprehensible. But he knew how the world functioned, and that men were compelled by images that flashed on that tumultuous private stage, the human mind. He also knew that emotions could not easily be controlled, and that the mind is subject to weathers—not unlike a ship at sea.

He and Toby drank more than their share at local bars, sitting with other sailors at bamboo tables on the streets near the docks, listening to a bright cacophony of tongues—Portuguese, French, Spanish, English, and Dutch. They smoked rude cigars purchased from passing vendors and felt worldly and wise. Tandoo joined them, too: he had become increasingly friendly over the past weeks, as H.M. had sought him out periodically.

"I am liking Rio," said Tandoo. "These ladies, Brazilianas, they are so beee-utiful. And so many, and so cheap." He licked his chops in the most ridiculous fashion, which appalled Toby.

"You have a good eye," said H.M. to the harpooner, shocking Toby, who could not unfrown himself.

Now Jack Hall joined them as well, preferring the company of

ordinary seamen to that of fellow officers. He talked of "the abominable Pease," recalling famous mutinies: always a staple among seamen. But the vehemence of this storytelling worried H.M., who
could not imagine such a challenge to authority. For better or worse,
the captain was captain—the man in charge. Authority was something terribly fragile, difficult to achieve, and so it must be respected.

H.M. had been a captain of sorts only two years before, at a
school in the Berkshires at the foot of Washington Mountain, to the
southwest of Pittsfield. It was a remote setting, and the school had
no pretensions. Two boys in his class, Ed Sherman and Sydney
Franks, had taken a dislike to Mr. Melville, mainly because Herman
took his job seriously and asked them (*all* of them) to study hard and
report on their newly acquired knowledge. The trouble began with
wisecracking in the classroom, which spiraled out of control as Herman attempted to tamp it down; these disciplinary efforts led to his
being waylaid on the way home to his cottage at the top of a
wooded hill. Sherman tackled him by the ankles, while Franks pum-
meled him. But H.M. was stronger than he looked, and he began
to enjoy himself as he fought back, blazing with fists and kicks; he
left the two of them squealing for mercy. It was a brave performance, and battle scars in the form of black eyes and facial scratches
would survive for weeks to embarrass his pupils. At once he found
himself wholly in command of his classroom, and he thought of this
now, smiling to himself. He had been no spineless Ichabod Crane
in Sleepy Hollow, and H.M. might still be a schoolmaster had the
pay been adequate or, indeed, forthcoming. As it happened, the
local school board ran entirely out of money before the year ended.

Captain Pease did not allow his men to rest for long in Rio, to
the annoyance of all. When a crew worked as hard as this one had,
shipping so many barrels home in triumph, they expected a substantial break. But Pease, buoyed by his success, insisted on continuing after only three days in port.

Heading into fierce winds, the *Acushnet* tacked awkwardly through Guanabara Bay and turned south along the coast. Its narrow shingle trailed off starboard like a green bannerol, the mountains rising beyond them. One could sense the resentment of the crew as they went about their routines in silence, many of them wishing they had jumped ship in Rio. There was a bad feeling aboard, which Herman shared, and Jack Hall (as ever) put into words. "I do not like what I feel," he said.

The first night out, as H.M. sat at the base of the foremast and smoked cigars with Tandoo, the Indian grumbled, more to himself than his listener: "He is paying for this, Mr. Pease. He is paying!"

The ship hugged the coast for several weeks, picking up speed, nearly schooning as it ran downwind toward Tierra del Fuego, which Magellan had named so memorably this "land of fire." The explorer thought that local Indians wished to ambush and murder him, but that was in 1520, and this was more than three centuries later. The native population nowadays welcomed American and European ships, most of which were whalers rounding the Horn en route to Pacific cruising grounds.

This was a good time of year to make your way around the Horn, as Hall explained to H.M. and Toby. He liked to play the schoolmaster, telling them about the short, cool summers and breezy winters typical of Cape Horn. As he spoke, he gestured grandly toward the littoral with its seething pebbles and green-gray shimmer that hinted at multitudinous life—the invertebrate life of limpets, snails, slugs and starfish, urchins and sponges, pale sea cucumbers, mollusks and crabs of endless shapes and sizes. Beyond the shore were tracts bristling with canella and evergreen forests, and what Hall described as "a thousand strange birds."

One night, in hiding from a storm, the ship lay at anchor in a bay not three hundred feet from the coast, and Herman found the night strangely quiet, with the water almost too smooth, as if solid. Once in a while a school of fish whisked along the surface, but this only accented the silence, the solidity, the huge depth of darkness in this part of the world.

A few years earlier, Hall had passed some memorable weeks on Isla Grande, the main island, where he feasted on delicious beach strawberries. This island was, he said, "a marvelous waypoint, where a fine meal could always be found." He apparently dropped this morsel of information into the captain's ear, but Pease had no intention of stopping for a bit of tourism or good feeding. His mind was all whales.

And so they rounded the Horn, with its blades of moss-covered rocks pushing through folding and unfolding seas, each girded by a lace of foam. Cormorants rode the swells, craning their oily black necks. The sky was screech-blue, with herring gulls pinned against clouds. Once in a while you could see flag trees, permanently misshapen by their life in these windy straits. Before long they passed Staten Land, an outcrop like an iceberg of granite. H.M. fixed on this landscape and found consolation in the solitude; the world seemed to cast up these emblems of isolation, each of them calling to Herman's deepest nature.

He felt isolated, yet he wished for a closer friendship with Toby Greene, this kindred spirit. The possibilities shone in odd moments. Indeed, once Toby had put a hand on his shoulder, squeezed it, and said he understood what it felt like to have a stronger, more aggressive older brother like Gansevoort. (H.M. had spent many nights on watch complaining about Gans.) This opening passed swiftly, however, and Toby remained unapproachable in most ways. He read his Bible daily before dawn, and he was apt to refer to Scriptures quite often to support a piece of common wisdom. Somewhat disconcertingly at times, he gave only the name of the book, with its chapter and verse numbers, assuming that H.M. could summon the language in his own heart. (Toby favored citations from Deuteronomy and Exodus, with Leviticus running a close third.)

Toby had also come to dislike Captain Pease. "A right fool, he is," he would say, under his breath. He hoped that Herman would concur, but H.M. said nothing explicit about Pease, as it would never change anything and he felt uneasy about disparaging an officer. In any case, Pease paid no attention to H.M. or most of the crew. It was largely the 'Gees whom he abused in public, ridiculing their lack of English, their cowering posture, their failure to respond to his every command, however arbitrary. The men generally did not object when Pease persecuted these outsiders, who could hardly defend themselves. To many, the Azoreans were a subversive and possibly threatening clique. Why did they huddle on deck as they did, whispering in their strange tongue, snickering and winking? The songs they sang made little sense. Why could they not learn English as every other foreigner aboard the *Acushnet* had done?

Stories about Pease, true and less true, began to circulate among the crew. His perfumed presence only added to the dark rumors, and his lack of sociability fueled the animosity that rose in flames around him, devouring his authority. Jack Hall was the main source of anti-Pease gossip, and ordinary seamen in any case tended to believe tales arising from an officer.

"He is dangerously peculiar, I fear," said Hall one day, abaft. "We must put our heads together about Pease or trouble will come." He leaned nonchalantly against the coaming and smoked a fat cigar, addressing the third mate, Wilbur Mallon, a slight fellow from Nantucket, who stood at the helm and nodded.

As ever, Hall's voice was a deep bell, and the remark drew affirming looks from a number of seamen.

H.M. worried about this, as one did not say such things aboard ship without consequences. Mutiny took different forms, yet it was always a grave offense. Pease might be mad, even a little cruel, but he was no tyrant. Apart from the 'Gee whom he had forced into a whaleboat with a broken arm, he had not, as yet, terribly endangered anyone. He was surely a pompous fool, too fond of his rank and its authority, but he remained a businessman at heart, someone who wanted whales above anything else, as their oil could be sold for huge profits on the world market. It was, as he said, "a form of liquid gold." In this obsession, he seemed no different from captains of other whalers. One could see the rewards of successful whaling expeditions in the pastel clapboard houses of former captains. Their fanciful latticed porches and peaked dormers overlooked the rocky New England coast from Maine to Connecticut.

H.M. was increasingly afraid of Jack Hall, who spoke too freely and vehemently about Pease, denouncing the captain loudly on the foredeck. A swell of annoyance with the captain had begun to build, and there was no telling how this feeling might crest. A range of scenarios flashed in Herman's mind as he kept a wary eye on the captain, whose nervous tics (a snap-twitch of the eye and ripple in the left cheek) grew more intense as the *Acushnet* sailed around the Horn and turned north along the black mountainous coast of Chile. It comforted no one that Pease talked to himself when alone on deck at night, gesticulating and perorating—a character who raged like a younger Lear. One never wishes for a mad captain, especially in sharp seas or heavy weather. Yet Herman had some trouble deciding how mad his captain really was. Hall was not, he decided, a reliable judge of character, the sort of second mate a captain could trust in a storm. His animosity toward Pease exceeded the circumstances.

Soon enough the *Acushnet* moved into familiar cruising grounds, where it might gam with another whaler. That is, two vessels would draw close, and the captains would retire to one ship, the mates to another. The crew would mingle as well, if they could.

There was so little in the way of social life aboard a whaler that such occasions provided a welcome shift from the usual routines.

On principle, Valentine Pease hated gams and resisted them. "A waste of good time," he would say loudly. "We have a larger pursuit, have we not? It's whales for us, men. Whales!"

Jack Hall would shout in wry imitation, "It's whales for us, men!"

And the men would laugh.

As the journey lengthened and grew (at times) monotonous, Herman depended for diversion on the stories that older sailors told at night, deep in the forecastle, often in a soft rumbling voice, so that those who wished to sleep could do so. (There was an old cooper called Toothless Tom, who never tired of recalling his younger days on tropical islands, where he had fallen among cannibals.) Men who could not sleep would prop themselves on an elbow and listen intently. The tales were often, of course, risqué, with images of palm trees and nubile women, all naked and supposedly available for anyone who should wish to make use of their taut, trembling bodies. The South Seas with their lush, savage islands beckoned, a dream that would, in the months to come, become substantial. Already H.M. could smell the sweet blossoms and see the exotic fruits on trees and bushes he could never name. He could feel the hot sand under his bare feet, the warm sudsy surf like milk around his ankles.

Perhaps the most reflective hours occurred on night watch, under a snow of stars. He and Toby connived to take watch together, and they would sit cross-legged on the foredeck and talk in low tones about the nature and purpose of life. H.M. grew to admire, even to love, Toby Greene, peeling away at the young man's bark, digging into the soft pulp below. Toby was deeply religious at heart, and he longed for God. H.M. too felt a thirst for the eternal, and he had read Ralph Waldo Emerson. A volume of his essays was tucked into a canvas bag near his bunk; he found the language stirring. Looking up at the starry heavens, he wanted, as did Emerson, to enjoy an original relation to the universe. He could intuit the unity of creation, the fact that we are all part and parcel of God. He wanted to trust his instincts, to follow his thoughts, his feelings, toward some ineffable state, something akin to enlightenment.

On the other hand, he distrusted all creeds or specific religious practices, drawing a line here between himself and Toby Greene, who still clung to the conventional forms of Christian practice. As Herman explained to Toby, Emerson had warned his audience, in an address to the Divinity School at Harvard only two years before, about the complacency of traditional worship, encouraging them to pursue something wilder, something that would take one deep into the center of Truth.

"To be frank, I have never heard of your Mr. Emerson," said Toby.

H.M. found it a little frustrating that his friend had heard of few authors, and that he approached religion in such a matter-of-fact way. But Toby had moments of surprising spiritual awareness, as when, one night, he said, "I don't think we listen enough to God."

Herman realized the truth of that remark, and he determined to remain open to such a voice and its redemptive possibilities. He had no wish to whittle away at Toby's faith in the goodness of the Creator or to dislodge his belief system, but he knew he could never get close to the bone without burrowing into places that might feel uncomfortable. So he challenged his friend, inviting him to confess his darkest yearnings, even his sexual frustrations, his hopes for what some day might lie in store for him.

"I would like a young girl to lie beside me, a wife," Toby admitted.

This comment struck Herman as remarkable in its lack of affectation, though he couldn't resist an urge to tease him.

"Why do you require a wife?" H.M. asked.

"I do not want to disappoint God."

"Oh, please, Toby!" Herman had lost the direction of his friend's thinking. "Do you think God really cares if you marry or fail to marry?"

"I do."

Herman suggested that God might have other things on His mind.

Back and forth, their conversation edged closer to formulations that for a young man felt like ultimate truth. By the time of eight bells, when the watch ended, they often felt as wise as Plato at the conclusion of a grand symposium, their heads full of glimmers of divine reality, their bodies alert and quick, nerves struck and humming like tightly wound strings on a beautiful instrument.

As they sailed near the Galápagos, stories resurfaced of the *Essex*. Within miles of these rocky islands, in November 1820, that ill-fated vessel had been hit broadside by a ferocious, self-destructive, monomaniacal whale. It punched a deep, fatal hole in the ship's hull. Bizarrely, the whale refused to desist, attacking again and again, as the frantic crew abandoned ship, manning the whaleboats, in which they drifted for weeks without sustenance, at last driven to the point of murder and cannibalism.

Versions of this macabre tale sprouted and grew into scarcely recognizable forms. Indeed, Jack Hall had absorbed, and transmogrified, countless variants of the original tale; with his brassy voice, in the best Queen's English, he held H.M. and Toby (among others) in thrall one night under a full yellow moon. "There is no telling the lengths to which a desperate man will go," he said. "God himself cannot understand the infinitely depraved depths of His creation."

"Oh, I think He does!" said Toby, with puppylike earnestness. "He is omnipotent."

Hall looked at Herman with baleful eyes, as if to say, *How do you deal with this boy's ignorance?* But H.M. kept his own counsel, offering no opinion of God and no criticism of Toby.

Tandoo looked on, staring through a haunting scrim of moonglow, silent yet somehow bemused. H.M. could see a glint in the eyes of this muscular Indian—not uncommon in Tandoo. Herman would sometimes wink at him, as if to acknowledge their quiet sense of amity and collusion.

Meanwhile, the *Acushnet* spotted any number of whales in the distance but—to the annoyance of Captain Pease—managed to catch only a few of them. The Pacific had thus far proved strangely sparse as whaling grounds, especially when they gammed with other vessels and heard about the rich hauls that were, in theory, available. Rumors circulated among the crew that the *Acushnet* was jinxed.

"I should not have killed that albatross," said Jack Hall, confusing poor Toby.

"He refers to a poem by Coleridge," said Herman. "But I should not put it past him. He is capable of slaughter."

In late October, they cruised among the Encantadas, a cluster of stark, uninhabited islands that, to Spanish chart makers, seemed to appear and disappear at will, as if their existence defied marking. Now these black rocks multiplied into a series of volcanic mounds in dark waters, with pale buff cliffs that seemed to break off jaggedly. H.M. scouted the islands in a whaleboat, drawing up to Redondo Rock one morning just before dawn, observing the contrast between the bare island and the seas around it, which swarmed with protean life.

Astride the equator, called simply the line, the *Acushnet* hung in seasonless austerity—beyond cheer or sorrow. For three days at one stretch the winds simply died, as in the Coleridge poem. It was weirdly, even terrifyingly, calm now. H.M. wrote in his journal: "No breezes for days that hang like months, immovable. Sails sag. The sun blazes, a gold coin nailed against the sky, too bright even to behold. There is silence everywhere. Even Jack Hall says nothing, as if embarrassed. The captain paces madly, abaft, self-absorbed, a head full of undiscovered whales. I fear for his sanity."

"It's the captain," said Jack to Herman one night at the taffrail. "God does not like him."

"God has no interest in Pease, nor us. He has a rather indifferent streak, I fear."

"Perhaps He does not exist."

"Perhaps *we* don't," H.M. added quickly. "This whole thing often seems like a dream to me."

"God is dreaming us, I should think."

"If so, He's got something of a nightmare under way."

Their banter continued, but Hall returned compulsively to Valentine Pease, even as the winds picked up and the sailing vessel resumed its usual slow heave. Dissatisfaction with the captain had been smoldering since Rio, with talk of his madness and cruelty. Hall's doubts about the captain were kerosene applied to dry kindling, and the flames of dissatisfaction roared. There was talk of desertion in the forecastle. Of course it was not uncommon for men to desert a whaling ship in the middle of an expedition that could take as many as five years, depending on circumstances. Few captains expected to come home with their original crew, although a mass flight from the *Acushnet* would certainly disable the enterprise. Pease, however, had no idea that his men disliked him so thoroughly; he continued to stroll the deck with blithe self-absorption, barking commands, indifferent to the hostility around him.

H.M. wondered if Pease could really be considered cruel. Now and then Pease ridiculed a seaman who failed to perform some menial job for him. He had broken the nose of that unfortunate Azorean and shouted rudely at one or two others. But these displays of bad temper hardly counted as cruelty in the context of seagoing, where brutality was the currency of everyday life. Officers not infrequently abused their men, especially captains who had a less than perfect grip on their own authority. In many ways, Pease was just a petty, ineffectual, run-of-the-mill bully—one who lacked force of character. On the other hand, he never actually put the ship in jeopardy, nor did he misdirect the venture in any selfish way. He wanted to kill whales, which is what everyone wanted, especially the owners of the *Acushnet* back in New Bedford and Boston. All they required of Pease was oil—as much as he could produce.

Herman understood that a whaling expedition was a business proposition; nevertheless he disliked this particular captain with an intensity that surprised him. By the time they crossed the equator, he already knew in his heart that he would never complete a circuit of the globe aboard the *Acushnet,* at least not in the company of Valentine Horatio Pease. He might never get to the South Seas again, and he wished to make the most of the prospects for adventure that loomed, an improbable kingdom in the middle distance of his imagination.

Herman had disliked Pease from the outset, and his impatience with the captain's pretensions and self-involvement only grew as he listened to the complaints of those around him. It did not help that one could smell Pease from twenty paces, a result of the unctuously sweet lotions he applied to his hair and skin, as if he were about to court some invisible lady. The crew scurried to elude him, ducking behind the yardarm or disappearing into a hatch.

For his part, Pease grew increasingly frustrated. In the best of times, he had difficulty with summoning men to action, but the problem had worsened lately. "Where are you, sailors?" he would cry. "Stand, ho! Do you hear me? Stand, ho!"

Rarely did sailors materialize: a fact that began to prey on the captain's mind. Quite rightly, he began to suspect that Jack Hall had poisoned the ship against him. So he determined to do something about this problem lest it put the entire venture at risk. To manufacture a loss for his investors was beyond the pale, as he would never win command of another ship if such a thing were to happen. This was his last chance to prove himself. And failure would not happen.

The weather turned in late August, with squalls rising off portside. Thunderheads balled their angry fists in the sky, and a dark curtain of rain approached from a few miles away as the burgee snapped aloft, a yellow warning. All was not well. The surface of the waters roiled, with whiteheads running. The *Acushnet* bucked and rolled in ways that frightened those with experience of these waters. (As Jack Hall noted, one should always retreat in the face of a tempest. It was standard seamanship.)

Yet a distant sighting of sperm whales excited Pease, who commanded the ship to tack into the storm, in pursuit of what Hall described to H.M. as "a fantasy school of whales."

"There are no whales in that direction, sir," Hall said to Pease.

"What, Hall! You contradict me?" He stepped back, with a puff of air in his cheeks that suggested rage. "Do you *dare*?"

A pause followed, then Hall said with a derisory grin, "I believe we could use our time more wisely."

At this, the captain erupted, slapping Hall on the cheek with a leather glove that had been tucked into his belt. It was a humiliating gesture for Hall, one that horrified everyone in sight of it, including Herman. A captain did not strike a fellow officer. Such behavior went against what Captain Marryat in *Mr. Midshipman Easy*—a book that H.M. kept in his ditty bag and was currently reading for a third time—had called the hard unwritten code of the sea.

Hall turned a fine shade of rosy-purple, the color of a bad bruise. His eyelids fluttered as he drew his lips into a grimace—a futile attempt to stabilize his features. Unable to control himself, his lips trembling and white, he reached forward and grabbed the captain's lapels, staring into his gray eyes. Violence was beyond recall, so he managed to back off, sucking a breath—though murder flashed in his face.

The captain was not a man who tolerated any form of insubordination. "You will retire to your quarters at once, Mr. Hall," he said. "I shall deal with you later."

The second mate's mutinous behavior pushed the idea of whales far from the mind of Valentine Pease, and he changed direction at once, away from the storm, southward. They ran hard, on a direct downwind course, as if the weather understood that urgent matters lay before them. The unsettled crew, the mad captain, and the disgruntled, humiliated second mate compacted problems aboard the *Acushnet,* which suddenly had ceased to become a threat for any whales in the vicinity. Soon hardly a voice could be heard, aloft or below, although Pease often stood alone on the quarterdeck with his lips moving.

"Captain Pease, he is speaking to himself only," said Tandoo to Herman.

"Not a pleasant conversation, I should think," H.M. replied.

The weather improved markedly as they approached the Peruvian coast, with the sea blushing like a pink wine at evening, the winds steady, undemonstrative but propulsive enough to keep the vessel on track. The agreeable nature of this climate, with the sky like a soft, warm cheek, seemed at odds with what had been happening aboard ship in recent days. One felt the absences of the captain and Jack Hall. But these were hardly painful for Herman, who noted in his journal the "warmly cool, clear, ringing, perfumed, overflowing, redundant days" that tumbled, one after the other, as the *Acushnet* headed into the harbor.

They anchored off Paita, a port familiar to all whalers, widely known for a cluster of lively brothels and bars behind a filthy breakwater. Half a dozen vessels, including the *Hobomok* (Falmouth) and the *Alexander* (New Bedford), lay at anchor in the turquoise bay, with anchor lines tightly drawn, decks patrolled by the handful of resentfully sober sailors left to mind their ships. The town itself consisted of two dozen or so tumbledown buildings clustered along half a mile of ragged coastline, with a plateau behind it like a high silver plate raised to the crisp blue skies by some invisible waiter. Herons swarmed the rocky beach, and local fishermen picked at their nets under tall, bony palm trees. Rickety docks arose from the surf to meet boats unloading crews eager to set foot on land again.

In the silence of his cabin, Captain Pease had drawn up the complaint against Hall that he would lodge with Francis Wilders, the American consul in Paita, who was an acquaintance from earlier visits. Wilders would deal with Hall or (as seemed more likely) do nothing. It hardly mattered, as the captain well knew. To remain in Peru and pursue a charge of mutiny was beyond him at this point; he needed to cross the Pacific as soon as possible, to get to better whaling grounds. The important thing was to relieve himself of an underling who had shown an instinct for rebellion. This expedition was, after all, a business proposition, not a military operation. One had to keep one's mind on whales. Anything else was a distraction, likely to reduce one's profit and damage one's reputation as a man who could generate profits. He needed to rid himself of Hall, once and for all.

The whaleboats were lowered, and the *Acushnet* emptied, with giddy sailors loyal to Jack Hall beating ashore at once—in advance of Pease. H.M. was swept along with the pack as they made their way to the American consul's door to complain about the captain before he could complain about them.

The American consulate occupied a two-story wooden house in a bay of palms. Any number of flea-bitten horses were tethered outside and there was a fire in the yard, or the remains of one, warm sticks with diced turtle meat in a fly-speckled heap beside it. Somebody had recently had a meal and, perhaps under threat, disappeared. A single gourd-faced Indian in a colorful blanketlike shawl sat on the veranda with his back against the wall. He smoked a mule cigar, blowing rings in the air.

The sailors rushed past the Indian, confronting the consul in the front hall. Wilders had experienced such things before and remained silent, listening and nodding in a professional way—as if the world hung on what these men told him. He was a lanky man who held himself high, his cropped silvery hair balanced on his head like a tray. He was also a worldly man, someone who had spent large swathes of his long career in squalid outposts. As such, he understood at a glance that trouble lay before him. Such men, minor officials in remote places, always loathed anything resembling trouble. A quiet dissipation was all he sought, and Captain Pease was, if not a friend, a man—like himself—upon whom fate had bestowed authority. It would never pay to side with those wishing to challenge this authority.

The crew introduced themselves one by one, stammering out their names as Wilders stroked his beard and narrowed his gaze. Only the 'Gees—two of them—stood to one side in the shadows of the ill-lit room, saying nothing. A lamp burned on the trestle table, sulfurous, with winged termites around the flame. There was a damp smell of spent firewood and balsam oil.

The men complained of their captain's cruelty and madness. Jack Hall had been severely abused, they said. The ship had recently been directed into a storm, as if whales were more important than human lives. Any number of large or small complaints had, indeed, been accumulating for months, and their ostensible content masked the core of their problem with Valentine Pease: he was a peculiar, self-satisfied, pompous fool.

H.M. was the last to speak, and he spoke his name firmly, with pride. This caught the consul's attention. It so happened he had been a young man in Boston when Thomas Melvill oversaw the port, as customs inspector, and he asked H.M. if he were any relation to Major Melvill.

"He was my grandfather, sir," said H.M. with pride.

"An American hero," said the consul.

The others looked at Herman with fresh interest. They had assumed he was, like them, another of the unwashed masses. But they also understood that whaling attracted a range of men from various backgrounds. (Indeed, it was Jack Hall who often recalled a voyage at the beginning of his career when he discovered, in the forecastle, a young baronet from Wiltshire. The rebellious peer had begged him not to reveal his true station.)

Now the consul singled out H.M., asking him pointedly if the captain of the *Acushnet* had behaved in ways that endangered the ship. Toby Greene looked at his friend intently.

"I *do* think he's a fool," said Herman.

"Ah, yes. That we must allow. But has he acted in ways that deserve official rebuke or censure? I should like to know what you honestly think, Mr. Melville."

H.M. fingered his beard, hesitating. "He has slapped our second mate," he said, "that is true. And he makes strange speeches, shouting at the night skies like Tom O'Bedlam. But he has injured none of us gravely."

"I see," the consul said, his eyes like coals lighting the room's soot of darkness. "That is a thoughtful perspective, Mr. Melville, and very well said."

To his relief, H.M. saw that he had not upset or disappointed his fellow sailors. They saw, at a glance, that he belonged to another class of men, and that he had an alliance with the captain and the consul that had something to do with tradition, with a feeling of solidarity. They could not hold this against him, yet he would from this point forward have to stand by himself. He was no ordinary seaman.

Jack Hall, by this point, had come ashore and disappeared into the Peruvian masses. He would doubtless emerge in due course, find a ship to Liverpool, resume his life elsewhere, perhaps in another line of work. Certainly he would no longer serve as second mate aboard the *Acushnet*—much to the relief of Valentine Pease, who later heard about H.M.'s speech to the consul from Wilders, who told the captain over a quiet dinner to "look out for this excellent young man, whom you must consider a friend."

This news surprised Pease, but he made a mental note of the exchange, and determined to reward this unusual young man when he had an opportunity to do so. The main thing, from his viewpoint, was that Hall had disappeared from his life. The South Seas, with their populous schools of sperm whales, beckoned.

*Though our Handsome Sailor had as much of
masculine beauty as one can expect anywhere to see;
nevertheless, like the beautiful woman in one of
Hawthorne's minor tales, there was just one thing
amiss in him. No visible blemish indeed, as with the
lady; no, but an occasional liability to a vocal defect.
Though in the hour of elemental uproar or peril he was
everything that a sailor should be, yet under sudden
provocation of strong heart-feeling his voice, otherwise
singularly musical, as if expressive of the harmony
within, was apt to develop an organic hesitancy, in fact
more or less of a stutter or even worse. In this
particular Billy was a striking instance that the arch
interferer, the envious marplot of Eden, still has more
or less to do with every human consignment to this
planet of Earth.*

H.M., *Billy Budd*

5.

Malcolm had only one friend who mattered: Norbert Hillsdale, whom he called Bertie. Bertie was, as Herman put it, "something of a champagne flute," elongated, thin, elegant. He had a quiet effervescence, too. His soft voice was bubbly, and he could be heard in Mackie's room quite late at night.

"They chatter too much," H.M. complained, as he wrote poetry at his desk, the lamp burning, too late at night for a man with work to attend in the morning. "I hear their voices into the wee hours, especially Bertie."

"They have much to discuss," I would say.

"What can they possibly discuss?" Herman would reply. "Malcolm has nothing much to say."

I knew better, of course. The boy had nothing much to say to *him*.

Bertie worked for our old friend Mr. Lathers, as did Mackie, and they shared a desk in the insurance office. The young man had

come to Manhattan from Connecticut, and so he rented a bedroom
at a boardinghouse on Seventh Avenue. It was said to be a "wild
house," as the landlady was rarely present to restrain her brood. But
Mackie dismissed such a notion as rumor. "Only a few boys live
there, and they are discreet," he told me firmly. "And Bertie is, I
would say, something of a recluse among them. The revels, such as
they are, amount to nothing more than a card game on weekends
and, perhaps, cigars with a swig of brandy."

I only half believed him, but it never worried me. A young man
in full view of his nineteenth birthday should have a degree of freedom. I tried my best to convey this idea to my husband, but it was
never worth talking to him about the children. He had fixed ideas,
even though he himself as a young man had lived a most indiscreet
life among cannibals in the South Seas. (That he never referred to
these exploits only cemented, for me, the notion that he had
behaved in ways that no gentleman could admit, even to himself. It
had driven him mad when reviewers dared to mention his infamous
exploits or referred to him simply as "Typee" instead of Herman
Melville.)

Bertie came home often with Mackie, and they would dine
with me in the kitchen. Herman dined alone, as he came home so
late. His night wanderings remained a mystery to me, but I was not
going to inquire about their exact nature. "I was out with Duyckinck," he would offer, if I dared to inquire. He knew I approved
of Evert Duyckinck, who edited various magazines and moved
among the better crowd of literary types in New York. But I suspected he did not spend as much time with Evert as he pretended.
He had his private life, apart from mine, and it was easier to say
nothing about such things. In truth, I preferred a meal without his
glowering presence at the table.

I should add that Bertie was a most wonderful raconteur after a
glass of wine, holding forth on politics—he had wry things to say

about our feckless president, Andrew Johnson. "He will almost certainly be the first president to be tarred and feathered," said Bertie, who noted that Johnson, a former senator from Tennessee, had been very quick to appease the South after the war. "I do suspect he actually *liked* slavery," said Bertie. He would never have spoken so freely in the presence of my husband, who had become a dampening influence, all scowls and demurrals. It was as if he resented the fact that Mackie had a social life and he lacked one.

On a Friday or Saturday, Bertie would spend the night, sleeping in Mackie's feather bed. I could hear the two of them giggling behind the oak door, and it pleased me to think that my son had acquired such a good friend. They would sleep late on Saturday or Sunday morning, and so I insisted on quiet in the house, as it would never please them to have their dreams so rudely interrupted. Boys need their rest. For his part, my husband was gone at eight-thirty on a Sunday, keeping to his routine. He said, "I'm an old sailor, and so I set sail." He might well drift all the way north to Central Park, which held a certain fascination for him; but I never asked him about these voyages in Manhattan. "Enjoy your day, my dear," I whispered, and kissed him on the forehead. "And do come home for dinner, if you can manage such a thing."

On Sunday nights, he usually had dinner at home. It was the one reliable meal in his life, a time when I could expect him in his chair at the head of the table, a hungry man who had gone into the broad daylight and returned, having seen many things I would never hear a word about. After dinner we would sit in the parlor by the fire and read aloud from Dickens or some other author. It was a pleasant time, and Bertie—now a fixture in the house—proved an able reader, capable of entertaining everyone, even Herman. He would do the different voices in a tale with true thespian vigor, taking on a range of accents, raising the pitch if a woman or young girl spoke.

My daughters adored him, and so did my mother-in-law. Even our shy, glum Stannie could be heard to express a laugh, sometimes very loudly indeed. (It was such a pleasure to see him laugh, and the smiles relieved his natural expression, which gave him the appearance of an unhappy child—a thought I could hardly bear.)

"I do believe our Mackie has a considerable affection for this young man," H.M. said one night, as we lay in our iron bed, peering through the grate at our feet, listening to laughter down the hall.

"This is all very good," I said.

"I had such affections, when young," he said.

"Indeed."

"There was a young man aboard the *Acushnet*."

"Toby Greene," I said.

"Yes, Toby."

"I am well aware of Toby Greene," I said, trying not to sound too cynical. Toby had appeared from nowhere in the days after *Typee* was published, providing public evidence that my husband had not simply imagined his time among the cannibals of the South Seas. Toby had been there, and his testimony as to the truth of what happened had gone a long way to appease Herman's most vehement critics.

"He was a good lad, Toby, aye."

"I dare say."

"A delicate smile, when cheerful."

"A smile is good."

"It's such a pity, the whole thing. Mackie is a puzzle to me."

"What is there to pity? I cannot follow you."

"I cannot follow myself," Herman said. "This is the tragedy. I have never followed to the end of anything. I leave off in mid-flight. There is a lack of completion in the arc of everything I describe."

"You make my head spin with your dithering."

"I suppose it's the general sadness of it all," he said, but he was not talking to me. He had a private audience who listened to him, nodding in the shadows, shaking their ghostly heads, twisting their mouths or perhaps shutting their eyes. They provided a kind of mental Greek chorus, and he relied on them as he never had relied on me, on his mother, or on his children. They offered counsel, affirmation, or disapproval—depending on the subject at hand.

"And there was Eli Fly," he said, rather brightly.

"I know of Mr. Fly."

"Oh, you know his name. You didn't know the boy, the face, or the laugh. It was the laugh of his, you see, and a sidelong smile. He was a whip, he was."

"A whip?"

Herman chuckled, then settled into a loud sleep, snuffling, coughing, rasping, grunting, even giggling at times. It was like sleeping with any number of men at once, each of them trying to communicate some emotion or discomfort. I suspect that tobacco and drink played a part in this noisy drowse, which I didn't call sleep. He would sometimes shout strange things, shocking me into full wakefulness, causing me to tremble. And he cried out various names, few of which I recognized. There was a mysterious John, for instance—an English fellow he had met in the Sandwich Islands long ago. He would not talk about this John, but he dreamed of him, I had no doubt about that, although I was privy to only one side of these peculiar dream conversations! Several young men had made a very deep impression on my husband, and they lived with him, strange but often friendly spirits. I could nearly see their bright faces flicker on the ceiling of our bedroom.

Why I continued to sleep in the same room as my husband was a good question, and it cannot easily be answered. I seemed by nature a dutiful wife and accepted my role, this peripheral part in Herman's tragicomedy. Although sorely tempted to flee, I had made the choice to remain as Mrs. Herman Melville. For better or (mostly) worse, I had determined to play this part until H.M. was nothing but a name, letters etched on a tombstone at Woodlawn or on the spines of books long abandoned by their maker and certainly by the historians who keep track of such things.

I supposed I would have some quiet years by myself, after his death. That was usually the case, as women tended to outlive men by a decade or more: we must count ourselves the stronger sex. And I looked forward to those years of freedom, wondering when they might begin, how long they might stretch, and whether a form of sadness would ultimately prevail. I did not think so. As a child, I had savored solitude, practiced its art. In another century, I would have made a good nun in some contemplative order, a denizen of silence. Life would have been easier without the commotion of men, their insistent needs—although once in a while I took pleasure in the simple sight of them.

Once, for instance, I caught a glimpse of Bertie Hillsdale on a Sunday morning in the heat of August. It was late, almost time for lunch, and I assumed that the boys had gone for a walk, as they sometimes did on a bright day. Bertie lay there naked on the bed, on his stomach, and the sight took away my breath: such beauty in a man-child with his straight-cut body, where no excess of flesh could be found. His lean legs stretched along the cotton sheets, with light covers bunching at the bottom of the bed. His blond hair was silky on the pillow. His narrow buttocks rose at the base of his spine, however slightly. I wanted to walk in there, to put a hand on those buttocks, to feel the swell, the taut skin, to press my fingers into the sweet hollow of his spine. I saw not a hair on that body—like a young girl he was. I understood exactly why my boy admired him and kept to him with a singular devotion. It was only natural.

"Mother!" cried Mackie, coming up behind me in a dressing gown.

I think it embarrassed him that Bertie lay in such a state in full view of any passerby.

"You have had a bath?" I asked.

"Yes, I have."

His hair and beard glistened, and his eyes were like chips of ice, blue and hard—the eyes I had loved so much when he was a baby. In fact, I could see the child in him, even now, swaddled in adulthood like a soft blanket.

"Your friend," I said awkwardly. "He is asleep."

"We had a bit of Father's brandy last night, I'm afraid. Not much is left in the bottle."

"He won't mind."

"He will never know."

I pressed his dear wrists with my thumbs. "You can trust me, darling."

He kissed me on the cheek, as he often did, and my heart beat rapidly. What a lovely, pure, dear, innocent boy!

I never quite anticipated a military turn, but Mackie came home one evening with Bertie and both were in uniform, shimmering and forceful. He and his friend had joined a volunteer militia, and they planned to spend their weekends in the country, training with their company, shooting rifles at defenseless trees and swinging sabers at each other. They would march and parade, doing all the nicer things that soldiers do in times of peace. I had no objection to the uniforms, though I did worry that they both carried pistols, which they swore would never be loaded in the house.

H.M. merely scoffed at what he called their "martial pretensions."

"Oh, let them play at this," I told him. "It's good for Mackie to have an interest outside of work."

"One should not play at soldiering," he said. "That is a most serious business—an unhappy one, too."

It had been a huge relief that my boys had not been old enough to serve in Mr. Lincoln's bloody and protracted war. So few young men came home unscathed, and even those who escaped a musket ball suffered from instability and grief in unimaginable ways. To be frank, neither Mackie nor Stannie was cut out for combat, however much they assumed otherwise. I had watched them in Pittsfield as they played among country boys, and neither could happily enter into the fray. As H.M. remarked one day when they returned home in tears, "They should be playing with dolls. They are little girls at heart."

Overhearing this, my tactless mother-in-law said, "Boys will be girls."

Like her son, Maria knew exactly how to annoy me.

I could hardly wish for my sons to behave like girls; on the other hand, it came as a relief that they refrained from hand-to-hand violence with ruffians in the Berkshires. They rarely caused trouble at home, nor did either boy raise a voice to his father in anger. He was their master, their God. Herman ruled the house, and they understood this arrangement and accepted it without question. We bowed, all of us, before the great H.M., who had only his mother to answer to, the Goddess Maria. A withering look from her at the breakfast table could ruin his day. With a simple flick of the hand, she might dismiss one of his grand ideas. "Oh, this constant reading you do! It has never been good for you, Herman. Just look at your eyes. You're making yourself blind! Let your wife read for you. Let *her* eyes do the work!"

"I am no wife to Mr. Milton," I said.

"I can read myself," said Herman, glaring at Maria, who crossed her arms. She came alive in the midst of arguments and looked for ways to provoke them.

My husband's eyes were, indeed, his weakest point. They had been a problem from childhood, causing him considerable anxiety and suffering. Yet he insisted on reading by lamplight into the late hours, underlining his beloved volumes of Milton and Shakespeare, Lord Byron, Plato and Emerson, writing in the margins. He paid dearly for these efforts now, wandering the streets of Manhattan in dark glasses, hiding under the brim of the largest hat he could find. I wondered if he ever really saw my face, or the look of pain in my eyes, in the eyes of the children. He talked over us, mostly—a high cloud rushing past.

Once H.M. hoped for a presidential appointment, perhaps as consul in Florence. It was the city of his dreams—the place where Dante had caught a glimpse of Beatrice on a bridge, thus changing his life forever. The air by the Arno was sweet, he told me—an elixir that inspired visions. On a visit there in 1856, he had sat day after day in the Caffè Doney, drinking cups of granular coffee, scribbling in his journal, sketching stories or ideas for stories, listing titles of possible books. He felt he must, somehow, get back there.

Surely he could get such an appointment in Florence, or so H.M. believed with his usual iron whimsicality. He would summon into action on his behalf a handful of illustrious associates, such as Richard Henry Dana, Jr., and David Dudley Field, perhaps even Nathaniel Hawthorne himself. Hawthorne was his dearest friend, his ally in the world of letters, his peer atop Mount Parnassus. He thought so, in any case.

The monarch of American literature had lived, ever so briefly, in a small red cottage near Lenox. He and Sophia, that peculiar wife of his, kept mainly to themselves, disdaining the locals while spoiling their children to an extent that horrified the county, which fed on gossip about them. I don't know why they chose to live in the remote Berkshires. It was not suitable for them, as the winters were long and unforgiving. Even in summer, one had to contend with pesky mosquitoes and the ravages of hay fever. Needless to say, the possibilities for genteel or literate conversation were few, during any season.

Of course the consulship in Florence never materialized. Why would it? Herman was hardly a natural diplomat—anyone could see that, and it would have been foolish to recommend him to Washington. H.M. came home unhappily from Europe to a country nearly at war with itself over Abolition—a subject that tormented us all.

Soon thereafter my darling father fell ill on Mount Vernon Street. I rushed to be near him, summoned by my stepmother. Bringing him a tray of tea and toast one morning, I saw at once that he had ceased to breathe, and what remained were body rags too trivial to consider. A good deal of commotion followed, as it would, culminating in a huge public funeral for this hero of the Commonwealth. The casket was covered with black velvet and studded with silver nails. He lay in state for two days under the dome of the capitol, and thousands of ordinary citizens came to pay homage, despite a driving wet spring snow. At the service itself, we sat in a daze in the freezing church, with Herman squeezing my hand as the distinguished Dr. Dewey gave a long and incoherent eulogy that nevertheless (to my relief) acknowledged H.M. as a beloved son-in-law and writer. The eulogist dropped the names of others in the room, including Lowell, Holmes, and Longfellow—the holy trinity. He seemed particularly impressed by the presence of white-haired President Felton, who had led the Harvard contingent. "And their works do follow them," Dr. Dewey said, quoting from the Good Book. He referred, I'm sure, to my father's excellent works, but I saw Herman nodding eagerly.

Would *his* works follow him? It seemed, at least to me, unlikely—as already his novels had begun to fade. And the fading would continue.

When eventually the war began in earnest, Mr. Lincoln called for volunteers. Even we in the remoteness of Pittsfield felt the tug of battle, a dark transfer of energies, as young men marched away from their idyllic farms in fresh blue uniforms. It was a ghastly period, and I clung to my dear sweet boy, Mackie, who wanted badly to fight for his nation. "I shall go for a soldier," he said. "I do hope the war lasts a very long time."

"You must support Mr. Lincoln by going to school," I told him. "Do your best in whatever you do. Only your very best."

I was among countless mothers in every state saying the same thing to boys who had watched young men march off in glory, smartly uniformed, proud and brave. Even H.M. was on the militia roll, although he was hardly fit for service, as everyone knew. He had "nervous problems," as his mother put it. His eyesight was dreadful. He would never make a soldier, and nobody in their right mind would ever want him in their regiment.

We struggled during the war years on many fronts, it seemed. What money we had came mostly from my inheritance, which appeared in irregular installments, lifting us over humps in the road. H.M. managed to summon a few royalties from the work of his pen, but this was never enough to satisfy our needs.

Yet that is not why we left Arrowhead.

The truth is, Herman could never keep a farm, not without hired men. In addition to having fallen off a wagon—he was the least responsible of drivers—he had acquired a rheumatic affliction that made it difficult for him to walk any distance or lift heavy things, and there seemed no choice now. We had to put the Berkshires behind us. Reflexively, perhaps, we drifted to Manhattan—always "home" for my husband, a New Yorker in his soul. He had important friends there, such as Evert Duyckinck, and it seemed likely that some form of employment could be found in that city without extraordinary efforts. In any case, this was the center of his emotional world, a place where he could linger in galleries and museums, staring at pictures that thrilled him, puzzled him, challenged him, and inspired him. There were booksellers galore, where he could squander what little was left of my father's money. That I much preferred to live in Boston meant nothing to him.

"Boston is too far north," he said. "I am very tired of Massachusetts."

For me, Manhattan did offer the prospect of decent schools for the boys. I wanted them to live among their social peers, to learn to speak as they should speak. I sought a broad general education for them, and this would never happen in Pittsfield, where a single schoolmistress held sway over twenty or more ruffians, who recited their lessons without real understanding, eager to get out-of-doors as soon as possible. That was the way with country boys, and it didn't matter what sort of family connections they could boast. Willy-nilly the country turned them into rubes.

It was, I confess, somewhat galling to sell the farm to my obnoxious sister-in-law and her prosperous husband, Allan. Jane Melville had no idea how ridiculous she seemed, referring in her letters to "poor simple Arrowhead" and wondering how she might "bring it up in the world a notch or two" so that her children did not have to suffer the indignities which I and my children had suffered. She remade the house so entirely I could scarcely recognize it, filling the rooms with furnishings that seemed wholly inappropriate for a Berkshire farmhouse. One did not require Persian rugs or finely crafted chairs in the chimney room! The view of Mount Greylock beyond the north parlor did not improve if the windows were dressed in velvet curtains. But I held my tongue. I had become an expert at holding my tongue.

· · ·

Things went badly wrong in late summer. I don't know when I first understood that trouble lay before us, but I think it happened when, on a hot morning in early September 1867, I heard the distant slamming of a door. Bertie had been with us since Friday night, although the boys had gone to their training camp outside of the city. We had become quite familiar with their military affectations: the way they called each other by their last names or shouted orders in the hallway or brandished swords in the kitchen, terrifying the maids. This seemed all in good fun. But Mackie had been mooning about the house lately, missing work because of headaches.

I should have guessed that something was wrong when he missed three or four days of work in the week before. He was not really ill—I felt quite sure of that—but sat with a glass of brandy in our bedroom at his father's desk, leafing through the pages of *Typee*. Before this he had never shown the slightest interest in Herman's work, and there was no reason why he should suddenly take a literary turn.

"Is this a true story?" he asked.

"I don't think so," I said. "Your father has a robust imagination."

"I believe it's true," he said. "Father is an unusual man."

I nodded.

"Do you love him, Mother?"

Such a question!

"I do," I said. But what could I say? How could I begin to explain to Mackie what it meant to love this intense, sullen, amusing, difficult man, his father?

"I do not understand about love," he said.

"You will have your time," I suggested, brushing a lock of hair from his beautiful eyes. "You're only a boy."

"I'm a man," he said.

"After a fashion, I suppose so. Unless I'm mistaken, you will soon be nineteen."

He continued reading, and I left him there by himself.

One evening he did not come home after work as usual. He had left no message, and Herman began to worry about him at ten o'clock when he did not appear.

"He has become quite impossible," H.M. said.

"Perhaps he and Bertie have gone for a stroll."

The warm September nights were perfect for strolling, and I knew they often liked to walk in Battery Park under the stars.

"He and Bertie have not been getting on lately," my husband said.

"That will change," I said, surprised that Herman should have noticed as much. He rarely showed interest in the lives of his children—not on this level of particularity.

I waited up for Mackie, as I always did, sitting in the parlor, expecting his footsteps in the hall at any moment. I knitted anxiously, drinking cups of tea. The grandfather clock gonged thickly, resonating in the hallway: one, two, three. I determined to remain in place on that sofa until dawn, if necessary. It would, in any case, have been impossible to sleep. I had never known my son to stay away from home like this, and made every effort to refrain from drawing dire conclusions.

Soon after three, the telltale clomping in the hallway startled me. He was home at last.

"Oh, Mackie," I said, taking his hands.

"I'm sorry, Mother," he said. "I was in Yorkville, with friends. There was a bit of entertainment."

"Entertainment?"

"A little music, some dancing." He shifted from foot to foot. "I'm sorry," he said again.

"You must get some sleep," I said. "You have to go to work in a few hours."

I doubted he had taken much drink, though one can't always tell. I tried hard not to notice. The odor of cigars on his breath was certainly strong, and I shied away when he kissed me on the cheek before ascending the stairs.

I watched him climb, more slowly and deliberately than usual, as if uncertain about his balance.

In the morning Bessie as usual prepared breakfast for her brothers, and she tried to waken Mackie at seven by rapping on his door. He could not get up without some exhortation on the best of days.

"Go away!" he cried.

Herman sat up in bed now, startled, and I told him what had happened.

"The boy was drinking," he said. "I have suspected as much. A drink or two on the weekends can only be a good thing for a boy of his age. But he should not drink so much when he has to go to work the next day. That is irresponsible!"

"He was not drunk," I said.

"No matter."

"Let him sleep," I said.

"Mr. Lathers will be upset."

"Yes, he shall. I don't care."

Herman grunted his disapproval and got dressed for the day.

The day proceeded as usual. H.M. set forth, making his rounds of the wharves. He had a drink after work at Duyckinck's house on Thirty-fourth Street—or so he claimed. Fanny and Bessie went to visit a friend in Brooklyn for the afternoon. Maria, thank goodness, was not with us that week but with a cousin in Albany—a brief respite from her presence. I attended a midweek service at All Souls, and later I called on Mrs. Watson, a widow who lived nearby. She and I had been friends for several years, and we sat on a church committee that met on Wednesday afternoons at her house. It was a relief to be among her bright colors: yellow and peach walls, with lacy curtains and red chairs. H.M. would never tolerate such colors. He wanted drab, drab, and drab.

When I got home, I saw that Mackie's door remained shut, so I knocked loudly. "Come down for a bit of tea," I said. "We must talk before your father gets home."

He failed to answer, and reluctantly I let him sleep. I suppressed a feeling of panic, deciding that he must indeed be ill. A fever or stomach ailment or some such thing had obviously overtaken him. And this was not unusual, as he was a fragile young man, susceptible to these things. It seemed wise to let him rest.

Herman arrived home at seven-thirty in a gruff mood, his eyes red and full of mucus. He must have been worried about Mackie, as he inquired about his whereabouts when he stepped into the front hall. H.M. could be difficult in these circumstances, even harsh. I had not looked forward to the encounter between my husband and Mackie. The boy had not yet developed an ability to withstand the onslaughts of his father, and there had recently been several clashes that shook the walls of our house.

When I explained that Mackie had not yet stirred, Herman's expression darkened. He was worried, I could tell. Somehow I had put my concern to one side through the afternoon, stopping at the Fulton Market before coming home. I knew that Mackie, much like his father, always enjoyed a good piece of cod, and it would brighten the mood generally at dinner. I had even bought a cake at Morgan's, on Broadway—a chocolate one with pralines and vanilla icing.

"He cannot be sleeping," said Herman.

"I suspect a fever," I said.

"He has no fever."

"He did not look well last night."

"He was drunk."

"This isn't fair."

"Fair is fair," he said, although what he meant by this expression eluded me.

Herman climbed the stairs at a pace not seen in many years, and I followed, out of breath myself as my husband knocked firmly on Mackie's door. He called the boy's name, turning the handle back and forth. It was obviously locked—a peculiar thing, indeed. Herman struck the door harder, using a flat palm, hoping to raise the boy from his stupor.

"Malcolm, wake up! Wake up!"

Now Bessie and Fanny appeared in the hallway, wide-eyed and worried. I gave them a fierce look, so they would not come too close. This was probably unnecessary, as they knew enough of their father's potential for outbursts to remain at a safe distance.

Herman could be a bull, and he became one. He seethed visibly, glowering; then he lowered his right shoulder and plunged, again and again, breaking the door from its brass hinges, a wild splintering of oak.

I did not try to stop him, though I could imagine the humiliation of the poor dear boy as he lay there, desperately ill, unable to arouse himself in time to satisfy his father.

We said nothing, standing together at the foot of his bed. I don't even recall walking into the room. But we stood there, aghast, seeing the pistol still in his right hand, our dear boy dead.

A bullet had opened a wide hole in his skull above the left ear. He was soaked in his own blood, which had pooled widely, a sight as ugly as any mother in the history of time has been forced to bear. He was dressed in the uniform of his militia—a pale blue jacket with dark cuffs and three brass buttons. My eyes turned from the wound, following the dark stripe down the legs of each trouser. He wore his boots still.

Herman did not move at first, and could not avert his eyes.

Then I heard his rumblings, a gusher of sound that seemed to draw from his heels, rise, and erupt. The cry spouted, a spray of agony too deep to imagine. I had not thought my husband capable of such anguish, such ferocity and pain. His voice filled the room, so that it seemed to shake, to quiver. The red sun glowered on the sheets now, on my son's dear lifeless face, with its look of terror which I cannot forget, will never forget.

I don't remember how it happened but I found myself being pulled by my daughters from the bed, where I lay and held him as the damp bloody sheets churned like a sea around me. Bessie was firm, shouting, "We must go, Mother! We must remove ourselves!"

The doctor came, but there was no point. He could do nothing for Mackie. They took him away on a litter, taking the bloody sheets with them. In one corner of the bedroom Herman stood alone, straight-backed, arms folded across his chest. He was his own Ahab now on the quarterdeck, watching as his vessel sank, swept by invisible waves, washed in the sorrows of circumstance, lost in the depths of silence, which is the language of limitless grief.

I did not in fact believe that Herman Melville would ever speak again.

*Weary with the invariable earth, the restless sailor
breaks from every enfolding arm, and puts to sea in
height of tempest that blows off shore. But in long
night-watches at the antipodes, how heavily that ocean
gloom lies in vast bales upon the deck; thinking that
that very moment in his deserted hamlet-home the
household sun is high, and many a sun-eyed maiden
meridian as the sun. He curses Fate; himself he curses;
his senseless madness, which is himself. For whoso once
has known this sweet knowledge, and then fled it; in
absence, to him the avenging dream will come.*

H.M., *Pierre*

6.

The *Acushnet* cruised for sperm whales, sailing beyond the Galápagos, moving into remote grounds by late spring. Few whales appeared on the horizon, and Valentine Pease—who grew less and less balanced as the paucity of whales became apparent—secluded himself in his cabin, waiting for the telltale cry from the lookout. He would prowl the deck at night, the heels of his boots clacking. On several occasions he again chose to head into a storm, convinced that whales lay on the other side of a squall or thunderhead, taking the ship into dangerous seas. Herman began to dream of Pease as Satan, with horns on his head, teeth of fire, a pitchfork in hand. The captain seemed to want whales so badly that he would trade the welfare of his crew for a few hundred barrels of oil. The men understood this, and they despised him for it, as month fell to month and the atmosphere aboard grew malignant.

In late spring H.M. wrote in his journal: "Six months out of sight of land, under the Line's perpetual unforgiving sun-blast, and we rolled on the Pacific's wide billows, with sky and sea around, an unforgiving landless world. Provisions dwindled, as they must; the supply of salt-horse and sea-biscuit causing great anxiety among the men. It has been some time since a potato or yam had been offered at mealtimes. What I would give for a piece of fresh meat, roasted, with gravy and pearly onions." He worried that someone might casually peruse his journal, which he kept hidden beneath his mattress. It was easy to accuse someone of mutiny, and he wanted none of this for himself, not now.

His friendship with Toby deepened by the day. Herman often felt giddy in his company, acting foolish. The nonchalance of Toby's manner appealed to him—his innocent blitheness. He merely tossed his head to the side with a rueful laugh when problems occurred. His frowns easily upturned, became smiles, with teeth so white and clean. His laughter was like coins dropped in a brass bowl.

H.M. watched the shenanigans that took place in the forecastle below with distaste. It was awkward to have twenty or so men, most in the prime of youth, in a cramped forecastle. The talk of sex was ceaseless, as were the jokes. Priapus reigned. At night, in the darkest corners of the room, sailors touched each other in forbidden ways that relieved tensions, for a time. Herman himself attracted the predations of Martin Wilson, who had shadowed him for weeks. He was a compact fellow from New London who had been a surveyor before going to sea, so he and H.M. had something in common. A pimply-faced youth, he had masses of wiry red hair and foul breath. "Claw me, and I shall claw thee," Wilson whispered in a husky voice one night to Herman, who grabbed him by the neck and pushed him against a wall with a force that surprised them both. "Do not talk to me in such a manner!" H.M. said, barely controlling his anger.

From that point on in the journey Wilson avoided him resolutely.

. . .

By early summer, the *Acushnet* had moved into the green waters of the South Seas, where occasionally the captain would allow a gam with some kindred vessel, such as the *Ontario* of Nantucket or the *Columbus* of New Bedford. These opportunities to exchange stories excited the crew, who heard astonishing reports of beautiful nymphs who populated the islands not far away. The Marquesas held an allure, the name itself summoning visions of palm-lined groves and cannibals feasting on the flesh of enemy tribes. In his bunk, H.M. dozed in his off-hours, dreaming of sunlit valleys, towering bread-fruit trees, bamboo temples, and bowls filled with exotic fruit, the tastes of which could hardly be contained by English words. He had read about such things in libraries, but he wanted badly to experi-ence them for himself. This was his time, his real life.

"What do you think, Toby?" he wondered, as they stood watch under a bright moon that widened a golden path on the sea before them.

"Think about what?"

"We could jump ship in the islands, run about. See the world!"

"I've already seen the world. I didn't like it."

H.M. gestured toward the moonlit path. "What lies beyond interests me."

"You've been reading again."

"I've been dreaming," said Herman.

"I have no desire to offer myself as Sunday lunch to savages on some remote island."

"You would make a fine feast."

"Such flattery."

"Do you like this ship so much?"

A long pause followed, as Toby considered his options. "I am bored with the *Acushnet*."

"But you admire the cuisine."

"I could use a good beefsteak, with potatoes. A tankard of cold beer would improve my mood as well."

"The cooks are apparently quite good in these islands. I shall put in a request for you."

They bantered so, edging more closely each night to a decision to jump ship. This was ordinary talk among sailors long at sea. Everyone knew that one could always find a berth on another whaler, as these ships were leaky buckets, and the captain of any expedition spent a good deal of time topping up his crew. In the case of Pease, who had no leadership skills to speak of, everyone assumed that a hefty percentage of the crew would never return home at his side.

The *Acushnet* had nearly run out of supplies, and Pease understood he had no choice but to abandon these cruising grounds for a spell, putting in among the islands, where he could acquire fresh vegetables and fruits, even meats. The natives often waited for ships to anchor in their harbors, and they eagerly sold whatever provisions they had for glass beads, mirrors, brass buttons, tobacco, or colorful bits of cloth. The winds favored such a retreat, in any case. So the ship glided on a direct downwind course toward the islands—a period of surprising leisure, with the crew largely abandoning the forecastle to sleep on deck under sheets spread before the mast to form an awning.

H.M. himself lay there day after day, an immovable object, as the bow of the ship cut through seas with a low hiss that mingled with the sighs of the sleek dolphins who chased the vessel like friendly companions.

Valentine Pease stood on the quarterdeck with a spyglass, looking for the telltale horizontal shadow of an island.

"Land ho!" was heard, at last, and H.M. hastened to the rail, where Nuku Hiva Island rose from the water, with its black sands and high green hills. A welcome committee of gulls and sea hawks landed on the yards and stays, squawking and bawling. Plankton washed about the ship's hull, smelling of land. The sun widened its big eye.

Herman whispered to Toby as they leaned over the rails, "Our new home, I believe."

Toby winked at him. With Pease standing nearby, Toby certainly didn't want the captain to get wind of their plans.

Nuku Hiva spread before them as they tacked closer. It was larger and greener than Herman had imagined.

"The Typees eat people," said Herman, casually, referring to one of two native tribes on the island. "They roast their neighbors in great fire pits."

"Tastes like pigeon," said Toby.

"How do you know that?"

"It's what they say."

"They say a lot of things," H.M. said.

They turned in to a cozy blue harbor, where six French vessels lay at anchor, including a black flagship with the tricolored flag draped gaudily over her rails. "As we advanced up the bay," Herman later wrote in his journal, "numerous canoes pushed off from the shore. Sailors, we found ourselves amidst a small flotilla of nymphs, all struggling to come aboard. It beggared belief." H.M. knew already about this infamous school of girls, the "whihenies," who swarmed any new ship, offering their bodies without reservation. They were young—barely women, in truth—lovely, nut-brown, lithe, with long black or brown hair. Their eyes burned like coals.

What happened aboard the *Acushnet* defied easy description. H.M. decided against being too explicit in his notes—the details could hardly be inscribed without venturing into the arena of pornography, and he worried about future readers, especially his mother, who had warned him about "the pitfalls of carnality." If this was a pitfall, he told himself, he was ready for the dive.

The girls danced, in blithe nakedness, around the men, singing in their odd, sibilant language. They kissed the sailors greedily, running fingers through their crude beards and unkempt hair. They lifted shirts and unbuckled trousers. A wild scene followed—the massive unrestrained orgiastic pulse of bodies on deck, in every corner or nook. Only the captain remained absent, in his cabin—as he knew he must. The men would scarcely have tolerated the presence of Valentine Pease on the quarterdeck, his arms akimbo as he surveyed these revels with contempt or fury. H.M. recorded what happened as the hours passed: "After we had come to anchor, the deck was hung with yellow lanterns on lines strung from mast to mast, and our little band of sylphs, tricked out with pink or yellow flowers and dressed in robes of tapa cloth—or wholly undressed without shame—danced for us and sang. They could not stop dancing and singing. Our ship gave over to every species of riot and debauchery."

Could he ever tell the world about this scene from a Roman orgy, one he might have found in Petronius? Here was something wilder than what he had witnessed on frescoes in the London brothel a few years before. Unlimited gratification is rare in life, and yet H.M. was himself gratified. Even Toby Greene succumbed, falling into the arms of a maiden with breasts like melons; she pushed him backward to the deck and fell upon him, taking him into her lean body, devouring him greedily, rising and falling, moaning happily. She could hardly have been as innocent as Toby, but she glowed with candor and freshness. He held her rocking buttocks with both hands.

"I'm afraid that I betrayed my Christian principles," said Toby, a few days later.

Experience is a gift to memory, and Herman knew he would never forget what happened that day aboard the *Acushnet*. If he lived to be a hundred, the images of that afternoon would remain in his mind. No fantasy or dream would ever match its sweet reality.

Late that night, as the men lay in their hammocks on deck, sated and sleeping, H.M. found Toby near the yardarm, in a pensive mood. The sky dangled its star hairs, and the moon—full and yellow—transfixed him, turning the bay into a bronze shield. The girls had since fled the *Acushnet,* returning to shore, adorned with rings and trinkets from the ship. One could see a lonely fire on the beach, and it was easy to imagine these nymphs in a circle of deep but happy sleep. They had, indeed, played themselves out.

"So, my friend," said Herman, adopting an avuncular poise. "You have lost your innocence."

"I acted in ways that surprised me."

"You're a man, Toby."

"I am a fool."

Herman put a hand on his friend's forearm. "We must get away from this ship tomorrow. We've been given leave by the gods."

Toby and Herman had resolved to jump ship at the most convenient moment. Now the opportunity lay before them.

"Be ready to go tomorrow," Herman said. "I shall take almost nothing—a ditty bag, my journal."

The consequences of desertion would be insignificant, as captains of whalers asked few questions when they picked up strays. Now and then a man would spend a few days in irons, but even that consequence was rare. Pease, in any case, had acquired a foul reputation—gamming had confirmed that few sailors had respect for him. Other captains avoided him, as he avoided them. The wonder was that anyone remained aboard the *Acushnet* at this point, more than a year and a half into the expedition. Only the natural pessimism of this crew prevented mass desertion: they seemed to believe that one captain was as bad as another. "You can switch horses," said one old salt, "but it's always the same cart."

The plan was as follows: Herman and Toby would go ashore the next morning with six or seven men, part of the starboard watch; they would then unobtrusively break with the company and head into the hills on their own, losing themselves in the dense underbrush. A party might be sent in pursuit: Pease was unpredictable in this regard, and seemed possessive of his crew. Yet they would push deep into the interior, overland for perhaps a week or two before joining another whaler in one of the island's several bays. They had no worry about food—a tropical island is a natural cornucopia, as Jack Hall had told everyone in one of his know-it-all monologues.

H.M. and Toby had no plan to "go native," as the saying went. Men did this regularly, and on most islands in the South Seas one could find a light-skinned, bearded man in beads and loincloth. Often a native girl could be found nearby, with several tow-haired children. The temptations were obvious. Why not exchange the strictures of European or American life for something akin to paradise, a world of bamboo temples and fruit, sweet coconut milk and intoxicating drinks, unabashed sexual freedom and the perpetual midsummer of life near the line? Why not avoid the grind of day-to-day commitments, the lockstep schedules of chartered accountants, schoolmasters, and commercial travelers? Clock towers never chimed in this timeless universe.

Toby brought a ditty bag with him into the boat—a quiet signal that he would jump ship as planned. For his part, Herman had provisioned himself as best he could, stealing handfuls of sea biscuit and salt horse from the galley. He had tucked into a roll as much tobacco as he could lay his hands on: the inch-thick plugs would come in handy with the natives. He had in his pockets a small supply of trinkets, for bartering.

And so they came ashore in late afternoon, with Captain Pease watching them from afar, alone on the quarterdeck. The plan was to spend a few days on the island, gathering supplies.

Even in paradise, dark clouds will appear, and they did. In the tropics, rains switch on and off suddenly. As they rowed to shore near sundown, raindrops prickled the water's surface like gooseflesh. Making landfall, Herman and Toby stepped into the tepid, milky surf, knee-deep in foam, glad to feel the earth underfoot again. One forgot what it was like to stand on a level plane. Herman felt his head sway, and he nearly lost his balance. As Toby tumbled into the water, Herman extended a hand.

"On your feet now, Greene," he said.

He held on to Toby's hand longer than was necessary, and Toby did not withdraw it.

With evening approaching, the men hastily constructed a shelter of palm leaves, using driftwood for timber, as a wall of rain swept across the black sand of the beach in torrential sheets. A stiff wind lashed them, and the men cursed their bad luck, but Herman and Toby felt only relief. The weather would provide a perfect distraction.

This makeshift haven was hardly proof against such a downpour, and yet the drumming rain on the palms proved soporific. Before long the larboard crew fell asleep—a kind of group hypnosis. Toby and H.M. seized the moment, slipping away into the night. With Toby in the lead, they beat a path toward the grove behind them, following what seemed like a natural path that moved steadily upward. By dawn, the rains abated, with a screech-blue sky overhead; the deserters—exhausted but too excited by their escape to fret about the lack of sleep—could just make out the ridge ahead, their goal. They passed several clusters of wattle-sided huts with thatched roofs and dirt floors covered in tapa rugs, but they were able to slip by these dwellings without detection. Before long they found a trace that appeared to rise toward the ridge. All the while neither escapee spoke.

Silence sealed their pact, or so H.M. believed.

He and Toby would rise or fall together.

After climbing through the whole of morning in humid, bright air, they arrived at a plateau—still miles from the ridge itself. Ahead rose a solid curtain of yellow reeds.

"We are bucked," said Toby.

"Nonsense. Let me go first."

Herman was the stronger of the pair, and he used his bare hands, pulling the reeds apart like prison bars. Eventually he took out his knife—he was glad he'd brought it—and cut as best he could, weakening the wall before him, creating openings. The task grew tiresome after a short while, yet H.M. bulled his way forward. It was his nature to do so, and he pushed and trod, knocking down the dense curtain. He sweated and huffed, while Toby followed close on his heels, a beneficiary of Herman's efforts.

Nothing must stand in his way, Herman told himself; the summit would be his that afternoon.

He and Toby clawed and hacked their way to the top, where they would spend the night under a lean-to assembled by laying branches over a sturdy fallen coconut palm propped up by a large boulder. The roof complete, they lined the floor with feathery blue-gray ferns. Herman felt quite satisfied by this handiwork (he and Eli Fly had once constructed a similar shelter in the Adirondacks), and he decided they should feast on moist biscuits and shreds of salt horse, with fresh guava for dessert—he had harvested the fruit earlier in the day, with an eye toward dinner. They would drink milk from coconut shells, washing everything down with water from a nearby spring.

As they ate, the sun slid down the sky, sweeping the floor below as they looked out from what must have been the highest point of the island. The bay of Nuku Hiva blazed below them, with the *Acushnet* visible, a dot among the other dots. The view toward the interior spread over a vast green valley, with a farther distant ridge in the evening mist, barely visible. Herman and Toby had hoped to see the bay of Happar in the distance, but this was not the case. They would have to proceed on faith, believing in the reality of things beyond view.

The valley opened gradually to Herman and Toby, who had slept deeply after their long hours of unabated climbing. The day had broken hot from the outset—a lovely warming heat with the sun like a griddle—and it felt good on their bare arms and faces. They had breakfasted on biscuit, which had been reduced to a mush in rain-soaked folds of cloth. H.M. checked to see if his journal had survived the transfer from ship to shore, and it had: he had wrapped it carefully in waxy paper. It attracted Toby's curiosity.

"What is this writing of yours?"

"I keep a journal."

"You will publish our adventures to the world, eh?"

"I shall tell the truth, Toby."

"Not that!"

"All right, the half-truth."

"Call it a novel."

"Or a memoir," H.M. responded. "Everyone knows they are made up. Only novels tell the unadorned truth."

They found the downward trek hard on their knees—much harder than climbing. As expected, there was an abundance of fruit to pick, and they stopped to gorge themselves on unknown morsels of many shapes and sizes. It was clear that someone had passed this way not long before: a fresh print in the mud revealed as much. They knew that a fair population of natives—Typees or Happars—

lived in these jungles and some were hostile; accounts of brutality and cannibalism were common fare aboard whalers—the usual stories told by sailors during evening watch, probably embellished. (Toothless Tom—the oldest man aboard the *Acushnet*—had reveled in tales that made the blood curdle, and the details he provided were such that none doubted their authenticity. You could not invent such things.)

To press on steadily seemed the only option, as Pease could well have sent a search party after them. What they had not quite counted on was the steep and slippery path, which drew to a halt on a sharp cliff, with a dizzying drop below. They rested there for a time, dangling their legs over the ledge. It was Herman's contention that no obstacle was insurmountable; ingenuity was all. And soon enough he found a ropelike vine and lowered himself over the edge. Toby followed, grasping another vine. They found a footing and leaped from rock to rock, holding to various plants and exposed tubers that provided a kind of matting to the slimy hillside. Roots dangled and dripped, but they conducted H.M. and Toby downward to a path that would lead into the thickets.

They paused briefly to look back, upward.

"I don't think we're going home that way," said Toby.

"Unless we grow wings," said Herman.

In midafternoon, exhausted, they paused at a point where several streams converged and poured into a deep gorge—a beautiful site, with surrounding rocks sleeved in leathery moss. Toby and H.M. decided to spend the night in a nearby cave, where at least they would not have to sleep in full view of the native population. They could sense a thousand eyes burning in the green shade, under leafy boughs or behind thickets.

"Why do I think we're not alone?" Toby wondered.

"Because God is with us," H.M. said, to tease his friend.

Herman was not especially afraid, being confident of his survival skills. He would not succumb to these savages, however strong or clever they might prove. That was simply not the fate he had imagined for himself. Everything that happened here was part of a larger narrative, and he saw himself inside an evolving plot that never failed to absorb him. All he had to do, at this point, was imagine the ending.

The cave was shallow, as they discovered, its entrance masked by shrubs with a eucalyptus tang. H.M. and Toby soon made themselves comfortable, arranging a bed of dry palms and propping their heads on the ditty bags. The day had been sultry, even sweltering, and they welcomed the cool interior, with stony walls that dripped into the dirt floor. There was a gurgling sound deep in the hillside, almost a sucking noise. But they fell into a swoon almost at once.

In the morning, the young men stepped into the jungle light, struck by the wondrous scene. Coming upon a stream, where a deep pool gathered under gray rocks, they stripped to bathe. H.M. watched as Toby lowered himself into the foaming waters, going under for a full minute, rising with a burst through the surface, splashing. He seemed childlike in his love of water, swimming from one side to the other, hauling himself onto a flat stone, where he baked, a lizard in the sun. Herman pulled himself up beside him, and they lay there for a while, enjoying the evaporation on their skins.

But a nearby swishing sound in the bushes startled Herman, who sat up. He thought he saw a face in a briary thicket, though he said nothing about it to Toby. They were probably in the midst of Typees or Happars, he decided. How else to account for the footprints, so omnipresent in the dirt? He had heard from Toothless Tom that these tribes loathed each other and would perpetrate the most hideous affronts on those captured in their regular skirmishes. Torture, for these natives, was apparently a preoccupation and pleasure, and they spent a good deal of mental capital on devising ever more brutal ways to abuse their enemies.

"I would love to stay here," H.M. said, "but we should press on."

Toby noted that the island was obviously bigger than they had been led to believe, and it might take several days to cross it. Their plan, fashioned on insufficient knowledge, had been to quickly travel to another bay, where whalers arrived at regular intervals. The fact that jungle paths rarely plow ahead in a direct fashion had some-how failed to register.

"There's a lot of underbrush," said Toby.

"And overbrush as well."

Herman didn't mention the eyes in the foliage, nor did he say that during the night he thought he heard a distant drumming. Indeed, he might well have imagined these things, as his own excitable nature—a tendency toward "enthusiasm," to use his mother's word—tended to create omens. It was quite possible that he had invented the eyes, even the drumming, in the fantastical the-ater of his mind, where all sorts of mischief occurred.

Toby understood the need to press on, and they resumed the trek, moving downhill into the jungle, coming to a ravine that seemed yet a further stepping down of the valley. They paused to look, awed and terrified by what lay before them. Four mountain ranges appeared, one behind the other, in different shades of teal. Had Herman and Toby been giants in one of Gulliver's improbable travels, they might have stepped from peak to peak and avoided the thickets that fell between them; as it were, they would almost certainly have to clamber up and down the sides of several valleys to find the bay where whalers might appear and rescue them.

It was good, however, to find abundant water to drink and fruit to pick—purple guavas in profusion, breadfruit and coconuts, tiny tomato-like fruits that smelled foul but tasted delicious, yellow man-gos and green plums of one kind or another. Toby had a passion for such things and seemed willing to swallow any object produced by a tree or bush. In Herman's view, a good portion of this fruit reeked of carrion or old socks, but his hunger was such that he suppressed his revulsion. Even a plantain smothered in ants was tasty if one felt hungry enough.

"Think of the bugs as bits of chocolate," Toby suggested.

Uphill and down, they gave no thought to turning back. The bay of Nuku Hiva lay improbably far behind now, a path impossible to retrace. Day after day for a week they pushed slowly through the jungle, feeding on whatever lay close to hand, sheltering in caves that appeared at nightfall with miraculous ease, as if prepared in advance by a mad hotelier. Nowhere did they encounter Happar or Typee tribesmen, although the evidence of their proximity mounted.

"I'm starving," said Herman, after hours of hiking.

Toby handed over a green branch, whose soft bark was sweet as honey. Herman tasted it, but it lacked substance, and he longed for something more substantial than berries and fruits or the sap of branches. He wanted a piece of rare meat, warm biscuits or buttery rolls, yellow turnips, potatoes with gravy. A succulent bird on a platter—roast chicken or pheasant, perhaps a duck breast in cranberry sauce—would be marvelous for the sort of breakfast that Mr. Pickwick and his friends enjoyed on their rambles through the English counties, where they stopped at thatch-roofed inns that boasted oaken tables laden with quail eggs, pigeon pies, rashers of bacon, hams, salt herring, lamb chops. The English know how to have a good breakfast, H.M. thought.

"Do you know Mr. Pickwick?" he asked Toby.

"Where does this fellow live?"

"He never lived anywhere. But he is very much alive, you can believe me."

Toby looked at him with unease, as if his traveling companion had suddenly lost his mind.

As they continued their descent to the bottom of a valley, the path widened, with so many footprints in the mud that neither Herman nor Toby could doubt the presence of human life. Soon they walked into a clearing amid a fringe of coconut palms. To one side they saw a bamboo hut overlaid with flaxen roofing. Drawing close, they peered into the dim interior: the hut was empty, but there was evidence of recent occupation, as a fire dwindled in the pit outside. They saw a pair of sandals beside a mat, and a bowl of water with flowers floating on the surface—a strangely civilized touch that H.M. found comforting. Surely people who put flowers in their huts would not wish to eat their fellow creatures for dinner.

Herman stared into a grove where among the scrappy silver-leaved pandani, he could see two natives—tall, slender figures that looked eerily alike, a boy and a girl. He moved toward them, holding out a handful of trinkets as bait. After hesitating, they stepped forward, their hair rich, curly, and full. It draped in ringlets over their tawny shoulders. They wore only the slightest garments: girdles of bark, from which hung the leaves of breadfruit trees like green swords. They shimmered, unadorned: Adam and Eve in their innocence and glory. H.M. could detect a residue of fear in the shyness that hung about them, and he smiled, hoping to reassure and welcome. He offered red beads to the boy—he must have been fifteen or sixteen—who took them in his hands, unsure whether to eat or wear them.

Now others appeared, stepping forward into the clearing. They encircled Herman and Toby, drawing close, curious. One older woman actually touched Herman's beard, trilling her tongue. The others laughed. Herman assumed they had few visitors, and so the sudden presence of white men with beards in ragged clothes amused them greatly.

One man of middle age, a stocky fellow with a fierce look and necklace of bone-white shells, his chest and arms tattooed in the most exotic fashion, stepped toward them with belligerent forth-rightness. He held a spear in his right hand and was perhaps a chief. H.M. decided to offer him a plug of tobacco, and he unrolled the precious substance from his frock, holding it before the chief, who sniffed it, stepped back, and stared coldly. He shook his head slowly.

"He doesn't smoke," said Toby. "But they seem friendly enough."

"Let's just say they haven't eaten us yet."

"Happar or Typee?"

H.M. motioned for Toby to be still. It could not be a good thing to signal an understanding of the tribal complexities of Nuku Hiva.

The chief looked soulfully at Herman, as if to say: *What do you take me for?*

"Typee?" asked Herman.

Some instinct had been at work, and it proved a decent impulse, as the chieftain smiled, his teeth like rusty screws in his red gums.

"Typee!" he cried.

A dozen men began to clap, shouting in unison: "Typee! Typee!"

The chief put his hand to his breast, saying, "Mehevi."

H.M. understood. "Herman," he said. "Her-man."

The chief tried, without much luck, to mouth the word. He called him "Hevi."

Herman grinned, accepting the name—so close to that of the chief. And from that time forward, he was known as Hevi among these people. The Typee seemed to relish the name, and they repeated it often.

The exchange of names established a pact of sorts, and friendly relations followed. Mehevi led H.M. and Toby into the bamboo hut, where they sat on mats and received any number of visitors, all eager to exchange names, which seemed a ritual of high importance among this tribe. Merriment prevailed, and the islanders laughed hard and shook their heads and danced in circles. The white sailors were brought a meal in a great calabash: *"poee-poee,"* it was called. Herman bent to feed, later recording his impressions of this dish in his journal in a tiny hand, making sure to use every bit of the page:

> I plunged my hands into the yielding mass of *poee-poee,* a bread-fruit jam not unlike binder's glue. Withdrawing my hands, the jam stuck to my fingers in lengthening strings. So stubborn was its consistency that, in putting my hand into my mouth, the connecting links almost lifted the calabash from the mat. Toby joined me in this embarrassing act of eating, with a group of perhaps a dozen Typees watching, convulsed in laugher, pointing and yipping. Bemused, Mehevi soon demonstrated how properly to eat this local delicacy, swirling a long forefinger in the dish, drawing it out covered with the yellowy goo. He licked this finger clean.

In the evening Mehevi ushered H.M. and Toby to one corner of the hut, where they were to sleep on mats. They lay down, whereupon an elderly woman with long white hair ceremoniously covered them with blankets of tapa and then extinguished the tapers that burned in small pots beside them. Herman half expected a bed-time story.

The week that followed seemed less than real, a fantasy of easy days in paradise, in which they were shown the considerable plea-sures of Typee life. They feasted on an array of delectable fruits, and they watched with fascination as the young natives walked to a nearby stream to bathe beneath a waterfall. All were naked, male and female, splashing in the water or lying about on warm rocks. From what H.M. could tell, the young men were lazy fellows, and he called them "roistering blades of savages" in his journal. They took turns holding hands with young women, running fingers through their long hair, smoothing their skin with their hands as if polishing the bronze surface. The girls liked this attention and glowed.

H.M. and Toby went bathing as well, naked like the others. This pool reminded H.M. of a particular swimming hole in the Adirondacks where he had swum naked with Gansevoort one summer when he was eleven or twelve. He took a special interest in the two lovely savages he had seen in the grove, and whose names, as far as he could discern, were Far Away and Fawn Away. They must be twins, he decided. He could hardly distinguish one from the other, except by their genitalia. They stood taller than the rest by several inches, with lean and smooth bodies, wonderfully graceful. Hair cascaded over their shoulders, gleaming and wet. They smiled at H.M. adoringly and asked perpetual questions he could neither understand nor answer, although his silence afforded no obstacle to their interrogations. He lay on a warm rock between them and ate a banana that Far Away—the male twin—had peeled for him in the most loving manner. It was more delicious than anything he could recall, and he ate greedily, as Fawn Away, with her delicate fingers, stroked his beard and chatted.

"Life was not meant to be like this," said Toby, enjoying a massage of his shoulders from a young woman who had taken a shine to him.

"I don't see why," H.M. said.

"They must have a god, or gods, who disapprove."

"It's our God who disapproves, not theirs."

"He is not happy with us, I fear."

"But we are," Herman said. "Just don't tell your mother. It's not what a good Methodist would do."

"I won't tell a soul, if we survive."

"Oh, we'll survive."

"You hope so."

Their dialogue unfolded—slow, mundane. They lived as if

awake but dreaming, accepting this pageant of life among the Typees. They were a novelty of sorts, a wonderful adjunct to the Typees' lives.

Now he reciprocated the strokes of Fawn Away, feeling her damp hair and twirling her ringlets with his forefingers. She was all mud and sunlight and smelled of hibiscus, with her necklace of blossoms. Her brother, Far Away, also wore flowers. They were perfect creatures, unblemished and fresh. Only age could diminish them. In the meanwhile, they seemed oblivious to the possibility of demise or decrepitude, inhabiting the day itself, wearing its raiment of sunshine, its cloak of shadows.

Finding the sun too hot after a while, H.M. slipped into the water beneath the falls. He skimmed the sandy bottom, opening his eyes to a profusion of minnows, pink and gold, then let the bubbling spring lift him. Far Away and Fawn Away waved, and he swam toward them, keeping his head above the surface. As he approached the ledge, he felt something sharp running along his leg on the inside, from ankle to mid-thigh. A mysterious plant pricked him like barbed wire: a snag in paradise. He hauled himself onto the flat rocks to inspect the damage: a red line like a scratch from a thumbnail. It stung, forming a welt in crescent shape.

This wound, however slight, proved a crack in the teacup that widened into a chasm.

H.M. thought nothing about the scratch again until the next morning, when he found it difficult to walk. By noon, his leg had swollen below the knee, with the wound forming a small pillow of flesh that looked worse than it felt. Now a large young man knelt beside him and motioned for Herman to mount his shoulders. H.M. was a little baffled, and he eyed the fellow suspiciously: he was colossal, with broad shoulders—Brobdingnagian was the word that floated into H.M.'s mind.

"Kory-Kory," he said, touching his chest with blunt fingers.

"Me, Hevi," said Herman, imitating the gesture.

Kory-Kory—who had clearly been assigned to look after Herman—liked this exchange and showed his pleasure by saying, *"Humpa humpa."* Only this gentle giant, Kory-Kory, seemed acquainted with this word, and he used it frequently.

After dinner that night, a fever seized Herman. Sweat lathered his beard, and his teeth clattered. He shouted for his mother as Toby applied a wet cloth to his forehead. Kory-Kory grew increasingly agitated as the evening wore on. At one point he disappeared into the dark for an hour, returning with a fat-necked medicine man called Manuhela, a stump of a fellow with painted cheeks and a beard like fungus. A session of chanting followed, after which Manuhela dribbled a bittersweet ooze into his patient's mouth, and H.M. did not resist. How could he? He fell at once into a stony sleep, as if drugged.

Two days later he awoke, perilously weak, unable even to sit. Toby and Kory-Kory crouched at either side of him.

"I am going to die, Toby."

"You will be fine," said his friend, without conviction.

"Listen to me. You should go *now*. Get help, and some medicine. These savages will kill me with their foul brews."

"The chants are probably *more* dangerous," Toby said, not entirely in jest, as he had a superstitious nature.

H.M. smirked, and Toby was relieved to see his friend had not lost his humor. Reaching for Herman's hand, he squeezed it. "I promise: I'll be back."

Toby kissed him lightly on the forehead—a gesture of affection that H.M. would remember.

"Goodbye, Toby."

"I'll come back. Trust me!"

Kory-Kory appeared to understand the nature of this exchange between H.M. and Toby; under his breath, he let out his usual expression: "*Humpa humpa*." What he meant puzzled Herman. In any case, the giant remained at his side, making no effort to alert anyone to Toby's behavior as he gathered up his ditty bag and slipped away into the bush, determined to return as soon as possible with help.

Nobody called attention to the disappearance of Toby Greene, at least not in the presence of H.M., although he did notice that his hosts seemed to guard him with fresh vigilance. Far Away and Fawn Away had obviously been assigned to him as well, for they rarely let him out of sight. Appearing soon after breakfast, they remained beside him until he lay down on the mat in the evening. Kory-Kory, as usual, acted as devout manservant, fetching drinks and meals, even brushing his beard and hair. When things went smoothly, he would say, *"Humpa humpa,"* leaving it there. (He rarely spoke to his fellow savages—a curious fact that began to prey on Herman's mind. Was the fellow a simpleton? Was he merely shy? Had he, perhaps, been captured from another tribe and forced into the role of slave? Indeed, his size alone set him apart.)

The Typees treated H.M. like a visiting head of state. His every wish they anticipated, bringing him gourds stuffed with fruits and compotes, few of which he could identify. A plate of roasted meat appeared one afternoon, much to his surprise; he could not quite identify its origin, but it tasted of venison, perhaps a little gamier. He didn't quarrel with this, as he felt starved for meat. Manuhela turned up every morning after breakfast, applying a smelly poultice to Herman's leg. He would also perform various chants and dances for good measure. The leg seemed no better but no worse, and this comforted H.M., who knew about gangrene and its horrors—experienced sailors aboard the *Acushnet* often referred to men who lost limbs to this disease. Other infections posed a threat, too. It seemed that everything in the tropics was subject to rot, even one's own flesh.

The centerpiece of Herman's day was the afternoon, invariably spent bathing at the waterfall. Kory-Kory carried him to the edge of the rock pool, where he would lie naked among other nymphs and swimmers. Fawn Away paid close attention to his every movement, to his delight. He loved her oval face, wet lips, and the glisten of her teeth. Her hair was black but could also seem chestnut—the color depended on the angle of light; lush ringlets fell over her shoulders, and her small breasts were always pointed, as if perpetually in a state of arousal. That she had beryl eyes—a peculiar shade of blue-green—interested him: everyone else among the Typees had black or brown eyes. (Even Far Away had deep brown, nearly black, eyes.) She did have a number of tattoos, but less so than her twin, her lover—whoever he was, this beautiful young man who allowed only a little distance to gather between them.

H.M. could not stop watching them as they played in the water, splashing each other, kissing. He often lay between them on the hot rocks, his head in her lap or his. Fawn Away would massage his bad leg, applying mud: a cure-all that seemed popular among the Typees, many of whom had slabs of pink-gray mud applied to their skin in some place. Kory-Kory had recently smothered his throat in this mud, making him look like a rooster with his neck like an old nail pulled from his shoulders. This procedure apparently pleased Kory-Kory, who stepped back in admiration, uttering his all-purpose groan of satisfaction: *"Humpa humpa."* (Alas, when Herman used it once as Fawn Away massaged his leg, it only produced guffaws.)

H.M. would lie on his mat in the early evening—propping himself on one elbow, making notes in his journal. "Flora is their jeweler," he wrote. "Sometimes the islanders wear necklaces of tiny carnations, which they string like rubies on a fiber of tapa or display

in their ears—a single white bud, the delicate petals folded together
in a beautiful sphere, not unlike a drop of the purest pearl. Chaplets, too, resemble the strawberry coronal worn by the English peer-
ess. Composed of twined leaves and blossoms, they often crown
their beautiful temples; bracelets and anklets of the same tasteful pattern are commonplace."

Gradually H.M. found himself able to walk on his own, with
less pain every day. He wondered, however, if he should reveal the
extent to which he had actually improved. The savages guarded him
lightly, believing him too lame to disappear into the bush as Toby
Greene had done. One day Mehevi led him along a jungle path on
the shoulders of Kory-Kory—not the usual sort of excursion. They
descended into a glen, across a flinty stream. In the tall palms one
heard racketing parrots and tropical songbirds whose trilling resembled that of the martins that H.M. had liked so much in the Adirondacks. They passed through a flurry of white butterflies like summer
snowflakes. All the while Mehevi rumbled on, explaining things to
H.M., who had only begun to find the language less than thoroughly opaque. He supposed that, should he remain in place among
the Typees, he would at some point understand what they said. A
foreign language is like that, he concluded; you listen for a length
of time, in a mist of incomprehension, and suddenly the babble dis-
solves. Words become things.

Kory-Kory stopped amid a grove of high breadfruit trees.
Mehevi bowed, his arms folded at his chest. He uttered a brief
chant. This was a sacred wood, H.M. assumed, a place where the
Typees enacted tribal rituals, perhaps abominable rites. Half hidden
in the shrubbery were altars, blocks of polished stone, one upon the
other, all perilously balanced and rising to perhaps fifteen feet. A
rustic temple rose, surrounded by a curtain of bamboo. A putrefac-
tion of some kind lay on one of these altars, a decaying mass of veg-
etable substance. Eerily shaped wooden figures leaned toward the

center of a circle, where a stake in the ground was draped with flowers. In a nearby shed, H.M. was shown an array of muskets (of more antiquarian than real value, and doubtless obtained from European or American ships in exchange for who knew what), rows of spears, axes, war clubs, and javelins. This was the armory of the tribe, and Mehevi would almost certainly have a reason for showing this store of weaponry to his captive. Was he suggesting that Herman should think twice before trying to escape? Perhaps he simply wished to boast, saying: We are stronger than the Happar tribe, are we not?

Mehevi lifted a spear from the rack, and he touched the blade to the palm of his hand.

Whatever the chief's motive now, H.M. wore an appropriate look of deference. What he saw impressed him, and he had no desire to end up at the wrong end of a spear.

"Typee, powerful," Herman said, hitting his chest with a closed fist.

This provoked a ripple of nervous laughter in Kory-Kory. Mehevi followed with a gutsy laugh, and he touched Herman on the forearm to register his approval.

A few days later, H.M. heard what could only have been war drums, an ominous throb in the distant bush. Within half an hour, a small gathering arrived in the clearing that Herman had made his home for some time—he'd lost track of the calendar and could not decide whether he had been a captive for two weeks or two months. Local drums answered the distant drums, a pattern of call-and-response; before long a dozen youths—Far Away among them—in full body paint appeared, armed with spears and hatchets. The women gathered in a circle around them, ululating. Herman understood from the sober look on the face of Kory-Kory that serious business lay ahead for these warriors, who now rushed into the jungles with sharp cries.

Hours passed, and whatever battle took place occurred far from

Herman's encampment. But he sensed the danger: its aura filled the air. The women sat around working anxiously at their beads, cooking. Older men paced in silence. Kory-Kory fell into a vague trance, his legs crossed as he leaned against a mud wall with shut eyes, occasionally mumbling what may have been a prayer.

At sundown, the band of warriors returned, several of them with severe gashes and bruises. H.M. recognized most of them, as they had joined him on previous days for afternoon swims. But he wondered about Far Away, who was nowhere to be seen. Had anything happened to him?

The young men were served large wooden trenchers heaped with steaming meat, and the tribe gathered around, feasting and feting—a few of them bursting into cries or cackles. H.M. thought, at first, this was surely cannibalism on display. How else to account for the uncouth noises, the barbarous undercurrent he could sense? But as he drew close, he realized that, in fact, a wild pig had been caught and cooked. He recognized the familiar smell of roast pork, and with gratitude he accepted a platter of meat from Mehevi, who looked on with amusement as H.M. consumed the dish with peculiar gusto. He had not tasted anything so good since the *Acushnet* left port in Peru.

Later that night, as he lay half asleep on his mat, H.M. heard a quiet throb of drums, the shaking of gourds filled with dry seeds. The gourds rattled, almost hissed, and chants arose. He wanted to watch the proceedings but assumed that his presence would not be welcome. He did manage, however, to catch a glimpse of a procession through the open door of the hut: the returning warriors moved in a slow train, carrying what was surely the body of a slain Happar. The corpse was slung on a pole, shouldered by two stout fellows. The ceremony lasted only a few minutes, after which the crowd dispersed. H.M. felt quite sure this body had been taken to the sacred grove.

He slept badly that night, in a sick sweat that lathered his mat with damp. His dreams were so terribly violent that he actually preferred waking to sleeping. At least as he lay awake he could vaguely control the direction of his thoughts.

The next day was something of a high holiday, devoted to hours of rituals led by a man who had appeared from nowhere: a small-boned, white-haired high priest called Kolory. Everyone paid him respect, bowing and scraping as he passed, falling silent or muttering praise. He led what Herman came to regard as the Feast of Calabashes. Overflowing dishes arrived in long bottle gourds, and prayers lifted to the heavens. All and sundry danced in slow circles, chanting. Fawn Away seemed disconnected, dancing by herself in a small circle of sorrow. Now H.M. knew that something had befallen Far Away, who had not appeared in several days. He wished he could speak the Typee language, could talk to her plainly, offering condolences. But he felt impotent, unable to comfort her in this time of grief and disarray.

Fawn Away's distress grew by the day, and Herman's inability to communicate with her drove him mad. One night in sympathy he put his arms on her shoulders, and she leaned her head against his chest, with her small breasts pressing to him. She invited him to lie beside her in a hut some hundred yards from his usual dwelling, and he consented, following her closely, ignoring the frowns of Kory-Kory.

The night passed in surprising and intimate ways, as Fawn Away opened herself fully to her friend. They wrestled like children, biting and clawing, kissing, teasing. Herman came up behind her and licked her neck, burying his face in the lush ringlets of her hair. She thrust her buttocks in a way that invited him forward, and he did not refuse the invitation. He loved what passed between them, and would have died happily that night if fate had commanded such. He lay with her till dawn broke, observing with a sigh the elegant slope of her spine as it dipped into a valley in her lower back before a sudden rise to perfection. He decided that a naked woman on her stomach, asleep, was the loveliest thing in the world.

At this point a sleepy Kory-Kory—who had crouched outside the hut all night—called to him, with a sense of urgency: "Hevi—*bunga vo!*"

Herman had come to trust his faithful cicerone and understood what he meant by this. He followed him into the misty dawn, returning to his hut, where he lay beside Kory-Kory and slept a few more hours, waking to another drumbeat in the bush.

"Happar!" Kory-Kory intoned.

Another phase in the continuing war between Typee and Happar warriors must have begun, and H.M. reckoned these hostilities could only spell danger for him. Again he watched the young warriors assemble in the clearing for a blessing by Kolory, who threw powdery handfuls of seed in their hair, one by one. This was perhaps a way of empowering them—or some equivalent of the last rites of the Roman church. Meanwhile, a dozen elderly men crouched on the ground behind them, offering an uninterrupted monotonous chant as elderly women with breasts like heavy sacks beat the air with grass fans. Herman and Kory-Kory stood to one side, observing the scene. A short while later, H.M. took out his journal to record his impressions.

His writing puzzled the Typees, who often gathered to watch over his shoulder as he scribbled. He wondered if they understood anything of what the act of writing meant, how it engaged body and soul, this discipline of seeing and saying. Certainly they had their own arts and crafts, though such activity seemed the province of women. H.M. had observed the weaving of tapa or painting on gourds or clay pots. They created intricately beautiful necklaces and bracelets from shells. Many had a gift for arranging flowers into chaplets or chains for ceremonial events or personal decoration.

They were also expert at tattooing, and their elaborate designs were much coveted by young warriors.

Soon after the warriors departed, Kory-Kory offered Herman a pipe, and he smoked happily, the dry blue-gray leaves more like an exotic tea than tobacco. It was called *bonugo,* and he had smoked it several times in the past. The sweet smoke made him drowsy, and he wondered what it was exactly—he thought seriously about importing its seeds. Surely this would secure the fortune that he intended to amass at some point, preferably earlier rather than later. He determined *not* to end his life as his father had: sunk in debt, with an anxious brood of children, attended by a desperate wife who wondered how to pay the rent or feed the family on a negative income. He would accumulate a nest egg, using whatever means lay at his disposal as a bulwark against the world and its indignities.

The *bonugo* smoke sent Herman into a swoon, and he was nearly unconscious when a tap on his shoulder alerted him to Fawn Away's presence. He wondered how long she had been there.

"*Ne-meni,*" she whispered, with a knowing look.

She led him through the bush into the sacred wood, where tapers burned on low altars, although the temple was empty. Fawn Away took him into a hut where, on a slab of polished black stone, a dozen skulls glistened. In a box nearby were human bones picked clean, probably not by birds or animals. Her big eyes met his, and he nodded to show he understood.

The message was unmistakable: he would be eaten soon. If the war with the Happars did not go well, what would stop the Typees from offering to their gods a very handsome morsel of American flesh as a sacrifice? Fawn Away whispered in a way that required no literal translation. He listened to the sound of sense, with meaning carried by the inflection, the urgency. Her attempt to inform him struck a chord, and he kissed her mouth—a lingering hard kiss, with a clatter of teeth. He would have made love with her on the floor of that bone shop had she allowed it; but she held his hand and pulled him from the hut into the dusky jungle, where it was suddenly cool. Winds riffled the high palms and brought gooseflesh to his skin.

A drumming could be heard, faintly at first, growing louder quickly, and they crouched behind a thicket of vines, shielded by ferns as tall as themselves. Fawn Away motioned to Herman to keep his head down, and they watched as six Typee warriors passed nearby, with the corpse of a dead Happar slung from a pole, bound by his wrists and ankles. They took him into the sacred grove, into the bone shop, where a strange unearthly chanting began.

"*Ne-meni,*" whispered Fawn Away.

He replied under his breath, but in English, "I must get away from here. Home! I must go."

She understood. He knew this because she led him along to a branch in the path, where the left fork dropped steeply into a valley. She pointed urgently, and he realized she had revealed an escape route—a path to his earlier life, if he chose to take it—a road home. And he must take it, as he could never live happily or permanently among the Typees. This was not his life, and they were not his people; their ways were alien, at times repulsive. Even if they should not actually wish to eat him, he could never rest easy among them. Their appetites and secret ways frightened him. Perhaps more important, he understood that he could only occupy the position of outsider for so long without discomfort. He liked to feel a part of the world around him, not an onlooker.

Now Fawn Away led H.M. back to his hut, where he settled quietly beside Kory-Kory, though he didn't dare sleep, lest he should dream. He knew that in dreams he would see Typees peeling flesh from the slain Happar warrior or roasting hunks of flesh or licking his bones clean. Another skull would shine on that horrid slab—and the collection would surely grow.

As he stretched out on the mat, he listened to the usual jungle racket outside—a million insects working their tiny engines in the night, feeding and mating. Did he just imagine the swish of bodies through the sooty air, the click of bamboo? At first, he thought he heard drums again in the middle distance, a subtle but dire pulse. Then he realized that what he heard was his own heart, which knocked in his throat, its echo rising in the round dome of his skull.

To soothe himself, he tried as best he could to recall the comforting details of his home near Albany, with its garden in the back, a shed full of tools. He moved in his mind from room to room, noting the brown wainscoting, the ivory trim on the doors, the yellow-and-blue flowery wallpaper and brass sconces. He could see the wide pine floorboards, which he had sanded and stained himself. Having exhausted this tack, he recalled long afternoons of fishing in a swampy inlet of the Hudson, a summer of skinny knees and swimming naked with Eli Fly. Then he brought to mind certain galleries in Manhattan, where he liked to wander on visits to the city, and where he dreamed of being able to purchase paintings one day—canvases in gilded frames, Venetian views perhaps, something by the great Canaletto—his favorite artist of the previous century. Ah, to own one of these paintings would surpass any dream!

He tried to imagine a future for himself in the realm of literature. One day he would be a famous and wealthy writer, and the world would wait eagerly for each book. "Have you read the new Melville?" they would ask, in elegant parlors or smoky clubrooms. "I do believe he's outdone himself."

Perhaps he would live in Venice and write novels or long narrative poems. He might occupy a series of sumptuous rooms in a villa overlooking the canals, or with a view of the Lido, or perhaps San Marco itself. He should have no less of a life than the great Lord Byron, whom Lady Caroline Lamb once described as "mad, bad, and dangerous to know"—if he could believe what Gansevoort had told him. (How was it that Gansevoort knew everything about the lives of authors?)

For two days he bided his time. It was clear he must go, and that no other option presented itself. Indeed, on the night before his departure, he dreamed that a procession of warriors arrived to bind his ankles and wrists; they strapped him to a pole, carried him to a ceremonial grove deep in the bush—a place he'd never seen before. They slotted each end of the pole into a crutch of sorts, lighting a fire beneath him. No matter how he screamed, they stared at him coolly, smacking their lips. He would make a lovely meal, they believed—a very tender and tasty meal. At daybreak, he woke to a hovering Kory-Kory, who applied a cloth to his forehead, offering a gourd of water flavored with the smoky leaves of papal. He drank with trembling hands. The nightmare had been far too real, and being a man who trusted his dreams, he took this vision as a warning.

Yet in the commonsensical light of day he wondered that a tribe should really want to consume a man they had welcomed so completely. His mere presence seemed to amuse them, as they frequently laughed at his behavior, especially when he ate. (The art of Typee etiquette had eluded him.) He certainly had not found them reluctant to bestow sexual favors; for these people, sex was hardly a mysterious or evil thing, something one swept under the rug, practiced in secret, or confined to the marital bedroom. Among the Typees, the usual boundaries that exist between men and women in the West simply disappeared. Typees thought nothing of behavior that, in Europe or America, would have led to deep censure, even prison. He had seen young men, for example, walking in the lush groves, hand in hand, even kissing. The things sailors did in the darkest corners of a whaling ship were done innocently here, without fear or shame.

It occurred to him, however, that men and women of a certain age on this island formed an alliance akin to marriage. They behaved more or less as long-wedded couples, although men often seemed to have two or three wives. He would have liked to remain among them for a year or two—enough time to study their ways, their odd habits, their religious beliefs, their fears and animosities (their hatred of the Happar tribe amounted to an obsession). A very important and popular book might emerge from this research. He might even spread his fame and make a good deal of money by traveling about the United States, giving lectures, as so many had done. If he could bring home a spear or two, a headdress, even a drum, he would have striking visual aids for these lectures.

Fawn Away hovered near him, sighing, pining for Far Away. The exact nature of her relationship with her twin eluded him, and he wished he could ask some questions of her. He wanted more than anything to understand the details of her life, the nature of her feelings, the substance of her thoughts. But the language barrier remained a fairly thick membrane between them. She looked at him beseechingly now, and he took this to mean she understood he was in terrible danger and hoped he would make a sensible decision and flee.

He resolved to leave at dawn the following day, well before Kory-Kory—a heavy sleeper—woke. He would make his way into the bush, following the fork in the path that Fawn Away had shown him. The Typees might choose to pursue him, or they might leave him to his fate among the Happars. The Happars were, at least by reputation, a gentler people. He had already experienced the most threatening group of islanders—if he could trust the collective wisdom of sailors. Many of them would never believe that he had somehow managed to survive, even prosper, among the Typees, as well as he had done thus far. That he entertained, however briefly, the notion of remaining among them forever would certainly astonish them.

He needed no alarm to waken. It was perhaps an hour before dawn when, stealthily, he abandoned the hut that had begun to feel like home. Kory-Kory had smoked a good deal of *bonugo* the night before, guaranteeing a secure sleep; he snored loudly at present, a rattling, scraping sound that comforted H.M. as he had packed his ditty bag and slipped, undetected, into a thicket behind the hut. The Typees had begun to take his presence for granted, and somehow they didn't imagine he might wish to escape. Why would an honored guest choose to abandon their generous company? What could the world beyond the Marquesas offer that they did not possess in abundance?

As he stepped behind a large banyan, looking for cover, a voice startled him: "Hevi!"

It was Fawn Away, who waited for him in the bush. Had she been there all night?

She spoke rapidly, in a husky whisper, gesturing in the direction of the jungle. He followed her, limping (his leg still was not perfectly healed), descending without a word into a broad, misty valley. Herman felt a tremendous swell of sadness as they walked, aware that he would never see her again. She would be fixed in lithe girlhood, a memory he would never lose, an ideal of sorts, a site of permanent longing. Once they stopped to kiss under a huge gum tree, and it was a long, deep kiss, a kiss of parting.

We must go, she seemed to say, pointing to the path ahead. He understood and he followed, struggling to keep up with her as they dropped into the valley. It amazed him how she moved effortlessly through the bush, avoiding low-hanging limbs, skipping over streams. Big-finned palms swayed overhead, making an ominous hiss. Coconuts rained down unpredictably, and H.M. could hear chirping noises in the middle distance—Happar warriors, perhaps. He assumed Kory-Kory would alert the others to his absence, and a party would set off in pursuit. They would have guessed at once that Fawn Away had told him how to get to the coast, as he could never make such a journey without a guide, and he worried about what consequences awaited her for this act of treason.

The path turned sharply northward as they approached the beach, and H.M. could see the bay below—a thrilling sight. Even more heartening was a tiny black dot on the water that would probably be a whaler. He prayed it was not the *Acushnet*! If so, he might well choose to return with Fawn Away to his fate among the Typees. On the other hand, this was surely *not* the bay of Typee before him, and he assumed the vessel in view was something else. They would surely welcome him aboard, as an experienced hand could only add value to any expedition.

Within the hour they made it to the hardscrabble beach, its black shingle pitched at a slight angle toward the water. The ship lay at anchor, a compact whaler with a low-slung hull blackened by time, its rigging bleached by exposure to the tropical sun. It was definitely *not* the *Acushnet,* which was all that mattered to Herman.

He and Fawn Away were not alone, however, as a band of islanders materialized from another point along the beach and began to rush in their direction. Herman assumed they were Happars, though it hardly mattered. Fawn Away seemed quite upset by their presence, urging him to run ahead, shouting what he took to be the Typee word for "hurry." He obeyed, driven by unalloyed terror; he could no longer even feel his legs as they churned beneath him.

A small whaleboat manned by five tanned fellows had come ashore, and the men stood about as if waiting for him. Picking up speed, H.M. passed Fawn Away—reaching his hand to touch her as he passed her, shouting "Thank you!" as his fingers grazed her shoulders. He wanted to stop to kiss her, to hold her; but he knew that everything—his future itself—depended on his rapid transport to the vessel just offshore, whatever it might be.

The men at the whaleboat understood, nodding as H.M. gestured toward the whaler. He began to push the whaleboat into the warm suds, shouting orders in a commanding fashion as his pursuers closed on him, only a hundred yards away, skimming over the hot black sand and shrieking. H.M. wondered what they could possibly want of him, but he had no reason to wait and see.

"Away!" he shouted. "Hurry!"

The tribesmen now reached the edge of the sea, three or four of them shouting, raising spears, hissing. It was terrifying, especially as one of them tossed a spear that narrowly missed Herman's head.

"Row, men! Row!" he cried, seizing an oar himself.

Two of the natives tried to swim after the boat but could not catch up, as the wind pushed the whaleboat away from the beach and the other rowers pulled hard now. They had no wish to deal with these savages, who might well like to snatch a Western sailor, whom they could exchange for beads or trinkets, antique muskets, plugs of tobacco, or whatever.

The swimmers abandoned their chase, and H.M. looked back with a mixture of relief and sadness, seeing Fawn Away in the distance, where she stood by herself, arms folded at her chest. Her features grew less and less distinct as the green hills of the island rose up behind her, steamy, overwhelming.

Within half an hour, the whaleboat drew alongside the *Lucy Ann,* an unimpressive Australian ship—as H.M. could tell from its bleached flag. A number of sailors peered over the rails with mild curiosity. Who on earth was this ragged fellow with long brown hair and an unruly beard who wished to board, asking to speak with the captain? There would surely be a tale here, and perhaps a good one, too.

The truth seems to be . . . that, when he cast his
leaves forth upon the wind, the author addresses, not
the many who will fling aside his volume, or never
take it up, but the few who will understand him, better
than most of his schoolmates or lifemates. Some
authors, indeed, do far more than this, and indulge
themselves in such confidential depths of revelation as
could fittingly be addressed, only and exclusively, to the
heart and mind of perfect sympathy; as if the printed
book, thrown at large on the wide world, were certain
to find out the divided segment of the author's own
nature, and complete his circle of existence by bringing
him into communion with it.

Nathaniel Hawthorne,
"The Custom-House"

LIZZIE

7.

We had heard for some weeks about the impending visit of Charles Dickens—or perhaps visitation is a better word. The great man would appear *in the flesh,* more god than man.

Mr. Dickens was coming to Boston in the depths of a dull winter, 1842. I wrote to my dear friend, Helen Melville (a frequent guest at Mount Vernon Street), suggesting that she stay with us, dangling the bright carrot of Dickens before her nose. "You will certainly meet him," I said. "Father hopes to invite him to the chambers of the supreme court."

Helen and I had been reading Boz for several years, and we adored him.

"He is the dearest man, I'm sure of it," she wrote, accepting my invitation "with fondness and gratitude."

In those days of innocence and enthusiasm, we lived and dreamed the inimitable Boz, who had conjured Mr. Pickwick and Sam Weller, Alfred Jingle, and so many others. He had put poor dear Oliver Twist before us, the sweetest boy who ever lived, and led him into the wicked hands of Fagin and his filthy tribe. He had given us *Nicholas Nickleby* and *Barnaby Rudge* and *The Old Curiosity Shop*—perhaps the noblest of his works.

It was the latter that seized the American public as they grew increasingly frantic for each installment—such was the gift of Mr. Dickens. Everyone was eager to learn the fate of little Nell Trent. I myself lived in the world of that curiosity shop owned by Nell's grandfather, her fond but woefully inept guardian. I grew to hate the hideous moneylender Quilp, whose machinations had inadvertently cast Nell into the streets. Of course I disliked it that her grandfather had so foolishly accepted a loan from such a man: everyone knows the trouble that loans inevitably cause. It is a foolish and dangerous habit that some men acquire—out of necessity, perhaps, or as a failure of character. It leads only to disaster, heartache, and desperation—as I later learned, in the years with Herman.

As *The Old Curiosity Shop* moved inexorably toward a climax, throngs of Mr. Dickens's most devoted readers in New York City, men and women alike, waited impatiently at the dock for the latest installment to arrive by packet ship. They would cry out to those on board as the vessel approached, "Is she dead? What news of little Nell? Is the poor girl alive?" That a novelist should possess the power to command an audience through sheer artifice fascinated me. Little Nell, or Quilp, or Mr. Brass, or Kit Nubbles did not exist—not in reality. But Mr. Dickens had roused them from the void where all souls must dwell until summoned, by hook or by crook. He had made them live and breathe, walk, strut, sing, sigh. He had created a world equal to, perhaps more vivid than, the one in which we moved and breathed. His world made ours more real, more significant—if such a thing is possible. His big heart enlarged our own, added colors to the rainbow of our feelings. He made us see, think, hear, and taste life with more acuity.

How could one not love such a man?

Helen arrived a week early, her suitcase full of books and magazines. (She was my elder and her knowledge of literature was intimidating, although I managed to hold up my end of most conversations.) We spent long afternoons in the sitting room by the fire reading aloud from *Pickwick*. I found it delicious, and so did she. We had each known versions of Job Trotter, Mr. Jingle's horrid servant, who conceals his wiles, feigning meekness. The amiable Augustus Snodgrass, the poet, was an ideal traveling companion, having no force of his own to countermand a situation. (On some occasions, my own father—with his cherubic smile and white whiskers—seemed like a slightly more determined version of Snodgrass. They had portliness in common, and a kind of universal geniality that buttered every occasion with a bluff bonhomie.) Being young women, we had of course encountered versions of the flirtatious wag Mr. Tupman. Indeed, Helen and I often dubbed any sportive or teasing young man a "Tuppie."

We once thought of forming our own Pickwick Club, only it would consist of young women of a certain background and temperament. We might travel about New England by coach, having adventures. I wanted adventure badly, having spent far too long in my father's house. Life on Mount Vernon Street had acquired a tedious predictability, even though my father brought decent young men to the dinner table most weekends, perhaps hoping that something magical would happen, and that one of them might request my hand in holy matrimony. I had myself expected this to happen in due course, though any number of eligible men came and went without a single proposal of marriage. The situation had begun to unnerve me slightly. I wanted children, not unlike most young women, and therefore I required a husband.

Helen brought news of her mysterious brother, Herman, who had set sail a year ago aboard a whaler, visiting such exotic places as

Rio and the coast of Peru, and those strange, bare islands—the Galápagos. He had recently landed in the Sandwich Islands—or so Helen said. The family waited upon the post, desperate for word of the prodigal son, who had refused the ordinary confinements of work in a landlocked life. The death of his father had made it necessary for him to abbreviate his schooling, though everyone knew he had intellectual gifts, even a scholarly disposition. He had been variously a bank clerk, a purveyor of dry goods in his brother's store, a teacher of wild schoolboys in the Berkshires, and a student of engineering and surveying. He never lasted long in these environments, as his wish to fling himself about the world had always overcome the inertia of any situation.

In most of us, inertia steadies and cools, holds us firm.

"I shall faint in front of Mr. Dickens," said Helen. "He is the sun itself. I shall suffer from too much light."

"And I shall suffer from too much of you," I said.

Five years my senior, she nevertheless seemed like a young girl who had still to confront the difficulties of life—what my stepmother called its "variable contours." Nevertheless, I admired Helen's excited way of talking, her frankness and foolery: she said whatever leaped to mind, blurting out truths that most would try to suppress. She dearly loved Herman, her younger brother—that was evident as she repeated his stories. Although he could fall silent for long stretches, in brighter moods he became a teller of tales, an exaggerator, with a rich vocabulary at his disposal. I had not yet had much in the way of personal experience of H.M. and his habits, but I grew to love him through his sister.

"You and Herman would make a perfect couple," she said one morning as we sat in the garden behind my house. "Well," she added, "almost perfect."

I did not like that *almost*.

My dear father understood our affections for Mr. Dickens, and he took it upon himself to see that we got to meet him. One could count on him on these occasions, as he liked to play the role of facilitator.

"I am John the Baptist," he would say. "I pave the way for great men."

I didn't much like the allusion, as the Baptist's head was famously handed to Herod on a silver platter.

We attended a performance in Mr. Dickens's honor at the Tremont Theatre on the night after his arrival. It was thrilling to see the man himself when, to frenzied cheers, he emerged from a side door and was led to a gaily decorated box by several managers and local worthies, including Mayor Chapman (whom my father detested). The young novelist was about to turn thirty, but he looked like a teenager to me, almost girlish with cascading brown hair that brushed his shoulders in a fashionable manner. His quick eyes surveyed the scene with keen interest, and he occasionally waved to someone in the crowd.

The applause continued for several minutes after Boz and his wife took their seats; indeed, great waves of cheering broke over the author's head, demanding a response. So Mr. Dickens stood, taking several dramatic bows, smiling broadly and waving. When the thunder of approval died down, the orchestra played "a Boz Waltz," composed in his honor. The poor fellow tried to sit calmly through the waltz, but this would never do. The audience brought him repeatedly to his feet with cheers of "Boz! Boz!" I felt embarrassed by this behavior, which could never have occurred in a London theater. The English know how to behave in public.

I confess that I liked the looks of Mr. Dickens very much. That hair! It was thick and voluptuous, wavy and rich—any girl would thank God for such tresses. The mobility of his face should have surprised no one: his eyes glittered, and his mouth turned up and down as the fine lips tightened or relaxed. He wore a nut-brown frock coat with yellow buttons, a vest of bright red with a gold paisley print—so different from the black satin waistcoats that Bostonians preferred. I could see a double chain of gold, too. One might say, as Father did, "Mr. Dickens has a bit of the old dandy in him." But I liked this about him, as it suggested boldness, and this trait seemed to fit with the writing.

As I later discovered, the poor man had pushed his way into the theater through a mob of well-wishers who screamed, "Boz! We love you, Boz!" As one might guess, there was not an empty seat in the house.

As the play began, he folded his arms at his chest and inclined his head politely toward the stage. The bill consisted of one act of *Nicholas Nickleby* starring (and adapted by) Joe Field, the comedian. The ingenious Mr. Field had also devised a skit called *Boz: A Masque Phrenologic*. At the outset, he recited a witty poem supposedly in the voice of Boz. It was full of sly jokes about Mr. Dickens's obsession with the cause of international copyright, making light fun of his public (and highly controversial) wish to be paid for his work in North America:

> Besides, I'm told they rather *read me* there,
> For *nothing* too! yet not for that I care;
> Although, no doubt, their authors would delight
> To see me paid, *so* get themselves their *"Right"*
> But pshaw! I must not quarrel with the "Trade,"
> In golden smiles more richly am I paid;
> Happy, when gone, if they my wish recall—
> God bless their Lit'rature and bless them all!

It was all good fun, but I thought I could detect a slight pallor in Mr. Dickens.

Helen whispered in my ear, "This is *too* awful."

As I read in the papers, a delegation of young literary men had called upon the writer at his hotel one morning. The reporters saw Richard Henry Dana, Charles Sumner, and Henry Longfellow leaving his chambers. A grand luncheon was held on his behalf, with speeches and toasts, all of this conveyed in the papers. Another time Mr. Dickens paraded with his wife in the streets of Boston in a shaggy buffalo skin—an extraordinary wildness in this affectation. Young ladies swarmed whenever he paused, some of them furtively snipping bits of fur from his coat as mementoes.

On his last afternoon among us, he and Mrs. Dickens appeared in my father's private judicial chambers, a command performance. My stepmother sat next to me, with Helen Melville on the other side. None of us could speak—such was the extent of our adoration. Then again, one does not speak in the Divine Presence.

For quite some time, Dickens and my father were locked in conversation, with Dickens asking about the legal ramifications of copyright in the United States—a subject he seemed unable to put to one side. A waiter served tea in small china cups, and there were trays of butterfingers.

Suddenly my father ushered the novelist in our direction, introducing us one by one. Leaning toward me, Mr. Dickens looked deeply into my eyes, taking both of my hands in his, pressing them.

"This is such a pleasure," he said.

"I've read your books," I said.

"You're a lovely young woman, I do believe," he said, winking at my father.

"Oh, she's a pistol," said my father.

I could have murdered him, using such a phrase in front of Mr. Dickens!

He actually kissed the hand of Helen, after she brought it toward him in a manner that allowed no other option.

"I shall never wash this hand again," she said.

I gasped. Was she really teasing him?

"Oh, I do like American girls!" Mr. Dickens said.

Mrs. Dickens, however, scowled. It could not have been easy to play the role of wife to a man of such popularity, especially among younger women. Of course she could hardly have known the heights of fame and fortune that lay before her husband when they wed. I knew little about their social origins but my father said they were "from a modest background, both of them." As the papers noted, Mr. Dickens had begun his writing career as a parliamentary reporter. During these years, he wrote a number of sprightly sketches under the name of Boz. From there came *Pickwick,* and the heavens suddenly opened. One could hardly believe that a novelist could so visibly transform the sentiments of millions, softening their hearts, delighting them, terrifying them, appealing to their emotions in the most shameless ways at times, plucking the heartstrings. Mr. Dickens could do all of this, and even more.

We listened as Mr. Dickens recalled his recent voyage. They had encountered horrible storms on the North Atlantic, their steamship—the *Britannia*—pitching and reeling.

"I thought I should die," said Mrs. Dickens, moved to speech for the first time. "Mr. Dickens fed me brandy and water."

"She lapped it up," Mr. Dickens said.

"Nonsense," she said. "But I do like a drop now and then, I do."

"As an aid for digestion," her husband added.

My father took the hint, and he offered brandy to Mr. Dickens and his wife, who—to my surprise—accepted the offer without hesitation. My father joined them (against his habit at this time of day) to make them comfortable, although it didn't appear they required his company.

After a gulp or two, Mr. Dickens returned to the subject of their crossing, which had left a mark: "Ten days into the voyage it got so bad they had to lash the smokestacks to the ship with chains. There was some fear they might tip over and set fire to the decks. That would have done us, no doubt. The waves climbed to a terrible height, and the lifeboats smashed and shattered, still strung in their hoists. The paddle wheels nearly exploded."

"Tell about Halifax," said Mrs. Dickens.

"Ah, Halifax! We ran aground on a silt bar, I believe it was. Waves smashed over the sides. We thought we should have to swim ashore—that would finish us nicely, in that desperate water. But the captain remained calm, as captains do. They are paid to stay calm, and so he did."

"Very calm indeed," Mrs. Dickens added.

Mr. Dickens glared at her. "We dropped anchor in a backwash of some kind," he said, "with the tide ebbing. In the morning we had plenty of water, and could free ourselves."

"My word, what a frightening journey," my father said. "But we're so glad you made it."

"I'm a good swimmer," said Mr. Dickens. "My wife—not so much."

Mrs. Dickens held out her glass for a refill, perhaps unnerved by this talk of swimming.

Now Helen increased the level of anecdotal mayhem by pitching in. "My brother Herman has recently jumped ship in the South Seas," she said. "He was a prisoner among cannibals for some weeks."

"This is wonderful!" Mr. Dickens said. "I do *love* Americans."

"Even the English occasionally jump ship," said my father.

"But the cannibals!" he said.

"The English will occasionally find themselves among cannibals too, I feel quite sure of this," said my father.

Mr. Dickens bared his teeth. "The literary world of London is nothing but cannibals," he said.

"I'm not a literary man, Mr. Dickens, but I suspect it's much the same here. One cannot get a foothold without someone endeavoring to knock one off his perch."

"We like your city very much," Mr. Dickens said. "I had a long walk in the early morning, down by the harbor. The little streets are attractive: the signs are so bright, with their gilded letters. The red brick of your houses is so . . . red. The green shutters are so—"

"Green," my father cut in.

"Yes, green. In London, the paint is dull on everything. The soot has ruined the brick. Everything is old and worn. Yet here all is new, spanking new. The New World, so to speak."

It struck me that Mr. Dickens had a finer turn of speech in his novels than in person.

"I hope you will see a good deal of our country," my father said.

Mr. Dickens explained that he planned to visit factories and mills, homes for the insane, even a noble institution for the deaf and blind. A fairly complex itinerary had been planned for him, I gathered.

"You will find these sites no more cheerful than their counterparts in the Old World," my father said. "I'm afraid we have not lived up to our own expectations."

The remark, with its poignancy, created a gap in the conversation. This proved a natural turning point, and Mr. Dickens announced that he and his wife had to keep another appointment.

As he left my father's chambers, the novelist paused before a large mirror, noticing that a lock of hair had gone astray. He pulled a comb from his jacket, moving the hair back into place before he left, with a slight bow to everyone in the room.

"He is terribly vain," said Helen, later, as we lay in bed. "Did you notice the little thing with his hair?"

"I don't mind that."

"My brothers would *never* comb their hair in public."

"Authors are often quite vain, I believe," I said. "It's almost expected of them."

I knew whereof I spoke, having met quite a few authors at our dinner table. My father was especially fond of Richard Dana, who often came to lunch on Sundays. (I had an inscribed copy of *Two Years Before the Mast,* which my father considered a masterpiece.) Mr. Longfellow had dined with us a number of times, too, as had Mr. Gray, who ran the Wednesday Evening Club—a gathering of authors. My father also liked Dr. Holmes, who had written "Old Ironsides" and other well-known poems. He would turn up for lunch on Sundays at our house with copies of verses by younger poets of his acquaintance, including an eccentric divinity student from Harvard called Jones Very, who was a favorite of Mr. Emerson in Concord. Dr. Holmes would read these poems aloud in a most engaging manner, and we generally admired them.

But Charles Dickens and his books existed on a different plane. Even Mr. Longfellow, with his fertile brain and diverse talents, could not hope to compete. In any case, that was my thinking in 1842, having just shaken the hand of the messiah.

In later years, as Mrs. Herman Melville, I wondered that I should have been so fascinated by Boz. He was just another author, after all—a fine one, of course. But that he should have been treated like Prince Albert himself by the whole of Boston amazed me. No author in our time compelled anything like this adulation.

I have since known many famous authors, including Mr. Hawthorne. Herman worshipped him, much as his sister had worshipped Mr. Dickens. But Nathaniel Hawthorne had no charm. He was a drab, overly serious, self-important fellow whose conversation seemed quite ordinary. I could never understand my husband's obsession with the man or his work. If H.M. had met Charles Dickens, he would have been thoroughly absorbed. We would, perhaps, have followed him to England, where Herman might have strolled in Piccadilly Circus in a shaggy buffalo skin with cascading hair. It seems quite possible he would have realized that an author must at least *try* to please his public. Contempt for one's readers is poor salesmanship. I always tried to tell him this, but he would shrug me off. "My readers," he said, "need very little in the way of coddling."

Alas, they were few in number.

A long calm in the boat . . . It was airless and profound.

In that hot calm, we lay fixed and frozen in like Parry at the Pole. The sun played upon the glassy sea like the sun upon the glaciers.

At the end of two days we lifted up our eyes and beheld a low, creeping, hungry cloud expanding like an army, wing and wing, along the eastern horizon . . .

Here be it said, that though for weeks and weeks reign over the equatorial latitudes of the Pacific, the mildest and sunniest of days; that nevertheless, when storms do come, they come in their strength: spending in a few, brief blasts their concentrated rage. They come like the Mamelukes: they charge, and away.

H.M., *Mardi*

8.

There is nothing worse than a captain without authority, and Henry Ventom was such. On the deck of *Lucy Ann,* he adopted a swagger that fooled no one. A Cockney by birth, with filthy ringlets of auburn hair and breath like a pigsty at high noon in midsummer, he spoke in a rumbling, slurry voice, with a fruity grin that showed any number of teeth like black raisins. His instincts for whaling were unsound, and yet his whims had been realized in excursions that had taken his vessel far afield of the usual cruising grounds of whalers. His motley crew of English and Portuguese sailors considered him a thoroughly dangerous, unpleasant madman, prone to strange resolves. Indeed, it was in the aptly named Resolution Bay on Santa Christina that eight members of his crew had jumped ship, leaving the captain desperately short of hands. Even the first mate had deserted, which left Ventom's dipsomaniac chief officer, James German, as second officer aboard this hapless vessel.

I am back on the *Acushnet,* thought Herman. Only this time the captain is truly farcical and probably murderous.

German—a pale ghost of Jack Hall—was sober enough to realize that Ventom not only showed a weakness of character but was probably dying of venereal disease. The yellow ooze in his eyes told the story. They rolled in his head like sick globes, and the captain had begun to drool and stagger, clutching the ornately carved taffrail in desperation, howling orders into the wind. He seemed confused at times, and believed he could hear the banging of the Great Bells of Bow in London.

"Ring, ye bells!" he would cry.

"Wring your neck," James German would say.

Ventom was also given to meaningless commands, as when he stood on the quarterdeck and began to shout, "Away with the sails! Canvas, ho! Away with ye bastards!"

The men, quite rightly, had ceased to obey his commands, even when they sounded vaguely sensible.

H.M. had been ushered into the captain's quarters by the obsequious Mr. German soon after boarding off Nuku Hiva Island in such melodramatic circumstances, pursued by natives. He was offered a glass of pisco, a strong Peruvian drink, and a chair. For some time the three of them simply absorbed the alcohol, staring ahead as the ship moved into open water.

At last, German confronted Herman. "What on earth were you doing on Nuku Hiva?" he slurred.

Herman leaned back, telling German and the stupefied captain a little of his ordeal among the islanders. He confessed to having deserted the *Acushnet,* guessing that honesty might work best—these men would have known the truth in any case. One did not accidentally fall among cannibals on Nuku Hiva.

"Such honesty is not required," said Ventom. "I will assume you wish to ship aboard the *Lucy Ann*? Do you, what say ye? Speak, boy!"

"I do, sir."

"Ah, *sir,* is it? Good man!"

German examined his own fingernails and said nothing.

Ventom pushed the ship's articles under Herman's nose, dipped a quill in the inkpot, and beckoned him to sign.

"Can you write your name, sir?"

"Oh, aye. I can do that," said Herman, suppressing a smile.

"Is something wrong with your leg, man?" the captain wondered. "I saw you walk a bit of a gimp. I was noticing as much, I was."

"You are quite right," said H.M. "I acquired an infection on the island. My leg was swollen for a week or two but seems to improve each day. It will not affect my duties."

"We shall have no slackness aboard, sir! Not on this ship."

"No, certainly not."

"Work hard, play hard," said German.

"We welcome you, Marvel," Ventom added.

"Melville."

"Indeed, aye."

The captain poured himself another tumbler of pisco and swilled it greedily. German did the same, spilling a quantity of the precious fluid on his lap. H.M. refilled his own glass, too, though he already felt giddy, even light-headed.

After another round of silent drinking, German showed H.M. to his bunk, asking him if he had enough clothing and other personal effects. H.M. admitted that, apart from a small ditty bag, he had few possessions, and so German offered him an array of trousers and shirts, all left behind by men in a rush to desert the *Lucy Ann.* "I dare say, you won't need much, it's so bloody hot in these climates."

German kept a bottle of pisco in a hemp bag slung over his shoulder, and he offered Herman another swig. They crouched

together in the dark forecastle and talked, while men clambered up
and down the scuttle. It was rare for an officer to present himself
below, under any circumstances, and H.M. was experienced enough
to intuit that this German lacked a sense of decorum. He pushed
the boundaries—or failed to discern them. Such indiscretion or
ignorance could only lead to trouble in the tight, fragile society of
a whaler.

Herman required little in the way of clothing. Most of the crew
walked about in loose cotton pantaloons, rarely bothering to put on
boots or shirts. Needless to say, discipline aboard the *Lucy Ann* was
beyond slack, as H.M. discovered. It was a miracle that this spidery
wreck of a ship moved forward through the water in an intentional
direction. Many of the sails hung loose, their hanks broken. Herman wondered if he had not signed on to a ghost ship that would
sail away into eternity.

The dismal state of the crew worried him, as many already
seemed posthumous: figures who moved about the ship in slow
motion, responding to no external stimuli—certainly oblivious to
orders from above. A fair number were ill from venereal disease,
which seemed the eventual fate of most sailors who stayed in this
profession for long. It was thought that the disease largely originated
from ports in South America, although the contagion had swept the
world, spreading widely among the islands of Polynesia, where sexual practices had none of the Puritan lines of demarcation that kept
European and American males relatively free of disease (if also
devoid of pleasure). Racking coughs were normal with most of
these men, as common as breathing itself. And most were troubled
by red blotches, carbuncles, scabs, running sores, body lice, and
other ailments of the skin.

H.M. went to sleep at once in his squalid bunk and did not wake
for twelve or thirteen hours. Toward morning, in the tenderly pre-
scient moments before dawn, he climbed the scuttle to the foredeck,

where a pristine world greeted him. He could breathe here: safe and free. The trades blew softly, putting a mild strain on the canvas overhead, the vessel heading into indigo waters. The watch slept, half a dozen men in a state of disarray, slumped on the deck with bottles of pisco beside them. Even the man at the helm dozed, one foot on the rudder, leaning against the capstan, snoring loudly. The *Lucy Ann* sailed itself, in effect, and H.M. determined to get away from this disastrous vessel and crew as soon as possible. In the meanwhile, it would provide necessary transport into the depths of paradise.

The black gulf of water amazed him as it sucked under the bowsprit with a loud slush. A gull flapped about in the rigging, making a strange barking noise—very like a spirit calling to him, an otherworldly presence. But little of this charmed him, as it might have months before. He had experienced enough of nautical life, its tedious rounds of starboard and larboard watches, the weight of officers who strutted their authority, and the daily discomforts of the forecastle and stale biscuits for dinner. He had wasted enough time already among the world's riffraff—men down on their luck for good, destined for early death, misery, deprivation, and bouts of dissipation. He had witnessed this form of life at close hand, and enough was enough. He had somehow to return to the United States, to resume his actual life, not this waking dream.

He hoped eventually to live in the country, perhaps near his uncle's house in Pittsfield, in the glorious Berkshires. Memories of lazy summers in the shade of Mount Greylock lodged in his head. He would live there, among his own family, surrounded by love. He would write books of his own—a long shelf of them. He would be a gentleman, a significant cog in the wheel of society. Nothing could stop him, as he was strong and intelligent, widely read, a descendant of important men and women who had helped to shape American history. Why should he not reap the benefits of such a life in this ample young country of the United States? He would think back on these adventures in the South Seas as a phantasmagoria. He was in the act of producing future memories each day, and he determined to record the details in his journal, as they would provide a gold mine in decades to come.

He must surely record any detail of Nuku Hiva he could recall. His experience among the Typees, and his affections for Far Away and Fawn Away, would shape him forever. He knew that now. But already that island felt insubstantial, more like a brief fantasy that might arise in the moments before waking: apparently real but, in truth, fantastic. He began even to doubt what had happened to him, wondered if his mind had played tricks.

But what had become of Toby Greene? Had he simply disappeared in the South Seas? Had he lied to Herman about his true mission? Did he get caught by the Happars, and had they murdered him, cooked him, or turned him into a god of some kind? The questions only multiplied, and he wondered if answers might ever come to him.

As the sun rose over the blue-vermillion water, H.M. felt revived by intimations of his future in the world. It would take years to absorb and understand whatever had happened to him, and he well understood this. He also knew it would be difficult to talk or write in a genuine way about what befell him. Travel books of the kind he had read and (mostly) admired—Mungo Park's *Travels* or Washington Irving's *Alhambra*—were charming enough, breezy and entertaining, their prose like cold running streams with eddies and whirlpools that caught the effluvia of exotic experience in a fashionable way. Yet he wondered if he could write about his experience like that. Such a book might feel disingenuous, a pale version of the thing itself. Yet he sensed a tremendous power within him, and he believed firmly that, if harnessed properly, this energy would lift him on wings over the fiery seas. He might fly close to the sun and, somehow, survive.

H.M. saw that a shadow crossed his body, and he squinted into the sun. A figure loomed.

"I say, you and I may be the only able-bodied men aboard this ship," said John Troy.

"Perhaps *you* are," said Herman.

Troy smiled. He was obviously English, taller and younger than H.M., with bronze skin and frizzy hair that absorbed the sun. His erect stature caught Herman's attention: the tautness was unusual, almost military in bearing. And it was clear from half an hour of idle conversation on the deck of the *Lucy Ann* that, unlike Toby Greene, Troy would prove a durable and complex companion. He was a literate fellow with an easy, expressive manner of speech, liberally versed in politics and the arts, ready with opinions yet willing to debate issues such as the French influence in Polynesia, which had become oppressive in recent months, threatening an age-old way of life.

"This is paradise," said Troy. "Only the intrusion of Western ideas of order can ruin it."

H.M. had not heard this formulation before, but he concurred. These dwellers in Eden would have been far better off without Europeans or Americans trying to civilize them, to set them straight.

Troy filled Herman's ears with tales of crude attempts by French commanders to intimidate the population of various islands, including Tahiti. Papeete was the capital of the island, first settled by William Crook, an English missionary, in 1818. The beautiful Queen Pomare IV lived there, in a palace (one of several)—a revered figure among her people, much beloved. Troy had a bountiful fund of stories about her royal highness, and he loved good stories.

To refresh his fund of narratives, he began to extract the particulars of Herman's recent sojourn among the Typees. And H.M. fed this furnace happily, refusing to trouble over the facts. Indeed, he confessed to wild amorous exploits that titillated his new friend,

who came from an innocent small village in West Sussex. Sexual
stories were the aces in Herman's deck, and he didn't mind slapping
them on the table in the right circumstances. Cannibalism was yet
another trump card, one that rarely failed to interest an audience.
But it was sex that focused the attentions of John Troy. He wanted
to hear about nubile young females without the usual Western inhi-
bitions, and Herman could hardly refuse to supply the lubricious
details.

James German soon began to envy the friendship that H.M. had
developed with the young Troy, and in drunken forays among the
crew he dropped insinuating remarks, hinting that H.M. may have
an "interest" in Troy. "She's a lovely one," he whispered to Herman, winking. His words drew the ripe blood of embarrassment to
Herman's cheeks and ears.

But H.M. made no response. He refused even to acknowledge
that he understood the tenor of German's rude comment.

It worried him, however, when it became clear that German
had begun to assume greater control of the ship as the captain grew
less coherent and responsible by the day—a pattern that seemed
eerily to retrace his experience on the *Acushnet*. Must *every* voyage
yield up mad captains and overreaching mates? Was there, perhaps,
something within the whaling industry itself that seemed to darken
and twist those under its murderous spell?

"We may have a mutiny on our hands," Troy whispered to
H.M. one morning.

"I have seen it before," Herman said. "Walk *very* carefully."

If Ventom lost control of himself, he would certainly lose his
command, and no court would consider this mutiny. But he seemed
to revive in the days following the departure from Nuku Hiva,
ordering the ship into cruising grounds far to the east, where no
whales had been found in recent years. On the quarterdeck, Ven-

tom braced himself with both hands, babbling commands to the men below, who stood with gaping mouths, arms akimbo, shaking their heads. The experienced sailors aboard the *Lucy Ann* realized that the captain's plan to revive their whaling adventures had little hope of success. Whales had eluded them thus far, and it was foolish to imagine they would magically present themselves in grounds more famous for impossible weather and dangerous currents than for schools of whales. The peeling copper on the vessel's hull told a sad story of decay and foreshadowed disaster. As anyone could see, the *Lucy Ann* was hardly bound for glory.

One day German—himself emboldened by drink—took a wild step, deciding that he would face up to the captain in view of everyone. He told Ventom (who was incoherent that afternoon) to get back to his cabin, calling him "incapable of command." They were heading into harbor in Tahiti, a short distance away, and they would take Ventom to "a proper doctor" there for medical treatment. The whaling expedition would then continue under German's leadership, he declared, speaking loudly, in stiff sentences, propping himself up with difficulty.

Ventom listened, wide-eyed, swaying. It was difficult for him to understand what German meant by any of this, and he flashed an oblique smile, raising a finger in the air. "I will not be defied!" he shouted before he sank, with a thud, to the planking. His eyes rolled back in his head, and his tongue lolled to one side. Foam drooled from his lips.

German bent to listen at his heart: the captain was alive but seriously ill, he explained to the men.

"I hereby take control of this ship!" he shouted.

With the help of the ship's carpenter, a droll Scot called Willy Menzies, German carried the limp captain to his quarters.

This was not mutiny, German explained to several of the crew that night as the ship lunged over black water, running fast down-wind. Captain Ventom was incapacitated. He was merely going by the book.

The men nodded in agreement, many of them thrilled by the change of direction. They liked the idea of Tahiti, although nobody cared for German. His inebriation concerned them, and they found his peremptory manner, the way he assumed control of the ship with a swagger, distasteful. As H.M. guessed, many of them would desert the *Lucy Ann* at the harbor in Papeete.

H.M. himself was delighted by the prospect of Tahiti. He had read George Robertson's famous account of a visit in the 1760s aboard the *Dolphin,* always assuming that magical island would be part of his experience of the Pacific. He also knew something of Louis-Antoine de Bougainville's travelogue. The French explorer had landed there in 1768, and he later published a lively account of Tahiti, which he considered an earthly paradise, a place where the natives lived in robust innocence, free of Western corruption or restraints and in easy commerce with the natural world.

Herman found himself a popular addition to the crew of the *Lucy Ann*, and he spent hours before that mast under starry skies, regaling the men with stories of his life as a captive among the Typees. In particular, he enjoyed telling them about their tapa weaving and tattooing. These intricate native arts had been brought to a point of perfection of Nuku Hiva, he explained. They preferred, of course, to hear about the young women of the island and their libertine disposition, and Herman did not disappoint them. He began to perfect his stories, expanding and contracting them as needed, enhancing their shape, sharpening their detail. He saw that different kinds of foreshadowing and twists of plot worked better than others, and he revised his tales before their very eyes. Nobody troubled to call him on the discrepancies, as they understood that truth requires a certain boldness of invention, a willingness to remake reality.

"You must write down some of these stories," Troy told H.M., who confessed he had been keeping a journal along the way, and managed to procure another notebook from Troy, who had acquired a stock of them from Peru. They had flaky white pages with stiff boards for covers, and H.M. sighed with gratitude to receive them. That very night he began to record his impressions of the *Lucy Ann* and its crew.

He developed a routine, waking early, ascending the scuttle to the foredeck to sit before the mast with a pencil in hand, a blank journal open on his lap. He wondered if he should fashion his own version of *Two Years Before the Mast*. Or should he make a novel of these adventures, filling in with fancy where reality had failed him?

"The problem may be," said Troy, "that nobody will believe your stories. They go beyond the boundaries of memoir."

"And what are these . . . boundaries?"

"Everyone knows that the truth can't be told, not in historical writing. You have to make it up, else nobody will believe you."

It was a comely paradox, and H.M. grinned. His new friend had put the matter succinctly. He would try to remember this, should he decide to venture into this realm.

He was happy as he stood at the rail and smoked a pipe, watching the blue-green sea of early morning tilt and slush. The sails snapped in fresh winds, the ship heeling as Tahiti loomed with its jagged peaks like obelisks of teal against the sky.

As they drew near the island, the wind shifted and slowed to a sweet drawl. The ship seemed to stall. This was a harbor one approached carefully. H.M. later scribbled in his journal: "Papeete Bay is considered a ticklish one to enter. It was formed by a bold sweep of shoreline, protected seaward by a coral reef upon which the rollers break with great violence. After stretching across the bay, the barrier extends on toward Point Venus, in the district of Matavai, eight or nine miles distant. Here there is an opening, by which ships enter, and glide down the smooth, deep canal, between the reef and the shore to the harbor."

It was late September, the sky as clear as gin over the harbor. H.M. studied the prospect of Tahiti, with the coral outcrop of Moto-utu glimmering and pink. Behind it lay the harbor of Papeete, with clusters of white houses and one or two church steeples. High palms crested, feathery, in rows. Fiery-winged gulls looped and landed on the yardarm and topmast of the *Lucy Ann,* while H.M. and Troy noted a variety of other ships, including a man-of-war, a frigate, and a dark corvette with French flags flying. A canoe drew beside the *Lucy Ann,* with a naked boy in the bow, an elderly man aft in a frock coat, without trousers. His bony knees were red, and one could see his dangling male part, which he took no trouble to conceal. The old fellow wanted to pilot them into a safe anchorage— for a fee, no doubt. German waved him off.

Tahiti was currently in the grips of political turmoil, Troy explained to H.M. as if lecturing to a crowded theater. (A few members of the crew did gather around to listen.) The French had designs upon Tahiti and the Polynesian isles, Troy declared. Queen Pomare IV was a woman of considerable luster in the South Seas. She actually preferred the British colonists to the French, and had allowed Protestant missionaries to establish chapels in various communities. It would be an exaggeration to call them towns, as they were generally clusters of open-air shacks.

As the crew of the *Lucy Ann* would soon learn, one of the ships in the harbor, the *Reine Blanche,* was under the command of an ambitious and blustery admiral, Abel Aubert Du Petit-Thouars, who threatened to bombard the island if the queen—vastly pregnant at the time—did not cede Tahiti and its neighboring island, Eimeo, to *his* monarch, Louis Philippe. Under duress, Queen Pomare signed the papers presented by the admiral, and she was forced to retreat to Eimeo, where she occupied a royal compound on a choice peninsula—a palace of interconnecting huts under a broad canopy of coco palms, mango, and breadfruit trees. From there, she could gaze back on Tahiti, perhaps longing to regain control of her demesne.

"I should think she is miserable," said Troy. "One always wants most whatever one has lost, however trivial."

Having anchored, German sent word ashore that the captain was ill. An elderly physician, Francis Johnstone, was brought on board to examine him, and he insisted that Ventom be taken ashore at once. The consul on the island, George Pritchard, was in London at the time, and Charles Wilson—a diplomat of middle age— stood in for him. As it happened, Ventom and Wilson were friends, and the latter insisted that Ventom move into the British consulate with him. German agreed to this, but it worried him. He needed to control the shape of this narrative himself, lest charges of mutiny arise.

Such fears proved sound. After listening to his friend's woeful story, Wilson boarded the vessel to get a fuller sense of the atmosphere aboard the *Lucy Ann*. He mustered the crew aft to discuss the situation, asking pointed questions. The men explained their reluctance to continue a whaling expedition under German's erratic command. They had of course signed articles to serve under Ventom, and as their captain had been removed from the vessel, they considered all contracts null and void. They further explained that bronchial illness had swept through the forecastle in the past weeks, and few of them felt able to sail anywhere at present. They required medical attention.

Wilson listened with professional intentness to the men, and he took into consideration what Ventom had told him as well. (H.M. remembered the consul in Peru, and he wondered about these diplomats: so bland, tolerant, helpful, and shrewd. It was a breed to itself.) He retreated into the captain's quarters with German, where they talked for more than an hour. German must have sounded convincing, as Wilson later—after several days of thought—returned the verdict that German could serve as captain of the *Lucy Ann*. He further declared that any men whom Dr. Johnstone saw fit to work must continue on the whaling cruise, as they had signed a contract. As Troy explained to H.M., Wilson just wanted to get the ship on its way. The harbor already teemed with hostile vessels, and another crew of malcontents was unwelcome on Tahiti during these strained political times. It was best to clear them out.

H.M. and Troy resigned themselves to this fact, thinking they might jump ship at a farther point along the way, in less troubled waters. But they were swept into a small rebellion, as ten crew of the *Lucy Ann* took issue with Wilson, refusing to lift a finger under the command of James German, who rushed to the consulate to level a charge of mutiny. The men in question were put briefly into custody on the *Reine Blanche* in what amounted to a strange collusion between British and French authorities. This incarceration didn't work, as the French released them after a few days (they had their own schedule to keep, and were heading for Valparaiso). By now H.M. and Troy had resolved to end their attachment to the *Lucy Ann* and informed Wilson of their decision. "I hereby arrest you both," said Wilson, without conviction. The whole business of the *Lucy Ann* had become a frank annoyance.

The rebels (now including Herman and Troy) were duly marched to prison along Broom Road, a scenic pathway through a tunnel of feathery sago palms and breadfruit trees that continued over several wooden footbridges. The British jail, known by one and all as the Calabooza Beretanee, lay about a mile to the north of the village on a promontory with a wide-angle view of the bay. It was a lovely spot by a stream that flowed from a nearby mountain; the water guzzled into the sea: "a gleaming, sinuous thread that lost itself in shade and verdure," is how H.M. described it in his journal.

The jail was a husk of thatch on bamboo struts, open to the four winds, which circled its single room with a lambent movement, cooling its inhabitants, who slept on tapa mats. Tufts of grass sprouted here and there in the floor. The structure was devoid of furniture, apart from a series of stocks used to lock prisoners in place for the night. These artifacts of the British penal system consisted of two timbers, twenty feet in length, laid in parallel lines. They held a man in place somewhat crudely, although the rebels of the *Lucy Ann* knew it was there mainly for show, and they would never really suffer themselves to lie in this unholy position, locked in place by the ankles.

Their jailor was Captain Bob, a jolly native with a voluminous belly and legs like stilts. He seemed reluctant to clamp the stocks or to insist on much of anything. He was a plump fellow of indeterminate old age, with close-cropped white hair and a triple chin that seemed indistinguishable from his neck. He spoke a version of the English language, modified by Tahitian dialect. "Not to worry!" he kept repeating, and the men laughed; nobody worried much in the Calabooza. It was a place of rest and rumination—a respite from the hard real world beyond its airy confines.

H.M. relished his Calabooza nights. The sea was close enough to provide a soothing purr, with the lapping of waves on smooth sand, the swish of palms and hedgerows alight with fiery red blossoms. Captain Bob fed himself and his charges on gourds of succulent Indian turnips called taro, which had been baked and covered with sweet oil. He produced little treats like honeyed seedcakes on wooden platters, and the men consumed them greedily. Now and then a plate of roast chicken would appear, or bits and pieces of pink meat that had no obvious origin in the animal kingdom, although its smoky flavor was satisfying. There was, of course, plenty of fish as well.

The prisoners slept uncomfortably in the stocks the first night, shifting every few minutes to reposition cramped muscles, but after that ordeal of initiation Captain Bob relaxed his discipline, saying, "Oh my, oh Mamma Maria, these stock no good for leg of sailorman, make blister. Finish!" (He often invoked the Virgin Mary in this way, signaling his Christian affiliation, of which he was proud.) "You boys no run, so? I will make change to this. Thank you, Captain Bob." (He always ended his perorations with a note of thanks to himself.)

In the morning Captain Bob initiated a ritual of bathing in the stream that appeared from a crevice half a mile above the jail and gushed into a limpid pool before trickling away to the sea. The men walked in line, following the captain, then undressed and bathed; after perhaps twenty minutes in the water, they sunned themselves on flat rocks nearby, gleaming and naked. Bob joined them in the water, splashing and laughing. It was good fun and reminded H.M. of bathing among the Typees, only here there was no hint of sensuality. The men kept to themselves, although H.M. looked furtively at the shining bodies, several of which caught his attention—especially John Troy's. H.M. moved to sit beside him, glancing at him cautiously. The human form always appealed to him, whatever the sex.

Troy was oblivious to these glances from H.M., breathing deeply, his chest rising and falling in a relaxed manner. He had not shaved in a very long time, yet his beard remained only a ghost of one, barely visible on his cheeks and chin. His hair was a crown of golden frizz caught by the intense sun. He seemed electric, tense and bright: a streak of tamed lightning.

After a long rest, the prisoners marched in single file like schoolchildren to an orange grove, where they filled baskets with enough fruit to keep them happy through a day of easy living. They would play card games, sleep in the shade of palm trees, tell stories, or entertain guests from a nearby village. The English doctor, Francis

Johnstone, became a regular visitor—there was obviously not much to occupy him elsewhere. ("I can't speak their bloody lingo!" he said.) He showed an eagerness for company, and there was a hopefulness about him that seemed at odds with his actual prospects. H.M. understood only too well that cheerfulness could be a ruse, a way of hiding one's melancholy. From a cloth medical bag, Johnstone fetched an assortment of salves and pills, which he freely administered, saying "God save our gracious queen" as he did so. It was doubtless a novelty to have a queen instead of a king, and he seemed to delight in the fact that Victoria had assumed the throne.

Herman's leg caught the doctor's attention, as the swelling had not subsided entirely and a rosy patch had formed. Johnstone produced a native blend of herbs mashed in mango paste, instructing the American sailor to apply a little of the balm each night at certain points along the leg. It would, he explained, "draw the inflammation."

Conversations in the Calabooza—especially after dark, when hearts and minds opened—generally enchanted H.M., who could not remember a more genial time. In particular, the ripening friendship with John Troy pleased him. He liked being with someone whose family and education differed so markedly from his own. As Troy put it, he had experienced "a mild and sufficient childhood" on a small farm, where his father worked a plot of land that had belonged to the family for generations. His mother, a weaver of tapestries, had something of the artist about her, and her reputation had spread from West Sussex through the south of England. Troy was no intellectual titan, but he had attended a local grammar school—a feather in his cap—and there, like Shakespeare, he had acquired a little Latin and less Greek. He talked easily and freely of books and authors, and he seemed especially fond of William Blake, the poet who had lived in the village of Felpham—not far from the Troy farm. H.M. confessed to his ignorance of Blake.

"He was a poet and visionary, and a painter as well, so I believe," said Troy.

He referred to a posthumous volume of Blake's poetic "songs," reciting a few stanzas of one, about a tiger. H.M. listened, struck by the ferocity and beauty of the lyric. He loved poetry, and thought of himself as a poet, although he had tried his hand haphazardly, writing occasional verse. He liked to read novels and memoirs, travel books, and essays, but it was poetry that lodged in the heart. He had by rote a small anthology of poems by Sidney and Shakespeare, Collins, Akenside, and—most recently—Robert Southey. He tried one or two of these on Troy, who wondered if William Wordsworth was among his favorites.

Troy considered Wordsworth a spiritual master, but H.M. resisted this judgment, having found the language insufficiently weighted, a little too easy—although he had memorized the poem about London seen from the bridge at Westminster in 1802. "The river glideth at his own sweet will," he said, quoting the poem as he lay beside the stream with Troy. What pleased him was that Troy recognized the quotation and challenged the masculinity of the river Thames. "I think of her as a lovely woman," he said.

H.M. saw an opening here. "Have you had much experience of women?" he asked. (As he asked this, it seemed that Billy Hamilton's ghost peered over Troy's shoulder with a sweet smile, as if summoned.)

Troy confessed to having a limited knowledge of "the fairer sex," as he put it, but he admitted to interest in the subject. "I have been tempted along these lines," he said cautiously. "One or two girls in West Sussex have stirred the old pot." Troy admitted that opportunities had arisen at various ports of call en route to these islands. In Rio, he had paid a visit to a brothel, although he had not "exercised the license" that had been available.

"I dare say, you will have further opportunities," Herman said.

He alluded to the subtle beauty of women in Polynesia. They had such firm bodies, an easy and open manner. They were quick to smile, and they had such ivory teeth.

A shadow passed over Troy's eyes, as he seemed to delve in amorous thoughts or fantasies.

H.M. would not let the subject go, however, turning the conversation to such things whenever he could. It excited him to excite John Troy's imagination in these ways, and Troy seemed not unhappy with the prodding, though Herman knew he might easily overstep a boundary and create tension between himself and Troy. He could detect a strain of irritability, a hesitance to engage too freely in sexual banter. Herman guessed that what lay before him was the fabled English reserve.

He and Troy preferred to sleep outside the Calabooza, on the soft, finely woven mats that Captain Bob had supplied. There was a thatched bit of roof that overhung the main structure on narrow struts; this could serve them well on rainy nights, or during periods of downpour, which often occurred in the midst of an otherwise dry spell.

"I wish I could live out-of-doors," said Herman, a bit too wistfully.

Troy said, "We have houses because of the endless discomforts of nature—even in the tropics."

Herman understood the point here, watching a large red-and-blue spider cross the grass near his hand.

But it was worth putting up with the insects to sleep outside, thought H.M. They would pull the mats onto a mossy slope beyond the roof, where the sky domed over them, such a gaudy display of stars that Herman could hardly begin to imagine what it all meant. Did each pinprick in the cloth of night actually signify a universe of life and light? What importance could the brief life of Herman Melville have when measured against the infinity of time? Questions loomed, unanswered, perhaps unanswerable. He had heard preachers in Albany and New York talk of eternal life and damnation, and these sermons had sunk to a gut level, where he still worried about the possibility of hell. Heaven was out of the question: he did not have that sort of hope for himself. He was only half a believer, but with this believing half he believed passionately.

He loved to sleep beside his friend, to hear the lull of his breathing. For the most part, it was enough to lie beside him, within inches of another human being, occasionally brushing against him. At times they whispered into the morning hours, revealing secrets, hopes, dreams, ambitions. The world was all before them, thought Herman. It lay open and dangerous, wild, uncertain, thrilling. The life of the beachcomber, the *omoo*—that was the local term—was precarious but appealing, and he could see that any number of men had come to this cul-de-sac in paradise to make a profession of lassitude.

"We should try to live here," said Troy. "I don't think we need to find another whaler."

Herman agreed. They should try to find work that would sustain but not deplete them. He could imagine staying in these islands for years to come. His mother would never understand, but he had something here more intense, more compelling in all ways: John Troy.

One morning Captain Bob introduced them to Zeke and Ezra Foster, American twins in their mid-thirties (from Rhode Island). They lived on the nearby island of Eimeo, where they had leased a plantation. They were seeking help and offered what they called a "stake" in the farm to all who signed on.

"But we're jailbirds," Herman said, with a sly grin.

"You will speak to Mr. Pritchard, the Englishman, and he will listen," Captain Bob said, delighted by himself as usual. "Thank you, Captain Bob."

Troy lit up, more than eager to leave the Calabooza, where he had grown a trifle bored of life in paradise.

For his part, H.M. could happily have remained longer. He adored the lazy days and lush nights of lying beside Troy. The problem was that his friend had lately—at least Herman thought so—cooled to his gestures of affection. He wondered if, indeed, he had gone too far one night, letting his hand brush against Troy's thigh, allowing it to rest there for a long time. H.M. knew that men aboard whalers often "helped" each other, touching in the most intimate ways, releasing anxieties in the way men do. One evening under his breath he recalled this practice aboard the *Acushnet*. Troy scoffed at this information, calling such activities "heathen." Herman took this as a rebuff, and he determined not to let his hands wander again. The next morning, Troy seemed unusually aloof, averting his gaze whenever Herman tried to snag it. Once, gingerly, H.M. put a hand on his friend's back in a friendly way, but Troy twisted away.

Herman was convinced now that he and Troy had reached a border that could never be crossed.

This was in fact the day the Foster brothers appeared, and Troy agreed to join them as soon as possible on Eimeo. H.M. feigned interest, although the prospect of farming potatoes held no appeal for him. But he would follow John Troy to the ends of the earth, if need be.

That night, Captain Bob announced that George Pritchard had returned from London a few days before. The elderly consul had no interest in looking after a ragtag group of prisoners, Bob explained, as problems with the French delegation had increased exponentially. "You may go to him, if you like," he said to H.M. and Troy. "It will never suits us here, you see. We have more fish in the sea to fry. Pritchard, he very bored to run a jailhouse." Licking his lips, he exclaimed, "And thanks you, Captain Bob!"

Troy and Herman left the Calabooza the next day after breakfast, making their way straight to the consulate, where they found the lazy Pritchard half naked and asleep in a hammock on the veranda. He was a portly fellow, with a swollen belly that rose and fell as he breathed. A clay container, a *botija* of pisco, lay beside him on a knee-sized table. In late morning he seemed well past retrieval.

Troy drew close, staring at the consul.

"Aye, boys. Aye!" he shouted, opening one eye.

"I am John Troy, sir. My friend is Herman Melville. Lately of the *Lucy Ann*."

"Mutineers, aye! Wilson has told me!"

"We bear no ill will toward Captain Ventom."

He swung to a sitting position, rubbing his eyes. "Have a drink, boys. It's bloody hot."

Troy lifted the *botija* and drank, passing it to H.M., who obliged the consul.

"I served in Peru," said Pritchard. "Damn good drink, pisco. Grape liquor, don't you know?"

"I do like it," said Troy.

It so happened that Pritchard had a distant uncle in Aldwick, near Bognor Regis, in the vicinity where Troy had been raised, not far from the coast. They chatted warmly like members of a secret fraternal order, exchanging signals that H.M. found difficult to understand. It was always this way with the English, who had a dizzying range of gestures and harrumphs, silences, winks, and sly grunts.

"And what do you want, lad?" the consul wondered aloud. "Be frank, old thing."

"My friend and I hope to work on Eimeo."

"It's a rat hole."

"I'm sorry to hear this."

"Go, dear chap, if you like. You are free." He waved his hand like a priest, making the sign of the cross, closed his eyes, and fell back into a deep sleep at once. His chin sank into a fat neck that rose like a surf beneath his skin.

With a glance, Troy motioned H.M. toward the path, and they walked slowly away, as if expecting a shout behind them, or some officer of the consulate to force them to a halt and clamp them in shackles. Within minutes, they felt wonderfully free, almost giddy with a sense of release. They made their way to the harbor, where— at dusk, after a dinner of fire-roasted fish on the beach under coconut palms—they enlisted a dilapidated bark to take them across the water to Eimeo, which lay just beyond them, its single peak rising like a fluke from the jungle, almost unnatural in its height and severity.

Bamoo, the boatman, was an old fellow, bamboo-thin, with a wispy beard and moss-colored eyes. He had acquired a handful of English words over many decades of life in a port town, and he repeated them in nonsensical fashion, convinced of his ability to communicate.

"I am *you*," he said, with conviction.

"Yes, indeed," Troy said. "And we are *us*."

Bamoo nodded. "Eimeo, hot, cold."

"More hot than cold, I should say."

The boatman grinned. "Fish, bird!"

"Bird and fish."

He pointed to the moon, waning but still bright and gilding the waves with a golden phosphorescent shimmer. "Moon," he said.

"Yes."

Bamoo smiled, revealing pale gums with only a few teeth like pegs driven into spongy white gums. "Yeth, yeth," he cried.

His inarticulate babbling continued across five leagues of bright water. Above them was slung the vast tropical night, its shawl of purple sequined with stars. As the three peaks of Tahiti rose behind them, barely visible, the spire of Eimeo—its so-called marline-spike—sharpened in the moonlight. The island was a mirage, vaguely realized. But H.M. kept his eye trained on a pale line that he assumed was beachhead. Soon enough, its reality dawned and before long they found themselves gliding into a tiny harbor that had been formed by a coral reef that looped around from the jut of land.

The calmness of the bay seemed a good sign to H.M., who believed in good omens, inklings of fortune. He had lived his life on them, leaning into the future with a blithe self-confidence, believing that the best lay ahead. For him, Eimeo was all promise.

There were no hostels for these young adventurers, but each carried a roll of tapa as well as his ditty bag. Soon they spread their mats on the beach, a quarter of a mile below the cluster of ram-shackle huts above the harbor that formed a kind of village—one of the few on the island. Troy and Herman bathed in the moonlight under the stars, the water as warm as the air. They splashed each other, making jokes, and thought they might stay forever on Eimeo. This was, indeed, paradise. As they lay on their mats, still naked, under a swishing breadfruit palm, H.M. exclaimed that Eden itself could hardly have been sweeter.

The next day, however, they realized they had landed some-where east of Eden. They found themselves joining a group of natives in the work of clearing a hot, reeking field. The Fosters had lodged them in a smelly bunkhouse with four other men, including Jimmy Strong, a red-haired Cockney in his mid-thirties who had lived on Eimeo for six months, a true *omoo* who made his way from job to job, day to day, among the Society Islands; he moved from place to place with the nonchalance of a tumbleweed. Lately, how-ever, he had found a friend in Zeke Foster, who made him into a kind of foreman. He claimed that Eimeo was "home."

"We're in 'eaven, mates," he said.

"Or hell," said Herman.

The idea, as Jimmy explained to his crew, was to clear away the roots of guava bushes, which had tangled in the loamy dirt. "We're making way for potatoes, lads," he said. "They grow like warts in this soil. Once they get going, you can't stop 'em." There was apparently good money in potatoes, and the Fosters promised to share the returns with their Anglo-Saxon associates. The natives could, as usual, forget any notion of profiting from their labor.

This blatant inequality galled H.M. as he worked, wondering about the blatant unfairness of the world. How was it that the rich only added to their fortunes, while the poor shifted in the usual way—unnoticed, underfed, and certainly underpaid? He hacked at the thick, hairy roots with a mattock, while Troy gathered up the debris behind him with a shovel, heaping them into a barrow. The field was immense, the roots infinite, and the project formidable in the ardent heat of a tropical sun, which by midmorning seemed monomaniacal. In the afternoons, however, after a lunch of fresh fish, breadfruit, and sweet potatoes, with gourds full of spring water, the exhausted workers retreated to the bunkhouse for a siesta. In a hammock slung between posts, Herman lingered over the pages of Captain Marryat's *Phantom Ship*—a book that someone had left behind, "another random Cockney," as Jimmy recalled.

One way or another, H.M. often came upon yet another sea story by Frederick Marryat, and he read them eagerly. Here were tales of adventure equal to his own experiences, even surpassing them. It didn't surprise him when he learned, from Troy (who had an uncanny knowledge of such things), that Marryat was a good friend of Dickens.

Yet Troy was dismissive when it came to Marryat. "The old captain is slightly ridiculous," he said. "He churns the plot."

"One man's plot," said Herman, "is another man's bad luck."

They argued about the merits of *Mr. Midshipman Easy,* Marryat's popular tale of a young man of high birth who nevertheless believed in human equality to an extreme degree—a view held by his noble if somewhat muddleheaded father. Easy befriended any number of lower-class seamen aboard ship during the Napoleonic Wars.

H.M. defended Easy's radical ideas, even though the midshipman modified his notions by the end of the novel.

"I do believe," Herman said, "that a man's a man, as Burns would say. No man is better than another."

"Robert Burns was a fantasist," said Troy. The weight of the Old World seemed to sit on, to round, his shoulders.

H.M. decided it was good for him to rub against such a tough-minded fellow. John Troy would make a good teacher, he thought. Yet his lack of formal qualifications would hold him back, especially in Britain, where such things mattered.

The days multiplied, and the work was physically harder than anything Herman had done before; but in the early evenings, H.M. and Troy had time to themselves. They took long walks along the beaches of Eimeo, bathing in a clear stream that gushed into the bay below a sheer limestone bluff. These cooling baths after a day of labor delighted Herman, mainly because he got to talk at length in privacy with Troy. He admired the Englishman's clarity of manner, his independent spirit. He wished for greater intimacy with his friend, but this proved impossible. The trembling nights spent outside the Calabooza had frightened Troy, who withdrew to a degree that dismayed Herman. He wished he had not allowed things to reach this point. He and Troy continued to chat about matters of life and literature, but the restraints of gender were such that one could only go so far. Herman felt the distinct limits of their friendship, and this proved almost too painful to bear.

One night, at the violet hour of dusk, they sat on a mossy ledge under a half-moon. A number of fishing boats lay at anchor, bobbing in the lee of a coral reef. Waves on the broad shingle below them provided a backdrop of sound—a lapping sound, a low consistent slur. H.M. tried his best to pick open the heart of his friend, and he marveled at the difficulty.

"You have been a lucky thing in my life," he said, taking a risk. "If you had been a woman, I think I should have proposed by now."

Troy waited for a time, saying only, "Aye." He didn't look at Herman as he lit a stubby cigar that Jimmy had given him after dinner. Soon a smoke cloud shielded him from excessive scrutiny.

"I could live here," H.M. said.

"Your mother wouldn't like it, would she now?"

"I don't care."

"But you do. I know that much about you."

This remark puzzled H.M., who had not talked about his mother at length to Troy. But it was true enough that Maria Melville remained a fierce presence in his life, her voice sounding in his head at the edge of sleep. He had not had a father when he most needed one—on the very cusp of adolescence—and Gansevoort had never managed to supplant him, though he made gestures in that direction. His uncle Tom in Pittsfield had been a major figure in his life, and Herman felt gratitude to him for that. Yet this was no substitute for a genuine father, someone who could hold the line, who could protect him from his mother. That was what he knew he had lacked: a buffering presence.

He wrote to his mother when time allowed for it, aware that postal arrangements were uncertain, at best, in the South Pacific. Letters entrusted to ships on their way home were messages put into bottles. They might—or might not—wash up on the appropriate shore. As a result, it was best to say little of substance. Herman had sent over and again the same message: *all is well*. He had received only two letters from his mother since boarding the *Acushnet*—these delivered during gams off the Encantadas. He had found them unnerving, summoning emotions that he did not like to entertain, even acknowledge. He suppressed them, for the most part, though once he had wept openly on the foredeck, sitting cross-legged before the mast, wondering why on earth he had left home. In truth, he missed his mother horribly. He had often, as a teenager, been unsure where he began and she left off.

He wondered about simply disappearing into the tropics forever. This was not uncommon, as sailors often died at sea or decided to slough off identities, their old lives. He could roam from island to island until the ideal situation presented itself. He could marry a local girl, live in royal fashion on a plantation, where a white man enjoyed a kind of residual authority. He might well become, like his father, a merchant, exporting exotic goods or spices or native art to the West: a fortune could be made, perhaps. There would be no struggle in the tropics to make ends meet or, at least, create a body of wealth equal to one's imagined place in society. In these parts, one did not have to worry about the next meal—it fell from the trees. One did not require coal or wood for heat. One did not actually need a substantial house. It was enough to live in the wind.

H.M. always liked the experience of meeting an *omoo*, one of those lost souls who flew about like birds of paradise, looking for a perch. The islands teemed with men who had simply shrugged off Western life with its serial obligations. Why bother about securing loans to purchase a "proper" house? Why support a wife and children, a mother or father? Who needed a closet full of fine clothing? Why should one accept the rigidities of married life, where sexual impulses—ever mysterious, ambiguous—found a narrow bed to lie in? And why worry about one's status in the social world? H.M. would never fit the profile of a gentleman. In truth, he found it difficult to sustain conventional relations or to make polite conversation. He hated tea parties and such. He had suffered, briefly, the regimens of office life—as a teenager, he had worked in a bank in Albany. It had been memorably oppressive. With further training, he might have become a surveyor, but the economy of the United States had declined precipitously, and he saw few prospects for himself.

Perhaps he could become an author. That seemed a likely turn, given his love of reading and writing. He could become the next Marryat or Dickens, spinning tales like a web from his guts. The untapped powers of invention surged within him. Sentences formed in his head like dew on the grass at summer dawn, sparkled in his imagination, although by noon the language evaporated. He must write down these sentences, he knew as much: thoughts fly away, but writing remains. And it was not enough to make random jottings in a journal. He must begin a book as soon as possible. His adventures among the Typees were an obvious place to start. Who would not adore such a narrative, if suitably enhanced by invention? One could hardly tell the whole truth of such an experience—even readers of novels were not so liberal-minded—but he could gesture in the direction of truth. The readers he cared about would read between the lines, as reading was all hints and guesses.

One evening, as H.M. and Troy approached the bunkhouse, Herman seized the wrist of his friend. He looked at him yearningly. He wanted to tell him that he loved him, although the exact words didn't form on his lips. He held on very tightly, however, and Troy understood what was meant.

Troy allowed a lapse of time, his gaze steady, meeting Herman's eyes with apparent ardor.

"Our friendship means . . . a good deal to me," H.M. said, in a weak voice. His knees almost buckled.

"It's been a long day," said Troy, with his schoolboy slump. "I find myself weary in the evenings, and my back has been tricking me."

"I have a weak back myself."

"You have a good steady rhythm when you work."

"I do?"

"I watch you with admiration."

"As I work?"

"With your trusty mattock."

H.M. felt dizzy, dislocated. Troy had veered sharply from the subject. But had there really been a subject? "I like to hack away at roots, I suppose."

"You are a marvel," Troy said, unable to contain his cynicism.

With that, Troy walked ahead of him rapidly, and H.M. understood that it would never do, being so explicit or emotional. The love he felt for John Troy, however profound, had nowhere to lodge. He could not possess him. He could not live beside him forever. Their friendship itself had stumbled into a ditch, and it would be difficult to get out. The truth was, there was nothing to sustain their contact over a stretch of years. Troy was an Englishman who wished, in his own way, to cling to the conventions of male behavior. He understood about friendship, but only to a limited degree. The depths of human intercourse would never interest him. He could remain a friend, but no more. There would never be talk of affection, and no exchange of intimacies would follow. One could show the quality of one's affection to some extent, obliquely, but that was it.

In truth, H.M. had done with obliqueness.

His dizziness did not disappear as he walked toward the bunkhouse. The stars suddenly began to wheel overhead, pulsing in great legendary patterns that he could not interpret. He heard a loud hissing, as if some rising surf of feeling threatened to overwhelm him. Unable to proceed, he fell to his knees, dipping his forehead to the grass. He could feel the long rivers of night churning through him, the tears of the world gathering and pushing against a dike that might well burst, at which point he would break apart and scatter, float in a million pieces, sucked into the blackest void ever imagined. He might never again assemble in the hirsute, ungainly sack of skin known as Herman Melville. And that might be a good thing, he thought, a very good thing indeed.

It is impossible to talk or to write without apparently throwing oneself helplessly open . . .

H.M., *Pierre*

9.

"Hello!" Herman called, banging on the door too furiously.

What was he *thinking*?

My stepmother's footsteps clattered on the floor, and she seemed quite pleased if somewhat surprised to see him. He might have been a prodigal son returning, not a suitor for her stepdaughter.

"What a shock!" she said.

He had been nearly four years at sea and, to be frank, I hardly recognized him. He was much taller, fuller, and broader, sporting a thick unruly beard and cascading hair that fell over his shoulders in womanly fashion. His face glistened a deep russet like apple skins, the perfect color for October. His threadbare tie—why did he bother?—hung rakishly askew, the collar unbuttoned: one could easily imagine a hairy chest beneath the shirt, and I did. (The idea of a hairy chest always appealed to me, a nest for my eager fingers.) His high boots needed a polish, and his jacket of blue serge had seen better days. As I said to my stepmother, he looked like a pirate.

"But my child," she said, "he *is* a pirate."

It took some decades for the truth of that statement to achieve its full weight. H.M. went to literature for the same reasons that Henry Morgan went to the Spanish Main.

He turned up at 49 Mount Vernon Street on one of those sticky Indian summer days when the flies no longer felt sure of their flight as they bumbled and droned at the windows, sometimes falling to the floor, where they buzzed in mad circles until expiring. Our cats slept on the porch in direct sunlight, as if aware that such brightness would soon pass. Already the geese had begun their journey south-ward along the Atlantic coast, bleating in loud V after V—the sad-dest sound in the world to my young ears, a sign of passing youth. The last of the season's flowers brought color to our garden out back—asters, goldenrod, harebells, and yarrow. A humid breeze moved off the sea, swirling around Beacon Hill, dislodging the yel-low or scarlet leaves from the maples, elms, and beeches. Even in such heat, one could already believe in winter and its dull finalities, when the sky presses down with a hard gray iron lid over the city and when hope fails.

The year was 1844, three years before I married him. At twenty-two, I had only just put girlhood behind me. My heart hid somewhere, out of sight, a little haven where I gathered a sense of myself as someone intelligent, quick, and strong. Marriage was hardly paramount in my thoughts, if present at all, although my step-mother would refer to what she discreetly called "my possibilities."

In defiance, I took to referring to "my impossibilities."

"Oh, pay no mind to her," my father would say, at dinner. "She will marry a man of some importance. Watch!" He was a man of importance himself, possessed of such good cheer that nobody could run against him for long. What he said tended to happen, although many would argue—many did!—that Herman Melville was hardly a good match for me. His talents, such as they were, did not impress everyone. My brothers, in particular, remained skeptical, noting that any number of their friends would "have me." I did not want to be "had," I told them.

I caught a glimpse of Herman from the west parlor, where I lay on the couch with a novel in hand—the latest by Dickens, I suppose. I put down the book to listen to him talking—his voice too loud, the speech tumbling forward as if under pressure, a small waterfall of elocution and exclamation. (He reminded me of Mr. Dickens, in fact. They blazed before one, with a propulsive voice that held the ear and stirred the heart.) He dropped a number of familiar names, which were his calling card. My friend Helen was among them, his dear sister. From her letters I learned that he might well reappear in Boston, a sailor home from the sea. The name of his older brother, Gansevoort, rang out, leaving no doubt in my mind about this gentleman caller.

But had he called for me?

He had come home from fabulous adventures in the South Seas and Sandwich Islands—the exotic, incalculable hoard of experience from which he would extract a lifetime of writing. Helen had written from Lansingburgh with tales I could scarcely believe. (The Melville family, all of them, tended to exaggerate; indeed, any ordinary rug of truth became a colorful afghan in their mouths.) It had occurred to me that I might encounter H.M. in the not so distant future; that seemed a likely prospect. Yet here he was, Herman himself—unannounced, a manifestation. It was obvious, to me at least, why he came. A girl of a certain age, in my circumstances, is alert to motives.

The idea of marriage to Herman had never before crossed my mind, but it was apparent that afternoon, when he appeared unexpectedly, the fulfillment of a dream I had never had. It was all suddenly obvious to me and seemed inevitable. And he was infinitely more fetching than the young lawyers who apprenticed themselves to my father, many of whom had already darkened our doorway with intentions.

My stepmother led him into the kitchen with its tall ceiling and hanging brass pans, where she often entertained guests informally at the trestle table that once occupied the center of her mother's kitchen at Cape Cod. It could seat a dozen easily, so it became a place of daily conversation, especially when casual guests appeared: a neighbor or good friend, one of her extended family. (The fact that she brought Herman straightaway into the kitchen was a sign of family ties, a decidedly intimate gesture on her part, although I'm sure he didn't quite understand this.) While pushing cups of tea and sesame biscuits under his nose, she listened eagerly to his stories, extracting further details by subtle smiles and winsome head tilts. I stood by the kitchen door, out of sight, embarrassed to assume the role of eavesdropper. But how could I not listen to him? It wasn't as though handsome young men so often came home from sea and appeared at our house to recount their perilous and enchanting adventures.

In retrospect, it is too easy to see myself as young Desdemona standing there, listening to the great Moor, who had suffered much, experienced more.

And, to be sure, I loved him for these extravagant adventures, and he—before days had passed—loved my loving him for what had befallen him. He understood, in his broad intuitive way, that I provided an affectionate and guileless audience. At least in the autumn of 1844, I was all ears.

When I sneezed, the point of hiding vanished, so I stepped into the kitchen, feigning surprise to see Herman Melville at the table.

"A visitor!" I said.

"You will remember Mr. Melville?"

I nodded.

"Lizzie is learning the violin," said my stepmother. It was a most peculiar thing to say.

"Oh, yes," I said, not wishing to embarrass her, drawing an imaginary bow across invisible strings.

In truth, I had not picked up my violin in several months and had abandoned formal lessons over a year ago.

Herman stood, bowed ceremoniously. "The violin is the songbird of any orchestra," he said.

Songbird, indeed!

"I actually prefer the cello," I said.

"Ah, the cello," he replied.

I could hear the grandfather clock in the hallway as it ticked, supplying a backdrop to the lengthy pause that followed.

"Lizzie is twenty-two," my stepmother added, oddly and inappropriately, as if to excuse my behavior.

"Ah," he said.

"I believe you have been at sea, Mr. Melville?" I put in. "You have gone a great distance."

"Around the Horn," he said. "I'm just returned, not a day ago. Various ships, in essence."

"He began his adventures on a whaler," my stepmother said.

"The ship itself, the captain . . . proved less than agreeable." He offered a nervous laugh. "It's a very long story. A good one, too."

"Do sit," my stepmother said to Herman, as I took a seat at the long table. "We don't stand on ceremony." She looked at me searchingly, as if I was meant to read her mind. "Will you have some tea, dear?"

"Please, yes," I said.

Her hands trembled as she poured from a heavy brown teapot— a rare sign of anxiety in her. I wondered if she felt so desperate for me to marry. Somehow I had not realized this.

"You will be seeing your family soon, I suppose," I said.

He nodded awkwardly. "They are in Lansingburgh still. I have a brother in New York."

"I'm sure you do," I said, as if I didn't know that Gansevoort was in New York City.

My stepmother dipped her oar in the water again, as if embarrassed by me. "Mr. Melville's poor mother doesn't even know he's arrived!"

"Tell no one," he said, looking at me in a conspiratorial way. "I hope to surprise her in a few days. But I need first to get my land legs under me. When I walk, I tend to pitch and roll."

"I explained to Mr. Melville that Oakes's room is free," my stepmother said, "and he should feel welcome here. There is no point in wasting money at a hotel. We're chockablock with bedrooms."

By my count there were three empty bedrooms upstairs. As Oakes had the finest room of us all, this meant that mother wished to impress Herman. He would be treated like royalty.

"Do stay, Mr. Melville," I said, too quickly, as he turned quite red in the ears.

"Oh, yes. I will stay. Two or three days, perhaps."

"Good!" said my stepmother.

Arrangements were made, and we sent around to the hotel on Tremont Street for Herman's few belongings, which arrived before dinner in a battered case and a cloth sack that he called, after the fashion of sailors, his ditty bag. As we soon learned, this bag contained the better portion of a human skull, which he produced at the dinner table that evening. "It comes from a remote island in the South Seas," he said, with a glint. "The poor man was perhaps somebody's lunch."

How could one not love a man who could make such pronouncements at dinner on Beacon Hill, with the chief justice of the Massachusetts Supreme Court presiding?

Father, as he would, relished such nonsense. He wished for a skull himself, he said. He would place it next to his gavel in the courtroom, and it would put the fear of God into supplicants at the bar.

That night, over dinner, I got to see at first hand the remarkable Mr. Melville, who told wild, inappropriate stories with charm and understatement. He was full of wry remarks of the kind my parents liked.

"You must write down these stories," my father said.

"Oh, I've kept a journal. I have one or two books in mind."

One or two? I was impressed by the casual confidence of this declaration. He just assumed that he could write a book, even two of them. I knew at once—as did my father—that he meant this, and that he would do as he said. It seemed, briefly, as if an American Dickens had materialized before us, and I could imagine him strutting down Commonwealth Avenue in a cape, with eager readers trailing behind, desperate for a lock of his hair.

"A splendid young fellow," my father said to me, later that night in the hallway, squeezing my wrist—as if I were somehow responsible for Mr. Melville and his splendid nature.

Those three days linger in memory, elevated above the years and decades to come, the falling seasons. They were dreamlike hours, when the first tender feelings of love for H.M. began to root in what was fertile soil, as I had entertained few gentlemen thus far in my short life and had certainly loved none. How irresistible I found his conversation, with its fund of rich expression. At once I saw—alas too clearly—that Herman Melville would never make an easy choice as regards a husband. He was opinionated, willful, and oblique, with a stormy intelligence; this proved an affliction more than a gift, as he often saw around corners that did not exist. Nothing quite satisfied him, and he could rarely settle on one thing or another. He was, at heart, something of a pagan, which is perhaps why he got along so well among the native population of the South Seas.

I was and remain a devout Christian, and so Herman's faith-lessness created an irritation, a point of contention. In later years we often lay in bed, after the lamp had been extinguished, debating the merits of the Almighty, as though it were up for grabs.

"God? There is no God," he would say. "This is why I so dis-like Him!"

His whole life was one extended quarrel with the Divine. An easy and settled belief never appealed to him, and he referred to reg-ular churchgoers as a pack of lemmings. By instinct, he mistrusted everything, and this held especially true for men in clerical garb—he called them "divine poseurs." For discrete periods he would attend church with me, but he could not sustain the commitment and soon fell back upon his pagan ways, taking long walks on Sun-day mornings, sometimes stopping at the back of a strange church to listen to the music. He suggested that God spoke in the poems he liked to read, and so he would spend an hour or two in his study on the Sabbath, reading the poems aloud as if in prayer. Behind his study door one often heard snippets of Herbert, Crashaw, Thom-son, or Edward Young, whose peculiar *Night Thoughts* he could recall in astonishing detail, quoting long passages verbatim. "It offers the comforts of religion," he would say of that poem, "but without the hocus-pocus."

He always doubted the depths of my love, though I tried over many years to reassure him (especially after I decided *not* to aban-don him, as the scandal would have been unbearable for everyone concerned). I tried to ignore the fact that he had repeatedly run us into debt, borrowing tidy sums behind my back. And there was his drinking, too, which grew worse during our lonely years in the Berkshires, where he had no access—or little—to manly friendship (unless you counted Mr. Hawthorne, who lived briefly among us and drove Herman nearly mad). We had little money, barely enough to keep up, if we did even that. It did not help that his books never

sold enough to make a difference. His pretense to being a professional author was exactly what it seemed: a fantasy. There was
scarcely a living in those books and stories. His poems proved just
another expense that my indulgent family would have to bear.

When I think back to those days in mid-October, so long ago,
I realize that H.M. set about with real deliberation to seduce not
only me but my parents as well, especially my father, who had a special fondness for him. Father may have felt guilty about the fact that
he had not helped Allan Melvill's family sufficiently after his friend's
premature death—I don't know. My hideous mother-in-law had
certainly been left with her hands full, with liabilities beyond her
means. The possibility that she could climb out of debt without
massive infusions from friendly sources did not exist.

"Herman is not like his father," my father would say. "He has a
steely side, a determined aspect, and that's a trait of the Gansevoorts.
The Melville side is soft, even complaisant. Poor Allan . . ."

On his last night with us on Beacon Hill, Herman produced
further recollections of the South Seas, where he'd been taken a prisoner by cannibals. It amused me to think that my father, for all his
experience of the world, had nothing as strange as this to proclaim.
He questioned my future husband with a prosecutor's relentlessness.
Did Herman really believe these innocent islanders could *eat* him?
What evidence did he have for this? What sort of diet did they usually pursue? Was the skull he showed us one of those found in a jungle lair? Why had this servant called Kory-Kory been assigned to
guard him? How did Herman communicate with these infidels?
What did their language sound like? What gods did they worship?
Had he noticed anything on the island that resembled a church or
a temple? Did conventional families exist among them? Had they
anything like the courtship rituals and exchange of marriage vows
that exist in the Western world? Herman replied at length, having
an array of details and pithy anecdotes at his disposal. It was frus-

trating when, only twenty minutes after dessert and coffee had been served, my father insisted that Herman join him in his study for brandy and cigars.

From what Herman later said, I gleaned that my father fired off a fusillade of questions of the type that men would only dare to ask in a room without ladies. Did the women wear clothes? What sort of mating habits did he observe? How many wives did a typical native have? How attractive were the younger women? And so on. I knew Father would pummel him with this sort of inquiry, as—I could guess as much, having heard him with his friends—he retained a robust (if prurient) interest in such things.

As any married woman knows, men focus on their physical needs somewhat relentlessly for many decades. After sixty, the demands tend to ease—my stepmother had once suggested as much. In Herman's case, I doubted that he would *ever* relax about sexual matters. After death, he would rattle his coffin for some years. Woodlawn would tremble!

Before his departure the next day, Herman and I made idle conversation in the garden, on a bench under a spreading chestnut tree—the big leaves were growing brown and golden at the edges. The chestnuts nestled in the grass, shiny and delicious. At one point H.M. began to touch me, more intimately than I would have thought possible in broad daylight, in my own garden, after such a brief courtship—a matter of days! The wind circled warily, as I let him reach beneath my blouse. His palm opened on my breast, and he drew shallow breaths. Shocking me, he pulled my hand toward the buttons of his trousers, and I could feel the hardness, the life of his manhood. I don't think we spoke, even breathed, for a very long time, hovering in each other's presence, touching and kissing. I wondered what on earth the neighbors, if they should chance to see us, might think. This was all *so* improper!

"You are beautiful," he said.

I was not unpleasant to look at, not then, having a crisp brow, an aquiline nose, and deep-set eyes. Nevertheless, I found his remark rather conventional for a man of his linguistic gifts. He guessed at my unspoken disapproval and tried again.

"I admire the way you devote your days to study," he said.

That was stretching the point, perhaps. I did tell him I had been reading Dickens, Miss Catharine Sedgwick, Charles Brockden Brown, and Washington Irving. Recently I had seen a boring play by Royall Tyler with my father in Cambridge. But it would be a stretch to say I devoted my days to study.

Like most girls of that age, I wasted much of my time. After breakfast, I sat in my boudoir, fussing and fretting, considering myself in the looking glass. I combed my hair in ways that suggested I didn't care how it fell about my head or put white powder on my face. It was fashionable then to look pale, wan, even ill—and I was à la mode. My dark eyes looked even darker when I put zinc below them, so that they rested on a fluffy white pillow of cheek. My lips, however, needed nothing to deepen their hue; they glowed quite naturally, a sanguine shade that bespoke my youth.

"How do you spend your time, when you are not engaged in reading or music?" he asked.

"I prefer to walk on the Common," I said.

This was true enough. Quite often in the late mornings I sat alone on the Common that fall, watching the swans in their beauty on the flashing ponds. Red and yellow maple leaves fluttered around the bench where I lingered or scraped along the pathways, often whirling in currents of low wind that caught and chilled my ankles. I felt isolated, unnoticed, insignificant. It saddened me to note the demise of summer, my dwindling girlhood; the womanly adventures that lay before me seemed impossible to imagine. I did not even try. Instead, I looked backward to a decade of innocence, wishing for something more but wholly unfamiliar with the possibilities that adult life afforded. Certainly I had entertained no thoughts about Herman Melville, who burst into my life with such immediacy and fury that I was barely able to comprehend what had befallen me. It was as if I had simply been picked, and there was no real choice on my part.

The decision was somehow made. I didn't mind this decision, nor did I fully understand its implications.

"I like the Common," Herman said. "It was a place for public hangings until quite recently."

"Really?"

"As a boy, I used to watch them from a distance."

"How awful!"

When I asked my father about this, he said there had been no hangings on the Boston Common for twenty-five years or more. Herman suffered, he said, from "an overheated imagination." Perhaps Herman meant that his father had watched these hangings . . .

"I will think of you," said Herman, as we parted company.

"Think of me, indeed. But will you write?"

"Oh, yes. And I shall come back to Mount Vernon Street as soon as possible. Perhaps even sooner than is possible."

"That is quite soon."

"Yes," he said. "Do you love me?"

"You must not put such a question before me, Mr. Melville," I stated flatly. He needed to learn a bit of manners. It was far too early in our association to use such language.

"Call me Herman," he said.

I did not tell him to call me Lizzie. But I kissed him on the forehead to show a degree of approval before we parted company. Soon thereafter, I bid him goodbye from the front steps, then watched him descend into a carriage with his case and ditty bag. From my limited viewpoint, he seemed the handsomest sailor in the world.

Boy, take my advice, and never try to invent anything but—happiness.

H.M., "The Happy Failure"

INTO THE BLAST

10.

Having abandoned Eimeo and John Troy, Herman made his way by sea to Oahu, hiring onto an English clipper as a deckhand for the duration of the journey, where eventually he signed aboard the frigate *United States* as an ordinary seaman for three years of cruising. By now, he was eager to get home.

"You *must* come home!" his mother had said, in a letter that reached him poste restante.

At this point in his adventures, he fully agreed. He had wasted enough time in Hawaii, where for months on end he circled the island like the wind itself, aimless, missing Troy horribly. So horribly that he consoled himself in the brothels of Water Street in Oahu, where local whores charged a pittance for the right to explore their most intimate portals, at least until the cocks crowed. H.M. spent everything he had within these dank hovels, often recalling the line from Shakespeare's sonnet about the "expense of spirit in a waste of shame" being "lust in action." This was, he decided, nothing more than rampant lust; as such, it had given precious little in the way of relief to a young man who guessed he would never again see the friend who mattered most to him. Never would he forget the love that had been his, however briefly, in this paradise of his youth, on those succulent, savage islands.

Troy had remarked in passing that he hoped one day to return to West Sussex, where he would inherit a farm. He also said that Herman would be welcome in those parts, and that he should plan to visit. The invitation was well intentioned, but H.M. understood the truth of such things. Once the years of travel fell behind him, H.M. would settle permanently into middle-class life in Lansingburgh or New York, perhaps in Boston. His mother would expect nothing less of him. It was his destiny as a Melville and Gansevoort.

"Your father was a pillar," she would say. "You must be a pillar as well."

Oh, I'll be a pillar, he said to himself, hoping never to look back at the ruins of Sodom.

He had arrived on the island of Oahu with empty pockets, filling them with change earned by cadging a day's work here or there, often at the docks, where his broad shoulders and big hands were always welcome. He had been forced to lie low when, to his horror, the *Acushnet* hove into view one morning. H.M. thought, at first, he was having a vision, a waking nightmare. But careful inspection revealed that this really was the *Acushnet,* with its parched sails and bleached rigging. Within hours his former shipmates wandered up and down the streets of Oahu looking much the same as before, neither more nor less venereal or pocked or vengeful. Once he actually saw Valentine Pease in a barber's chair, having his beard trimmed. There was no mistaking that head, like a block of cheddar, his blood-bright nose reflected in a large mirror. It seemed he could smell the man's perfume, although he was too far away for that.

This accidental sighting of Pease frightened him, and for a week or more he stayed in his rented room off Water Street. The legal ramifications of desertion were uncertain, but he would not test the system. He had no wish to land in some filthy Hawaiian brig, where conditions would never meet Tahitian standards of insouciance. God forbid, they might insist that prisoners remain within prison walls!

When Herman saw the *Acushnet* sail away one morning, his spirits improved. Within days, he found work in a bowling alley, setting up pins and rolling balls back to the players. The sport held a mild fascination for him, and the atmosphere was lively. The alley itself was near the beach, and before work H.M. spent bedazzled hours observing local boys on their boards as they rode the surf with courage and abandon. He would sit under a leafy coconut palm to watch them, this flock of young seabirds, clustered and waiting for the right wave. When it came, they rose on their boards, crouching, agile in the foaming water. Their black hair was visible above a far-off wave when it crested. And they might ride for a mile or more from the farthest sea bank, before collapsing in knee-deep surf. They would drag their boards behind them as they came in, sipping from split coconuts that little boys would bring to their heroes. Herman guessed the boys were anywhere from twelve to nineteen, all lean and brown, talking rapidly, laughing and teasing. They ate and drank with gusto, and (if what Herman had heard was true) made love with abandon, ignoring the dour Protestant missionaries who had infested the island in recent years, supplanting the more genial Catholics with their Calvinist gloom.

Although not in literal control of the government, the missionaries had acquired uncanny power. They could be seen any day as they rattled about the streets like potentates in native-drawn carts called *kanakas*. They lived in well-appointed homes in the better parts of town with small armies of maids and gardeners at their service, and their wives often employed "coolers" with broad manila fans to keep the breezes coming, even when nature refused to oblige them. As one wag quipped: "The missionaries came to do good, and they did right well."

H.M. disliked organized religion, and yet he sometimes attended the Seaman's Chapel, where a genial missionary by the name of Samuel C. Damon had become a friend. It was Damon— a towering New Englander with bushy white eyebrows and considerable warmth—who brought him to the bone-white chapel overlooking the bay. The blue Bethel flag snapped in the high breeze above the cupola, reminding Herman of the verse in Genesis: "And Jacob called the name of the place where God spake with him, Bethel." That verse was stamped in his brain, and he impressed Damon with the quotation.

Damon had wandered up to him on the beach one afternoon, and they sat together on the sand, admiring the acrobatics of surfers.

"They are my sea nymphs," said Damon, a confirmed bachelor with an eye for beautiful boys.

Having studied the classics at Yale, Damon liked to recount the ancient myths, especially those that involved the rape of someone or other by Zeus or Apollo, who seemed perpetually on the lookout for prey. These tales also appealed to H.M., who knew he had not read enough of the Greek and Roman authors. He borrowed volumes of Homer, Ovid, and Catullus from the mission library in an anteroom of the chapel, most of them with Damon's nameplate on the title page. The pastor recommended *Metamorphoses* as "the place to begin." Ovid retold all the great stories, he explained, though he warned Herman against believing in a world where "so many disagreeable gods could be found." He wagged his finger, half in jest. "There is one God, and only one."

H.M. confessed that he wanted to believe in the Almighty. He thought he *did* believe, in some instinctual way; but for him God was a sensation, not a construct resulting from a process of rational thought or actual practice. When he applied reasoning to his beliefs, it was usually at the expense of these beliefs. "I don't really know what to think about God, or how to talk to Him," H.M. said.

"Don't talk to Him. Listen!" Damon said, reminding Herman of Toby Greene, who had made a similar remark.

H.M. worried that he could not find a space where such intense listening might occur.

Damon suggested that quietness, in due course, would come. "The soul calms itself when the time is ripe." God would be there when H.M. needed Him, he explained; otherwise, He might well remain out of sight and silent. Now and then, Damon overdid it, saying that God was "the still center upon which everything else rested" and that His "long roots dug into the earth, became its point of balance, its source of life." But, for the most part, he refrained from grand formulations.

Although he liked the few sermons he heard from this lanky preacher, who tended to dwell on vivid passages from the Old Testament, H.M. found it difficult to give himself wholly to the order of service. It seemed as if God were almost too present for him, an ever-present annoyance, inescapable. The ritual of worship felt perfunctory, reductive, beside the point. God would never require such nonsense, Herman felt quite sure of that. Nonetheless, he could sense the ubiquity of the Divine, the holy presence in the world's infinitely rich surfaces. God was a low, continuous murmur in the back of Herman's head, the spiritual equivalent of strong surf with a fierce undertow that threatened destruction to the casual bather. At times, H.M. felt that God spoke *through* him, in the words he wrote in his journal or in fragmentary lines of verse that arose in his mind, grand if not grandiloquent.

He was a poet at heart, he told himself; it was the rise and roll of the unfolding line that appealed, with its glide and glitter, its unexpected turns or abrupt halts in white marginal space. He liked the feel of language that echoed and chimed, its heft and cadence, with meaning amplified by resonance: the poem as a system of linked sounds. But he longed to tell stories, too. He had always been an excellent purveyor of anecdotes, so had no trouble attracting an audience of eager listeners. His hours before the mast had been a kind of school wherein he perfected his craft, learning from others what worked or didn't. A few wondrous storytellers had entertained him under starry skies from Rio to Oahu, and he had practiced the art himself before listeners who would detect any false note.

Now Damon's narrative powers intrigued him. The pastor had a prodigious trove of anecdote and incident in his keeping, as he'd listened to countless sailors in his years of missionary work. One night over a bottle of brandy (Damon called himself a "lapsed non-drinker"), he told H.M. about Luther Fox, for instance: a green boy from the Albany region who had, in a fit of rage, murdered a ship-mate. Fox had been called to work somewhat rudely in the middle of a meal, and he struck the unfortunate man sent to fetch him with a blade used to chop whales into sections for rendering. The poor wretch emerged from the gangway with blood pulsing from a gash above the knee, whereupon he told the horrified captain, "Young Fox has cut off my leg with a mincing knife." This put the matter bluntly. The man died in agony two hours later, and Fox was taken from the ship in irons, then hanged—a prisoner of his own inex-perience in dealing with injured feelings. It was, Damon ventured, "a case of wounded masculine pride."

"I understand the boy's flaw," said Herman. "My own blood will boil at times, and I don't trust myself. I have, on occasion, struck a blow."

Damon's brow lowered. "Be slow to anger," he said. "So the Good Book tells us. This is the beginning and, perhaps, the end of wisdom."

Another tale that Damon relayed with force involved one Captain Sherman of the *Parker,* an ill-fated whaler from New Bedford. The captain's monomania in the pursuit of sperm whales had led to his destruction in the South Pacific. He had fastened his whaleboat to an especially massive and desperate whale, refusing to let go—even when the others begged him to cut loose. The creature dragged Sherman and his crew among a frenzied school, where another whale's fluke overturned the boat, stove and shattered it. The captain himself was last seen grasping a fragment of the boat, foundering in a whirlpool, hurling curses as he sank. The main vessel, under the command of its first mate, had thereafter split apart in a sudden squall after dashing against the blades of a coral reef. A contingent of survivors managed to piece together a raft from the remains of the ship, whereupon they floated with insufficient food or water for eight days before washing ashore at Ocean Island, a bleak outcrop, where they fed off seafowl and seals for six months before a passing whaler rescued them.

A passionate Christian, the first mate—George Smith by name—had presided over daily services, reciting long passages from the Bible by rote, with the appropriate commentary. On Sundays he invariably raised the bethel flag (exactly how he managed to have such a thing in his possession was a point that puzzled Herman, although he didn't trouble Damon with this little inconsistency: a story is a story, after all). This tale brought tears to the pastor's eyes as he retold it for the umpteenth time, and the narrative sunk deep in Herman's memory. It was a kernel that, perhaps, would grow into a full-blown tree one day, even a forest.

"Will you chase more whales?" Damon asked young Herman, who seemed never to tire of his stories, especially when they involved whaling. "I would imagine it's in your bloodstream. I've seen many a good man lost on the whale road."

H.M. shook his head. Whaling—and the extreme discomfort

of the forecastle, its perpetual gloom and reek of human failure—
no longer interested him; he wanted only to get home. And he
would seek an easier way to get home than aboard a whaler.

"You will have few options," Damon said.

"Oh, ye of little faith," Herman responded.

And then, as if summoned by his faith, the *United States* sailed
into the harbor at Oahu one afternoon, flying the Stars and Stripes.
She was an impressive vessel at 178 feet from bow to stern, with her
main mast rising more than a hundred feet. In addition, she had a
good deal of firepower from the spar and gun decks, although
Herman hoped not to require this. Her crew formed a small floating city, complete with barbers, policemen, coopers, cooks, and a
clergyman. Military life was generally off-putting to H.M., whose
natural anti-imperialism had been inflamed by the way the English
and the French had bullied the naïve, gentle inhabitants of the Sandwich Islands. Hawaii was hardly a native zone any longer, despite
the royal presence of Kamehameha III. His capitulation to the missionaries had been a sign of weakness, as his subjects understood perfectly well. Lately he had planted a gigantic cross of bamboo outside
the royal compound, insisting that wreaths of flowers drape it every
morning, and that naked girls dance around it every Sunday.

"So much for the risen god," said Herman to his missionary
friend.

"I shall miss you," Damon said, planting a kiss on Herman's
forehead. "Most of the young men tossed up by the sea are dreary
and dull. You are neither of these things, although it would not hurt
if you bathed a little more often."

H.M. promised to bathe that very night. He said he *wished* he
could stay on the island forever, if only to amuse Damon, but he
longed to see his mother in Lansingburgh.

"She is a lucky girl, your mother," Damon offered. "I suspect
you will not *like* your compatriots, however: not very much. They

are grasping and tedious, on the whole. But you must go. Those who remain on this island tend to rot from the inside out."

"Like you?"

"You flatter me. I am rotting from all sides."

The enlistment happened with shocking speed, as the *United States* was short of hands. Herman was summoned at once to the sick bay, where the ship's doctor commanded each recruit to strip. The order surprised him, as nobody stripped on a whaler, at least not for medical purposes. But the navy would not admit to its ranks the usual run of motley and diseased seamen who populated whalers. Venereal afflictions were deeply unwelcome on a naval ship, as they implied degeneracy and a lack of self-discipline. H.M. stood in embarrassment as the cadaverous surgeon poked and prodded him with a variety of cold instruments, looking for pubic lice, piles, hernias, and diseased gums.

"And how is thy urine, man?" asked the doctor.

"She is fine, sir," said Herman. "Glorious, in fact."

The medic didn't like the attitude embodied there, and he remarked sternly, "Sailor, you will do well to keep yourself to yourself, and to mind your tongue in the company of officers."

Herman held the man's gaze for a long time.

The truth was, he liked being at sea again, feeling the sway of the ocean underfoot, the forward plunge of a ship at full sail. He had almost forgotten what it felt like to walk on spongy knees, absorbing the rhythm of the swells, feeling the pliability of the ocean, which wrapped the earth in its capacious silky shawl and changed colors minute by minute, its mood unreliable, shifting from sanguine to choleric, with few stops between. The green of the South Pacific, and its florid equatorial breezes, appealed to him; the Atlantic, by contrast, seemed gray and unyielding, the appropriate surround for discontented Separatists such as Governor Bradford and his puritanical lot.

Almost at once Herman found himself in a comfortable harness aboard this well-run ship, although he was a military man at present, subject to disciplines that were previously unimaginable. In fact, not two days after the *United States* moved into open water, a command rose from the boatswain: "Punishment, ahoy! All hands on deck!" The captain came forward from his cabin and shouted, without conviction, "Master-at-arms, bring up the prisoners!"

This was not a good way to begin a voyage, H.M. realized, having heard a good deal about ritual punishments that formed the basis of naval discipline. He had no wish to observe the flogging of unfortunate sailors, but the drill was set, and everyone must assemble as commanded before the hatchway, where the captain, Mr. Armstrong—a colorless man with a shock of prematurely white hair—presided in desultory fashion, as if the whole proceeding bored him. The day's punishments began with two boys called Eli and Billy, accused of fighting and cursing. The smallest one, Billy, appeared no more than thirteen, although a faint mustache could be detected on his upper lip. He wept profusely, begging for a pardon. "I am not to fault!" he wailed, his high voice cracking. In a gesture that impressed H.M., Captain Armstrong put a hand on his shoulder, as if to say, "Not to worry, lad."

The boys were stripped to the waist, fastened to a grating designed for this evil purpose, and flogged six times with the legendary "cats," as they called these whips. The lashing drew bloody welts on tender backs. The shrieks and subsequent wailing of the boys was pitiful, and H.M. began to doubt the wisdom of his decision to join the navy, however temporarily. A merchant ship might have been much easier. He felt sure of this after witnessing the brutal floggings that followed, a consequence for smuggling liquor aboard the ship and drunkenness. Such behavior apparently warranted a dozen lashes, which reduced the backs of the offenders to patches of bloody pulp.

That evening, in moonlight that turned the deck into yellowy strips of planking, Herman wrote in his journal: "It was brutal to endure these lashings, even to watch as the boatswain's mate combed out the nine tails of his cat and then swept them round his neck, bringing them with the whole force of his body upon the tender backs." He found his sense of indignation swelling as he wrote: "Irrespective of incidental considerations, it seems obvious that flogging is opposed to the essential dignity of man, which no legislator has a right to violate for any reason; that it is oppressive, and glaringly unequal in its operations. It is utterly repugnant to the spirit of our democratic institutions and involves a lingering trait of the worst times of a barbarous feudal aristocracy. In a word, I denounce it as religiously, morally, and immutably *wrong*."

The firmness of this passage pleased him, and he noted the date: August 20. Despite what he had been told, he wondered how long it would take to get home. Sea journeys were, at best, unpredictable, and he had no wish to emulate Ulysses. He also wondered what strange things might happen en route to Boston, where he would have to negotiate release from the navy (an officer had assured him this would present no difficulties). Often it seemed as if nothing had gone as planned since leaving New Bedford in the winter of 1841. H.M. certainly had never imagined that Valentine Pease would prove intolerable. He could not have foreseen his jumping ship in the Marquesas, nor the train of circumstances that would tumble from that decision. No matter: he had narrative gold in his pocket, especially the stories about life among the cannibals of Nuku Hiva. He had been to the interior, where few white men had gone before him. And he had lived to tell the tale, one that grew more elaborate and interesting with each retelling.

Day after day now he sat before the mast with a rapt audience

at this feet, most of them hungry for stories. His length of stay
among the Typees had grown from weeks to months. He had
begun to see Fawn Away in fresh ways, and she became more and
more attractive in retrospect—a mermaid of sorts, a Siren who
tempted him to remain among the Typees forever. Never did he
mention Far Away, her lovely brother—that would arouse sus-
picions. The hovering of Kory-Kory always intrigued his audience, and they liked to hear about his tattooed body as well as his
excessive concern for Herman's health. H.M. found himself
remembering, or inventing, a thousand details about this proud if
primitive tribe. He would linger dramatically on his fear that his
hosts might eat him, and that proved a wise ploy, as cannibalism held
their attention.

It annoyed him when skeptics among them asked awkward
questions, such as how it was possible that he could understand their
language, however partially, on such a brief acquaintance. Patiently,
he explained that he had "a gift for languages," and that Fawn Away
spoke in such a clear and deliberate fashion that one could understand her without knowing the meaning of her exact words. "It was
all in the tone," he explained, adding that she was also adept at sign
language. This helped a great deal as he worked toward understanding their difficult tongue, which he proceeded to demonstrate,
offering whole paragraphs of Typee while gesticulating. He suggested that, had he remained among these people for another four
months or so, he might have written an epic in Typee, making the
sounds of their words conform to Roman letters. (He soon developed a side lecture on native linguistics of the Society Islands that,
to most ordinary seamen, confirmed his status as genius.)

He thought hard about narrative deployment, and realized that
storytelling involved asking questions and (very gradually) supplying the answers. He also thought about drawing characters. Bold
strokes would sometimes serve, especially with lesser figures. In this

regard, Kory-Kory—a hulking silent creature with his elaborately tattooed back, arms, and face—proved an ever-reliable prop. The underlying question about him seemed unanswerable but fascinating: Was he a servant or a guard? There was the matter of Herman's status among the Typees, too. Was he a guest or a prisoner? How free was he to do as he pleased? Could he abandon the tribe if he chose to do so? Perhaps he was mistaken about their intentions and they simply meant to absorb him into their community, turn him into a good and decent cannibal! Herman enjoyed these queries, responding to each questioner in a thoughtful fashion. At times, he assumed a professorial tone, in imitation of the Reverend Samuel Damon, who could chatter in splendid detail for hours about nothing—always a useful talent for a cleric or teacher.

His shipmates questioned him about the particulars of his sojourn, including the problem with his leg, the peculiar food, the religious rituals, the Happar wars, the making of tapa and tattooing of bodies. What seemed most to intrigue his listeners was the amount of leisure that the Typees enjoyed. They had no need to work for mere survival by the sweat of their brow, like the fallen children of Adam and Eve. Instead they merely plucked the fruit of the land as required or killed the odd pig or snake for meat. They spent inordinate amounts of time lounging by a waterfall, bathing and sunning their beautiful bodies on warm rocks under the shade of palms. They suffered few (if any) restrictions when it came to sexual pleasure. On this topic, H.M. found himself willing and able to conjure a wild range of amorous activities, although he feigned slight disapproval as he described these practices with clinical detachment, implying that as a good Christian he would never himself willingly indulge in liberties so readily assumed by these natives, who knew no sexual boundaries.

As a teller of tales, he knew enough to leave plenty of room for guessing about his own level of participation in the scenarios depicted. Perhaps he had been thoroughly indulgent, acting as the natives themselves did, taking pleasures wherever they arose. Maybe he stood to one side, disapproving or shyly restrained. One or two shipmates challenged him openly on this matter, but he deflected them with a teasing wink, a wry shrug, a glancing laugh. To the most aggressive questioner he said, "Well, matey, that's for me to know and you to guess." This had drawn considerable applause, as well as laughter.

It occurred to H.M. that no better audience existed for his stories than his shipmates. They were young and sexually deprived. The most experienced among them had consorted with any number of whores in various ports from Rio and Valparaiso to the Sandwich Islands. But the general run of ordinary seaman aboard this frigate had experienced little in the way of sex. They found a good deal of relief among themselves, of course, in the forecastle. It was commonplace for them to touch each other in the night, "lending a hand," as they put it. Actual buggery was rare, though not unknown, and some ships were apparently worse than others for this practice, H.M. was told by one old salt, who claimed that one infamous British ship was known as the HMS *Sodom*. Occasionally a desperate man would force himself upon another in a dark passage, but it was useless to complain to the authorities about these petty aggressions. Experienced officers turned a blind eye, as it was hardly worth troubling about the sex lives of sailors. All that concerned them was the spread of disease or any outbreak of violence, and the sort of activity that happened in the night below decks was relatively healthy—that is, it led to no obvious ailment, such as syphilis. It also kept the men in a calm state, less prone to fisticuffs or mutinous thoughts.

Belligerence, however, was the currency of military life. H.M. realized he was no longer whaling when, at the end of August, in open water (and with no other vessel in sight) the ship's drummer mustered all hands on deck. It was gunnery practice at sea, shadowboxing with nonexistent foes. Herman watched openmouthed as a muscular black man rammed and sponged a thirty-two pound cannonade. The blasts were thrilling: even a jaded seaman such as H.M. found it bracing to experience the pitch of battle, however imaginary. In his head it summoned picture memories of famous sea battles, such as Trafalgar, which had involved a flotilla of twenty-seven British ships under Admiral Lord Nelson. They had defeated thirty-three French and Spanish ships, although poor Nelson lost his life in the process, having been hit by a cannonball.

When Herman was a child, at bedtime his father had often recalled that the admiral had turned to his friend Captain Hardy as he knelt on the deck, fatally wounded, and said with enviable calm, "Hardy, I do believe they have done it at last. My backbone is shot through." He died three hours later, in agony, and his last words (according to Allan Melvill) were: "Thank God I have done my duty."

Overall, H.M. disliked heroics. He most certainly disdained naval protocol and procedure, however useful in the prosecution of warfare. He could see that, apart from these imaginary battles, the ship had no real purpose in this world. The voyage home would largely prove boring as Herman retraced his path around Cape Horn and began the gradual process of forgetting, and reshaping, his own past.

While still in the South Seas, however, he suffered from the absence of John Troy, although this wound required concealment, as it defied the usual conventions. It was not manly, even appropriate, to pine for another man. But thinking of Troy, H.M. often found himself unable to breathe. He wanted only to lie beside him on the soft mat outside of the Calabooza, to watch him while he slept. He wanted to see him bathing or sunning himself on a flat rock or digging a ditch for yams in Eimeo. He missed his friend's rough-hewn English accent, the angle of his chin when he told a certain kind of story, his quick smile and hunched walk. He had come to adore Troy's sleepy odor at dawn or his sweat during the day, when they worked side by side through a long afternoon in the remorseless sun. They had furtively allowed their affections to find expression in physical ways, but Troy had been like a pony, easily scared.

H.M. knew that their friendship had reached its outer limit. Whatever had happened between them on the islands belonged deeply in the past, where it must remain. Yet Herman could not accept the hideous and unthinkable finality of this separation. He cursed his life, and this unenviable turn, which could take him only in the direction of conventionality.

These feelings intensified as the *United States* approached Tahiti, whose peaks were visible from a distance of fifty miles. The longing induced by this sight nearly overwhelmed Herman, who found himself damp-eyed at the starboard rail, barely able to control himself. He felt alone on the ship except for one man, Jack Chase, an officer (captain of the maintop) who moved happily among those below him in rank, a natural democrat whose openness delighted Herman. He sought him out one day, comforted by the officer's genial, avuncular, and thoroughly benign presence.

Chase was a Briton in his early fifties, a bachelor and professional naval man who stood over six feet, with a roan beard that jutted forward from his chin. His auburn hair mixed with silvery strands, giving him a prophetic look. His nose was beaked, chapped, and blistered, and his nostrils flared when he laughed. And he laughed easily, priding himself on his wit. When H.M. noted the benefits of experience, for instance, Chase had quipped that age and decrepitude were "far too dear a price to pay for wisdom."

But Chase had earned his maturity. Being an Englishman in the American navy, he was a genuine oddity—at least to Herman. The navy accepted all nationalities (they could hardly afford to be picky) but it was a little strange to have an English officer in the ranks of a ship called the *United States*. As one discovered from Chase's stories, he had broad experience of naval life in far-flung places. As he liked to recall, he had witnessed the Battle of Navarino in 1827, during the Greek War of Independence. An armada of British, Russian, and French men-of-war—all of them sailing ships—had vanquished a fleet of Turkish and Egyptian vessels. This had, indeed, been one of the last naval battles to be fought entirely by ships under sail, Chase mused. And it had been especially bloody.

Chase could easily have met Lord Byron in the course of this colorful war, and he regretted that the opportunity had passed him by. Like Herman, he adored the rakish poet's verse and could recite long stretches of *Childe Harold* and *Don Juan*. One poem he declaimed on more than one occasion, as a kind of warning (or so it seemed to Herman), was about John Keats, Byron's younger contemporary, who had died at the age of twenty-five in Rome, with so much promise:

> Who killed John Keats?
> 'I,' says the *Quarterly*,
> So savage and Tartarly;
> ' 'Twas one of my feats.'
> Who shot the arrow?
> 'The poet-priest Milman
> (So ready to kill man),
> Or Southey or Barrow.'

Chase seemed unusually wise to the devouring habits of critics for someone who did not write poetry or prose. Henry Milman, he explained to Herman, was a well-respected critic who had published a nasty review of *Endymion*; so had John Barrow and Robert

Southey—all eminent figures in London literary circles. Shelley had written to Byron to wring his hands over this matter, explaining that young Keats had burst a blood vessel in his brain and collapsed at the foot of the Spanish Steps in a fit of anxiety over reviews of his work in the *Quarterly Review* and other periodicals. "He was broken by his least intelligent readers," Shelley wrote. "Woe to any man who should wish to write poems."

"The fact is I wish to write poems," H.M. confessed.

"Ah, poor boy," said Chase, adding: "I hope you will be stout-hearted, and take criticism with a grain of salt. You know what you are worth. Nobody else can know . . . not ever. Don't believe their derision or accept their slander. They are envious creatures who must, above all else, sell papers. They wish to impress their peers as well, and derogation is the quickest route to success as a reviewer."

Herman absorbed this wisdom, nodding gratefully, but he secretly believed that everyone would love his work. (He loved it, of course, though it was as yet unwritten.)

Chase proved a godsend on this voyage, ever ready for intelligent conversation, happy to discuss literary and philosophical matters, keen to assume a fatherly role. He had been a schoolmaster in Brighton before joining the navy, and it showed. He liked to ferret out whatever knowledge H.M. had, and he sought the blank spots, which he eagerly filled. One afternoon between watches he gave Herman a tour of the ship's library, which contained a fair number of novels and books of travel, as well as volumes devoted to naval history. On its sloping shelves one could find moldy copies of Irving, Scott, Cooper, Bulwer-Lytton, Marryat, and other manly volumes. Among the newer writers that Chase admired was Nathaniel Hawthorne, who had recently produced a collection of stories, *Twice-Told Tales,* in two volumes. It revealed, said Chase, a writer of unusual talent, his style being wild, meditative, and allegorical.

"There is a purity in the writing," he said. "He sees everything double: the world and the deeper realities behind the world, which move in concert, the one amplifying the other." H.M. liked this remark so much that he scribbled its wisdom into his journal, wishing the ship's library contained these stories. It would be too long before he could get his hands on them.

Chase recommended a particular tale by Hawthorne called "Young Goodman Brown." It had been published in *New England Magazine* some years before, and the officer admired it so vehemently that he tore its pages out, keeping them in a folder by his bed. He loaned the story to Herman, who read the yellowing pages by moonlight under the mizzen. It startled him, with its unlikely compacted emotions, and he determined to write something as fine one day.

The young man of the title is married to Faith, a Christian woman who wears pink ribbons. He wanders from her one evening at sunset, away from the security of Salem, into the forest on some mysterious errand, which he seems not fully to understand himself. In the woods he meets a figure who is perhaps the Devil himself, although he looks uncannily like an older version of Brown. This figure beckons to him, but the good young man resists. The very possibility that he should consort with the Evil One is ridiculous to him, even appalling. His Salem ancestors would have no willing contact with Satan. At least he thinks so, until this ghostly one explains otherwise: "I have been as well acquainted with your family as with ever a one among the Puritans; and that's no trifle to say. I helped your grandfather, the constable, when he lashed the Quaker woman so smartly through the streets of Salem; and it was I that brought your father a pitch-pine knot, kindled at my own hearth, to set fire to an Indian village, in King Philip's war."

Brown drifts into a clearing where some unholy ceremony is

taking place, a meeting of witches and warlocks. To his horror, he recognizes his neighbors in the crowd, even his wife—all at ease among these satanic communicants!

Brown never understands the nature of his vision—or nightmare—but it haunts him as he rejoins the community, having had his testing time in the dark wood. The intolerance seen among his ancestors could hardly be avoided, as it nestled inside him as well, a black kernel that would blossom. In the end, he becomes what he abhors—or always was.

"Don't let Mr. Hawthorne frighten you," said Chase, when Herman returned the pages, visibly shaken.

"I don't understand the story," H.M. said.

Chase fingered his beard, as he did before launching into an explanation. "What I think it means is this: You must never be afraid to go into the woods at night, and yet—if you do—you must *not* believe everything you see and hear. The human imagination is a perilous zone. It can restore us, or kill us."

"And what do you make of the wife, Faith?"

"Keeping Faith," said Chase, with a smile. "You've heard the phrase?"

"She's not a real woman."

Chase studied his younger friend's face as if he examined a painting in a museum. "One can only arrive at the truth obliquely," he said. "Think how various and complex our life is, as when you look out to sea. How many colors are there in the sky, the waves, and the clouds? How many words do we actually have to describe them? Imagine what a fool's errand it must be to attempt to frame the variations of the human heart in human language. Writers gesture in that direction, awkwardly, but they depend on figures of thought, sleights of hand."

"Parallels."

Chase brightened. "A tale is a world unto itself, and other worlds as well."

"These stories," Herman said, "teach us something essential."

"Some do," said Chase. "Others just entertain us. And there is nothing wrong with that."

"We can't see ourselves without stories."

Chase nodded, offering a cigar to his younger colleague, a way of acknowledging his approval. As H.M. saw it, Chase was his Socrates: a worldly philosopher. One did not expect someone of his quality and interests on a frigate, and so Herman considered himself blessed.

On religion Chase inclined toward a kind of genial deism, *à la* Voltaire, so he found it vaguely unsettling when H.M. claimed to doubt the existence of God. Herman's skepticism seemed to provoke one of the officer's finer speeches: "Do you believe so firmly in accident? I can't imagine human consciousness as a random occurrence. The world is too intricate for that. When you sit on the maintop at night and see the heavens unfold in sprays of light, do you not marvel at the spectacle? Do you not wonder at the inventiveness that put such a gaudy thing on display? Those quiet voices in your head, are they all yours? We're part and parcel of the universe, dear boy. I believe that phrase belongs to Mr. Emerson."

Herman demurred, saying he had read Emerson's little book *Nature* and admired it, but he could not go quite so far. "Why put a name to our natural reverence for the physical world? Why say 'God' when you could say anything? Call it chance, if you will." H.M. grinned. "I will take my chances, as they say."

Chase frowned. "God is the center, alive in each of us."

"That would mean an infinite number of centers exist," Herman replied. "Is that logical?"

"Heaven's geometry is not ours."

"I'm confused."

"How excellent! A young man needs confusion in order to grow. It's the beginning of wisdom." Chase took a long drag on the cigar, blowing smoke rings into the air, watching as the wind dispersed them. "There is no end of anything, of course. No final shape or condition. Who can say that events do not unfold in a simultaneous manner, however much we believe in chronology? I would say I'm young and old, foolish and wise, everything at once."

H.M. liked conversational turns into places where the words themselves cracked at the edge of meaning, and so he looked forward to these watches, when Chase gave freely of his time and blew large quantities of smoky language into the air like well-shaped rings that rose and dispersed, leaving nothing behind but the faint smell of burning. Herman thought he overdid it, at times, but Chase's decades at sea had produced a mind rich in ideas, notions, and directions for thinking. His wide reading had shaped his understanding of how the world operates. He could quote poetry by the yard, even Camoëns, in the original Portuguese. He appeared to have all of Scott in his head, even minor characters and ballads. He could recite lengthy passages from *Paradise Lost*—such as Book IV, where Satan pays a slithering visit to Eden and turns envious at the sight of human glory. Yet Chase never forgot his official duties. To be sure, his top mates considered him a skilled and fair-minded officer, who listened to their complaints while retaining high standards for performance.

H.M. had felt quite lucky, being an ordinary seaman, to find himself among the experienced crew of this maintop, thus handling the lower sails, mizzen, and main sails (instead of working among the afterguard or, worse, below). His previous time on whalers had been taken as useful experience, and his interview with the officer in charge of new recruits had gone well. Once under way, he had proved himself quickly, showing off a grasp of the elements of seamanship. He took pains not to embarrass himself in the company of officers, among whom he behaved like the well-bred gentleman that, indeed, he was. The forecastle of the *United States* was, in any case, superior to anything he had seen on the *Acushnet* or the *Lucy Ann*: no disease-ridden vagabonds there, and fewer criminals and liars. Nonetheless, these were young sailors, many of them inexperienced in the ways of the world. So they looked up to H.M. as someone who—having lived among cannibals—had walked on the dark side. He had gone into the forest like Goodman Brown, and the experience had transformed him.

On their zigzag across the Pacific, the *United States* passed the Society Islands, standing off Anna Maria Bay at Nuku Hiva for a night. As before, H.M. admired the view of that island, with its steep sides, its green peaks, and the veils of mist that hung in its humid valleys. The French—nosing around in the South Seas, ever looking for ways to add geographical mass to their empire—had arrived before them, and they could be seen building huts along the shoreline. Several of their men-of-war lay at anchor with their strident colors flying. Within hours, the American frigate was boarded by the infamous Admiral Dupetit-Thouars—a preposterous little man who bowed ceremoniously to all and sundry. Captain Armstrong had an acute sense of naval protocol, and he ordered a salute of twenty-one guns.

Jack Chase whispered to Herman, "I fear we shall run out of ammunition if we come upon too many admirals on the way home."

The next morning, Herman strained to see the natives on the shoreline, wondering if by chance—by a miracle—he might glimpse the woman who had so enthralled him.

Either he imagined it, or he actually saw her. Certainly a woman very like Fawn Away waded into the water to her waist, and she appeared to gaze at Herman from afar. Was that a child behind her, on the black shingle? Could H.M. possibly have fathered a child during his passionate weeks among the Typees? Surely not enough time had lapsed for such a thing. Was he peering into the future? Or was he looking into his own heart, wishing for a child? Or simply hoping for a connection to this island? In any case, he felt heartsick, thinking of his time among these kind (if terrifying) strangers, wondering if he would know such ease again, such thrilling openness to the physical aspects of life. It seemed unlikely, as he would soon return to a world haunted by the ghosts of Puritan New England. He would move to the center of his own Salem, whether in Massachusetts or New York. And he would live with the hard emotional residue of his experiences among the Typees and with John Troy.

As the ship drew away from Nuku Hiva, and the outline of its peaks receded, H.M. could hardly tolerate the intensity of his feelings. His heart was broken, and he wept at the taffrail. He could hear Nathaniel Hawthorne's laconic voice in his head now: "A stern, a sad, a darkly meditative, a distrustful, if not a desperate man did he become from the night of that fearful dream."

"You'll be fine," Chase said, appearing at his elbow, unbidden. "But you must avoid nostalgia. It's a kind of sickness. The word itself suggests pathology, a manner of disease: the pain of getting somewhere that does not exist, *home,* perhaps, or a place that one tries to substitute for home. One can never really feel at home in this life. That's the one thing I believe with absolute certainty. The English language, perhaps, is the only home I know."

Herman knew there was something odd about Jack Chase, something remote and rhetorical. Chase could be a windbag. Yet Herman forgave these flaws, if they were flaws. His own dear brother Gansevoort could take flight as well, spinning paragraphs of sentiment, barking up trees that nobody else could even see. The important thing was that H.M. talked freely with Chase. Indeed, anyone listening would suspect he had swallowed more than his share of grog.

One evening, on watch under a harvest moon, H.M. told the older man about John Troy, wondering how he might survive in the deep void created by their separation. He wondered if Chase had ever experienced such a thing. Was the whole wrenching experience a piece of foolishness, a perversity, a curse upon his soul? Was it perhaps a sign of his active recruitment by the Devil? Would the pain go away, or would he have to live with the agony of Troy's absence?

Chase usually responded to questions without hesitation, but he waited, looking upward at the heavens, listening as the black-and-gold seas rushed beneath the keel, creating a sound like an infinitely long sheet of paper tearing. The sails were full tonight, as a strong breeze came from behind, and the ship sped forward at great speed, as if frantic to get home.

"We're making up for lost time," Chase said.

Herman nodded, waiting for a response to his confessions. At last, it came.

"I have had various . . . affections," Chase intoned, dropping his voice to the level of a stage whisper, making sure they had no eavesdroppers. "It is often like this, I think, among naval men, who must live without women for many years. So unnatural, this way of life. There is a need, a feeling of ill-content, in the male breast."

Herman dug the tips of his fingers into his palms.

"It's more complicated still," Chase said, "and more confusing. I don't want to make light of what you have told me, Herman. I take this information as a sign of friendship."

"That was my intention."

"I see that well," he said. "And will admit I have been in similar straits. I've been a single man, at sea, a long time. It would never have done for me, an ordinary life at home, a cottage in the dale, with simple board and bed, perhaps a few children playing about in the garden. I wanted that, of course. We all do."

"Yes. I do."

"Aye, and you shall have it! I will say as much."

"But my sadness?"

"Sadness?" He stepped back. "It is the way of things. Those who experience these . . . affections . . . have no choice but to keep them in small boxes, label them, align them on a shelf. Believe me, there is neither male nor female in the heavens above. The matter of reproduction requires it, on earth; but it's an artificial distinction. Human feeling is a wind that blows where it will and lands willy-nilly." He paused now, biting his lip. "There is really no way to explain what I hope to say. I'm talking in circles, am I not?"

"You make sense to me."

Chase lit a cigar, a delaying tactic, allowing words to rise slowly in the mind's well.

"I appreciate your frankness," Herman said.

Chase drew close to speak. "I have had attachments to young men in my time. That is blunt, sir. I will be blunt, as we are friends. I've had similar affections for one or two young ladies, and there was talk of marriage in one case. These are sad memories. I live with them. Sometimes I see the faces, and their voices rise in the wee hours, like ghosts. Overall, I think we are blessed by our attach-ments. Life, you see, is a lonely business."

Herman had never experienced this side of Chase, and the con-fessional nature of these remarks astonished him. Yet he felt much better. His dilemma had been put forward, set upon the table, exam-ined. It was not such a hideous thing as he had imagined. Jack Chase had held a mirror before his soul, and the reflection was not appalling. It was something normal, even typical, if rarely named or analyzed.

"I'm grateful for what you've said," H.M. declared.

Chase responded by putting a hand on Herman's wrist, leaning into his face with a smoky breath, speaking forcefully. "When there is a storm, it's best to turn into the teeth of it. Don't fly away, allowing an evil wind to come upon you from the stern. That's our weakest part. We're rib cage and metal up front. The bow is always best. Head into the blast, son. Into the blast."

The *United States* stood for a night off Eimeo, snug in the small harbor at Taloo, having left Anna Maria Bay in early October. It was as if H.M. could not escape his past and would circle forever in this groove, in and out of the Society and Sandwich islands, never forgetting the encounters, the couplings, the strange affections, the perfervid nights and shimmering days, when body encompassed soul, dissolving the distinctions between them. He had never lived so physically, so fully in skin and bone, tooth and nail. In these islands, the sun shone as if from within, the moon burned in his brain. Water became sky, and night exchanged its sultry qualities with day. All the world's angels had sung in his ears these several months, when he had lived on the salt edge of the breeze, with sails full and tight, keening. He had tasted a fruit so sweet, so ripe and perfect, that it seemed unlikely he would ever encounter such a thing again in the brief life that lay before him.

But Eimeo was hard to ignore, only two hundred yards away: a sleeping leviathan. John Troy would be there, he was sure of it. He would perhaps have made a home for himself among the islanders, as he fit in easily wherever he landed, a chameleon of sorts, taking his color from the land itself, its mood and people. He might have made another close friend by now. For a perilous hour, Herman stood at the rail and thought of diving into the moonlight, breaking its reflection on the water, shattering his course of life. He might have drowned himself or swum to shore. On Eimeo, he would almost certainly have made his way back to Troy. It would not have taken long to establish their old connection once again, despite the awkward parting.

Herman could have made a home there, allowing himself to forget about home and hearth, the noble lines of Gansevoort and Melville, the connections in Boston, in the Berkshires and New York. His mother would gradually realize he was gone for good; but she had other sons and daughters. It was not unusual to lose a son at sea: one half expected such a thing to happen. Once a neighbor in Lansingburgh had "lost" a son in this way. He had gone whaling, hoping for profit and adventure. But the letters had stopped in Peru. No further word came, and the family could discover nothing more about him: no report of drowning, no mutinous behavior. His shipmates said he disappeared into Lima, and they presumed him dead. There it lay until a dozen years later, when he knocked on the door of his old house in Lansingburgh: Rip van Winkle himself. But his poor mother and father had passed to the other side by then, and his sisters (who occupied the house with their own children) had little or no interest in his fate.

H.M. nearly leaped over the rail, but something mysterious fixed his feet to the deck of the *United States*. He could never bear the thought of his mother's agony if he should disappear: she was strong but not that strong. And he sorely missed his brothers and sisters, uncles and aunts, even his cousins. He was hardly alone in this world after all. He was part of a glorious, populous, and noble clan. And his worldly prospects, in fact, were considerable. He might go into business with his brother or apprentice himself to a law firm. If Benjamin Franklin could arrive as a young man of nineteen on Market Street in Philadelphia with nothing but a few loaves in his pockets and prosper, then so could he. He had more than a few loaves in his pockets. Most important, he possessed a rich imagination and the ability to write. His chances of success seemed better than even, and he would make the most of whatever talents lay at his disposal. He felt a coiled energy within him, and knew in his heart that he would surprise the world one day. They would remember the name of Herman Melville, the grandson of Revolutionary War heroes on both sides, a hero in his own right.

"Goodbye, John," he said, in a low voice, calling over the indigo waters that fell between them.

It hurt to say that phrase, with its finality. He knew he would never forget his dear friend. He also understood that he would mourn this terrible loss as long as he lived. That was a consequence of any great affection. He would not have missed it for anything.

I don't know but a book in a man's brain is better off than a book bound in calf—at any rate it is safer from criticism. And taking a book off the brain, is akin to the ticklish & dangerous business of taking an old painting off a panel—you have to scrape off the whole brain in order to get at it with due safety—& even then, the painting may not be worth the trouble.

H.M. to Evert Duyckinck,
December 13, 1850

LIZZIE

11.

We married in the dog days of August 1847, when not even a cool bath provided more than a few moments of relief as the dust on Mount Vernon Street invaded the house, churned up by passing carriages, especially with the coming and going for my wedding. For months I had kept the reality of this ceremony, its dislocation and terror, out of my mind. But it lay before me, a result of my own decision. I had made a choice, and I would live with it. I would become Mrs. Elizabeth Shaw Melville, for better or worse.

My stepmother had engaged half of Boston's unwashed masses to assist us in the preparations, and they moved through the house for days on end, arranging flowers and polishing floors, cleaning windows with ammonia, repairing broken steps, clipping hedges, lining the edges of the garden path with white-painted stones, and hanging paper lanterns in the ash trees. Father laid in cases of wine from Morton's, including enough champagne to float a ferryboat.

So much for the idea of a small wedding, I thought, sitting on the porch at night with Father a couple of days before, sipping lemonade, teary-eyed. It was not easy to leave home after more than two decades in the familial cocoon. My father would be a difficult man to replace. There was nobody like him in the world of my acquaintance, so gentle and self-controlled, brilliant and judicious, with the Commonwealth of Massachusetts at his feet. Herman Melville—with his volatility and uneven education, with his uncertain profession as author—was a pale substitute.

But, as Father said, he was "a promising young man from a fine family."

That Herman's father and my father had been close friends had tipped the balance for me. I was marrying a kind of cousin, a name that had been part of my childhood, and someone whose sister I treasured. Romantic love was not part of the equation, not precisely, but I didn't mind this. Novels gave young ladies the wrong idea about men and marriage.

My father had been my only teacher, my instructor in the world's ways and means. I could expect reading material to appear beside my plate at the breakfast table, for later discussion, as when he put into my hands a copy of the *Democratic Review* one day, where the publisher, Mr. O'Sullivan, rattled on about what he called Manifest Destiny. There was a disagreeable lust for blood and territory in Washington, especially since Mr. Polk had taken office. "If these politicos had a decent home life," my father opined, "they would cease and desist from this expansionist madness."

H.M. was, of course, an author—that had been part of the attraction. (*Typee* was published a year before our marriage.) But he rarely talked about books and bookmen, although he seemed to move easily in that world, and one of his best friends was Evert Duyckinck, a dashing gentleman with silky hair and beard. He edited the *Literary World* and (as my father recalled) had assisted Edgar Allan Poe in putting together a volume of his frightening

tales. We joined Mr. Duyckinck one afternoon for tea at the Little-
ton Hotel near the courthouse—my father met us as well—and I
was pleased to see my fiancé talk knowledgeably about the latest
novels and poetry. Mr. Duyckinck took pleasure in Herman's enthusiasms and egged him on, asking his opinion of Professor Longfellow from Harvard.

"I don't see why the world bends to him," Herman said. "The
man is an intelligent fellow, a scholar with intellectual resources, but
he is not an original poet."

"Oh, but he's the best we have!" Mr. Duyckinck said, taunting,
his gray eyes glinting.

"Then we have not much to say for ourselves—as a nation,"
H.M. said.

My father, who worshipped Mr. Longfellow and often dined
with him at Craigie House in Cambridge, could barely suppress a
scowl, although he admired Herman's independent streak. "Oh,
you're too hard on Longfellow," he said.

"But *he* is hard on us," said Herman.

"Do we have no excellent authors?" my father asked.

"We are lucky to have Nathaniel Hawthorne among us."

"And Mr. Emerson?" asked Mr. Duyckinck.

"Emerson," said Herman, "is a genius. But we can only read
him intermittently. His prose does not move. It stalls within the sentence. You can always quote him—they are perfect and memorable
sentences, aphorisms each. One can frame them, pin them to a wall.
But there is no movement."

My father listened with intense pleasure. It impressed him that
Mr. Duyckinck admired and respected my fiancé. Here was a most
reputable person, a graduate of Columbia who had studied law with
John Anthon, Father's old friend in New York. After admission to
the bar, he had traveled widely in Europe and had edited various
journals before taking over the *Literary World*. His brother, George,

was perhaps even more eminent as a man of letters, but Evert displayed a quietly judicious nature and impeccable manners.

Nobody remarked upon this explicitly, but it was obvious that my husband-to-be had avoided the usual paths for well-bred young men. He had barely any formal education, though he read books on learned topics with the vehemence of an autodidact. He seemed to know *everything* about whaling ships and naval protocol—he could talk about these at tedious length. I wondered how I would fit into his mental scheme, whether I would count, as I had grown used to counting.

I had watched my stepmother closely over the years, as she played the role of Mrs. Shaw. She usually agreed with Father, who would have found it difficult to live with a woman who opposed him consistently. On the matter of the Mexican War they formed a united front in public, mowing down many of our friends and neighbors, among whom there were some who had the temerity to admire President Polk and General Taylor!

At this point, as a young bride-to-be, I wanted to support H.M. and to provide gentle resistance at appropriate moments, but I didn't know where my future husband stood on the major issues of the day. One would guess, from a reading of *Omoo* (published only months before our wedding), that he disliked most forms of colonialism, which he regarded as efforts by the powerful to suppress those without the means to resist domination. But Herman generally held his cards close to his chest on politics, as with most things. When my father railed against the war, H.M. stared ahead, refusing even to grunt his approval. He could wax eloquent about the French in the Sandwich Islands, although this was not an *American* problem, as I pointed out one night, much to his annoyance. A woman, in his view, should have no opinions.

There was an innate stubbornness in his manner. "We are in

this life alone," he would say, betraying a melancholy that eventually would swamp his fragile craft.

Allan Melville, his younger brother, was not melancholy. He was, indeed, the one bright spot in the family, and he would soon marry the daughter of wealthy New Yorkers. In some ways, I felt better about H.M. because of Allan, and often thought I had attached myself to the wrong Melville. Allan was the opposite of his brother, with an acute sense of fiscal responsibility. He liked to socialize with the very best of New York society. (It helped, of course, that his wife, Sophia, had grown up in a fine house on Bond Street, with ties to the right sort of people, none of them "artistic.") At dinner at the Tremont House on the night before my wedding, Allan delighted my father by railing against what he called "these pig-headed autocrats" who had declared what was called "an executive war," prosecuted by a White House that had never sought the consent of the governed when it came to Texas or Mexico.

My father quipped that war "will usually find a way to succeed."

It could hardly be stopped, remarked Allan, adding: "In this, it resembles love."

"My wedding is tomorrow," I said. "We should talk of love in less violent terms."

"Marriage is about love and peace," said Herman, needing to add his voice to the debate.

"We cannot have peace when our nation is at war," I said.

Herman did not respond but looked at his plate.

"Oh, my dear Lizzie," Father said. "Whatever shall we do with you?"

I was already a figure of suspicion in Boston circles because of my engagement to Herman Melville. The papers reported with mischievous glee that the daughter of Chief Justice Shaw had consented to marry the man they referred to as "Mr. Herman Typee

Omoo Melville." One wag in the *Evening Transcript* suggested that a native girl called Fayaway might be suing Herman for breach of promise. I never alluded to any of this silly gossip, as it was beneath such consideration. For all Herman knew, I never read the papers.

The wedding proceeded with a genial inevitability. Afterward, the men sat together under a spreading chestnut tree at the north side of the garden, drinking brandy and smoking cigars until quite late. One by one the carriages pulled away, the house emptied of guests.

I waited patiently for Herman in my bedroom, and he arrived at midnight, reeking of tobacco and alcohol. I might as well have slept alone, as he claimed to have mixed too many wines, and this had produced a "thundering ache" in his skull.

I put a wet cloth on his forehead and kissed his lips.

"I hope you forgive me, but I must sleep," he said.

I was only too happy to oblige him, as my own nerves had been frayed by the weeks of preparation. I could hardly face the strain of sexual congress that night, after such a frenzied time. In any case, it felt unnatural to behave like rabbits under the roof of my parents, losing my virginity in a room with all the trappings of childhood around me. The bed was far too narrow, with a pink headboard— an unlikely venue for copulation. I had worried about this matter for weeks, so it relieved me that H.M. had come to bed so late, with a headache, real or imagined.

Girls do whisper among themselves to an excessive degree about the mysteries of sex, and this chatter only adds to the anxiety that accumulates at these times. My friend Eleanor Conklin, who feigned broad knowledge of carnal affairs, told me in a low voice: "His male appendage will astonish and frighten you, especially in the tumescent state. We are never prepared for this intrusion. It hurts terribly, at least for a while. There may well be considerable bleeding as a result. Ask him to be gentle. In due course, all will be well. This is typical."

Herman was not in any way a typical man, nor did I imagine he was. I was taking a chance here. As Eleanor put it so dramatically only a week before the wedding: "You will have to measure up to those savages of Tahiti, and good luck to you."

She had no right to say such a thing.

After the wedding, she winked at me before she left our house late in the afternoon. I could see her mouthing a sentence under her breath: "Write to me!"

I left Mount Vernon Street the next morning with commingling thoughts, saying a long goodbye to my parents while Herman stood to one side, impatiently rubbing his hands together and sighing. It was difficult for me, as I had spent twenty-five years under the protection of my family, enjoying the safety, the feeling that nothing inappropriate would confront me if I behaved like any other girl of my station. In my heart I understood that the ease of my father's house lay behind me. Those years would be wrapped in the gauze of memory. I had made a choice, or—how to put this?—*fate* had pointed me in this direction. I could surely have turned away from Herman, refused his hand; nobody would have objected in the least. My options had not dwindled to such a degree that I had no other paths in life. But there was something thrilling if slightly dangerous about this man. I had married a volcano, my very own Vesuvius—*for better or worse,* as the Reverend Mr. Young put it, adding perhaps a little too much weight to the latter part of that equation.

We left by train for Concord, aiming for the White Mountains and Canada, with Quebec City our farthest goal. We would make our way home along the narrow waterway of Lake Champlain, with the Green Mountains to the east, the Adirondacks to the west, coming to rest at Lansingburgh, where the Melville house overlooked the Hudson and "had plenty of rooms with excellent views of the river traffic," as H.M. would say. There he planned to continue his work as an author, and I would do whatever wives do in these circumstances. It was impossible to imagine how my hours would pass, what I would accomplish, or who would provide the kind of lively and affectionate company I had enjoyed on Mount Vernon Street. I could not really *imagine* life in such a tiny hamlet, although Herman appeared to like it—especially as his mother would preside over the household.

"You must humor my mother," he said.

"I don't believe she likes me."

"She doesn't like anyone much. Don't take it personally."

I should have seen at once that Maria and I could not live under the same roof. This would always be her house, not mine—which was the case even when we lived in homes that I had paid for myself. But I knew deep in my heart that H.M. loved his mother, or feared her, or for mysterious reasons could not live without her.

"But what shall I do in this town?" I wondered.

"What does anybody do?"

After a while, he explained that Albany lay close by. It was, as he reminded me, "a major capital in a major state." His mother was friendly with the current governor, and "one could expect invitations to important events."

I'd had my share of invitations to "important events" in Boston, but rarely did I accept them. I preferred a quiet life, which is what I faced. Events at the capitol were not forthcoming, despite Maria Melville's august connections.

It had been my idea, going to the White Mountains. Three decades before, my parents had made this same excursion after their wedding, climbing the windy sides of Mount Washington with a small army of guides and packhorses, reaching the Crawford

Notch (still some miles from the summit) after many hours. My father often recalled that journey—a precious memory of his dear departed wife, my mother—and once remarked to me that a good honeymoon was the key to marriage. "Setting off on the right foot," he called it.

Travel had become easier lately, with the advent of railways. And there we sat in a wood-paneled compartment, watching the woods and fields pass swiftly, gobbling up the miles at stunning speed. The maize, by late summer, was chest-high—gleaming fields of green corn that held the wind and swayed. My stepmother had made sure that we had a basket full of delectable things to sustain us: hard cheeses, fruit, smoked salmon, a loaf of bread. An elderly Negro porter filled our pitcher of water at least once an hour, as the cabin was insufferably hot, even with the window open.

"Are you well, Mrs. Melville?" H.M. inquired, as we approached Concord.

I nodded. But it was so *peculiar* to hear my name transmogrified. My identity had changed, in a fell swoop. I had become Elizabeth Melville.

We traveled by coach to a romantic spot at the far end of Lake Winnipiseogee, arriving in time for dinner in the public dining room, where dozens of couples ate at separate tables and murmured in low voices. The Alton Cliff Hotel was full, but Herman had reserved an impressive (and much too expensive) room overlooking the lake, with mountain views—a vision of heaven through open windows framed by tall larches and drooping hemlocks. The lake began at the edge of a lawn, and it gleamed before us, a ghostly silver surface, serene and beautiful. I stood for a long time, watching as black geese cut across a moon so large and yellow it seemed improbable. A loon's cry doubled itself, echoing. I was dazed or dazzled: I don't know which.

The room was spacious, the walls papered in a flowery pink-

and-blue print. A brass bed stood against the wall opposite the window, covered in a white spread like a field of snow.

"I'd like a bath," I said.

"Take your time, Lizzie. I shall read a book."

We understood that, in a short while, we must consummate our
marriage. This was only natural and expected, and yet the prospect
frightened us both, I suspect. We had said shockingly little to each
other during dinner, and during the dessert course when I reached
for Herman's hand, I found it cold and damp.

I actually fell asleep for perhaps ten or fifteen minutes in the
claw-foot tub—my nerves had exhausted me, and I needed this
respite. Upon waking, I changed into a nightgown of Irish lace that
my stepmother had given me as a wedding gift.

"It will delight your husband," she had said, coyly.

The gown was lovely: sheer, with a neat pattern of tiny circles.
Quite on purpose, I wore nothing under it. My face in the mirror
looked especially pretty. I had expected dark circles under my eyes
and sagging cheeks, as the last few weeks had been trying, but the
bath transformed me. I felt a fine fresh tingling on my skin. The nip-
ples of my breasts already seemed tender, alert. My breathing grew
shallow, quick, and I saw that I wanted very badly to make love to
the man in the next room. As I turned the knob, I found my hand
shaking, my knees wobbly.

I had not expected that Herman would have stripped completely while I bathed, but he had. The sight shocked me, as I had
never seen a naked man before (a few awkward glimpses of my
father and brothers did not really count). H.M. lay on his stomach,
reading a book, on the white cotton spread. His broad shoulders
and narrow hips took my breath away, and I liked very much his
delicate bare feet. But what focused my attention were his buttocks,
larger and rounder than I had expected but muscular, well shaped,
shining in the lamplight. I drew close, sitting on the edge of the bed,

where I studied his form closely, allowing myself the intimacy of touch. I drew my hand down his spine to the small of his back, grazing his buttocks.

He seemed to quiver, turning over, so that I could see his male part, which curled to one side, hugely full.

I looked at him searchingly.

"Have I startled you, my love?" he asked. "If so, I'm sorry. I should have undressed in the bathroom."

"I don't know," I said, touching him where I never imagined I would, and without hesitation. "It is quite peculiar."

He laughed. "I love the way you put things."

"Things?"

"Come to me, darling," he said, opening his arms. "Let there be nothing but skin between us."

That was well said, I decided, and I lay down beside him, allowing him to kiss me deeply as his large hands moved under my nightgown. He touched my breasts and thighs, and I remember reaching for him. The rest was a blur, although I know he came into me gently. It didn't hurt nearly so much as Eleanor had said it would, although I confess it was not a perfect experience. Herman was a sinewy man, with quantities of hair on his face, chest, and stomach—some of it rather coarse. He moved with deliberation, heaving and thrusting. Then he stalled above me, issuing a sharp cry, as if in pain. Moments later, he collapsed on the bed beside me and began to weep.

"There is no need for tears," I said.

"I hope you like me, Lizzie dear."

"I love you," I said.

I stroked him to comfort and reassure him, rubbing his chest with an open palm. The immense strangeness of lying beside a naked man for the first time overwhelmed me as we snuggled on the bedspread without bothering to get under the covers, as it was so hot, and we had no need to hide ourselves—not any longer.

*Melville, as he always does, began to reason of
Providence and futurity, and of everything that lies
beyond human ken, and informed me that he had
"pretty much made up his mind to be annihilated";
but still he does not seem to rest in that anticipation;
and, I think, will never rest until he gets hold of a
definite belief. It is strange how he persists—and has
persisted ever since I knew him, and probably long
before—in wandering to-and-fro over these deserts, as
dismal and monotonous as the sand hills amid which
we were sitting. He can neither believe, nor be
comfortable in his unbelief; and he is too honest and
courageous not to try to do one or the other. If he were
a religious man, he would be one of the most truly
religious and reverential; he has a very high and noble
nature, and better worth immortality than most of us.*

Nathaniel Hawthorne,
notebook entry of November 20, 1856

DARK ANGEL

12.

In 1849 Herman left his young wife and six-month-old son, Malcolm, at the docks in New York and crossed the Atlantic on the *Southampton,* a seasoned topsail schooner. He had the American proofs of *White-Jacket* in his suitcase—money in the bank. His plan was to sell the book in England, where readers had welcomed his talents more heartily than their American counterparts. The British always adored anything connected with the sea, and they had been the first to celebrate his writing. *Mardi,* however, had met with sighs of disappointment, with one reviewer commenting: "One hopes that Mr. Melville will soon return to form, with a rollicking tale of adventures on the high seas. This novel runs off the rails, as if the novelist had drunk some strange herbal potion while afloat in the South Seas of his imagination."

H.M. promised Lizzie he would return "sometime late in the following year." That was a long time to be away from a young wife and baby, but everyone saw that Herman required a break from life as usual: his nerves were jangled and he slept badly most nights, calming himself with tumblers of brandy and bad cigars before going to bed. His eyesight had begun to deteriorate, and he suffered thudding headaches after only a few hours at his desk. Marriage had not improved things for him, as Lizzie had grown sullen, even morose, chafing at the demands of her mother-in-law, refusing to speak to Herman for extended periods. Helen Melville suggested to her brother that this was simply a normal consequence of pregnancy, but H.M. doubted this.

The reality was that Lizzie had not fit into the Melville clan as easily as expected, and no obvious solution to the problem could be found, though the arrival of Malcolm in mid-February had temporarily saved the day, as Lizzie focused her attentions on her "Barney," as she called him, tending the infant with a gleeful obsession.

So Herman relished the prospect of freedom from Lizzie and his mother as he settled happily into life aboard a schooner. Unlike on previous journeys by sea, he occupied his own cabin—one of the few single aft cabins aboard this ship. From what he could tell, he owed this luxury to his status as the author of *Typee* and *Omoo*—the captain had alluded to these books during their first conversation. He was clearly expected to sit each night at the captain's table, where his recollections of life in the South Seas among cannibals amused other passengers, a few of whom had actually read Herman's books. H.M. especially liked the company of Ted McCurdy, a sylphlike young man of twenty-one with a mass of black curls and a finely shaped nose. Teddy, as he preferred to be called, was the only son of a wealthy fur trader from lower Manhattan, and he spent hours after dinner over bottles of ale in H.M.'s cabin. The young man wanted to know everything about Herman's adventures among the "wild and nubile Marquesans," as he put it.

Herman enjoyed titillating the boy, though afterward he felt guilty, as he tended to exaggerate his tales. He could not, however,

resist telling these stories, since Teddy responded so well—his liquid brown eyes widened and his delicate eyebrows arched while he
lapped up whatever H.M. could give him. One night, quite late and
after many rounds of Scotch whiskey (Teddy had stowed a special
bottle in his trunk), they fell asleep together in Herman's bunk.

Herman startled when he woke at dawn with Teddy's arm
crooked around his chest, the young man's face turned toward him
so he could smell his rank breath, the dry sweat around his neck.
That aspect of the encounter was unpleasant, but he liked the boy's
long lashes, each of them distinct and slightly curled; he marked the
soft cheeks and slight goatee, more of a wisp than a proper tuft of
hair. He savored the weight of the boy's arm, and the posture he
and Teddy assumed reminded him of those blowsy Calabooza nights
in the Pacific, when John Troy stretched beside him, his lanky body
so clean and supple. He would gladly give away everything in his
possession for another of those nights with Troy.

The Atlantic crossing ended quickly, though Herman remained
in contact with Teddy and other passengers after disembarking—it
had been a congenial group aboard the *Southampton*. Soon he found
himself trying to flog his book among London publishers indifferent to his reputation. ("Ah, Millersville," said one of them, "I have
admired your book on Italian gardens. Have you got another of
those for us?") The role of door-to-door salesman fit him poorly,
and he could hardly expect to replicate the success of Gansevoort,
who, before dying of a mysterious illness that nobody could explain,
had managed to get *Typee* into the sympathetic hands of Lord
Byron's very own publisher, John Murray.

That was in March 1846, during Gansevoort's time as secretary
to the American consulate in London, and Herman thought of him
as he walked these streets, thinking his brother had been there only
a few years before. Everything had come apart unexpectedly as Gans
began to experience severe headaches and ringing in his ears—

a "tinny whine," as he described it in one of his anxious letters home during this period. A few weeks later his eyesight began to fail, with flashes of light in his peripheral vision. He grew unstable on his feet, and his hands shook uncontrollably whenever he tried to light a cigar. Fevers swept through him like tropical storms, leaving him wrung out, dazed, confused. In late April, his nose and gums began to bleed without provocation, and soon the far-flung provinces of his body went into revolt. The doctors threw up their hands, having never encountered such a peculiar collocation of symptoms. The word "typhoid" was attached to this mix of ailments, as the coroner had no better explanation. Dead at thirty, Gansevoort was allowed a brief funeral service at Westminster Abbey, with a drab handful of colleagues in attendance on a rainy Saturday morning. The body was shipped home in a lead-lined coffin aboard the *Prince Albert*—the cost of the passage borne by the embassy, although a medical bill arrived some months later from one Dr. Elton Bykerstaff of Chelsea, who claimed to have "treated the deceased for several weeks with a range of medicaments."

Gansevoort's death stunned the family, leaving H.M. notionally in charge of a sprawling, improvident clan without resources apart from its network of well-placed relatives and friends. In this vein, an encouraging note of condolence to Maria arrived in Lansingburgh from Judge Lemuel Shaw: "I can only say how sorry I am about your son's death," he wrote to Maria, "and I remain deeply attached to your family, as I'm sure you realize. I shall do whatever I can to help you and your children in ways that seem appropriate. Your family is mine, as I loved your husband as one loves a brother, and I miss him greatly. May God comfort you and your children during this difficult time. It is hard to imagine the loss of a child at whatever age—there is perhaps nothing worse."

A short while later, the eminent Judge Shaw was Herman's father-in-law, more willing than ever to help in whatever ways he could. He did not hesitate when, over a glass of port in his study in Boston, H.M. asked him to finance this transatlantic journey in search of an English publisher. As he explained, there was no substitute for standing face-to-face with editors who had already shown some interest in his work. Another reason for going to England, he told the judge, was to study at first hand the life of Israel Potter, a soldier in the Revolutionary War who had fought at Bunker Hill. Captured by the British, Potter was taken to England as captive, though he soon escaped into the countryside, where he pursued a career on many fronts over the next forty-five years. At one point, he had acted as a secret agent in Paris. In the course of his tumultuous life, he met the likes of Benjamin Franklin and George III, becoming a legend in his own time. H.M. argued persuasively that this story would make a salable fiction.

"You are an enterprising young man," said Shaw, agreeing to put an appropriate amount of cash into his son-in-law's bank account.

In keeping with his promise, H.M. made a few desultory inquiries about Potter—seeking material in the British Museum and a few libraries, visiting a dismal close in East London where the fugitive supposedly lived for several years in seclusion—but he found nothing useful. Nobody seemed to have heard of Potter. He guessed he could make it all up just as easily, perhaps drawing on Potter's own *Life and Remarkable Adventures of Israel R. Potter* (1824)—published shortly before his death. Anyone could see that Potter himself depended heavily on the techniques of fiction, such as foreshadowing and the conflation of characters. H.M. thought he would get to the heart of this tale more swiftly and truly by using his imagination, yet it might prove useful to absorb the sights and sounds of England, as not so much had changed since Potter's birth a century earlier. For future reference, H.M. bought a map of London in the eighteenth century. "Potter's is a fetching tale," he wrote in his journal, "being the story of a man whose revolutionary impulses lead him into poverty and the path of self-destruction. There is something vaguely glorious about self-destruction."

Herman remembered London from a few years before, when that ebullient dandy Harry Crawford had introduced him to the darker side of the capital; but that visit had been such a whirligig that the city itself remained a blur of parks, squares, and boulevards. Now he strolled in slow, careful strides, taking in the elegant Palace of Westminster (still under reconstruction after a fire in 1834), the majestic abbey, White Hall and the Strand, Piccadilly Circus and Trafalgar Square. He lingered before magnificent artifacts and paintings in various libraries and museums. In the new National Gallery, one or two Rembrandts caught and held his eye for hours at a time. And one day he took a horse-drawn bus to Dulwich, where he stood openmouthed before Titians, Claude Lorrains, and Murillos—the feverish glow of these canvases like waking dreams. In another life, he would have been a painter, he told himself. It would have been good to work solely in images, trailing the odor of oil and turpentine, not ink. A painting, unlike a novel or poem, has such an unmistakable physicality that cannot be dismissed.

He longed to visit Italy, but it was impossible on this trip. His funds were growing short. London had proved more expensive than he had thought possible, and he had barely enough to afford a skip to the Continent, where he would join the languorous Teddy McCurdy in Paris, Cologne, and Brussels. The possibility of trekking to the Holy Land as well as Italy had been broached by Teddy, but this defied reason: H.M. could not bear the expense, nor could he stay away from home for so long. Lizzie and Malcolm surely needed him. He found himself missing his young wife, and believed that soon they would move to the country, as city life had become expensive and distracting. They could live cheaply in the Berkshires, perhaps on half the funds required in Manhattan; perhaps their standard of living would actually rise, given that rural homes were roomier, while good food was accessible and inexpensive. One could plant a garden, tend a few chickens for eggs, and keep a cow or two in the barn for milk and butter. What more did one need?

Paris and Cologne pleased him, yet it was Brussels that pressed deep into his heart. By coincidence, the hotel where he boarded lay opposite Number 51, rue Ducale, a narrow apartment where Lord Byron spent a dismal week on his flight into exile in the spring of 1816. England had rejected his genius and him—he had become a sexual outlaw hounded by the public that once adored him. Here, in a state of dejection, he nevertheless wrote the Waterloo stanzas from Canto 3 of *Childe Harold,* which H.M. considered a lofty peak in English poetry. He had read Byron's masterpiece over and again, hoping one day to write a narrative poem along these lines in many cantos. It was the mark of greatness in a poet that he should create a long poem in multiple parts—like *The Faerie Queene* or *Paradise Lost* or, more recently, Young's *Night Thoughts.*

In a wide bed with an upholstered headboard and four fluted posts with fleur-de-lis finials on top, H.M. nestled beneath a gold-brocaded coverlet that was like a medieval tapestry. He cupped a glass of ruby wine in both hands and thought about Byron's extraordinary life, which had long attracted him. As a boy of sixteen, Herman had greedily devoured Thomas Moore's *Life of Lord Byron.* It was a cautionary tale of sorts, and one that struck him as incomparably sad: the story of a young aristocrat of intense feelings who had lost his father at a young age—the one figure who might have understood his deep needs and potential, who might have nurtured his growth. Byron's mother was, as Moore said, "a bossy woman of blinding egotism and dominant views." She had "more love for herself than her son, whom she regarded as an extension of herself, hardly a separate being in the world."

Byron's Calvinist heritage weighed on him, but he could neither accept nor discard the harsh God conjured by that strain of
Protestant theology. His sexuality troubled him, as his affections
veered awkwardly between the handsome young women and men
of his acquaintance. At Harrow, he'd fallen in love with a younger
schoolmate, John FitzGibbon, the 2nd Earl of Clare, and had written passionate verses to him. "My school friendships were, with me,
passions (for I was always violent)," Byron recalled in later life. At
Cambridge, he met John Edleston, a fifteen-year-old choirboy with
silky blond hair and a piccolo voice, describing their friendship as
one of "pure love and passion." After John's early death, Byron
wrote a series of elegies to him and wore his lost friend's signet ring
until his own tragic death in Greece in 1824.

Herman's thoughts turned unexpectedly to his father, and he
recalled the terrifying last days when Allan Melvill muttered to himself, shrieked at the family, and cursed God. H.M. had begged the
Almighty to take his father swiftly: the pain of *his* pain was too much
to bear. In the months after his father's death, Herman had asked for
comfort from heaven, though none came. He soon enough began
to question the usefulness of prayer. Was it possible to make contact
with this Supreme Being? Was his own mind simply a reflection of
God's? Some days he felt lifted, even carried, by God's overwhelming presence. Other days, he felt horribly alone, a speck of dust on
the enameled surface of an impersonal world. A line from one of
Voltaire's verse epistles stuck in his brain: "If God did not exist, it
would be necessary to invent Him." Is that what he, and his fellow
creatures, had done?

He felt glum, terribly alone. Even the presence of Teddy in the
adjoining room meant nothing. The boy was useless to him. With
his self-absorbed manner, he could hardly provide the kind of companionship H.M. required. What Herman hoped for was counter-
love, a response at once fresh and foolish, unadorned, selfless. He

had experienced something like this, all too briefly, with John Troy—at least he convinced himself this was the case, forgetting that Troy had held back, refusing to give himself freely and fully. And Lizzie (for all her energy and wit) had not quite satisfied him, as she seemed always worried about his mother's intrusions, ready to poke and prod, absorbed in her own dreams of marital bliss, which only peripherally seemed to involve Herman. To her, he was Husband, a generic version. Perhaps, over the years, he might whittle his way toward her, shaping himself to her desires, finding a way to approach her. But so far he had experienced a troubling remoteness in their relations, and when Malcolm had appeared, he began to worry he might lose the connection with her altogether.

In London again before Christmas, H.M. fell into a hole of sorts. "I'm haunted by the blue devils," he wrote to Lizzie, knowing she would understand.

They often talked of this haunting, which left him exhausted at times, unable to lift the window shades let alone charge into the broad light of day. Now as he walked the streets of London, the sky seemed dark at midday, a lid of lead. At one point, as he picked his way along the Strand through a crowd near Charing Cross, he felt dizzy and breathless; he sat on a curb, afraid to continue. Was his heart giving way? Self-annihilating thoughts clustered in the black branches of his mind, rooks with wings of soot. He thought of poor, dear Gansevoort, alone in London, dying. And he decided he must get home as soon as possible, get down to work again, safe within the family circle. Hearth and home felt like a secure port, a comfortable alternative to this misery that beset him.

He moved quickly to secure a passage home, boarding the *Independence* on Christmas—a day of high winds and frothy seas. This was a sailing vessel, as Herman did not feel sufficiently flush with money to spring for a steamer, but the prospect of a slower passage did not upset him. He had begun to make notes in his journal about another book, "a novel of obsession." It would focus on the mad pursuit of a white sperm whale, not unlike the famous old bull called Mocha Dick, who had entered into the mythology of whaling. This indomitable creature had survived countless hunts over many years. It had rammed many boats, splintering them, drowning any number of sailors in the course of a long life, with irons hanging from its skin like badges. A decade before, H.M. had read an account of this whale in the *Knickerbocker*; the germ of this narrative had slept for some time in the deep waters of memory, dormant; now it rose like the whale itself, blowing hard, a blast of potential meaning. At once Herman understood how to use this material. He could almost see the visage of some hoary, mad captain on a quest to kill the fabled whale, a man in the tradition of Shakespeare's Lear or Milton's Satan—a dark visionary, bent on destruction, willing to pull the whole world down with him if necessary in violent pursuit of this white creature: another allegory of self-destruction.

The Bible lay beside his bunk in the cabin, and Herman carefully reread the stories of Job and Jonah. Reading by whale-oil light deep into morning hours as the vessel leaped over the cobalt waves of midwinter in the North Atlantic, H.M. realized he must put Israel Potter to one side to write a whaling story. It would sit neatly on the shelf beside his earlier works, only it would have a much larger audience, he told himself. Who could resist a large-scaled adventure at sea?

What a spell of writing he had already had: *Typee, Omoo, Mardi, Redburn, White-Jacket*—all disgorged in only a few years. He repeated the titles aloud to reassure himself. In his tiny cabin, Herman hunched over a brandy, dreaming of the next marvelous book he would write. *Mocha Dick,* he said to himself, balling his fist. *Mocha Dick!*

. . .

The following summer, Herman found himself with a thickening manuscript on his desk: inchoate, often incoherent—the beginnings of a rousing adventure at sea. It lay beside a tower of recently acquired books on whaling, such as William Scoresby's *An Account of the Arctic Regions, with a History and Description of the Northern Whale-Fishery*. He knew he must include a wealth of details about the whaling industry in this novel, and he could not simply summon these by rote. And so he took notes, translating these into paragraphs, even whole chapters.

It proved difficult to work in the city, however; the heat seemed to involve everything. It wafted over the rooftops and between buildings, a high thin screech that never relented, even in deepest night, when H.M. and Lizzie slept (as best they could) beside an open window, coverless, dressed lightly in cotton undergarments. They woke on sweaty pillows, damp and bedraggled, forcing themselves through long days with their nerves increasingly frayed, even snapping. A plan soon emerged by necessity: they would visit Broadhall, the former Melvill farm in Pittsfield, as the Morewoods (the new owners) had encouraged them to do. "We're all family," said the unstable Sarah Morewood, thrusting herself into everyone's life. "You must come and go as you please at the farm. Broadhall belongs to us all."

"Sarah is mad," said Maria, repeating what everyone knew. Nevertheless, she went north in advance of her son and the rest of the family, eager to make contact with friends in the Berkshires, including Miss Sedgwick, the popular author, who considered Maria Melville among her ladies-in-waiting. Maria would make sure that, for her, this retreat in the mountains would serve her interests. Not long after arrival, she wrote to her son: "It's just as always—the cool breezes carry the smell of hay, with several mountain ranges one behind the other. You and Lizzie must come as soon as possible. Malcolm will thrive here. The air is clean and fresh, the

food nourishing and plentiful, and flowers bloom in this soil like
nowhere else in the world. You should see the cow parsnip on the
western slope, and the lilies, too!"

H.M. had planned for some months to move his family to the
Berkshires—not for a holiday (as everyone imagined) but for good.
The prospect would please his wife, as Lizzie adored Pittsfield—
and who would not? Its beauty ravished the eye, especially in the
summer months, when the old wood-framed houses breathed easily, the windows flung open, their lawns brilliantly green or covered with blue cornflowers or daisies. White picket fences
circumscribed each property in the town, but without a sense of
exclusion. Anyone could stop, peer over fences, converse with
neighbors.

Life in the city had grown tiresome, with its congeries of
thieves, raw immigrants, and harried citizens mingling on streets
rife with dust and carts, carriages, or wagons. The reek of horse
manure could reach frantic peaks in midsummer. Of course Herman loved Manhattan, in all its coarseness, and often wandered in
lower and midtown byways, visiting galleries and museums or
libraries, stopping for a beer in some isolated tavern. But he didn't
require a steady diet of urban life, and thought he would find it easier to write in the countryside, with fewer distractions. He might
enjoy wandering a thick woodlot instead, or sitting by a pond to
think and make notes. He liked the notion of hiking in the high
green hills by himself, allowing passages and plots, even poems, to
fill the well of his imagination like groundwater pouring in from all
sides.

As Herman boarded the train for the Berkshires, with Lizzie
and Malcolm already in their horsehair seats, Evert Duyckinck
handed him a copy of *Mosses from an Old Manse,* Nathaniel
Hawthorne's latest volume of stories, to review for the *Literary
World*.

"Something to read on the train," Duyckinck said.

Herman leafed through the book, curious.

"I believe you already know one or two of the stories, and I've heard you sing the man's praises. Now read him carefully!"

Hawthorne, as Herman knew, had moved to the Berkshires a few months before, and they would certainly meet in due course. Miss Sedgwick would see to that! It made good sense to read him carefully, as Jack Chase had suggested some years ago.

As H.M. learned from his mother, Hawthorne occupied a red-shingled cottage on the Lenox estate of wealthy Bostonians. He and Sophia, his lovely wife, and their young children, Julian and Una, had fled the sharp, salty winds of Salem, a town full of punitive ghosts—many of them Hawthorne's ancestors. Though humble in size, the red cottage in a grove of shagbark hickory and oak proved comfortable enough, with three bedrooms and a woodshed-cum-study that they called a "summer house." Hawthorne could work there with a view of Lake Mahkeenac, one of many pellucid spring-fed Indian ponds in the region. The bulk of Monument Mountain rose behind him, magnificent. Stockbridge lay nearby, a quaint village, perfect for family outings, and there were fields and streams in every direction.

Berkshire County attracted a range of writers, who liked the ease of life amid hayfields, dense woods, ponds, and sloping hills. Oliver Wendell Holmes and his wife, Amelia, had acquired a house in the neighborhood only a year before, and the eminent poet-doctor would entertain his literary friends there, including Longfellow and James Russell Lowell. And, of course, there was the infamous Miss Sedgwick, who lived only a few miles from Pittsfield with her brother Charles, occupying the center of a circle like a queen bee. Her fame had spread far beyond the Berkshires, engaging readers and writers alike. *Hope Leslie,* for instance—her novel of Puritan life in seventeenth-century New England—had inspired

Hawthorne some years before, and few Americans with any taste
for fiction had not dipped into this romantic narrative about Puritans in Massachusetts and their relations among the Indians.

At Herman's suggestion, Evert Duyckinck soon joined the
Melville family in Pittsfield for a holiday, as did Cornelius Mathews,
another of the New York literati. They made a peculiar couple,
Duyckinck being a pale, thin, elegant fellow, fond of monocles,
while his friend Mathews was short and disheveled, with a florid
complexion. But they were both excellent company, full of gossip
and witty reflections on the literary scene.

They had left their wives behind on what they considered a
manly adventure into the north woods, away from the "Babylonish
brick-kilns of New York," as H.M. put it. They put up at Berkshire
House, a genteel hotel in Pittsfield with a broad porch overlooking
the main street of the village. Herman dined on the first night there
with his friends as well as Dudley Field, a lawyer from New York
who had inherited a large family house on a hundred and fifty acres
near Stockbridge. A snob with literary pretensions, Field knew
every writer in the area, and he now conceived a fabulous outing
in the countryside where everyone would meet. "We shall climb
Monument Mountain!" Field announced.

Herman had rarely been so happy, as his friends talked endlessly
of books and authors, sharing tidbits of gossip. From a canvas bag,
Duyckinck fetched out the proofs of *The Prelude,* a forthcoming
book-length poem by Wordsworth, who had died the previous
spring—the grand old man of English poetry. This massive poem
had apparently been in the poet's possession, unpublished, for many
decades. It was, as Duyckinck told Herman, "perhaps the finest narrative poem since *Paradise Lost,*" a volume that traced "the growth
of a poet's mind." Its form was nothing if not radical, putting the
artist at the center of life, meditating on nature and spirit. Duyckinck read a few extracts out loud, with a slightly Anglicized accent.

Herman listened avidly, finding "grandeur in every phrase," begging to borrow the proofs. Evert needed this proof copy for a review, but he promised to leave the book with his friend, if he could get his piece finished before he left.

Dudley Field, for his part, didn't really care to talk about literature, not with any specificity; it was gossip about authors that interested him, and—in the role of master of revels—he explained that what he called "a great treat" lay in store for them all. Nathaniel Hawthorne would join them at the end of the week for a day's outing at Monument Mountain. "Expect lots of good food," he said. "My wife is a marvelous cook."

"I'm quite eager to meet Hawthorne," Herman said to Lizzie that night, in bed.

"He's not more important than anyone else," she said.

"Oh, I think he is."

"You foolish man," she responded, kissing his forehead. "I hope you don't see more than meets the eye in Mr. Hawthorne— although I'm told that in his case a great deal *does* meet the eye."

H.M. left Broadhall without Lizzie (Malcolm had a stomachache, and she would not abandon him to his grandmother), meeting Duyckinck and Mathews at the appointed hour, traveling by buggy to the station in Stockbridge, where Dudley Field waited beside James T. Fields, a Boston publisher, and his cheerful porcine wife, Eliza. Fields wore patent-leather shoes better suited for Commonwealth Avenue, a starchy shirt, a blue jacket, a pink paisley waistcoat, and a polka-dot tie—not exactly the right attire for scaling mountains. Dr. Holmes, as ever, traveled with a medical bag of glazed India rubber, as if prepared at a moment's notice to administer aid.

The company proceeded at once to Eden Hill, an estate at the foot of Monument Mountain, to wait for Hawthorne, who would come by himself on horseback—late but not egregiously so. Young Harry Sedgwick (a nephew of the novelist) waited for them with an empty hay wagon, chewing a long piece of grass. He was nearly twenty although he looked sixteen, with flaxen hair parted in the middle and delicate features; he wore a broad-brimmed straw hat with a peacock feather in the brim that made him look very much like an artist.

They passed around glasses of lemonade, as it was a humid day, and Dudley wanted everyone in a good mood.

"Hawthorne is late," Dudley said, annoyed.

Fields, Hawthorne's publisher, ignored him, talking excitedly about the success of *The Scarlet Letter.* "He's not a modest man," said Fields, working to control his excitement, "but that is fine. He understands his value. He is our greatest living author."

"Greater than Longfellow?" wondered Mathews. "Or Bryant?"

"Mr. Irving is still alive," said Harry Sedgwick, who was savvy enough not to mention his aunt—although many in the Berkshires put Catharine Maria Sedgwick at the apex of living authors.

Dr. Holmes said, "Hawthorne is excellent. That's enough, I should think. Comparisons are odorous . . . as Dogberry would say."

"Who is Dogberry?" Harry wondered.

Cutting short a response by Holmes, Nathaniel Hawthorne appeared on horseback in the middle distance, moving at a casual pace.

"Ah, the great man!" Duyckinck said.

H.M. studied the horseman as he approached. Wearing a black shirt and olive-gray trousers, Hawthorne was slender and tall, dark-eyed, arresting. Famously, a Gypsy woman in Brunswick, Maine, had stopped dead in her tracks upon seeing him, asking, "Is he a man or an angel?" H.M. had heard this story from Duyckinck, and it made sense now. Hawthorne was, indeed, an angel: a dark angel.

Hawthorne tied his horse to a hitching post, making no obvious gesture to acknowledge the group. His indifference impressed Herman, who considered himself too desirous of acceptance, ever nodding in the direction of those around him, eager to please.

"Allow me to introduce Herman Melville," Dudley Field said, as H.M. drew near, shy but interested.

Hawthorne brightened, extending a large hand. "I have admired your *Typee,*" he said.

"I believe you reviewed it."

"Yes, of course," said Hawthorne, as if suddenly remembering. "You had some fun among the cannibals, I should think. I'd have collapsed in fear for my life."

"They were quite tame, after all."

"Except for their appetite for human flesh."

"A meal is a meal," H.M. said, with a flash of embarrassment. It was not a clever remark.

"Have you yet had a chance to read *The Scarlet Letter*?" Fields wondered.

Herman nodded too quickly, too eagerly. "It's very fine. A work, you know . . ."

An awkward moment followed, as Herman fumbled to add something but failed. Duyckinck, as ever, burst forth with puerile enthusiasm. "It's marvelous, your book. I feel as though I know Hester."

"You married her!" said Mathews, stirring a ripple of laughter.

James Fields did not want the conversation to move away from *The Scarlet Letter* quite in this way. He explained how he had convinced the author to expand a much shorter piece of fiction that had "shown a good deal of promise."

"I owe everything to you, James," said Hawthorne.

Herman loved the way Hawthorne said that, with an ironic twang—not offensively but taking the man to task for overreaching. He also put everyone on notice, as if to say: *I hope you will choose your words carefully around me. I listen closely, and I care.*

H.M. could not stop watching Hawthorne, who compelled his attention by his looks as well as a pervasively droll manner. Every sentence arrived on his lips fully shaped, even lapidary. He stepped into the path with Sedgwick and Eliza Fields on either arm. Duyckinck linked arms with Eliza, and they formed a bright phalanx, beginning a steep ascent at a pace that left James Fields breathless and straggling.

"There is no need to hurry," Fields said to Herman, pausing to rub his side, which had begun to ache. "I'm afraid I'm not as fit as I was in my heyday."

But there *was* need to hurry, as a lavender-tinged thunderhead had appeared at the east edge of the sky, darkening the day. Thunder rumbled in the distance, and a swift low wind scudded along the ground, stirring up dry leaves, shaking the tall stalks of mullein that grew by the rutted path. One could hear the swish of trees overhead.

"Thunder!" Fields said, with a talent for the obvious.

"The old man is just clearing his throat," Herman observed.

"An odd thing to say, Melville," said Fields.

The rain held off, however, until the party reached a high ledge, from which they could see the sweep of the valley below. But the weather had deteriorated, the clouds releasing a warm spray of rain that swept in a slantwise manner in horizontal winds that lifted Eliza Fields's skirt. The gallant Dr. Holmes broke three branches from a bushy hemlock to make umbrellas, two of which he passed to Eliza and James, the most vulnerable members of the group. H.M. lifted his face to the wet, enjoying it thoroughly.

Hawthorne beckoned from a nearby ledge—a perfect shelter for the hikers, who rushed to stand beneath its overhang.

"We're all cozy and dry," said Holmes, pulling two bottles of champagne from his bag, popping the corks. "Sit down, everyone. Please! These are dry logs, conveniently arrayed. I see that others have been here before us." Holmes had a silver monogrammed cup, which he handed around. Hawthorne took it greedily and drank.

Herman stepped into the shelter, too, amused.

Hawthorne lifted the silver cup to Herman's lips. "The blood of our Lord," he said, as H.M. sipped.

Herman swelled, full of antic energy, ready to put on a show for the company. He leaped onto a nearby jut of rock, pretending it was a ship's bowsprit, hauling imaginary lines as if he were a deck-hand, singing an old shanty in his granular voice. This provoked cat-calls and laughter. "Hail, Typee!" shouted Hawthorne, goading H.M. to further foolery. With a dexterity that startled everyone, Herman swung from tree to tree on a vine, howling.

"An ape!" cried Eliza.

"A hairy ape," Fields added.

"Do they have *hairless* apes?" Hawthorne asked. "I should hate to encounter a bald ape, especially in these woods."

Wanting attention for himself, Cornelius Mathews dug from his rucksack a poem about Monument Mountain by William Cullen Bryant. Most of the company already knew this poem about a fraught Indian maiden who leaped to her death in order to escape execution by her own people—as she had fallen in love with a young warrior from an enemy tribe. She landed in a tree, which cushioned her fall; her tribe, in fury, set fire to the mountain to make sure she was dead. Later, her family erected a pile of stones in her memory—hence the name of the mountain. It was a fetching local legend, with perhaps a grain of truth at its core.

Mathews boomed the lines, the sound echoing in the cave:

Thou who wouldst see the lovely and the wild
Mingled in harmony on Nature's face,
Ascend our rocky mountains. Let thy foot
Fail not with weariness, for on their tops
The beauty and the majesty of earth
Spread wide beneath, shall make thee to forget
The steep and toilsome way.

"What rubbish!" Hawthorne said. He took another swig from the silver cup, wiping his mouth with the back of one hand.

"That's quite right," said Dudley. "It's dreadful, a piece of doggerel."

"Bryant is *too* boring," said Eliza.

Dr. Holmes feigned horror, raising an invisible cup to Bryant: "Long live the old poet!"

"To the old poet!" Mathews cried.

Everyone toasted, lifting imaginary cups.

Rains swept through the woods again, and even the overhang offered no protection. Lightning sizzled and cracked a huge oak— far too close for comfort.

"Retreat!" cried Herman.

Dudley agreed, suggesting they repair quickly to his house, not far away. So the party made a quick descent, slipping at times on the muddy path, tumbling over rocks, clutching roots and vines whenever they could. Herman was like a boy, springing ahead of the pack, shouting, swinging on vines, showing off for Hawthorne, who rewarded him with smiles, laughter, sly winks. At one point, out of breath, Fields had to sit on a large elephant-colored rock beside the path. Such excursions had been rare in his life, and he could only tolerate this adventure because the company impressed him.

H.M. sat beside him in sympathy. "Are you all right, Mr. Fields?"

"I am miserable, but no matter. I'm just a publisher. You are authors. Authors!"

Herman said, "I believe authors die as surely as publishers."

"It's not the dying that concerns me," said Fields. "It's the living I have yet to master." He wiped a gob of mud from one shoe with his handkerchief. "My shoes will not recover."

"But *you* will," said Dr. Holmes. He offered another gulp of champagne, which the publisher gratefully accepted.

"That's better," he said.

The rain switched off like a shower, and the sun burned a hole in the clouds. The wet leaves glistened around, and one could hear the gabble of a nearby stream.

Dudley conducted everyone toward the hay wagon, and the merry company proceeded along a muddy road, drawn by a huge draft horse that had known better days. They gathered for a late lunch at Dudley's farmhouse, where J. T. Headley—the popular biographer of Napoleon and George Washington—had shown up in a white jacket and blue cotton trousers. The group feasted on wild turkey and roast beef, mounds of red potatoes, cabbages, carrots, peas, and broad beans. The best wines were brought up from the cellar, dark dusty bottles that wore their faded French labels as badges of excellence, followed by more champagne, brandy, figs, and porcelain bowls heaped with peach ice cream that had been churned in the kitchen that morning. Sprigs of mint topped each bowl.

"Why do we not have a literature equal to the English?" Dr. Holmes wondered.

"Dear fellow, we have a splendid literature of our own," said Dudley Field, citing Cooper and Longfellow, Catharine Sedgwick, Irving, and others.

"I do think that Emerson is among the finest authors in the world," Holmes conceded. "Even the British would agree." He recalled Emerson's visit to Wordsworth in the Lake District, saying that Wordsworth had been quite impressed by the younger American.

Melville grew incensed as he listened. "I should think we have no need to take our place in the world behind the British. I know England very well. They overvalue their own literary products, and we simply agree with them."

"Bravo," said Duyckinck.

"I do love Charles Dickens," said Eliza Fields.

Melville said, "My wife shook his hand!"

"I kissed him," said the tipsy James Fields. "He was quite a lovely young man when he came to Boston. But his clothes! Quite ridiculous. I believe he wore a buffalo hide."

"You are drunk, Fields," said Hawthorne.

Melville spoke loudly: "*Copperfield*—the new one—it's the best of the lot. Better than *Pickwick*."

Hawthorne admitted he had not read the latest novel by Dickens, and he would probably *not* read it. "I do think one gets the idea—after one or two novels. Novelists tend to repeat themselves."

"You have somehow avoided that," said Fields, in full sycophantic mode.

"I very much doubt it," Hawthorne said. "I know only suffering and sin. That's why I'm such a merry companion."

Eager to get the party moving again, Herman suggested they proceed en masse to Ice Glen, only a mile away. Headley, who lived nearby, agreed. "What a splendid idea! I shall propose a toast to Ice Glen!"

By this time everyone was too drunk to resist any suggestion, so—after toasting—H.M. led the revelers outside, on a scramble over scree and mossy rocks, between boulders, through damp tunnels. Hawthorne admired the way Herman leaped and slid along the slippery stones, stripping and diving from a cliff into a rock pool at the base of the valley. Hawthorne stripped as well, diving in beside him. They treaded water, talking, while the others looked on, befuddled and exhausted.

"Jump in, Dr. Holmes!" Herman called.

Oliver Wendell Holmes shook his head, waving.

"I think we've left them behind," said Hawthorne.

Herman could feel the icy spring from below. "Do you like my glen?" Herman asked.

"It's as if the Devil himself had torn his way through here, leaving all jagged rocks behind."

"The pool is spring-fed."

"I like cold water, especially on a hot day."

"Will you come to the glen another time?" Herman asked.

"Of course. But you must pay a call on us at the cottage. Meet Sophia and the children."

Herman smiled. "I know the house—the red cottage, with good views around." He had visited the cottage as a teenager, with his uncle Tom, who knew an elderly spinster who lived there in summers for many decades. "I'm reading your *Mosses,*" he added. "It's wonderful."

"They are just stories."

"The one about Goodman Brown—it's a dream."

"A nightmare, perhaps . . ."

"There was an officer on a frigate—the *United States.* I was coming home from Hawaii—and he had cut the story from a magazine. He insisted I read it."

Hawthorne sucked in a mouthful of water, gargled, and spat. "I like this man already," he said.

"It stays in my head—the idea that evil is ordinary and all around us, and that we have to own it before it destroys us."

"Then I have succeeded, in a small way."

They swam to a slippery bank, where Hawthorne lifted his tall
frame from the water. His body shone in the late-afternoon sunlight. Hawthorne had no shyness, and Herman could gaze at him as
he liked, and he did. He had never seen such taut limbs on a man
of forty-six. His torso was relatively hairless, wonderfully smooth.

"I'm writing a book about whales," Herman said, still in the
water, "a novel."

"A whale of a book?"

Herman passed over this remark. "I'm devoting a whole chapter to the zoological classification of whales—the science of cetology."

"How could anyone resist?"

"You're teasing me!"

"I can't help myself. You're easy to tease."

Herman pulled himself from the water, using his big hands to
clutch a loose vine, which offered a bit of leverage. He sat dripping
beside Hawthorne on a patch of blue moss. Hawthorne glanced at
him sideways, as if unwilling to look at him fully.

"What are you writing?" H.M. asked. The question felt
generic, but nothing fresher occurred to him, and he genuinely
wondered about Hawthorne's latest project. He guessed that it
would be difficult, after *The Scarlet Letter,* to begin again. A masterpiece lies in the imagination's doorway like a massive rock at the
entrance to a deep cave and blocks the fresh light.

"You write books so quickly," Hawthorne said, not answering
Herman. "With me, each page is a painful extraction."

"I must slow down."

"You're a young man. Do as you see fit."

A pause followed, as Herman tried to guess what would open
the channel of discourse between them. He did not want to seem
facile, as this didn't really describe the way he worked. His books
had come to him with the force of revelation, but he couldn't say

this. It would have seemed self-serving. "I hope to move to Pittsfield," H.M. said. "Lizzie and I love it here, in the country. New
York has become hideous."

"I believe your uncle has a farm?"

"He did until recently. It's been bought by the Morewoods."

Hawthorne gave a knowing sigh. "Sarah is most peculiar."

Herman restrained himself. As he knew only too well, gossip
about Sarah Morewood was rife in Berkshire County. She was
extravagant in every way, prone to fall in love with ineligible (often
inappropriate) men. Her husband, Rowland, was a pale Englishman
of no particular gender, known for his ivory-handled walking stick
and silk cravats.

After he stepped into his trousers and buttoned his shirt,
Hawthorne turned warmly to Herman. "Why don't you stop by
tomorrow—or before you return to New York? I believe my wife
would enjoy a visit. She's more sociable than I."

H.M. could not disguise his delight, and he agreed to come
within a day or two.

Hawthorne put a hand on Herman's shoulder, a gesture of
affection that moved him. He believed that he and Hawthorne had
much in common, and knew in his gut that this friendship would
move rapidly to the center of his life. Hawthorne seemed, at least
on first acquaintance, infinitely agreeable. What H.M. most
admired was the firmness of his opinions. Hawthorne did not seek
the approval of those around him—a factor that impressed Herman,
who felt drawn to a man who seemed not to require his company nor that of anyone else. He appeared wholly self-contained
and self-sustaining—a rare thing in this world, especially among
writers.

"I would say Hawthorne is one of the most popular men in
New England," Duyckinck later remarked, riding to Pittsfield beside
Herman in a two-wheeled gig.

"And he *should* be," said Herman.

"In which case you will write a review of his *Mosses* for our paper—a glowing review. I will need it quickly, however."

"And you shall have it," said Herman.

Sophia Hawthorne wrote to her sister Elizabeth Peabody on August 12, 1850:

My dearest Ell—

Only last week we had a visit from Mr. Typee—you will have read about his adventures among the cannibals of the South Seas! He is most affecting, a fine specimen of manhood, hale and dreamy at once. (His eyes like blue diamonds.) I see Fayaway in his face—the beautiful jungle maiden. In all, he is very agreeable and entertaining, with life to his fingertips—earnest, sincere and reverent, very tender and modest. I am hoping that we get to see a good deal more of him.

He is tall and erect, with an air of freedom, brave and forthright. His nose is straight and handsome, his mouth expressive of sensibility and emotion, more like a woman than a man. When conversing, he is full of gesture and force, and quite loses himself in his subject. There is neither grace nor polish in his manner, and once in a while this animation gives place to singularly quiet expression out of these eyes—an indrawn, dim look, but which at the same time makes you feel that he is at that instant taking deepest note of what lies before him. His look is a strange, lazy glance, but with a power in it quite unique. He does not seem to penetrate through you, but to take you into himself.

I just sat back to watch and enjoy the spectacle, pushing plates of biscuits before him. Una, quite unusually for her, sat on his lap at his bidding, and she refused to budge. Dear Julian looked on warily. He could see that his father admired this man, and he should prefer his father's undivided attention, of course!

Nathaniel has taken to Mr. Melville, which is a rare thing for my husband, as you know. He does not seek the company of anyone outside his immediate family and spends most days in his shady woodshed, where he writes, or even by lamplight when he "gets a steam up," as he puts it. I wish he would not overwork himself. *The House of the Seven Gables* can wait!

I hope we shall see more of Mr. Melville soon. His family has always owned a farm in Pittsfield, and he intends to purchase one in the vicinity. He is working on a book of whales, full of his own recollections from many years at sea. Come to see us soon, and perhaps you will meet Mr. Typee in the flesh!

Your loving sister, Sophia

In late August, H.M. published his review of Hawthorne's book of stories, *Mosses from an Old Manse*. He wrote in the guise of a Virginian visiting Vermont in July. He began coyly:

A papered chamber in a fine old farm-house—a mile from any other dwelling, and dipped to the eaves in foliage—surrounded by mountains, old woods, and Indian ponds,—this, surely, is the place to write of Hawthorne. Some charm is in this northern air, for love and duty seem both impelling to the task. A man of a deep and noble nature has seized me in this seclusion. His wild, rich voice rings through me; or, in softer cadences, I seem to hear it in the songs of the hill-side birds, that sing in the larch trees at my window.

In a further paragraph he explained the degree to which he found Hawthorne's work moving—to a point of ecstasy:

I have just returned from the hay mow, charged more and more with love and admiration of Hawthorne. For I have just been gleaning through the "Mosses," picking up many things here and there that had previously escaped me. And I found that but to glean after this man, is better than to be in at the harvest of others. To be frank (though, perhaps, rather foolish), notwithstanding what I wrote yesterday of these Mosses, I had not then culled them all; but had, nevertheless, been sufficiently sensible of the subtle essence, in them, as to write as I did. To what infinite height of loving wonder and admiration I may yet be borne, when by repeatedly banquetting on these Mosses, I shall have thoroughly incorporated their whole stuff into my being,— that, I can not tell. But already I feel that this Hawthorne has dropped germinous seeds into my soul. He expands and deepens down, the more I contemplate him; and further, and further, shoots his strong New-England roots into the hot soil of my Southern soul.

H.M. called upon his father-in-law at the Curtis Hotel in Lenox, where Judge Shaw came once every summer to conduct his annual court session in Berkshire County. He found him in a wicker rocker on the front porch, the *Boston Gazette* spread across his lap. He seemed quite dazed by the heat, his eyes closed, oblivious to the flies that stuck to his lids.

"Hello, Father," said Herman, sitting in the rocker beside him.

That they were alone on the porch suited H.M., who had private business with the patriarch.

"What?" the judge cried. "Herman!"

"I have ruined your nap."

"Feel free to ruin any drowse of mine. I find the country air a trifle soporific, but in a good way."

"When does the session begin?"

Judge Shaw knew that Herman did not come to discuss his court session, but he answered politely. "How is the little fellow, our Mackie?"

"Malcolm seems to prefer the country to the city."

"It's quite fine in August. In January, well, I cannot vouch for the weather. Rather grim."

"I like the silence of the fields after a snowfall."

"A good way to put it."

Judge Shaw shifted in his rocker, hoping that his son-in-law would get to the point.

"We're staying at Broadhall."

The judge nodded. "A lovely house. The Morewoods bought it for a good price, I believe. Lizzie wrote to me about this."

Herman grunted, as the judge had raised a sore point. "I've been thinking about our situation. Lizzie finds it very difficult in New York—the commotion, the noise of traffic in the streets. There is not an easy place where Malcolm can run, when he is ready to run."

"I don't care for Manhattan myself."

"You haven't been to visit."

"Not yet, no."

Herman leaned forward. "I have wanted to speak with you, in particular."

"In person, so to speak."

"Face-to-face."

"Indeed."

"To be blunt: there is a handsome farm—across the road from Dr. Holmes, in Pittsfield. It adjoins the Broadhall estate at the rear, so—in a sense—it might be considered an extension of old family property."

"Is the house any good?"

"I think so. A doctor lives there—Dr. Brewster. Do you know him?"

"No."

"It's a fairly big house, very square, with a marvelous chimney. On the north side, it looks out over fields toward Greylock. One could make a fine piazza there. The village is not so far away."

"Is there land?"

"About a hundred and fifty acres, partly wooded, but one could certainly turn a profit. The hayfield is well placed. And there's a large barn. One could have cows and chickens."

"I have longed for chickens."

"Really?"

Shaw touched the sleeve of H.M.'s shirt, grinning. "I dare say, you can see me strolling in a barnyard, can't you? Old farmer Shaw!"

Herman didn't quite know what to say. "One must see a property like this as an investment."

"I'm sure you are right." Shaw puffed on his pipe as Herman looked on apprehensively. "And so you wish to purchase this farm, I should think. A summer place?"

"Not for summers alone. We'd all move—my mother and my sisters. There is plenty of room. You would never require a hotel in Berkshire County."

"What a pleasant thought."

"Unless you preferred to stay in a hotel."

"Not with you so close. I would muck in with you and Lizzie and Malcolm. I do like your mother, too. And your sisters."

"Dr. Brewster is asking $7,000," Herman said, bluntly. "I could offer much less, perhaps."

"Perhaps." Judge Shaw paused. "Do you have enough in your savings to buy such a property?"

"Not really."

"I should think not."

"We have the lease on Fourth Street—it should fetch a good amount. And Dr. Brewster would allow a mortgage of fifteen hundred."

"You've already discussed it?"

"I'm quite serious about this farm."

"You're a man of action, Herman."

H.M. shifted uncomfortably. "I have had two or three talks with Dr. Brewster. He's a friend of my uncle. I do think he will come down on the price."

Judge Shaw seemed quite amused by all of this. "I don't suppose I could offer you an advance against my daughter's inheritance?"

Herman looked nervously ahead. "That would be very helpful."

"Perhaps two or three thousand?"

"Three would be perfect."

"Three thousand, then. I hope I shall have a good view from my bedroom window. I should like to see Mount Greylock."

"There is no better view in the world," said Herman, barely able to contain his enthusiasm. "I guarantee it."

H.M. settled comfortably into life at Arrowhead—he named the house himself, having discovered a number of Indian relics on the grounds—in early September. He arrived three weeks in advance of Lizzie, Malcolm, Augusta, and his mother, hoping to make some necessary repairs. Everyone seemed quite happy about the move, and Herman stressed the possible benefits for his writing. "The success of my book will depend upon it," he explained to Lizzie and his mother over a late-night dinner at Fourth Street. "I find it impossible to work in Manhattan. There is always some distraction."

Lizzie felt only relief, having never found the city to her taste. New Yorkers were not Bostonians. That is, they were insistent, materialistic, what her stepmother called "grasping." "The Shaws do not grasp," Mrs. Shaw liked to say. The fact that the Gansevoort clan had deep roots in Manhattan was of little import to Lizzie. The family had outlived the value of the name—and most certainly the money associated with such grandeur. She and Herman could hardly afford life on Fourth Street without dipping repeatedly into her father's pockets, and this annoyed her, especially as her brothers made sotto voce remarks that her stepmother had conveyed to her, indiscreetly, in letters Lizzie concealed from her husband, whose pride would have been severely wounded had he discovered them. As she understood by experience, a man needs the armor of his pride intact to wage life's endless battles.

It was good that Herman felt at home in Pittsfield. Arrowhead was his own house, for the first time—not leased quarters; he was surrounded by fertile acres he could manage in whatever ways seemed useful or profitable. To make the transfer of owner-ship possible, Dr. Brewster made a generous loan to Herman, and he seemed happy to postpone repayment until the Fourth Street lease was sold. Apart from its views, there was nothing special about this seventy-year-old farmhouse, timber-framed, with a shallow piazza looking northward.

"My relatives will be turning over in their graves," said Maria Melville, upon first walking into Arrowhead with her son. As he explained to her, she would occupy a small bedroom on the first floor.

"You wish I would go away," she said.

"I wish you would be still. You make Lizzie uncomfortable, and she is my wife, the mother of my infant son."

"She does not appreciate you."

"Oh, stop it," he said.

But when he saw her eyes had become wet, he kissed her wide forehead, and she put her arms around him, and they were mother and son, as ever.

The rooms, indeed, had nothing about them to suggest architectural brilliance of any kind; in fact, the functional quality of the dwelling struck any visitor. A massive stone chimney created a hearth of considerable breadth and depth, and this would become the center of family life, especially in winter. Yet the views remained the best thing about Arrowhead, which perched on a hillock above the Lenox Road, with open fields giving way to woods. To the north, a series of mountains spread their arms, and H.M. chose a corner room at the top of the house for his study. It was only a short walk from the master bedroom, and it boasted a fine view of Mount Greylock—the highest point in Massachusetts.

H.M. wrote in mid-December to Duyckinck to explain the texture of his new life:

> I have a sort of sea-feeling here in the country, now that the ground is all covered with snow. I look out of my window in the morning when I rise as I would out of a port-hole of a ship in the Atlantic. My room seems a ship's cabin; & at nights when I wake up & hear the wind shrieking, I almost fancy there is too much sail on the house, & I had better go on the roof & rig in the chimney.
>
> Do you want to know how I pass my time? I rise at eight— thereabouts—& go to my barn—say good-morning to the horse, & give him his breakfast. (It goes to my heart to give him a cold one, but it can't be helped.) Then, pay a visit to my cow— cut up a pumpkin or two for her, & stand by to see her eat it— for it's a pleasant sight to see a cow move her jaws; she does it so mildly and with such a sanctity.—My own breakfast over, I go to my work-room & light my fire—then spread my M.S.S. on the

table—take one business squint at it, & fall to with a will. At 2½ P.M. I hear a preconcerted knock at my door, which (by request) continues till I rise & go to the door, which serves to wean me effectively from my writing, however interested I may be. My friends the horse & cow now demand their dinner—& I go & give it them. My own dinner over, I rig my sleigh & with my mother or sisters start off for the village—& if it be a *Literary World* day, great is the satisfaction thereof.—My evenings I spend in a sort of mesmeric state in my room—not being able to read—only now & then skimming over some large-printed book.

That Nathaniel Hawthorne lived nearby added warmth and interest to Herman's sense of the region. He called on him as often as he dared, not wishing to wear out his welcome, riding on Waldo (his horse, named after Emerson) along the road to Lenox, several miles away but hardly an appreciable distance. It was never easy, however: H.M. invariably felt apprehensive, like an intruder, and it dismayed him that Hawthorne refused to open himself fully. Sophia, however, adored his recollections of the South Seas, stories he would exaggerate for effect, once pretending to fight off hordes of cannibals with a sword—a bread knife drawn from a drawer in the kitchen of the red cottage.

That particular evening, Herman engaged in his usual version of amateur theatricals, leaping on chairs, cursing the infidels, slicing his imaginary sword through the air, and generally entertaining the household. The children adored these antics, and went to bed giddy. Sophia, for her part, encouraged Herman's antics, though Nathaniel himself took a backseat during these performances, watching with a bemused smile. He was, indeed, an undemonstrative sort of man, recessive by nature. Lizzie called him "the ice man."

What troubled H.M. was the lack of reciprocity in this friend-ship. *He* paid all the visits, and Hawthorne never came to Arrowhead, nor went so far as to suggest a meeting between the two of them alone. That was what Herman craved, and he told Hawthorne that a visit to Arrowhead "would be most welcome."

Hawthorne was busy with his novel, he said. He had to husband his energies, and what he called "society" did not appeal to him.

"But we live in the midst of a great forest," said Herman, with a dash of drama.

"This is the forest primeval," said Hawthorne, mocking a famous line by Longfellow from *Evangeline*.

"If I were Longfellow, you would visit me."

Soon after this exchange, they met one afternoon for tea at the Lenox Hotel at Hawthorne's invitation, and he showed considerable interest in Herman's work, asking pointed questions about the novel in progress.

"It sounds as if you want to write an adventure story, something that would appeal to readers of Captain Marryat. But I believe you have something larger before you—a great metaphysical romp. You are a man of the spirit, Herman. You are a poet. I should put everything you have ever dreamed in this novel. Every real book is a form of Scripture. Write your own Bible."

"That is to ask a lot of me."

"We must ask a lot of ourselves. We live so briefly. There is no point, otherwise. Every line we write should be sacred."

"It's a whaling story," said Herman, lowering expectations.

"I know, but what does the whale represent?"

One could hardly pin a literary symbol down in exact ways, as Herman explained, believing Hawthorne would understand this, as his own work blazed with images that occupied a symbolic dimension. But his ambitions for the novel grew as they talked, and he pressed his friend for suggestions.

Hawthorne obliged, focusing on Herman's subject, but he

found his younger friend's appetite for discussion rather daunting. He had self-consciously narrowed the range of his contacts, scrubbed himself clean of social ambitions. As he explained to Herman, he required only enough money to live a modest life within the circuit of his family. "The world is what it is," said Hawthorne. "It cannot be more."

"But I want more," Herman said.

"That's a function of your age," Hawthorne said. "Actually, you're a bit long in the tooth for such thinking. You should have settled into a groove by now. You've got a house, a family. You have more books under your belt than I do. Enough!"

Herman knew he could never have enough, not in this life. His nature demanded more, and more again. And he knew Hawthorne was right about this whaling book: he must push the boundaries, pressing to a point where the mind collapsed within itself, seeking that space where eternity shone at the edges of this waking life. He should allow spirit to penetrate matter, and matter to shimmer, a holy thing, the great manifestation of God in this world.

So the seasons shifted in the Berkshires, bright tinsel leaves scraping along the ground, with snow blowing its fine dust. The towering stone fireplace at Arrowhead worked overtime, though the house felt chilly most days by mid-December. The heft of winter surprised Herman, who had forgotten that cold could take away one's breath. He gazed at Mount Greylock from his study window, a luminous white hump on the horizon, watched as it turned violet in late afternoon and darkened into dusk. Snowdrifts soon billowed around the house, and undulating white fields recalled the watery main. But he loved it, even the bracing temperatures, the way water froze in the pail on the way in from the well. Icicles lengthened like barbarous daggers from each window.

Herman felt wonderfully snug in his study, where he wore gloves and wrote as fast as he could, trying to keep up with the tale, which gathered momentum as he worked, a bonfire of language feeding on its own flames. Even when Lizzie or his mother pounded on his door to summon him for a meal, he refused to break off, and sometimes he shouted rudely, "Away! Go away!" He would compose into the late hours by lamplight, letting sentences build and break upon the shores of his pages. Sometimes he woke at his desk at dawn, amazed to think he had managed a whole night in his study.

One snowy afternoon a knock came to the back door, and there stood Hawthorne, in a gray coat and heavy boots. He wore a coonskin hat and deerskin gloves, looking more like a trapper than a famous author, and had come for no obvious reason. Certainly H.M. had not expected him.

"My dear Mr. Hawthorne!" Lizzie said.

"Is Herman here? I hope I'm not the person from Porlock," he said.

"You are welcome, to be sure!"

She knew that Hawthorne meant so much to her husband that this unannounced visit would lift his spirits, and they currently needed lifting.

"It has been a frightful winter," Hawthorne said, taking off his coat and hat, stomping his boots so that a small snowfield gathered around him on the pinewood floor. "I found myself quite at a loss during this blizzard, so I thought I'd shatter the stillness of Arrowhead. I believe your husband has been quite engaged lately. There has been no word from him in over a month."

"He has been working steadily."

"It's perhaps necessary," he said. "As I get older, I find myself less capable of keeping in my chair for hours. I grow bored with myself." He bent to pet a shaggy dog that nipped at his ankles. "I dare say, Herman does not grow bored with Herman."

"It is a feature of Herman Melville," said Lizzie.

Maria swept into the room. "My dear sir, Mr. Hawthorne—what a surprise! We had not expected you!"

"I come unannounced, but feel very welcome. Where is my friend?"

"In his study, of course," said Maria, with a tinge of disgruntlement; she had hoped to sit at once with Hawthorne by a blazing fire, and to hear news of Lenox.

"Let me surprise him."

Lizzie said, "But you'll stay for a bit of supper, I hope. I don't want to send you back into the storm unfed."

"He must spend the night!" said Maria. "This is foul weather, and Mr. Hawthorne might freeze to death on the way home. Is your horse in the barn, sir?"

"I have put him there already, thank you."

Hawthorne was at ease among womenfolk, whom he took slightly for granted. He was the master of any room he entered, and he expected deference, which in his case was not difficult to access. His bearing spoke for itself. He was among the lords of this life, by natural endowment and temperament.

"I shall be glad to dine with you," he said, with a slight bow, "if it's not any trouble."

"No trouble at all, sir!" said Lizzie. "We have a pie in the oven, with apples from our root cellar."

"Ah, apple pie. My favorite thing in this world."

He went upstairs quietly and knocked firmly.

"Mother?"

"I am not your mother," said Hawthorne.

Herman opened the door. "Nathaniel!"

"I have been going slightly mad," said Hawthorne. "I don't know what it is—the weather, Sophia. Even the children wear on my nerves. I'm too old for the rigors of fatherhood."

"You're not old."

"You are kind to say that, but I have access to a calendar." He kissed Herman on the cheek, and Herman embraced him, perhaps a little too avidly to make Hawthorne comfortable.

"Come in! Sit!"

Hawthorne looked about the untidy room, abashed; he preferred order, but it didn't surprise him that Herman would engender chaos in his study, given the ruminative, disorderly aspect of his conversation. Indeed, Herman was everything he was not: tempestuous, roiling, and enthusiastic. He launched into areas of darkness without giving thought to consequences. How else could he have written *Typee*, a book that exposed him to all manner of suggestive readings and criticism? Pages lay crumpled on the floor now, and the manuscript on the desk was fanned in disarray. Herman had ink stains on his hands, and it occurred to Hawthorne that H.M. had not bathed in several days. He was redolent—like moldy potatoes. His clothes were wrinkled, soiled. His hair and beard could have used a good brush. And his boots had not been polished in a very long time.

"May I read to you from my book?"

Hawthorne understood Herman's wish to read aloud from a work in progress, as he often requested that Sophia listen to his drafts. One could easily detect false notes in a passage when they were tested on the air. He sat in a lumpy wing chair, feeling the springs like vertebrae under the limp cushion, and acquired a listening air.

Herman read in a strained, off-key voice: " 'What is it that in the Albino man so peculiarly repels and often shocks the eye, as that sometimes he is loathed by his own kith and kin! It is that whiteness which invests him, a thing expressed by the name he bears. The Albino is as well made as other men—has no substantive deformity—and yet this mere aspect of all-pervading whiteness makes him more strangely hideous than the ugliest abortion. Why should this be so?' "

Herman looked up, anxious for a response.

"This is about your whale?"

"My white whale, yes."

Hawthorne's brow wrinkled. "White is not so much the absence as the fullness of color, if my optics are correct."

"Black is absence, white is presence."

"I would suppose the Albino has drawn so much of life to himself that he terrifies and, to an extent, empties the observer. He sucks the life out of us."

"I like that very much."

Hawthorne continued: "Your whale is, of course, a symbol. We have talked about this before. But a blank screen. The word blank is, indeed, *blanc*. And there is mystery here." He rose, gazing through a frosted windowpane. "So much whiteness out there. The snow somehow allows, even encourages us to imagine the world from nothing."

"Or *as* nothing," H.M. said.

"White terrifies us. That's true, I suppose. A black whale would not do. No, not a black whale."

"Too real."

"Think of the white things in nature. There are not so many."

"I had my honeymoon in the White Mountains, but they were not white." H.M. shuffled through his manuscript. "Listen to this, yes. 'And those sublimer towers, the White Mountains of New Hampshire, whence, in peculiar moods, comes that gigantic ghostliness over the soul at the bare mention of that name, while the thought of Virginia's Blue Ridge is full of a soft, dewy, distant dreaminess.' "

"Yes," Hawthorne said, ambiguously.

Herman looked up. "I have a whole chapter, as it were, on the whiteness of the whale. It's an attempt to understand what it means." He shuffled through his pages again, looking for something, then grunted with satisfaction, reading: " 'Aside from those more obvious considerations touching Moby Dick, which could not but occasionally awaken in any man's soul some alarm, there was another thought, or rather vague, nameless horror concerning him, which at times by its intensity completely overpowered all the rest; and yet so mystical and well nigh ineffable was it, that I almost despair of putting it in a comprehensible form. It was the whiteness of the whale that above all things appalled me.' "

Hawthorne lifted an eyebrow. "That *appalled* me," he said. "It's again as Mr. Emerson has written, words are fossil poetry. That word 'appalled,' from the Latin word that connotes paleness. To make white, as we say. In a moment of horror, the cheeks go livid, we are—quite literally—appalled. We erect a pale—a white fence— around us to ward off the darker forces. The semantic roots tell all. You are a poet, Herman."

"You tease me."

"I'm serious. There is a poetic element in your prose that appeals to me. I do not work in the same way."

"You're good with symbols."

"Flattery—but I like it. I would tell you not to restrain yourself, but that would be pointless. So listen to me closely: Do not restrain yourself."

Herman beamed, opening a corner hutch wherein, among other bottles, was a bottle of whiskey. He poured a glass for Hawthorne and one for himself. "We must celebrate our reunion," he said.

"A good Scotch whiskey—how nice."

"What a peculiar life we've chosen," said Herman, sitting at his desk.

"It suits well enough."

"I should be hammering nails. At least when you erect a building, you can live inside it."

"Readers live in your head."

"I never think of readers."

"But you must. Writing is conversation."

"We only hear one side of it." H.M. finished the glass quickly
and poured himself another. "You will spend the night," he said
urgently. "It's foul out there."

"I don't think Sophia would mind."

H.M. could not disguise his pleasure. "There's a tiny room
beyond that door, with an even smaller bed."

"It will do for me."

"We must talk honestly, say exactly what we think."

"Of course."

"You are my dearest friend."

"That is your enthusiasm speaking. Remember that enthusiasm
is nothing more than hope with sleigh bells attached."

"We have a good deal in common," Herman said.

"We share a craft—that is the basis of everything."

"It's more than that—"

"But what?"

"It's love, I would say. Friendship is founded on love. Do you
agree?"

Hawthorne pondered. "I do. But love is a difficult word. It has
many meanings."

"Do you love your wife?"

"I do, of course."

"And your children?"

"Yes."

Herman rose, walked to Hawthorne, leaned over, and held his
hand. "I can say things to you that I can say to no other person in
the world, not even Lizzie."

Hawthorne squeezed his hand. "I like your frankness. But we must not say more than we mean, or reach too far. That is folly."

"Icarus and Daedalus."

Hawthorne absorbed the implications before responding. "That was father and son, and it resulted in the death of the son, as you will recall."

"We must fly near the sun and survive."

"*Near* is fine. *Into* the sun, well . . ."

"Let's talk through the night, if that pleases you. It would please me well."

"I may fall asleep at a certain point, but I'd like very much to talk. I don't get enough of manly company."

Herman went to the window and lifted it, allowing a swirl of snow into the room, with its ferocious draft. He leaned out on his elbows, letting the flakes attach to his beard. He sucked a long, deep breath. This was life, he said to himself. It was the life he'd chosen.

Nathaniel Hawthorne to Herman Melville, November 12, 1851:

My dear Melville,

I write in response to your novel, which I received only too gratefully. Your kind—far too kind—dedication of *Moby-Dick* to yours truly came as a surprise, a wondrous gift, and (like the best of gifts) wholly undeserved. You have been too generous, as usual. And I cannot easily reciprocate. It is not possible, for reasons you will understand without my saying a word; but I must say how much your novel meant to me as a reader and your friend. It is a fine and ferocious piece of work, and I understand (any serious writer must) what such a project extracts from your soul. You have given so freely of yourself, your heart and mind, every fiber.

As you will certainly know, each character in this novel is you. You are Ahab—the monomania is yours, the will to fusion with the whiteness of the whale, in itself a sublime idea. Ahab fits poorly in the industry of whaling, of course. He wants only one whale, whereas his investors at home desire many whales, as numerous as possible, redacted, rendered into oil. Ahab is Don Quixote, a fantasist. May I call you that as well? May I say you fit poorly into the economic machinery of our day, which wants to grind or boil us, render us all? As an artist you require the sovereignty of Herman. You also have the good sense to understand how this remains illusory. The imperial quest can only lead to destruction. You are Ishmael, too: the ordinary seaman who ends his quest for knowledge at sea, quite literally, as a lone man in a broken vessel, clinging to the remnants of his soul-brother Queequeg, whose coffin represents the fragmented self. Does this seem true?

You have split yourself into many parts, and summarized them again in your tale, set them in consort, in opposition, in a broad human dance. You hope (we always do) that this novel will suddenly free you from the demands of commerce; but I do not believe that will happen. Few readers of the moment can or will comprehend what you have accomplished, alas. But I remain in awe, as I have said and truly mean. *I know what you have done.*

I write to you in a state of exultation, having just completed the first of what I should think will be many readings of your novel. It is massive in the best sense, accumulating enough detail to stand in for reality itself, to comprehend it. It is an admirable if strange thing to add to this world of made things. Like every great and noble work of the imagination, it changes how we think, act, dream.

I write this with affection, in deep appreciation.

Your friend, Nathaniel

P.S. I often recall in warmth if not terror the night we spent in your house on a stormy winter's night some months ago. I should not have let myself open in that way, I tell myself. It was not like me. In frankness, let me say I regret that I cannot respond as fully to your affection as I should like. It is not within me, and this remains a fault of mine. You are blameless, a dear and brilliant man.

Herman Melville to Nathaniel Hawthorne, November 17, 1851:

My Dear Hawthorne:

. . . Your letter was handed me last night on the road going to Mr. Morewood's, and I read it there. Had I been at home, I would have sat down at once and answered it. In me divine magnanimities are spontaneous and instantaneous—catch them while you can. The world goes round, and the other side comes up. So now I can't write what I felt. But I felt pantheistic then—your heart beat in my ribs and mine in yours, and both in God's. A sense of unspeakable security is in me this moment, on account of your having understood the book . . .

Whence come you, Hawthorne? By what right do you drink from my flagon of life? And when I put it to my lips—lo, they are yours and not mine. I feel that the Godhead is broken up like the bread at the Supper, and that we are the pieces. Hence this infinite fraternity of feeling. Now, sympathizing with the paper, my angel turns over another page. You did not care a penny for the book. But, now and then as you read, you understood the pervading thought that impelled the book—and that you praised. Was it not so? You were archangel enough to despise the imperfect body, and embrace the soul. Once you hugged the ugly

Socrates because you saw the flame in the mouth, and heard the
rushing of the demon,—the familiar,—and recognized the sound;
for you have heard it in your own solitudes . . .

What a pity, that, for your plain, bluff letter, you should get such
gibberish! Mention me to Mrs. Hawthorne and to the children,
and so, good-by to you, with my blessing.

Herman

On a sodden Sunday in November, Herman rode over to the
red cottage, having heard from his mother (the source of all intelligence within the county) that Hawthorne had decided to move his
family to West Newton. He would be leaving the Berkshires for
good.

H.M. found Hawthorne strolling by himself, a mile from the
cottage on Lenox Road. He seemed much older than Herman
remembered, somehow chalkier of complexion, worn. Hawthorne
had a switch of ash in his hand, which he used for a walking stick.
It seemed that he nursed an injury, as he limped slightly.

"Herman!" cried Hawthorne.

H.M. stepped down from Waldo. "Is it true then?"

"What is truth?"

The remark irritated Herman, who had never experienced
Hawthorne in this perfunctory and supercilious mode, although
everyone spoke of it. "You know what I'm asking. We are friends,
I assume, and we should speak frankly. Only that is worthy of us."

Hawthorne seemed to look over his friend's shoulder. "It's a fact
that I am leaving the Berkshires," he said. "We are going to live near
Boston."

"And why is this?"

"It's not easy to explain," he said. "There is some truth, however, in the idea that another winter here would kill me. I don't know how you tolerate it."

"I like the cold."

Hawthorne rubbed his large red hands. "I'm beset by the wretched landlady, Mrs. Tappan. She claims we have 'stolen' her apples to bake pies. It is this sort of pettiness and absurdness that shames the entire county."

"Caroline Tappan is unstable. But there are unstable people in Boston and New York. Wherever you go, you will have to deal with pettiness and greed, confusion, even infamy. This is the world."

Hawthorne realized he could not outmaneuver Herman on such grounds. He must speak honestly.

"I have my own devils to contend with."

"I love you dearly," Herman said, his voice wavering.

"Please . . . We don't require such talk."

"It isn't a matter of requirement. It's being able to face the immensity of our friendship, our mutual . . . understanding."

"You have read my soul, and I have tried to read yours. The fine print, however, has eluded us."

"This is no time for comedy. Are you really going to leave me, and so precipitously?"

"Not *you*, Herman. I'm leaving Berkshire County!"

Herman put his head on Hawthorne's shoulder now, and he began to sob. Hawthorne, profoundly uncomfortable with this display of feeling, put his hand on the back of his younger friend's head and stroked his long, tangled hair.

"Why are you doing this?" H.M. asked, like a child unable to understand a parent's shift of plans.

"I have to follow a signal, a signal from within. I listen for these, and I obey them. You do the same, I'm quite sure."

Herman brightened, as this notion caught his fancy.

"I promise to write as soon as I secure the household in New-ton. You can visit me whenever it suits. I will always welcome you."

"I will not let you go."

"I see that." Hawthorne stepped a little backward, drawing an invisible line between them. "But there is nothing I can do at this point."

Herman mounted Waldo defiantly. "Goodbye, Nathaniel."

"Goodbye."

"You will remember me to Sophia and the children?"

"Of course."

And so Herman rode away, assuming a trot, then a canter, breaking into a full gallop within moments. He could not contain himself, and he wept profoundly, cursing the day he met Hawthorne in the first place. It had been all too much for him, the events of the past year. He felt broken inside, having suffered a wound that would never heal—not as long as he lived.

Dollars damn me; and the malicious Devil is forever grinning in upon me, holding the door ajar. My dear Sir, a presentiment is on me,—I shall at last be worn out and perish, like an old nutmeg-grater, grated to pieces by the constant attrition of the wood, that is, the nutmeg. What I feel most moved to write, that is banned,—it will not pay. Yet, altogether, write the other way I cannot. So the product is a final hash, and all my books are botches . . .

H.M. to Nathaniel Hawthorne,
June 1851

LIZZIE

13.

I never imagined myself as mistress of Arrowhead, but it was an improvement upon Fourth Street. I found those cramped quarters with Maria and her daughters—Helen and Augusta and Fanny and Kate—more than I could tolerate. My nerves frayed, and I was prone to headaches and dizziness. I could hardly breathe at times, and needed more space around me, and quantities of precious silence as well. At least at the edge of Pittsfield I could lose myself in the surrounding woods or spend a quiet afternoon with Miss Sedgwick, who never failed to welcome me.

Catharine was a feisty old thing, full of eccentric opinions, but I didn't mind that. She had shown force of character, founding a school of her own in trying circumstances. As a writer of novels and stories, she had acquired an audience far wider and more devoted than my husband's, though I didn't really dare mention this. He had no tolerance for comparisons.

"She is hardly a writer of the first order," Herman said of Miss Sedgwick.

"I'm sure not," I replied, and he understood that I disliked his tone. Why do writers so often wish they were alone in the world, the last one left on the planet? There is room for different kinds of writing. Yet the mere fact that people devoured Miss Sedgwick in large numbers annoyed him. And her close friendship with Mr. Bryant, one of the finest poets of America, surely provoked some jealousy. I had read all of her novels, from *A New-England Tale* and *Hope Leslie* through *The Linwoods*. (Mr. Hawthorne surely had learned how to write about the Puritans and their self-wounding theology by reading her!) I admired her stories, too: she knew how to catch and compel your interest in a short space. My husband had not always done that. Nor had Mr. Hawthorne, whose tales left me dissatisfied, even gloomy. What was the point in the purveyance of such cheerless copy? Art should uplift the reader!

One night in winter, not three or four months after we had moved to Arrowhead, Mr. Hawthorne appeared out of a snowstorm on his horse. His presence dropped the temperature in the house by several degrees. I will not forget his darkling brow, his grave but courtly manners, his unsettling idiosyncratic remoteness. It did not surprise me when I heard that he had offended many of the women of Lenox, who thought he would join their circles, dining and taking teas and attending dances. Mr. Hawthorne had no taste for society, and society found him less than delectable as well. As Miss Sedgwick put it: "Nathaniel requires only a well-polished mirror to keep him company."

Mr. Hawthorne entered the house quietly, barely acknowledging my presence. After a perfunctory exchange of pleasantries, he went upstairs to speak with Herman in his study. I had no idea what his business with my husband might be, but I assumed it was the usual chitchat that one hears between writers, talk of proofs, royalties, reviews, and so forth. Herman could drone on for hours about these matters, especially when Mr. Duyckinck appeared.

Kate, my melodramatic sister-in-law, swooned after meeting him in the hallway; we nearly had to revive her with ammonia.

Augusta said, "I shall die. He is more handsome than God."

Her mother snickered. "You have seen the face of God, darling? I shall inform the pastor. He is looking for converts."

The pastor was Mr. Thorndike, an intense young man with features bunched like broccoli and straight black hair, which he parted severely in the middle. I liked his sermons—the depravity of man was a favorite theme—and I did my best to get Herman to attend weekly services, though he would join me only now and then. He preferred what he called "the cathedral of nature." His interminable walks in the woodlands were, he said, "a kind of worship." I might have quarreled with him about this, but it would have been useless. He read the Bible more thoroughly than any of us, so one could not argue with him on scriptural grounds without suffering defeat. Many evenings in the parlor he read to us from Job and other oppressive books. He tormented us with dull passages, reciting the "begats" without a flicker of humor, as if the lineage of Israelite tribesmen from millennia past could interest us. None of us cared about family trees, apart from Maria, who regaled us ad nauseam with her Gansevoorts, Van Schaicks, Van Rensselaers, Van Vechtens, and Quackenbosses—a line of pompous poltroons that she found quite thrilling to recall. I was quite happy with my lowly Irish Shaws and O'Connors.

It so happened that my husband, in the midst of moving to Pittsfield, acquired an irrational passion for Mr. Hawthorne, whom Kate called "the Messiah" when her brother was out of earshot. They had met one morning on a hike up Monument Mountain, and it was love at first sight, at least on Herman's part. (What exactly Mr. Hawthorne got from this friendship puzzled me at first. Later, when I had read *The Blithedale Romance,* I think I began to see it. My husband was thinly disguised as the muscular and monomaniacal reformer Mr. Hollingsworth. It did not surprise me in the least when Miles Coverdale and Hollingsworth parted company abruptly. I had seen this happen in what we commonly refer to as "real" life.)

Herman became a passionate scholar of Mr. Hawthorne's works. He read and reread *The Scarlet Letter*—he must have got it mostly by heart—and those dark and twisted tales of dark and twisted people living in a dark and twisted world. Had our forebears really been quite so miserable, so prone to cruel, self-serving behavior and subject to such strange unnatural urges? I questioned all of this, but I kept my doubts to myself. H.M. wanted nothing but admiration for Hawthorne on the tips of our tongues at Arrowhead. Nathaniel Hawthorne was the godhead, the source of life.

Herman thought so, in any case. He derived a peculiar energy from this friendship—as the manuscript of *The Whale* grew to intolerable proportions on his desk. The novel once had a straightforward adventure at its narrative core. Everyone likes a good fishing story, my father remarked when I told him about this novel, but he didn't reckon on hundreds of pages of blather in the guise of metaphysics. (I cannot help but think that Mr. Hawthorne's influence on my husband was a baleful one in this regard.) And then there were the endless *facts*.

For reasons of his own, Herman wished his readers to know everything about whales and whaling, the science of cetology—it was a new word for me! I dare say many readers liked to tuck a few facts under their belts, but this encyclopedic aspect of Herman's novel wearied me. I should have seen it coming with *White-Jacket*, where he told you more about naval protocol aboard an American frigate than really was necessary. (Was there, in fact, a story in that book? If so, I failed to discover it.)

It's not that Herman lacked the ability to tell a story. Within the

family circle he proved the most charming of talkers, full of anecdotes and wry observations, able to recall dialogue as if he had
recorded it. Maria and his sisters hung on his words, gripping the
ledge of his conversation with desperate fingers. But he grew overly
excited with outsiders. Without question, he overdid *everything* in
the presence of Mr. Hawthorne, who drew out the worst in him,
turned him into a vacuous oratorical fool. The night of the snowstorm, for example, H.M. never stopped talking during dinner,
referring to Plato and Aristotle, Voltaire and Goethe. (He pulled a
copy of Goethe's *Italian Journey* from a bookcase to read a long passage aloud.)

"You should go to Italy," said Mr. Hawthorne. "I think the
effect on your soul would be appreciable."

"I shall, I'm sure of it," Herman replied.

Now Herman launched into a meditation on Raphael's painting of Saint Cecilia, which he considered the high point of his work
as artist. He described in some detail the nature of this work, and
how it had been painted on a visit to Bologna in the company of
Pope Leo X—the purpose of the trip had been to meet the king of
France. When his friend Francesco Francia saw the painting, he was
so moved he fell over dead onto the floor of the church. Herman
told this story with peculiar animation, mimicking the death of
Francia by clutching his throat and falling to the floor.

"My son should have been an actor," Maria said.

Of course we had seen Herman in this florid mood before—
erudite and excited, gesturing wildly, spitting his food across the
table as he talked. (Bread crumbs were like flakes of snow in his
beard.) He drank large quantities of wine to steady himself, but this
was not effective. Soon he began to slur words, losing his way in a
thicket of language. This was all very well, but I could see that Mr.
Hawthorne (however much he tried to conceal it) grew impatient
as he listened to my husband. Everything about Herman's manner

cut against his grain. One could hardly imagine Mr. Hawthorne clutching his throat in such a fashion. He would never fall to the floor to make a point. Drinking with care, he sipped a glass of claret, clutching his sobriety like a treasure.

Maria sensed the discomfort of our illustrious guest and intervened. "We should ask Mr. Hawthorne to tell us about his children," she said. "I believe they are quite darling, a little girl and a little boy. What are their names?"

"Una and Julian," he said, showing no emotion.

"I like his children very much," said Herman, glaring at Maria.

"Thank you," said Hawthorne, without expression.

At which point my husband launched forth on the idea of fatherhood as what he called "a metaphysical conundrum."

I saw very little about the act of raising a family that could be called metaphysical. The conundrum eluded me as well, but then— I am no philosopher.

After dinner, Mr. Hawthorne followed Herman to his study, where they apparently consumed an entire bottle of whiskey and another bottle of claret as well (I removed the empty bottles two days later). I certainly made no effort to stop them. Men like to drink, and they often prefer to do so apart from womenfolk, who have less tolerance for bombast and gesticulation. That much had been clear to me from the outset of our marriage, and I tended to believe the problem of these past years—several decades of misery, if I may speak frankly—owed not a little to my husband's lack of fellowship with gentlemen of a better class. He preferred manly adventurers and rogues of the sort he encountered in the South Pacific. He actually fancied himself a rogue, I fear. But he was *not* a rogue, not ever, though there was no convincing him of this. In later years, I might have spoken impertinently, saying, "Herman, you are a customs officer. You are a minor administrator, a cog in the great wheel of commerce, an agent of the state." But he would only have slapped me or pushed me down—especially after drinking to excess. It was better to suffer quietly.

I listened at the door that memorable night in Pittsfield, hoping to catch something of the conversation that could explain this odd friendship between my husband and the fastidious Mr. Hawthorne. Even without hearing the exact words, one gleaned a great deal: one cannot disguise tone, even when a door cuts off the words. Their voices rumbled in a low fashion, with occasional bursts of laughter, mostly from Herman. Mr. Hawthorne was restrained, less eager to unfurl the banner of his soul. This frustrated my husband, who wanted easy intercourse of a type rare among men. But they did not relate in this way. (Two decades or more in my father's house had supplied a fair sampling of male behavior: young law clerks, in particular, came and went from his study in a never-ending stream of sycophancy, and I often paused in the hallway to gather what I could. The conversation was rarely metaphysical.)

Content in conversation is one thing, style another. In truth, Herman was more like a woman in this regard, being excitable, even prone to tears. He laughed too easily at times, exposing immense needs, which he wore on his shirtsleeves like gaudy cuff links. I wondered what exactly drew him to Mr. Hawthorne. Surely he had met any number of reputable authors, and rarely had he shown this level of fascination. (He avoided Miss Sedgwick at every turn, and I seriously doubt he would have crossed the street to have tea with Washington Irving or James Fenimore Cooper.) There was something inaccessible in Mr. Hawthorne, something dark. He would peer through your skin, see your heart in its bone-cage, quivering and vulnerable. He knew more than he revealed. To be frank, he terrified me, though I never said as much. Herman could tolerate nothing but praise for his hero. In his opinion, Hawthorne surpassed Emerson or Whittier, Irving or Miss Sedgwick. He was the highest visible point in the Berkshires, above Mount Greylock itself.

I went to bed early that night, guessing that Herman would remain in his study with his friend. In his more excitable moods, he rarely slept at all, and I knew he must stay up late—perhaps all night, if Mr. Hawthorne would oblige him. At one point, perhaps at three, I found myself awake. The moon had arisen and it lit the snow beyond our bedroom window with a blue light, utterly beautiful and haunting. Quietly, I crossed the hallway and pressed my ear to the door. The murmuring continued, but it was more subdued and farther away, the low rumble of intimate agreement. I guessed that they had retreated to the little room with the camp bed, behind the study—more of a closet than a proper room. It was peculiar, to say the least. I grew intensely curious, yet it would have been offensive to knock, unthinkable to open the door.

I withdrew to my room, drawing the silky bulk of a heavy down cover over my head, creating my own warm tunnel of sleep.

Herman and Mr. Hawthorne did not emerge until after the breakfast dishes had been cleared. Herman came in advance, dressed in the same rank clothes from the day before. He looked the worse for wear, with red eyes and a scrappy beard which badly needed brushing. He smelled of candle wax, tobacco, and old sweat. There was an odor of spilled whiskey that I disliked intensely.

"Would Mr. Hawthorne like to have something to eat?" I asked.

"Mr. *Melville* would," he said, digging in the bread box and taking a slice of bacon from a platter by the stove.

"You should attend to your guest," I said.

"What have I been doing?"

"I've no idea," I said.

"No, I don't suppose you do."

"There is no cause for rudeness."

"You are driving me mad," he said, licking his fingers. "This house is driving me mad."

I refused to let this stand without a challenge. "As you may recall, you brought us here, into the wild north woods."

"Is it so wild?"

"*You* are," I said.

Herman pawed the floor like a bull, and I thought he would butt me with his head, but he preferred to focus on his breakfast. Food generally acquired his attention, and it was hard to distract him. He cut a slice from a loaf that Augusta had recently made and lathered butter and honey on it. Then he cut another slice, presumably for Mr. Hawthorne. He put this on a silver tray, with a cup of coffee, then disappeared upstairs. It was two hours before he came down again with his illustrious guest in tow.

I stood to one side as Mr. Hawthorne assembled his suit of armor—a gray woolen coat, coon hat, leathery gloves, and boots—for a brilliant wintry morning. It was a still day, with the snow in dunes around the house—an icy Sahara.

"It was very good of you to visit us," I said. "You must come again, and do bring Mrs. Hawthorne."

"It is difficult," he said. "The children insist upon a good deal of attention. I'm sure you understand."

I did, indeed.

My mother-in-law explained that Silas, our hired hand, had fed his horse, and Mr. Hawthorne nodded gratefully.

"I am sorry we didn't have a chance to talk," he said to Maria.

"Oh, there will be time, Mr. Hawthorne. We are only getting to know each other. We are neighbors."

He seemed less than willing to grant this, yet he bowed gracefully and took his leave. Either he kissed her hand or I imagined that he did.

Herman said nothing, standing in one corner of the kitchen. It was odd, the way he said nothing, not even goodbye.

I didn't ask him about this, nor did his mother. We had grown used to Herman's inscrutable ways.

The summer and fall of 1851 fetched nothing but misery. I found myself pregnant again the previous winter, and everything went wrong from the outset. My ankles and knees swelled, so I could hardly walk. My head ached, as did my back, and I felt sick in the mornings, vomiting or wishing I could. Maria fussed and fumed, alternately delighted at the prospect of another grandchild or furious with me for taking to my bed and drawing the household's attention to myself. Herman was no help, as he drove hard at his desk, bringing *The Whale* to conclusion, losing contact with everyone at Arrowhead. He saw Mr. Hawthorne now and then, but he was strangely reticent about their friendship, often seeming forlorn if not defeated. I could not discern what had happened between them over this past year and half, but it was not good.

Certainly Herman adored Mr. Hawthorne, even worshipped him. He sent embarrassing notes to the red cottage, fishing for invitations. Mrs. Hawthorne was an exceptionally private woman, as I discovered, and she did not deal very well with visitors. Once she wrote to promise she would invite us to come by for a "summer picnic." It was not an invitation but the promise of one: a peculiar genre. It didn't surprise me that this picnic never materialized. In any case, it would have been impossible for me, in my state of pregnancy, to attend such an event.

"Perhaps *we* should instigate a picnic," my husband said one morning.

"Oh, what a fine idea," I said, "a birth picnic! Everyone can gather around and *watch* as I deliver a child!" My contempt was undisguised, but I didn't care. With Herman, one avoided subtlety on certain matters.

Stanwix—Stannie, as we called him—arrived in October, early by several weeks, with complications for me. He was, from the beginning, a sickly child who fought for every breath; he rarely slept and nursed poorly, wearing me down. The doctor came and went from Arrowhead nearly every day for a month, as the infant hovered between the living and the dead. For weeks on end, I wept profusely. I could not help myself. But my husband's mind was elsewhere, dreaming of literary glory. He believed quite fiercely that he had written a masterwork and told me as much, saying that the gods had provided a kind of tailwind during the last weeks of composition, when he rarely came to bed before midnight, often sleeping on the cot next to his study.

On November 14, *Moby-Dick; or, The Whale* appeared from Harper and Brothers with an obsequious dedication to Mr. Hawthorne: "In token of my admiration for his genius." Needless to say, Herman insisted that he should deposit the book into the master's hands for "a proper celebration." He commandeered our rickety wagon, collecting Mr. Hawthorne for a dinner at the Curtis Hotel in Lenox—a rather fine hotel, well above our means, and Herman would undoubtedly insist on paying for them both.

Their appearance created a stir, as I learned from my friend Celia Appleton, who lived in Lenox and, by chance, was dining at the hotel that night. What a thing to witness, with Herman playing the grand seigneur, ordering this and that in a loud voice. They tucked in to course after course, with bottles of wine and brandy, cigars, everything. I can't imagine what it cost, but a penny was more than Herman and I could afford. We teetered on the brink of bankruptcy, as the lease on Fourth Street had yet to find a buyer. My poor father, once again, advanced money to sustain us, although this time I didn't even tell my husband. He seemed at his wit's end since learning that his beloved Mr. Hawthorne would be leaving the Berkshires, fleeing to the outskirts of Boston, where he would no longer have to worry about impromptu visits from Herman Melville.

Celia described the tableau to me (in my bedroom, while I nursed the baby), saying my husband grew quite agitated at one point, pounding his fist on the table, knocking a decanter of water to the floor. Mr. Hawthorne sat like a block of stone, staring impassively or nodding. Herman broke into tears at one point, and Mr. Hawthorne reached across the table, taking my husband's hand. It was quite bizarre. I can't begin to imagine what Mr. Curtis (the hotelier) and this roomful of wide-eyed, gossipy spectators thought as they watched this scene unfold amid the clatter of dishes.

My husband was no driver and had made a name for himself by racing horses along dusty or wet roads at impossible speeds, overturning buggies, jamming wagons into ditches, terrifying the county. (That he never actually killed anyone, or himself, remained a mystery.) That night, having dropped his friend at the red cottage, he lost his grip on Waldo somewhere along Lenox Road after midnight. I don't know exactly what happened and he wouldn't say, but he stumbled home at four in the morning, his back wrenched, his leg bruised, mud-caked and reeking of alcohol. There was a horizontal gash on his forehead, though he ignored this altogether. He dropped heavily into bed beside me and began to weep.

"Whatever is wrong?" I asked, with the baby crooked under my arm.

"I made a fool of myself."

"This is only a village," I said, "so the audience for your antics is small—thank goodness. A very small portion of the world will know whatever silly thing you have done."

Herman turned his back to me and continued to sob into his pillow. The baby woke, of course, and I had the two of them bellowing.

"What's wrong?" I asked. "Can you tell me?"

"I don't know . . . what to do."

"About what?"

"Does he care for my book as he claims? I don't think so."

"Who?"

"Nathaniel."

"Why does it matter? He is only one reader."

This apparently provided no comfort.

"Well, I quite like the book," I said. "You have a distinct voice in the narrator, Ishmael. Ahab is well-drawn, too—excessive, but memorable."

"There's so little one can do," he said, in a mumble.

"About what?"

Again, he would not say what he meant.

"You have written the book you wished to write," I said. "I should leave it there."

He turned toward me. "It's digressive."

"I told you that."

"But the digressions are necessary."

"Then you must stop this maundering," I insisted. "Stand by your whale!"

Herman sat up, leaned against the headboard. He wiped his eyes and chuckled. "You are quite wonderful at times, my dear," he said. "I'm a lucky man."

"And why do you say this?"

"You are wise."

"I doubt it."

"Hawthorne will be gone soon. And we shall be alone."

"Not a bad thing, perhaps," I said.

.   .   .

I knew Herman would react badly to the reviews of *The Whale*. Evert Duyckinck had collected and posted them from New York, with a false note of apology. "I was sent these from England, and they are quite foolish," he wrote. "It seems they have read a very different book from the one you have written." When Duyckinck's own review appeared, not long after, he showed only a touch more enthusiasm than the English critics, referring to the book as "an intellectual chowder." This was hardly the acme of praise my husband would have expected from an old friend.

Herman left the batch on a table in the chimney room for everyone to read. He wished to share his misery with the rest of us.

I knew H.M. well enough to foresee how he would react to this news. For months I'd been afraid for his stability. Since Mr. Hawthorne had left the Berkshires, Herman had brooded, slept fitfully, and kept to himself—even refusing to come to meals except when Maria prevailed upon him. (He *would* listen to his mother!) He walked for hours in the snowy woods in the afternoons, coming home after dark in a frightening state, with a fringe of icicles on his beard, his nose and cheeks blistered blood-bright. In the evenings he would retreat to his study, where he swallowed inordinate quantities of cheap brandy. He often shouted in the night as he slept in the tiny room off his study. It had been months since he slept with me—in our dear four-poster bed, with Stannie in the cot beside us. I missed him, though I did not think his night terrors would soothe the child.

One night Herman stormed into the north parlor, where Helen and Maria sat beside me at the fire, playing whist. Once it was a game that cheered him, but cheer had passed from his life. We all knew he had something to say, and waited.

"I am never going to write another word," he said.

His clipped statement hung in the air, shorn of all qualification or adornment. I had never heard him talk like this before.

Maria said, "You mustn't talk in such a fashion. Your wife may soon believe you."

"She ought to believe me."

"The reviews are not as bad as they seem," said Helen, unhelpful as ever.

H.M. held a breath tightly in his lungs, exhaled with a hiss. He could hardly tolerate his sister's remark, which was foolish; but she had been helpful over the past few years, copying the manuscripts of his novels, making fresh pages as he revised them, without complaint. Given the terrible state of his vision (I had begun to think he would go blind before long), he needed her more than ever, as I had little time for this work, with infants to look after.

Herman unfolded a review from his breast pocket, reading aloud in an exaggerated English accent: "The style of his tale is in places disfigured by mad (rather than bad) English; and its catastrophe is hastily, weakly, and obscurely managed."

This article, from the *Athenaeum* in London, had apparently been reprinted in the Boston papers. Its conclusion was devastating: "Our author must be henceforth numbered in the company of the incorrigibles who occasionally tantalize us with indications of genius, while they constantly summon us to endure monstrosities, carelessnesses, and other such harassing manifestations of bad taste as daring or disordered ingenuity can devise."

Herman crumpled the paper in his fist, tossing it into the fire. "Count me among the incorrigibles," he said.

"It's of no importance," Maria said. "English reviewers don't bother to read the book at hand. Evert has said as much."

"It's the luck of the draw, perhaps," he said, shrugging. This seemed, at least, a hopeful sign. He was trying to rationalize his situation. One could certainly not count on reviewers to read a book with sympathy, with the intention of actually trying to understand what the writer had sought to accomplish.

"You've not been lucky," Helen added, unhelpfully.

Herman had, in fact, found a number of sympathetic reviewers in obscure papers, but this scarcely helped the cause. Only a few papers mattered, and the *Athenaeum* was among them. And American reviewers, as if afraid to express themselves, parroted the British. But what especially galled Herman was that the British publisher of *The Whale* had accidentally omitted the epilogue, wherein the reader learned that Ishmael had actually survived the wreck of the *Pequod*. Reviewers took this error as a sign of Herman's incompetence as a novelist.

One critic, in the *Spectator*, had put the matter bluntly, insisting that "nothing should be introduced into a novel which it is physically impossible for the writer to have known: thus, he must not describe the conversation of miners in a pit if they *all* perish . . . His catastrophe overrides all rule: not only is Ahab, with his boat's-crew, destroyed in his last desperate attack upon the white whale, but the *Pequod* herself sinks with all on board into the depths of the illimitable ocean." One could almost hear the self-satisfied clucking in this wretched man's throat.

"Pay no attention to these people," said Maria.

Herman, in response, picked up a cup of tea and dashed it—cup as well as tea—into the fireplace. It was a peculiar gesture that made no sense, and he must have realized this, as he sulked out, letting the door slam. I could hear, and feel, the wind under the door in that drafty house.

Upstairs in our bedroom, the baby began to wail.

"Your husband is unwell in his mind," said Maria. "But I should ignore him and tend to the child. Herman will come around. He always does."

For, Nature, in no shallow surge
Against thee either sex may urge,
Why hast thou made us but in halves—
Co-relatives? This makes us slaves.
If these co-relatives never meet
Self-hood itself seems incomplete.

H.M., from "After the Pleasure Party"

PARABLE OF THE CAVE

14.

The last straw was a review of *Pierre* in Boston's *Daily Times* by one Charles Creighton Hazewell (his name almost a joke in itself). He ridiculed the claustrophobic group of central characters in Herman's novel, which had been written quickly after *Moby-Dick*. This tale satirized the literary establishment and portrayed a confused, agitated hero, Pierre Glendinning—a man with an overbearing mother and incestuous impulses. "The annals of Bedlam might be defied to produce such another collection of lunatics as the hero, his mother, his sister, and the heroine," wrote Hazewell. "Were there no mad doctors in that part of the country where they lived? Were the asylums all full? Was there nobody to swear out a commission *de lunatico inquirendo,* out of regard to the common safety?"

If *Moby-Dick; or, The Whale* had been a disappointment, with few sales and decidedly mixed reviews, *Pierre; or, The Ambiguities* had been a catastrophe. H.M. surmised it was not okay to jest about the American republic of letters, as they took themselves very

seriously—Evert Duyckinck surely did, and he had been thoroughly
unpleasant about *Pierre*. Further, it seemed the wider reading public had no taste for stories of incest. Had they somehow missed the
lyricism of the prose? Herman picked up his personal copy of *Pierre,*
and he read again the opening lines:

> There are some strange summer mornings in the country, when
> he who is but a sojourner from the city shall early walk forth into
> the fields, and be wonder-smitten with the trance-like aspect of
> the green and golden world. Not a flower stirs; the trees forget
> to wave; the grass itself seems to have ceased to grow; and all
> Nature, as if suddenly become conscious of her own profound
> mystery, and feeling no refuge from it but silence, sinks into this
> wonderful and indescribable repose.

Was this not as fresh as anything he had written? How could
Duyckinck, his friend and ally, have called the book "a psycholog-
ical curiosity"? "The object of the author," he wrote in the *Literary
World,* "has been, not to delineate life and character as they are or
may possibly be, but as they are not and cannot be. We must receive
the book, then, as an eccentricity of the imagination."

H.M. had tea at his friend's house in New York, where Evert
had said, "I do hope you didn't take offense. I meant no harm."

"But you *did,* Evert. You meant harm."

Duyckinck looked around, uncomfortable, stretching his long
neck. He adjusted his tie and offered Herman another biscuit.
"They are praline and chocolate," he said. "My wife is especially
good with praline and chocolate."

Only this past year had Duyckinck's once gauntly youthful face
begun to fill out, with a deepening in the brow, a slight bagginess
under the eye, and the faintest hint of a double chin appearing. This
was perhaps the result of his wife's expert ways in the kitchen.

"I'm hoping to sell books, Evert," H.M. said. "Reviews like yours do not sell books."

Duyckinck could not resist saying, "It is *books* like yours that do not sell books. You had better return to seafaring tales. You have a knack for them."

Only 283 copies of *Pierre* had sold in the first year, leaving H.M. with a negative balance at Harper and Brothers. The prospects for authorship, in his case, had never seemed less promising.

"I can find any number of books for you to review," said Duyckinck, trying to sound helpful.

"You can, but what can you pay me for this work?"

"Not a great deal. Do you require a loan? Never hesitate. I will be here, when and if you require my assistance. My father, as you know, left me not a little sum. I find myself comfortable."

Comfortable, indeed. H.M. envied his friend this large well-kept brownstone over several floors on Fourteenth Street. He admired the tasteful furniture that filled each room—much of it purchased on leisurely trips abroad and shipped home from England or France. Duyckinck had quite a number of good Italian paintings, and he obviously had a taste for colorful Oriental rugs, which covered his oak floors from top to bottom, lending a rich flavor to the house. Arrowhead, by contrast, was a bare old barn.

At home in the Berkshires after this brief visit to New York, Herman found himself unable to work, even ill. He felt sure that his heart would soon give out, as his wrists throbbed and his throat pulsed. A bad taste often rose in his mouth. To calm himself, he drank most evenings but slept badly, waking early, unable to remain in bed past five. In the early hours he wandered by himself along Lenox Road, as if in search of Nathaniel Hawthorne. Herman wanted, rather badly, to talk to his friend, to explain himself to him. There had been some terrible misunderstanding, and it must be corrected. He could not go to his grave estranged from him, and he was terrified this might happen, as his health had turned precarious. Hawthorne—a hale man if any existed—would outlive him by decades, H.M. thought.

The habit of writing is not easily lost, and Herman soon found himself making notes, writing in his journals. Vague ideas for stories appeared like strangers beckoning from the edge of a distant wood. He began to wave back at them in prose, and this activity carried him through squalls of feeling that threatened to overwhelm the vessel of his work. Arrowhead itself was a kind of ship, and he was its captain; if he could only keep his eye on the horizon, all would be well, or so he reassured himself. His pen dipped compulsively into the inkwell, and before long he found himself in the middle of *The Isle of the Cross,* a novel that would never see publication. It was based on the story of a disconsolate woman called Agatha, who had been hoodwinked by her unfaithful husband, a sailor—a story that had come to Herman's attention on a visit to Nantucket. The writing had never felt strong, even as the manuscript grew to a staggering height on his desk. On a visit to New York, Herman showed the book to one of the Harper brothers, who wrote back: "The problems in the story may never be resolved. In general, it lacks the usual energy of your prose." In a fit of pique one night, after he thought everyone in Arrowhead had retired for the night, Herman tossed the entire manuscript into the fire, watching the pages glow, darken, and curl, with flakes rising up the flue of the chimney like a reverse snowfall.

"What on earth are you doing?" cried Maria, entering the room with her jaw unhinged.

"The novel is worthless," said her son. "I have destroyed it."

He fell to his knees on a carpet, and his mother put her arms around him. She let him sob. "You will know best, darling," she said. "At least, I hope this is so. Do not tell Lizzie. She does not understand you, not as I do."

Herman wrote to Evert Duyckinck: "This has been a bad year. I've been churning in the whirlpool of a novel, a sad piece of writing, and without luck. A writer needs luck, and I do not have it. The tale has finally escaped me. I shall pass the bare outlines to Hawthorne, who may wish to make use of it. I wash my hands of it, like Pontius Pilate. I will have nothing more to do with this material."

Desperate for income, he wrote stories for magazines. In due course he returned to the novel about Israel Potter that had, years before, occasioned a trip to London. He thought he could spin a workmanlike tale from the material, and he did, with results that seemed of little or no interest to the reading public. "I don't believe it's really your voice," wrote Duyckinck, who could never resist giving advice to an old friend in need of his critical acumen. "It's tolerable work, with vigorous patches, but it remains somehow not quite yours. Readers always know when a writer is dishonest with himself, as you have been."

Another book, *The Confidence-Man,* puzzled the few readers who found their way to its pages. For this short novel, H.M. summoned a motley group of pilgrims, putting them aboard a steamer on the Mississippi. His cast included any number of quacks and swindlers, fake clergymen, charity agents, even transcendental philosophers. He set them against one particular swindler (the "hero" of the story), who stole onto the boat on April Fool's Day to test the confidence of those aboard. One British reviewer, in the *Literary Gazette,* described the book in these terms: "A novel it is not, unless a novel means forty-five conversations held on board a steamer, conducted by personages who might pass for the errata of creation, and so far resembling the *Dialogues* of Plato as to be undoubted Greek to ordinary men."

None of this literary work made any money to speak of, though each reflected H.M. in the way a kaleidoscope reflects, or distorts, some object in its view. He was present in everything he wrote, if altered in form. As Lizzie pointed out, he was surely the leading character in "The Piazza." Its narrator has put aside the life of action to laze on his porch or "piazza," looking north toward Mount Greylock, which in every season afforded luxuries for the imagination. Only once did he make a journey into the surrounding countryside:

> My horse hitched low his head. Red apples rolled before him; Eve's apples; seek-no-furthers. He tasted one, I another; it tasted of the ground. Fairy land not yet, thought I, flinging my bridle to a humped old tree, that crooked out an arm to catch it. For the way now lay where path was none, and none might go but by himself, and only go by daring. Through blackberry brakes that tried to pluck me back, though I but strained towards fruitless growths of mountain-laurel; up slippery steeps to barren heights, where stood none to welcome. Fairy land not yet, thought I, though the morning is here before me.

Herman's narrator ("in a pass between two worlds") stumbles upon a strange and isolated girl he calls Marianna. Still possessed by her aura, he retreats to his piazza at midday, hoping to slough off the world of fantasy and yearning:

> Launching my yawl no more for fairy-land, I stick to the piazza. It is my box-royal; and this amphitheatre, my theatre of San Carlo. Yes, the scenery is magical—the illusion so complete. And Madam Meadow Lark, my prima donna, plays her grand engagement here; and, drinking in her sunrise note, which, Memnon-like, seems struck from the golden window, how far from me the weary face behind it.

But, every night, when the curtain falls, truth comes in with darkness. No light shows from the mountain. To and fro I walk the piazza deck, haunted by Marianna's face, and many as real a story.

It was usually the "real" story that obsessed him. He had told it repeatedly, and he would continue to tell it, or so he said to himself at night, for comfort or solace. But comfort failed to come, and this unnerved him. He straddled some invisible line between reality and the imagination, never quite certain where exactly a foot fell, on which side of the line. Agitation overwhelmed him in the night, as he slept with one eye open, often preferring the little room where Hawthorne had stayed. The great man's ghost occupied that closet, a lively beneficent spirit that spoke to him clearly, saying, "Do what you love best, even if it is poetry you must write. Do not worry about money. Think about readers who will find you in a hundred years or more. They are your destiny—like Penelope, weaving and unweaving at her loom, waiting for the arrival of Odysseus."

This was easier said than done, of course, as money problems in the Melville household had been exacerbated by the failures of *Moby-Dick* and *Pierre*. A boyhood acquaintance from Lansingburgh, Tertullus D. Stewart, had secretly loaned Herman more than two thousand dollars—a considerable sum, although H.M. calmly believed that royalties from his books would allow him to repay the loan without his wife discovering it. This plan failed and Herman had been forced to reveal his financial problems to Judge Shaw as well as to Lizzie, doubling his shame.

In addition, the mortgage proved more complex than expected. Dr. Brewster had insisted on regular interest payments, which of course Herman failed to meet. He had briefly entertained hope that *The Piazza Tales* would generate substantial income, as the reviews surpassed any that H.M. had received for some time. The *Evening Traveller* called one story, "Bartleby, the Scrivener," a piece of fiction "equal to anything from the pen of Dickens."

This had pleased Lizzie to no end, as she had never lost her infatuation with Dickens. In fond moments, she imagined that Herman would become the American Dickens, and now she half wondered if, indeed, this were coming to pass.

H.M. had written that tale in a whirl of eleven days—a period when he could hardly eat or talk to anyone. He felt an almost infinite sympathy with his subject, the poor scrivener, hired to copy material he simply didn't wish to copy. "I prefer not to," he repeated, when asked to perform tasks by the elderly and sympathetic lawyer who had hired him in the first place. Bartleby faces his desk to the wall. He tries to blank out the world, as H.M. had done (preferring not to write stories that obviously would sell). H.M. preferred not to "make something of himself," as his mother and wife had urged. His isolation, already intense, had been exacerbated after the loss of Hawthorne. He preferred not to seek other friends. He preferred not to move beyond the walls of his study. Life, with its petty demands, its requirements for attention or mere attendance, defeated him. He had become a leper in his own household, requiring nothing but what lepers had: a blanket and a pillow, a bowl for bathing, a dry towel. He had these things and nothing more seemed necessary, at least for a while. But in many ways he felt more like the narrator of the tale than his charge—the middle-class lawyer who looked in upon this dark figure he had taken in, offered him a place, nurtured and encouraged him. H.M. had done what he could for the Bartleby who lived inside him, and he would not send him away. Nor would he inhabit him fully, exclusively.

Critics liked this new work, and there was talk of sales. But his hope proved short-lived; the tales sold poorly, doing nothing to restore the name of Herman Melville in the eyes of publishers. In frustration, Herman resorted to selling half of his estate in Pittsfield, eighty acres in all, which fetched $5,500. This money went straight to Judge Shaw, who settled the debts with Brewster and Stewart. Not a penny of the sale fell to Herman, but he was, at least, out of debt.

The problem with his nerves did not ease, however. His eyesight, always bad, worsened, so that he found it extremely difficult to work for hours without debilitating headaches. His chest tightened like a fist around his heart, and he broke into sweats at night, waking in pools of his own anxiety. His moods shifted rapidly, with spasms of ill temper, even violence. More than once he threatened Lizzie, brushing her aside in the hall, even pushing her onto the bed once in a fury. Often he would disappear into the surrounding woods, taking long hikes by himself, even though his legs had begun to fail him, and he experienced considerable pain in his hips and knees. Coughs and grippes circled in the wintry Berkshire skies, landed, took possession of his body. Once, in the middle of dinner, he fell to the floor, gasping for breath, convinced he was dying.

Dr. Edmonds, from Pittsfield, rushed to the house, and he declared that Herman required "peace and tranquillity above all." A change of climate was also recommended—perhaps a trip to Italy.

"Is that all?" H.M. asked.

Lizzie determined to secure enough funds to send her ailing husband away, to Italy or anywhere. It seemed essential for his stability (and hers). He had been a man of action in his youth, someone who adored travel. For all his love of Renaissance art, he had never seen the wonders of Rome or Florence, as she noted, suggesting that he take such a trip by himself, for health reasons.

As expected, Herman simply observed that they could hardly afford such a luxury. They had only *just* extricated themselves from crippling debt, and there was no good reason to plunge into the same again, as it would make matters worse.

Lizzie, however, explained to her father that there was some urgency in the matter. He could afford to help his wayward son-in-law, and he did so immediately, writing to tell Herman that he would support a passage to Europe or anywhere that seemed useful. "Your health is our chief concern," he said. "I want my grandchildren to have a robust father."

Herman was embarrassed by this generosity from Mount Vernon Street, but he did not object. It had been seven years since he had last set foot in Europe. Indeed, he decided to visit the Holy Land as well as Italy. "The Levant is not expensive," he wrote to his father-in-law. "I shall spend a brief while there, mainly to see Jerusalem for myself. The time I pass in Rome and Florence could serve as the basis for lectures upon my return. As you have often observed, there is a good income on the circuit. Think of Mr. Emerson!"

Herman crossed the Atlantic in October 1856, taking a second-class ticket to conserve his limited funds. He occupied a stuffy cabin on the *City of Glasgow,* a paddle steamer, but he knew he would have very little financial leeway on this journey. The date of his return passage lay open; but he was unlikely to see Arrowhead again before the spring or possibly even the summer of 1858.

His mother would enjoy being in command of the family, not having to look (however perfunctorily) in the direction of H.M. before acting on her impulses. Poor Lizzie would have to follow her lead, yet she seemed more than willing to let her husband go. "It will do a power of good for you," she repeated, perhaps too often. Herman of course knew he had only been a hindrance in the past two or three years, creating turmoil at home, terrifying the children, upsetting his mother and sisters. This unfinished business with Hawthorne had almost ruined him emotionally.

H.M. looked ahead, however: the immediate goal of his journey being Hawthorne himself, now in Liverpool. He would surprise Hawthorne, turning up on his doorstep. In a foreign land, they would have more in common than had been the case in the Berkshires. The possibility of a reconnection kept Herman in a state of fierce anticipation, so much so he could hardly sleep.

During the passage of eleven days, he reread a good deal of Pope's *Odyssey* (which rarely left his side now), disembarking in Greenock, making his way south via coach along the Tweed, where he stopped to see Abbotsford, the fanciful and extravagant house constructed over many years by Sir Walter Scott, who had died two decades before—his last years devoted to pulling himself out of debt as best he could. This story about Scott had seized Herman's imagination. He would try to accomplish something like this one day, writing himself into genuine prosperity and ease.

H.M. thought of Arrowhead, his own version of Abbotsford, though on a vastly reduced scale. And he thought about his modest shelf of books. Like Scott, he had sought a wide audience, and—at least with *Typee* and *Omoo*—had nearly found it. If only the publishers had worked as hard as they should, his financial woes might have disappeared, and he would not have been tied to the benevolence of Lizzie's father.

As he understood it, unless something shifted, he could not hope to earn his living as a man of letters. Another profession was required. Perhaps, like Hawthorne and his paternal grandfather, he could become a customs officer. He would prefer an appointment to an American consulate, perhaps in Florence, where he could indulge his passion for Renaissance art; but he did not have the political advantages of Hawthorne, whose closest friend at Bowdoin College had been Franklin Pierce, the fourteenth president of the United States.

It was always good to know a president, Herman thought.

But H.M. had no acquaintances on a par with this. Judge Shaw might intervene for him in Washington, but that was unlikely to matter any longer. The judge was old, and his party affiliations would provide no advantages for his son-in-law.

After Abbotsford, H.M. made his way to Liverpool, where in due course, with difficulty, he found Hawthorne's tall, narrow red-brick town house in Southport, some miles north along the icy coast. He knocked on the large blue door, his stomach roiled.

Sophia answered, looking haggard, blond hair strewn over her face and intermingling with strands of gray. She studied H.M. vaguely for a moment; then her gaze clarified. "Mr. Melville!"

"Hello, Sophia."

"It's you!"

"I thought to surprise you."

"Indeed!"

He stepped into the foyer, crushing a hat in his hands.

"Nathaniel will be pleased," she said, without conviction. "Whatever brings you to Southport?"

"I'm traveling."

"On business?"

"There were some medical problems, a bit of neuralgia. My head, you see. And my chest. I needed a warmer climate."

"Such as . . . Liverpool?"

He laughed. "I'm en route."

"I suppose that's true of us all," Sophia said.

She asked a parlor maid to get a cup of tea for their visitor, then led him into the sitting room, which had a defiantly rose cast, as the wallpaper swirled in deep hues. The carpet, too, had a slightly ruddy glow. Herman felt absorbed into a dusky flower of sorts, the soft petals folding around him. He found it difficult to breathe as he sank into a chair by the fire, which gave off more light than heat. There was a bombé cupboard by one wall, but it displayed only a few pieces of china. He noticed that several British magazines lay on an ebony table by the window, including the *Spectator* and *Athenaeum*. These had been the very papers that ruined the reception of *The Whale* in England, and it did not please him to see them so well displayed. He began to wish he had never come to Southport.

Hawthorne emerged only minutes later, drawn from his study at the top of the house. His cheeks seemed especially dark and hollow. He had not shaved in a day or two, and there was frosty stubble on his chin. He wore a blue serge jacket that had seen better days.

H.M. leaped to his feet. He found it overwhelming to occupy the same room as Nathaniel Hawthorne, after all this time and trouble.

"Do sit, Herman," said Hawthorne. "It's so good of you to come . . . and such a distance! I had no idea."

"I'm fond of surprises," H.M. said.

The two men said little at first, drinking tea in chairs, facing each other. Herman explained that he had been unwell, and that he required a period abroad—in the Levant, in Italy—to recover. He rambled on, wondering if Hawthorne had yet received the copy of *The Piazza Tales,* which he had sent from the post office in Pittsfield three months before.

"I have read it," said Hawthorne. "It is fine work."

"There is small audience for fine work," H.M. said.

Now Una and Julian entered with their mother. Una stood three inches above Sophia, and Julian was large as well, with some of the dark beauty of his father in his lineaments. They seemed quite happy to see H.M., and he planted a wet kiss on each child's forehead. Soon little Rose toddled in, with a nursemaid, and bowed politely.

"You have a wonderful family," said H.M. to Hawthorne.

"As do you."

"I have rather a full house these days," he said.

"You needed a break from the masses," said Hawthorne.

He insisted that Herman should move into his house for the duration of his visit to the Liverpool area. It was a large place, he explained, "and paid for by American tax dollars."

H.M. stoutly refused this hospitality, aware that the Hawthorne family valued its privacy. He had never found it easy to appear at the door of the red cottage, and there was awkwardness in the household that unnerved him. No, he insisted, he would remain where he was, at a nearby inn. It was cheap enough, comfortable in a frowzy way. He could only stay a few days anyway. His larger plan was to write some lectures about Italy or the Levant, and he might eventually collect these into a book one day. Another novel, or perhaps a long poem, might emerge in due course. As he talked, he grew excited about his prospects. Perhaps this journey was not, after all, a waste of time and Lemuel Shaw's money.

When they were alone again, Herman wondered if Hawthorne might help him to find an English publisher for a novel he had recently finished, *The Confidence-Man*. "I think it would amuse a British audience. They apparently admire their long-lost American cousins."

"I'll send the book to my publisher in London," said Hawthorne, without hesitation.

Tears came to Herman's eyes, but he said nothing. It was a relief to have this support from his dear friend for a novel not yet published. After a lengthy chat that centered on Herman's bad luck with his last few books, they agreed to meet the next day for an excursion. Hawthorne insisted on showing Herman the local sights, singing the praises of the Irish Sea. "It's rather desolate in its way," he said.

"A mirror of your soul," said Herman, wryly.

Hawthorne made no response.

After a large breakfast at Hawthorne's house the next morning, they set off through brisk November weather in a cabriolet, with the sun a thin disk behind wispy clouds. The road hugged the Irish Sea, where a salty breeze slid off of a bay bristling with whitecaps. Cormorants rode the swells, reaching their long necks upward.

"You will like the beaches farther along," said Hawthorne, paying the driver. "But we must go on foot from here."

They set off along a boulder-strewn prospect, stepping over loose driftwood, golden ventricles of wrack, shells, and crab skeletons. The odor of dead fish swirled in the air. A pair of oyster-catchers stood in a pool of tidewater, black-winged birds with massive red bills. With a relentless wind against them, H.M. and Hawthorne had to tilt forward, holding their hats. Hawthorne rushed ahead, with H.M. wheezing behind him. He was not as fit as he should be. Indeed, the older man put him to shame with his energetic pace.

"I could use a rest," Herman said, after nearly an hour of plunging forward. "My heart has been acting up."

Hawthorne led his friend to a hollow between dunes, where they found relief from the high wind. Marram grass protected them, forming a wall of sorts. Herman offered Hawthorne a cigar, and they smoked happily in silence, listening to the sea.

"I wonder about providence," said Herman, out of nowhere.

"You have not become a Christian, have you?"

"I'm a Christian, yes sir, but a heathen as well. I think of God or Allah in the same breath. I worship the sun. I worship the moon, the ground, this sand, its particles." Excited now, he spoke in rapid gulps, delving into the nature of reality, which he described as "inaccessible, intractable." He could not believe in a conventional God, he said, although this didn't preclude the notion of a spiritual center, even a Supreme Being. Any literal description of heaven seemed "intolerable, tedious." He thought Mr. Emerson had a grip on the most elevated aspects of super-reality; but he could not really imagine himself in a place "beyond time."

"Do you imagine that we simply disappear in death?" Hawthorne asked. There was an edge to the question that H.M. could not quite calculate.

"I have pretty much made up my mind to be annihilated," said H.M.

"Annihilation is a strong word."

"It's a strong motion as well. Think of it: the soul absorbed into the silence of eternity. I prefer this to any literal version of heaven."

"I don't know," said Hawthorne. "I dislike Emerson, as you know. He is so . . . abstract. There is a hell, you see: perhaps not a place of fire and punishment, but it's here. It's as deeply bedded as the kingdom of God within us."

"Sin is real, you say?"

"The world is a field of battle."

Herman demurred. He did not believe in these "intensities of light and darkness" that so enthralled the Puritans and American revivalists. He had seen a flicker of goodness in men.

"Men are wicked," said Hawthorne.

"And the same wicked men are angels," said Herman. "I'm an angel, and you are certainly one—a dark one, perhaps."

Hawthorne grimaced.

"I read the New Testament quite often, for solace. I admire the Gospels, as they tell us a wonderful story, and we like a good story, don't we? The letters of Saint Paul are feverish, perhaps. But he's a wonderful writer."

"Ahab would admire Saint Paul," said Hawthorne.

"I admire him, too, or part of me does. I am Ahab."

"And Ishmael, and most certainly Queequeg."

"You could play Starbuck any day of the week," said Herman, with a glint.

"I have played every character in your book. We have each of us done so, in turn."

"God does not especially like me," said Herman. "It's the one thing I know for sure."

Hawthorne shook his head. "He likes us equally. He despises us equally as well."

"I pray to God, you see. I do. But He doesn't listen."

Hawthorne said, "As I believe you told me once, prayer is a form of listening."

"In the Levant, I shall listen."

The tall grass held its breath. The clouds seemed hardly to move overhead.

"I envy you this trip," said Hawthorne. "The Holy Land often beckons."

"I will go to Golgotha and suffer."

"The place of skulls."

"And I will listen. I promise."

"I have high hopes," said Hawthorne, bemused. "I predict you will write something about the Holy Land that will count among your finest works. I have an intimation."

"Perhaps a long poem, one day." Herman looked searchingly at Hawthorne now. "Your stories are poems, they are."

"You flatter me. There is no point."

"I say what I believe."

"That is like you."

"What's wrong with me, Nathaniel? I can't settle on anything. I worship too many gods."

"You've probably written too much of late. Cultivate leisure. That is my advice, such as it is."

"Too much—"

"I don't mean to patronize you."

"You never do."

"But we go round and round."

"I do, in any case," said Herman. "I chase my own tail. It's a habit of mind, a foul habit."

"Nothing human is foul."

"Or unholy."

Herman lay back, gazing at the sky as clouds parted to reveal a strip of blue, and he felt in heaven here. The shrewdest and most inspired man in the world sat beside him, and they talked openly and honestly about what mattered most. Everything else fell away, as it should: the daily dismal world, its tedious details, its sham. H.M. turned to examine his beloved friend, older but still so handsome, so mysterious. In seeing Hawthorne again, he had already achieved the purpose of his journey.

H.M. spoke bluntly. "I suspect I frightened you a few years ago. You left the Berkshires so abruptly."

"It was the beastliness of the climate, nothing personal."

"I don't believe that."

"As you choose."

Herman said, "I chose to love *you*."

Hawthorne bit his lip. This manner of expression held no appeal for him. It was unmanly, and he would not respond.

Herman shrunk now, letting his head drop. Why did Hawthorne resist him? He tried once again. "You refuse to acknowledge my affections."

Hawthorne shook his head. "I don't really think you have the full measure of this."

"We lack the appropriate terms," Herman said. "That is true. But I say what I feel. Love is the only word that will suffice."

"I do understand. And I appreciate—"

H.M. put a hand on his friend's hand. "There is no need. You don't have to explain yourself—nor do I."

Hawthorne winced, struggling to find exactly the right words for what he meant. "This is not your fault, Herman. It's mine." He closed his eyes and put the fingers of his right hand to his eyes to shade them.

"See how I hurt you," Herman said. "I never wished to hurt."

"No, please. Let the discussion change its course. We have been together less than an hour or two, yet already we have touched on God and the Devil, time and eternity, the meaning of love." He turned fondly to Herman. "This is the age of steam travel and locomotives! Civilization proceeds, but I'm not sure that philosophy has kept apace."

"The fact that one can cross the Atlantic in two rather than four or ten weeks changes nothing essential," Herman said.

"I know, but—"

"You must not evade me."

Hawthorne drew a long, deep breath to compose himself.

"We have so few chances in this life . . . to connect," H.M. added.

"There is a pub nearby, in the village," said Hawthorne. "We can have a plowman's lunch, with pints of beer, and we can poke and prod each other as long as you wish. I have no desire to curtail you."

"We can talk of engineering if you like. They build marvelous bridges in England. It's bridges today and nothing else. A good bridge is the symbol of man's progress. I have always said as much. I would build a good bridge between us if I could, but I am no engineer of human spirits. I have never succeeded in touching anyone as vehemently as would please me."

"You invented a word for this: *isolato.*"

"Is that mine?"

"I think so. Yes."

H.M. could not help but smile. He liked that, having named something as peculiar and important.

With a sly smile, Hawthorne withdrew a small manila envelope from inside his jacket. He handed it to Herman. "A token of our friendship," he said.

The envelope contained a photograph of Hawthorne, done recently in one of the many establishments that had lately emerged on Regent Street in London. It was a trifle dark, ochre in tone— but then, Hawthorne was dark. It was also striking: the fierce nose and tight lips, the blazing eyes, the overall visage as handsome as the man himself, if not more so.

"I will treasure this," said Herman.

It was a cold morning in mid-November, with high cirrus clouds like wild brushstrokes of white against a blue canvas. Herring gulls hung in the air above the harbor. Meanwhile, the passengers boarded: a slow process that took much of a single morning. The *Egyptian* was a screw steamer, more than a hundred and fifty feet from bow to stern, with forty-three cabins on two decks. The journey would consume four weeks—sailing from Liverpool to Constantinople, arriving in Turkey via the Greek archipelago. The itinerary would all be new to Herman, and he relished the prospect. He certainly wished to leave England quickly, as nothing was served by remaining in Southport.

The meeting with Hawthorne had frustrated him, though it confirmed a sad truth: he and his friend could only meet tangentially. Hawthorne seemed to wear an invisible shield that protected him from contact with other human beings. H.M. could penetrate the armor here and there, find unlikely chinks, but the hope of genuine contact was slight. They would never meet on the most intimate levels, and the friendship was bound to thwart and dishearten Herman, who wished for more than could reasonably be expected from a man as diffident as Hawthorne. The promise of their friendship had come to nothing, apart from a fleeting sense of sublimity.

H.M. did not bother to look back as Liverpool disappeared. The friendship with Hawthorne had, or so it seemed, come to a conclusion of sorts. He went below to arrange his things.

His stateroom was comprised of two narrow bunks stacked along one wall in a cubicle with a rusty starboard porthole. This part of the ship smelled of burning coal, grease, and rotting hemp: an unpleasant combination, he thought, as he lay in the upper bunk on the first afternoon. His bunkmate had left his rucksack and satchel on the lower berth to stake out a claim, though he was himself nowhere to be seen. Out of the rucksack, enticingly, spilled any number of dense theological tomes, including Herbert C. Spiller's *Treatise on Biblical Sources* and a volume on Old Testament theology by Ernst Bertheau, a well-known scholar from Göttingen. Curiosity overwhelmed him, and H.M. leafed nervously through the Bertheau. The pages contained lots of marginalia: a good sign. The name Orville Clarence was inscribed in a bold hand inside each cover.

Suddenly Orville appeared in the doorway. He coughed to draw attention to himself.

"Ah, your books caught my eye. I hope you don't mind if I took a peek."

"You will find that a tedious study," said Orville, pointing to the book in Herman's hands. "Professor Bertheau is a typical Germanic scholar, all footnotes and fetishes."

"I am shameless, I'm afraid. My curiosity was aroused."

"No need to apologize," Orville said.

Herman introduced himself as a writer, piquing the young man's interest. Orville had never read anything by H.M., but he said he would do so at the first opportunity. His own reading of novels had been, as he put it, "patchy." He was a theological student at the Yale Divinity School and was already a graduate of Harvard. He hoped one day to pursue a research degree in biblical archaeology, although he would probably assume a pulpit in the near future, as his father (a minister in Boston) thought he should have practical experience as a parish clergyman before indulging himself with further study.

Orville led H.M. into the aft lounge, a sunny area reserved for passengers, with drooping, spidery potted plants, a tilt-top table laid with afternoon tea, and windows that looked out over the receding harbor. The *Egyptian* was already in motion, gliding without obvious friction over the leaden waters.

Herman listened warmly to the young man, who seemed eager for company. The boy—he must be twenty-three or so, H.M. decided—had brown hair with a reddish tint. His nose twitched involuntarily, crinkling into a snort at regular intervals. He had large milk-white hands, bony knees, and long legs. His voice was nasal, almost tinny. His cheeks gathered into dimples when he laughed, tilting his head to one side whenever he did. Orville wore a white tie, a high collar, and black woolen jacket—already in the guise of a clergyman. He used his hands expressively, sometimes slicing the air with one hand to emphasize a point.

Like Herman, Orville was en route to the Holy Land for the purpose of his own edification. He planned to see the well-known sites in Jerusalem, Bethlehem, and Nazareth.

"I would hope to walk where Jesus walked," he said.

"On water?"

Orville stared at Herman, uncomprehending, and this proved a familiar pattern: H.M. would say something wry or absurd, and Orville would nod coolly or just stare.

Meanwhile, the *Egyptian* plied its way toward the Mediterranean Sea, passing the Rock of Gibraltar one morning in late

November: the huge backlit mass in sharp outline. Soon thereafter
a storm blew up, tugging the ship violently from side to side. Orville
doubled over the portside rail, heaving his guts into the sea. H.M.
stood calmly beside him, offering such comfort as he could. What
shocked him was how Orville broke into embarrassed laughter
between heaves. There was a dislocation here, as if the young man
could not accept the simple fate of seasickness—a common malady
among travelers. He abstracted himself, looking upon his behavior
as ridiculous, making fun of his discomfort.

Orville was not an ideal travel mate, but it pleased Herman to
have a companion with scholarly interests. There was, in fact, hardly
another passenger aboard the steamer who interested him in the
least. Some were middle-aged ladies, mainly from England, in
search of mild adventures abroad. There were Americans as well—
one group of noisy Ohioans caught his attention. They belonged to
a Methodist association and hoped to see various religious and
archaeological sites in Turkey associated with Saint Paul, such as
Ephesus or Tarsus. Everything seemed to horrify them, especially
the state of the ship's lavatories. H.M. steered well clear of their
company.

A number of commercial travelers could also be found on any
boat like this. They seemed to know each other, keeping mostly to
themselves, drinking beer, playing cards, and smoking cigars into
the wee hours after dinner on the aft social deck. H.M. felt some
kinship with these men, but he stayed away from their games, as he
had no extra cash to gamble away.

The captain of this steamer was a portly Englishman called
Robert Taitt with a finely etched mustache. His florid cheeks often
puffed, and he exuded a kind of sweet odor—shades of Valentine
Pease, thought H.M. He found Taitt vaguely ridiculous, but he
made sure to befriend the captain of any ship on which he traveled.
Men of the sea recognize their brothers, and Taitt clearly liked Her-

man, reserving a place for him at his table. Taitt had sailed in the South Pacific as a young man, so he and H.M. had much to discuss. Young Orville also sat with them, at the captain's invitation, listening to these tales with amazement, especially Herman's stories of life among the Marquesans.

"These natives, especially in their youth, belong to no particular sex," said the captain.

The comment startled Orville, who said, "I don't really understand your remark, sir."

Herman put a hand on his sleeve. "He refers to the lithe and somewhat uniform nature of their bodies. The women are slender. The young men do not seem overly masculine, nor do they have beards."

Captain Taitt understood that Herman did not want to confuse the young theologian with further details.

"Your adventures among the Typees do almost beggar belief," said Taitt, with a wink.

"As I recall, there is a book about similar adventures," said Orville, in the cabin that night. "I can see in my mind's eye where it lives on my father's bookshelf, in his study. It is quite scandalous, apparently."

"I do believe your father is one of my readers," said Herman.

"You wrote this book?"

"I did, some years back. I was a young man at the time. Young men have fervent visions."

"I looked at this book myself," Orville said, with hesitation. "You had sexual relations with a young cannibal?"

"*Several* young cannibals."

The boy's expression froze in a mask of horror, and the lineaments of shock didn't disappear for some time. For his part, Herman saw he was going to enjoy his travels with Orville Clarence.

In early December the *Egyptian* entered blue Greek waters,

thrilling H.M., who had continued to reread Pope's *Odyssey* on the voyage out. It was not so good as his *Iliad,* but H.M. much preferred this epic to its predecessor. Pope had translated only half of the twenty-four books himself, or so Herman recalled. Associates had done the others, though H.M. assumed Pope had given them a final lick, as the poetry retained the author's usual wit and clipped brightness of style—the heroic couplet had never rested in safer hands. There was of course no other story like the *Odyssey,* which recalled the passages through time and turbulence of Odysseus, with his return at last to his wife, Penelope, in old age on Ithaca, and his resumption of his sacred marriage bed of oak, this rooted place, the center of his universe. In the end, Odysseus confessed all to his dear wife, then fell asleep, his story told: "He ended, sinking into sleep, and shares / A sweet forgetfulness of all his cares."

Herman had not experienced this "sweet forgetfulness" in his life, not yet. He seemed to remember everything, his multitude of sins, various moral infringements, lapses, and cruel unrequited longings. What he would not give to experience the ease that suffused Odysseus after all his wanderings.

The captain wakened him at dawn, as promised, on the morning of December 6 to see the outline of Mount Olympus against a pink-vermillion sky. It rose to nearly ten thousand feet, its prominent "nose," as the highest peak was called, dispersing rays of light through a glitter of ice: the home of the gods. A range of lower mountains was still crested with snow.

"So beautiful," Herman said to Taitt. "So *very* beautiful."

They docked in Salonika, a bedraggled port that reminded Herman of Paita, on the Peruvian coast. He spent the morning at a café near the harbor with Orville, and they drank granular Turkish coffee and ate bowls of creamy yogurt with honey. It was a cool but sunny day, with everyone out-of-doors, countless Greeks in local dress, some of the men with red conical hats. Young men walked arm in arm in the cobbled street and sat at tables devouring flaky pastries filled with dates and nuts and honey.

They would remain in Salonika for several days, a planned lay-over, and Orville and Herman had been invited by Captain Taitt to visit a friend of his in the interior.

"This is not to be missed," he said to Herman.

They rode for more than four hours over hilly roads to the house of John Abbott, a shipping agent from a wealthy Anglo-Greek family. He lived in a temperate valley, well below the snow line, with summer palaces on the nearby slopes of olive-tree-strewn hills. Tall cypresses shaded the road on either side. Herman admired the spring flowers everywhere in profusion and thought immedi-ately of Botticelli and his way of coloring the world so freely, so extravagantly. It seemed they had somehow stepped into a painting.

Certainly Abbott was a creature of fiction—perhaps a good sub-ject for a future novel, he thought.

Abbott had been educated at Harrow, the English boarding school, and now lived in Oriental luxury within a compound of dwellings surrounded by whitewashed stone walls and protected by armed guards in elaborate costumes. A wizened man called Alexio led them into the courtyard, his face like a brown walnut. He bowed and scraped, taking them to the master, who sat cross-legged in the manner of a pasha on a silk cushion, drawing smoke from a hookah. He was a handsome man of forty, strong-boned, tan. He had just returned "from a day's shooting in the Vale of Tempe, and whortle-berrying on Mount Olympus."

"I have never eaten a whortle," said Herman.

"I think you have, more or less," Abbott explained, summon-ing a small basket of them from a servant. The tiny blue berries brimmed the basket, and each of Abbott's visitors took a handful.

"*Vaccinium myrtillus,*" said Abbott, adopting a professorial tone.

"You call them blueberries or huckleberries in America, or blae-
berries in Scotland. Myrtles in France—but of course, the French
like to stand alone, don't they? Each fruit is perhaps a little different, but they come to much the same thing."

Herman had not encountered such opulence in a home before.
Everything appeared to be gilded or silk-covered, with vine leaves
over the lintels and colorful mosaics on the walls. The visitors were
each given rooms in a separate outbuilding, with a servant attached.

H.M. looked around the room with satisfaction, resting for a
while on a narrow but comfortable bed. After a warm bath, he put
on native clothing provided by Abbott and dined with the others
on brocaded pillows around a low table on a tiled floor. The table
offered a range of delicious things, including dates and nuts, sweet-
meats, and lentil dishes, with girls bringing sherbet in silver
cups. Scented candles burned, weaving the air with delicious
smoke. They drank prodigious quantities of wine, and later smoked
hashish.

This was the first time H.M. had smoked this particular plant,
and a trapdoor in his head seemed to open—not unpleasantly. A
rich, secure feeling flowed through his limbs, spreading to his fingers, to his toes. The world seemed impossibly benign and accom-
modating.

Herman asked Abbott to recall his schooldays, noting that Lord
Byron had attended Harrow.

"A few years before me, alas," said Abbott, lighting up. "He fell
madly in love with John FitzGibbon, the Earl of Clare."

"A fine chap, I believe," said Taitt.

"He was the love of his life," said Abbott.

"What about his sister?" H.M. asked.

"Well, I suppose he did love Augusta—perhaps to excess, given
their connection," said Abbott. "I will concede as much."

Abbott obviously relished the details of Byron's life at Harrow, and he regaled his visitors with stories about the young poet's struggles with his first tutor, his passionate opposition to the headmaster, and his difficulties with Lord Grey—who had rented the family estate in Nottinghamshire, and wished only "to sleep with the young peer whenever he came to visit the ancestral home."

Orville Clarence was wide-eyed, disbelieving—as he drew smoke from the hookah. He had never heard such things before, and he half doubted what he heard now. "The world is very wicked," he said, abruptly, choking on the smoke.

Abbott laughed heartily, filling the young man's glass with a clear liquor that tasted of licorice. "Wash the smoke down," he said. "Do you like Byron's poetry?"

"I'm not a reader of poetry, I'm afraid," Orville said.

"He is a theologian," said Herman.

"Ah, good! We have all manner of theology in this part of Greece. We have Christians and Sephardic Jews, and—of course— our Muslim brethren. And we have the gods of Mount Olympus, who chatter away in the still hours."

Herman felt expansive. "The Ottomans swept into the Kingdom of Thessalonica in the early fifteenth century," he recalled. "The infamous Sultan Murad II, I believe, was their leader. He had a harem full of dancing girls."

H.M. and Taitt drank more of the liquor, taking in breaths of smoke from the rattling hookah. A number of servants stood by, ready to assist in any way required.

Orville took another drink as well, wiping his forehead with a napkin, sweating though it was hardly a warm night. He found it difficult to follow the implications in Abbott's remarks, although the unholy undercurrents of the conversation were apparent enough, and troubling.

"Is it lonely, living in such remote quarters?" H.M. asked.

"I am never lonely," Abbott said. "Whenever I think of the alternatives, I thank the gods for my life."

"The whortleberries are wonderful," said Captain Taitt.

"There are many sweet things to taste, such ripe fruit every-where," Abbott said.

As midnight approached, Herman and Orville made their way to their rooms. The captain had retired an hour before, claiming exhaustion. Abbott had gone to bed some time ago, leaving his guests to "finish off the bottle," which they did. But the young the-ological student had grown unsteady, and he swooned in the door-way of his room, falling into Herman's arms.

Herman carried him to the bed and put a blanket over him— it would be very cold in the night.

The boy opened his eyes. "Thank you," he said, "I'm feeling rather . . . unwell."

Herman could hear a watermill that beat in a stream just beyond the wall of Abbott's compound. A scented candle burned in a dish nearby, giving off the earthy smell of myrrh, with overtones of vanilla. Through a small window he could see the night-blue sky, with its spray of stars.

"I have a most terrible thudding in my brow," said Orville, standing naked in the doorway of Herman's room, much the worse for wear.

"You must have a large glass of water," Herman said. "Help yourself, please."

He watched as Orville poured a glass from a clay jug into a silver goblet on a dressing table by the door. The boy had slender buttocks with barely a dip at the base of his spine.

"What was in that pipe?" Orville asked. "It wasn't tobacco, I'm quite sure."

"A kind of Oriental leaf," H.M. said.

Orville sat on the edge of the bed, unself-conscious about his naked state.

"Welcome to the world of Eastern splendor," Herman said. "Mr. Abbott has set himself up like a potentate."

"I feel so . . . unwell," Orville said.

"It will pass."

"I do not think Mr. Abbott is a Christian."

"Oh, I wouldn't go that far."

Orville stood, yawned, and stretched, then left the room.

Herman could not help but laugh.

The steamer pulled away from the dock in Salonika after dinner, on a bright crisp night with a yellow moon that made the water sparkle with a million facets. H.M. sat in a canvas chair on the bridge, with Captain Taitt beside him at the wheel, looking back at Mount Olympus, its icy peak against the navy-blue sky.

"You must leave the gods behind, I'm afraid," said the captain.

"It is the story of my life," Herman said.

They entered the fabled Hellespont two days later. H.M. stood on the deck with Orville, taking in the view—the rippling water and dun shoreline. Waves splashed against black rocks near the beachhead.

"It is well known," said Orville.

"Lord Byron swam these straits some time ago. He was about your age. He never forgot it."

"I would drown, almost certainly," said Orville.

"I also think of Leander, who swam these waters in a quest for Hero—although it's a myth, of course."

Orville looked at him blankly.

"Hero was a priestess," H.M. explained. "She lived in a tower on Sestos. Over there, I would guess." He pointed to a lonely scarp.

"Was Leander in love with her?"

"Painfully in love. It was agony for him. He swam the width of this strait each night, drawn by the light in her tower. Leander deceived her, however. He told her that, as a goddess of Aphrodite, she must not remain a virgin."

"I'm a virgin," said Orville.

"That is not the point, however. *Hero* was a virgin, but she allowed her suitor to make love to her. He stole her purity, her greatest treasure. But one night in winter a storm blew up in the strait. Stiff winds puffed out the light in Hero's tower, and so Leander could not find his way to her. He drowned in these waters. Hero was despairing, and she threw herself from the tower. A calamity all around, I would say."

"Love is difficult," Orville said.

"Have you been in love?"

"With Emily, yes. A rather . . . splendid . . . young lady from Boston, the daughter of a well-known clergyman, a friend of Father's."

"Oh dear. I married a splendid young lady from Boston. One should probably avoid the category."

"Do you not love your wife?"

"I love her fiercely. But it's as you say—love is difficult. I find myself unable to fit easily into the molds of husband and father, son, or brother. I live among a great menagerie of relatives, you see. I hide in my study most days. I write my books in the wheelhouse, taking my position from the stars. I swim the Hellespont every night, in a storm of sorts. I have only one light, which glows atop Mount Greylock."

Orville did not understand a word of this, but he hesitated to press for an explanation. H.M. was good company, and they had recently agreed to travel together through Turkey and Egypt, and to visit the Holy Land, too. As Captain Taitt had explained, this region, however holy, was dangerous. It was much safer to travel in pairs.

After four days in Constantinople, Herman and Orville boarded a Greek steamer called the *Alexandra* bound for Cairo, checking into the well-known Shepheard's Hotel—only eleven years old but already a legendary hospice on the banks of the Nile. It was a grand establishment, popular with Europeans, and known for its lofty ceilings, stone floors, and potted palms. In the rooms were iron beds with billowing mosquito nets draped around them. On a low table at the foot of each bed was a low table with fresh dates and water in stone jugs. A bottle of *zibib* stood by itself on another table, with a crystal glass beside it. With a mere clap of the hands, a servant in red pantaloons and white skullcap would appear, bow deeply, and offer assistance.

Herman and Orville had adjoining rooms, and they met on a shared veranda for drinks to watch the sun set on the Nile. A dozen feluccas with pink sails drifted by. Herman waxed eloquent, full of details about ancient Egyptian culture and religious practices. Orville nodded, but he did not like the idea that Osiris, as H.M. claimed, was "an earlier variant of the dying and resurrected god."

"Surely Osiris and Jesus have very little in common," Orville said.

"Have you read your Plutarch?"

Orville had not.

Herman explained the similarities. "Both gods died and were resurrected. They died for the sins of mankind. In both religions, believers count on the resurrection of a god to bolster the idea of their own immortality."

Orville was not open to such talk. "I don't believe he was born of a Virgin."

"His mother was a goddess, that's true. But myths never travel in exactly the same clothes. The form or shape of the tale is what matters—the backbone of the story. The pattern is the same: a god who dies, who is dismembered, returning from the dead with freshened powers. Remember that the Egyptians worshipped Osiris several millennia before Jesus . . ."

Orville disliked such talk. His life was devoted to the idea of Christ, and he did not really want this information about Osiris.

"Osiris moved among the people," Herman continued, "much like Jesus. He spoke to them in simple language, using parables. He was charming, I believe."

"Jesus was not 'charming.'"

"Nonsense. He was quite engaging, our Jesus. It was Paul who had no sense of humor."

"Saint Paul?"

"The man was a horror."

"How so?"

"His letters are full of strange notions. I don't know why they were put into the Bible."

"The Bible is God's word."

"It's an anthology of bits and pieces. They were gathered by a group of worthies in 325 AD."

"Nicaea."

"Yes, the Council of Nicaea. As you know, it was Constantine who ordered them to burn some three hundred 'heretical' versions of the Gospels."

"I heard nothing of this at Yale."

"Your professors are too pious, I fear."

Orville refused to question the authenticity of the Scriptures, and he told Herman so.

H.M. shook his head. "You misunderstand me, dear boy. It's not that I disbelieve. I believe too well, too much. I allow for everything. I refuse no advent of the spirit. God is everywhere, in every wind that blows. He shows himself in the sails of those feluccas, huffing and puffing. He inflates your chest, and mine."

The next day, a young dragoman took them to the Pyramids. H.M. mounted a camel, as did Orville, hanging on to the saddle for dear life as their guide led them in a large circle around this shining, improbable site.

That night, H.M. told Orville that he had found himself "oppressed by the massiveness and mystery of the Pyramids," overwhelmed by "awe and terror." Indeed, a tight feeling swelled in his chest, and he found it difficult to breathe. "It is all or nothing," he wrote in his journal. "It is not the sense of height but a feeling of immensity that arises. After seeing the Pyramids, all other architecture is but a pastry. As with the ocean, you learn as much about its vastness with a glance as you would in a month in the water, and so with the Pyramids. A glance will satisfy for a lifetime."

Herman had found he could only look at them for so long without closing his eyes. The brightness oppressed him. And the sun hung in the air like an orange kite over the desert. It was not terribly hot at this time of year, but the air tingled and wavered. Sands whirled around in a dry wind from the west. H.M. imagined himself at sea here, high in the crow's nest, swaying as the waves rose and fell beneath the pell-mell running ship.

As they traveled to Alexandria, H.M. assumed that everything else in Egypt, even the Holy Land itself, would pall beside the Pyramids. Nothing could compete with such terrifying monumentality. Exhausted by everything he had recently done, he lay in bed for two days in a dank hotel by the harbor in Alexandria, where an old goat coughed in the courtyard all night and H.M. could hear strange wailing in an adjacent room. Here he shared a room with Orville, but he was hardly able to listen to the young man as he talked of Jesus and the meaning of the Gospels in his most earnest and irritating way. Orville no longer interested him, but he would not abandon the boy until they visited Palestine, as promised. After that, he was on his own, and he made the point explicitly, saying he would go by himself to Italy soon after seeing the Holy Land. "Oh, I shall be fine," said Orville, his voice wavering.

They sailed from Alexandria on a relatively empty Italian ferry, disembarking at Jaffa. From there, they followed another scruffy dragoman on horseback to Jerusalem by way of Ramla—the legendary city that Napoleon had occupied briefly in 1799. The huge dome of a mosque appeared in the distance as they approached the city—its pale hump reminded H.M. of his great white whale. They spent the night in what Herman described in a letter to Lizzie as "an alleged hotel," a flea-ridden musty flophouse that doubled as a brothel. He and Orville shared a small iron bed, where they huddled against the icy night under a coarse wool blanket. While Orville slept, with granite imperturbability, Herman found himself anxious, with a peculiar tingling in his fingers and some invisible weight upon his chest. He felt impossibly old, and he believed he would die soon. He felt quite sure of that.

Toward morning, he got up to sit in a cane-backed chair at a bare table, where he examined the photograph of Hawthorne bestowed upon him by the master himself. It produced an overwhelming sense of loss, a little loss that stood in for the endless losses that marked Herman's life at present. The idea of writing more fiction seemed utterly hopeless now, although it felt impossible to give up writing altogether. It was his way of paying attention to the world, to the motions of his own soul.

He wondered if he should turn wholly to poetry.

He had been writing poems—or fragments of poetry—in his journal for some years, and the idea of writing a long poem in connected cantos was appealing. It could be his version of *In Memoriam,* perhaps, that wildly popular poem by Lord Tennyson—written in response to the loss of a dear friend. H.M. scribbled rough notes about his as yet unwritten sequence: "A sensitive young theological student visits the Holy Land. He has only begun to question his faith, although he can hardly bear to occupy this unstable ground. A lovely young man, of somewhat feminine aspect, he meets a young woman in the shadow of the Wailing Wall. He falls in love with her, attracted to her dark eyes, her sultry openness. The verses move briskly, a loose iambic tetrameter, assembling into cantos or books. The boy is scarcely aware of the complexities of love, its multiple demands. He meets representatives of different faiths, and this unsettles him. An older man arrives? This character seems, at first, to represent faith. He is strong, confident. They go into the desert together . . ." He broke off, unsure where such a story might go or what it meant.

He wondered if he could actually produce a narrative poem along these lines. It would require concentration of a kind that seemed beyond him at the moment. He would have to sacrifice a good deal of what, thus far, he had considered essential to the conduct of life. But, for the first time, he thought he might do this. He might fully embrace the life of poetry.

In early morning, within the high limestone walls of Jerusalem's old city, Herman walked into streets where vendors set up their stalls, getting ready for a day of hawking wares, foodstuffs, jewelry. He found the city affecting, with its sense of history as a honeycomb devoid of bees, the countless dark and empty pockets that once teemed with sweetness and light. Life was so perilous and brief, he said to himself.

He knew that, in a tick, he could easily be the *former* Herman

Melville, a faint memory in just a few minds. Another man, a traveler like himself from far away, would occupy this very space in Jerusalem at a future time. He would have no knowledge of Herman's furies, those insatiable creatures who flew after him day and night, pursued him to the edge of dreams and beyond. He would know nothing of Herman's ridiculous, sad, unquenchable desires. He might one day stumble upon a dusty book with Melville's name on the spine, but the letters would mean nothing to him.

The idea of "making one's mark" on the world was ludicrous.

There was some relief in this, however. Anonymity has its benefits, releasing one in peculiar ways. There was freedom there. But Herman was not free, as he could not shake Hawthorne's image from his mind. Not even the splendors of this ancient city replaced that burning visage.

Orville Clarence struck him now as a pitiful substitute for Nathaniel Hawthorne. It was Hawthorne he wanted, *needed*. And it was Hawthorne who consumed his thoughts as he rode on horseback, a few days later, through the dry Rift Valley along the Jordan River. He and Orville had joined a group of English travelers, most of them devout Christians from the Yorkshire dales, on a four-day journey led by an obsequious guide called Abdul-Hakim, which (he told them repeatedly as part of his habitual patter) meant, in Arabic, "servant of the wise."

But was Herman wise or foolish?

He was not a natural tourist, that much he realized. He could not wholly fasten his attention upon the surroundings, however spectacular, even searing in their waste and wonderful beauty. Barely clothed, he ran beside Orville into the buoyant water of the Dead Sea, floating on his back in the bright sun, much to the horror of the English Christians, several of whom covered their eyes. Abdul-Hakim had laughed, smoking a ragged cigarette, urging them on.

But he had not taken off his heavy robe. It was winter in the Holy Land—not a good time for swimming.

The party camped overnight at the base of the Judaean hills. They sat around a campfire of dry brush, where the talk inevitably turned to theological matters.

"It is wondrous to imagine our Lord in this desert," said one middle-aged woman called Margaret. She had iron-gray hair like a helmet and wore a thick woolly pullover.

"Indeed, Margaret," said her friend the Reverend Mr. Edgar Wilson, a retired Anglican clergyman from Wiltshire. "Our Lord may have swum in the Dead Sea, like our American friends, but He would not have been unclothed."

"Our Lord would have taken pleasure in His nakedness," said Herman, playing the devil's advocate. "I do recall that Simon Peter was naked when Jesus came along. He apparently liked to work without his clothes on."

Wilson corrected him. "This is true, but he put on his robe when Jesus appeared, so as not to offend Him."

"Our Lord was modest," said Algernon, another of the party, who rarely left Wilson's side.

"Our Lord was a man," said Herman. "Like all men, He had a body, and He used this body to absorb the world through His five senses."

"Our Lord was more than a man," said Wilson, with the barely repressed smile of men who have no doubt about the rightness of their position.

"Our Lord was God himself incarnate," said Algernon, tossing statements like darts, waiting to see if they stuck.

Herman said, "I do wonder if He was actually God—I mean, in a strict sense. We are all gods for that matter. He was the Son of Man, after all. So the Bible tells us."

This set the cat among the pigeons, and H.M. sat back to enjoy the scrabble that followed, with Orville taking the lead. He had only recently had a course on Christological matters at the Yale Divinity School, and he could cite chapter and verse, which he did for some time, captivating the English Christians, who nodded with approval at his erudition and added verses that bolstered the young man's arguments.

"Our Lord has many faces," said H.M., with detectable irony.

The others looked at him with horror, or sadness, or both. He was clearly a lost sheep.

"I do believe in Him," Herman said. "I really do. In fact, I've been a believer my whole life. It's just that I believe in everything. I reject nothing."

This was of course unsatisfactory to his companions, and more discussion followed, some of it quite heated, but Herman retired early, leaving them to it—including Orville, who apparently found Edgar Wilson appealing, even a kindred spirit. They would have to sort their way through this tangle of theology on their own.

Herman slept separately from the rest of the company, snuggling amid coarse blankets, resting his head on his rucksack, which made a hard pillow. He quite liked the snug desert floor, the dry air, and the billions of stars, which pricked through the high black heavens, revealing the light behind it. He fell into reveries of home, and believed that Lizzie lay beside him, her warm, soft body. Many a night in winter he snuggled close to her and was grateful for this union, its depth and even its drama. Life was there, in her arms, in the bosom of family. He walked in his dreams through Arrowhead, its many rooms, and was glad for their ample familiarity.

The cry of a desert bird awakened him, and at first he felt afraid. He was not in the Berkshires, not at home.

It was frosty, well before sunrise, and he pulled on a cap and his boots. Drawn by some irresistible impulse, he set off in the dark toward the Judaean hills, which rose steeply three miles to the west. He had noticed a ruined monastery in the low foothills, and was told that a community of monks once huddled there in silence, devoting themselves to prayer and meditation, but it had been empty for decades. He headed toward this site, wondering if he might find something of interest within those austere broken walls.

But he took a wrong turn and found himself on a steep ascent as the sky began to blush at the edges. Behind him, the Dead Sea shone, a black mirror in the distance. The desert itself was mauve and massive, unyielding in its immensity. He could see the far hills of the Jordanian desert to the east, a jagged outline of mountains beginning to yield to the light. H.M. recalled a line in Ezekiel about the "living water" that would flow from the temple in Jerusalem to the Dead Sea, making it fresh and bountiful—a source of life. That promise of fresh water had obviously not worked so well, as this was the least vital body of water in the known universe, a symbol of stagnation itself. Or was that a mistaken impression? He had liked floating in the briny sea, which supported him handsomely, refusing to let him sink. One could, perhaps, think of it in different ways, shifting the metaphorical frame.

He did not want to sink, not in life or death.

He wanted to rise and rise forever.

A passage opened in the cliff before him, and Herman's curiosity overwhelmed him. He adored caves, and this one had a lovely, fresh earthen smell, like a newly turned vase of clay. He could hear a lively sound within, the drip-drop of water, consistent, inviting. He moved forward into the dark recess without fear.

The cave dipped into the mountain, the descent steep, and he was hesitant, as it would be easy to stumble and sprain an ankle or worse. But his legs carried him along, his fingers grazing the cool northern wall, the wet sides of the cave providing guidance and comfort. A dizzying array of myths and antique allusions swirled in his head. Like Antaeus, Herman told himself, he felt strongest when attached to the earth. He also felt confident this labyrinth would not defeat or swallow him. No Minotaur lay breathing at the bottom, coiled and dangerous—as in the labyrinth at Crete. If anything, this was the Sibyl's cave—as mentioned in Virgil. Yes, this was *her* cave, Herman decided, fancifully. It could not have been here, of course; she had presided over a colony of Greeks who lived near Naples. But he felt her lively, welcoming presence in these depths, and he shouted, "Ah, my dear Sibyl. Speak to me!"

His voice poured down the throat of the cave and returned as echo, doubled if not tripled by the geological formation, which gathered and amplified this abrupt, loud, silly, vulnerable prayer.

Then a strange light appeared within the cave—a kind of glow.

Herman felt his heart stop. He was afraid for the first time. He would have guessed he was dreaming, but he touched the wall, and it was there, icy and immovable.

But fear vanished as the light increased, and rising from the depths of the cave he saw—was it possible?—the shape of a young man. A white gown of light surrounded him. His bright hair touched his shoulders, and his eyes burned a hole in the dark in the way great poetry burns a hole in a page. He walked toward Herman in a stately, graceful procession of one, slowly but with purpose. He was not more than eighteen or nineteen, a lanky and lovely boy, and Herman could see his legs below the knees, the delicate calves. His hands were milky and large.

He realized now that his life, especially his journeys, had been strangely full of elusive young men. Could this one be the ghost of Billy Hamilton, the boy from Manhattan, so fetching and fragile? Or was it Toby Greene, that wiry friend who had jumped ship with him in the Marquesas and disappeared into the bush, leaving him to fend for himself among cannibals? The fair skin, the hairless calves,

belonged most obviously to John Troy. The nose and high cheek-
bones seemed unmistakable as the figure drew nearer. Yes, he
thought, this was certainly Troy before him, or some phantom version. He wondered that his dreams, his waking dreams, had been so
populated by these figures, and how many of them—even the peculiar Orville Clarence—had touched him in affecting ways.

It was beauty, in its various forms, that appealed to him: masculine or feminine. He did not care about the gender. Beauty was,
indeed, a potent weapon—sharp-edged, ferocious. It could be tight
like a bow, all potential threat. It transgressed boundaries.

Then a voice arose, a fluting sound.

The ghost was singing, and with such sweetness that Herman
could not hold back tears of gratitude. He wept openly, as the voice
was so beautiful, being neither male nor female.

The lustrous figure didn't address H.M. directly, but he—or it—
paused for a moment in the passage, stood beside him, looked at him
as if wishing to speak, as if wanting to know what on earth brought
Herman Melville to a cave in the Judaean hills. He lifted one hand,
his right hand, and made a sign. It was not unlike the sign of the
cross, although Herman could not be sure. It was puzzling.

But he felt decidedly blessed. A warm glow rose in his belly, and
the taste of honey filled his mouth. Herman knelt, involuntarily. It
was as if he had to bow before this presence, which he knew was
holy, and he understood this encounter had come as a sign from
heaven.

The figure passed on, out of the cave, into the light, and disappeared.

At least Herman could find no trace of this vision when he
rushed to the mouth of the cave, hoping to see this ghost in morning light, whereupon it might lose its mystery. Might this be some
wayward shepherd boy or, perhaps, the child of a cave dweller?

The idiocy of that thought amused him. Such a figure would not blaze and shimmer, would not sing like a god.

Now the sun lifted itself above the hills, with the Jordan River flexing in the rush of daylight. A light breeze slipped among the weeds, rattled bushes, snagged and swirled, drawing lazy circles in the sand. The shrubs seemed to pulse, and H.M. recognized a single tree, a fig or almond tree, near the entrance to the cave. A large bird sat in its branches, and H.M. could not help but think this was the boy he had seen in the cave, however transmogrified.

The bird cawed, rose on leathery wings, moving in broken rings above the tree. H.M. could not tell what it was—a buzzard or booted eagle, some sort of desert hawk?

It didn't matter. Herman realized now that he would never die. He would live forever, in one shape or another.

Our Lord of Many Faces had given a sign.

Herman was no longer afraid of death, not now. The experience of the Judaean cave had changed that for good. He felt certain of it. Although he had not been lucky in his health, he hoped to live a few more years, at least. Somehow he had always imagined himself as an old man, heavy with years and accomplishment, walking the streets of New York or Boston, pausing to feed the pigeons, seeing everything, free of desire. That image came to him repeatedly in dreams: an elderly man walking alone in city streets, observant, alert.

He needed to cultivate leisure as Hawthorne had suggested, allowing the spirit to nest in him, to live and thrive. God seemed to speak to him, and he must learn how to listen.

Freedom from desire was the key, he told himself as he sat in his stateroom on the steamer in Liverpool, having secured passage

home on the *City of Manchester.* Hawthorne was coming for tea, to
say goodbye. As H.M. waited for his friend, he leafed through his
journal of the last year. The journey itself had been life-changing,
he decided. He had been so moved by the Holy Land—and his
experience in the Judaean cave—that he'd felt unable to absorb the
Roman world. He had toured on his own for several months, traveling to Naples and Rome, Florence, Venice, Milan, Genoa. He
had, indeed, traced the path of Byron, his dear Byron. He had felt
the poet's presence here and there, and he had plunged repeatedly
into the depths of *Childe Harold.* The idea of the Byronic hero
appealed to him: the man of the world, the exile, fully human in
every respect, civilized.

More and more, he wanted to abandon the groves of fiction
and to write poetry. He planned to compose a long poem of his
own, one centered on a spiritual quest. That much had become clear
to him in the Holy Land, and the journey had given him a subject:
the search for God. Was there, in fact, any other subject worth a
great deal of time and effort?

Hawthorne arrived late, apologetic and distressed. Sophia
was unwell, he said. It was a deep chest cold. The English weather
posed a grave threat to his family, he suggested, with only a slight
smile.

When a steward arrived with a tray of tea, Herman pressed a
small coin into his hand and thanked him. He poured a cup for
Hawthorne and one for himself. There was a plate of stale-looking
scones at the side, and he buttered them, handing one to
Hawthorne, who looked markedly older, even though it had not
been so long since he last saw him.

"You have gone all out," said Hawthorne, taking a bite.

Was he teasing Herman? A cup of lukewarm tea and day-old
scones was hardly going "all out."

"How was the Holy Land?"

"Holy."

"Did the Lord speak to you?"

"In His own way, yes. I think so."

"In what language?"

"An unknown tongue."

Now they talked of Jerusalem and Rome, though Hawthorne seemed remote, as if determined to hold himself aloof. His demeanor frustrated Herman, who wondered why Hawthorne could not open up to him, as he had that wintry night in Pittsfield, when they sat on the edge of the bed in Arrowhead for hours and poured out their hearts.

Hawthorne actually seemed afraid of him, which was absurd. What two men on the planet had more in common?

"I may not see you for a very long time," said Herman. "I want you to know that I value your friendship, more than anything in this world."

"That is kind of you."

"I mean what I say," said Herman, leaning toward him, trying to hold his friend's gaze.

Hawthorne's hands trembled as he lifted the teacup to his lips. He had to put it back into its saucer.

"I hope that, one day, we might find ourselves living in the same place again," Herman added. "That sojourn of yours in the Berkshires was all too brief. We hardly had time."

"There is never time."

"No, you're wrong," Herman insisted. "There is so much time, and so little to do. That is the great truth."

"I don't see that, not exactly." Hawthorne steered the conversation back to Jerusalem and Rome. He wanted to get what he called the "high points" of his friend's journey.

But Herman would not cooperate. "My dear friend," he said, "but *this* is the high point. This, now, here."

Hawthorne turned a shade of pink. He disliked these unmanly displays of emotion.

"I'm afraid Sophia will be needing my attention," he said, rising.

"Yes, of course. I'm sorry," H.M. said, and he rose, too. "One can never be too careful."

"Rather."

Hawthorne took a bold step and stood only a foot away from Herman, who lunged toward him, embraced him, resting his head on the older man's shoulder.

"All will be well," said Hawthorne, in his most priestly tones. He patted Herman on the back, cautiously.

"I suppose," H.M. said. He was weeping profusely, and he didn't try to suppress it.

Hawthorne said nothing, although he sighed audibly. A few minutes later, he simply nodded goodbye, looking away from his friend, closing the door firmly as he left the stateroom.

And this was the last time that Herman would ever see him.

How it is I know not; but there is no place like a bed for confidential disclosures between friends. Man and wife, they say, there open the very bottom of their souls to each other; and some old couples often lie and chat over old times till nearly morning. Thus, then, in our hearts' honeymoon, lay I and Queequeg—a cosy, loving pair.

H.M., *Moby-Dick*

LIZZIE

15.

I dearly hoped that Herman's travels in Italy and the Levant would revive his spirits: he needed this boost. He was exhausted in the months before he departed, and his sleeplessness, agitation, with bizarre shifts of mood, worried me gravely. He required a tonic— something strong. In the period soon after his return, I thought the excursion had done the trick, as he seemed oddly benign, prone to fits of smiling, even laughter. He rarely shouted at the children, and I never once felt threatened or judged by him.

He was "refreshed and edified" by the change of scene, so he claimed. And he did seem, somehow, a different man. Apparently he'd had some "illumination" while camping near the Dead Sea, though he could not quite describe what had happened except to say a shepherd boy had appeared to him in a cave.

A shepherd boy in a cave!

The fact that we had been forced by circumstances to abandon our life in the Berkshires had not made our transition to New York easier. We left Arrowhead without cheer, in heavily loaded wagons, arriving in Manhattan in November 1862. I felt quite uncertain about everything that lay before us.

I need not have worried about space, as there was plenty of room for everyone in the town house—our four children, Maria, and two of Herman's sisters—all of us arranged over three floors at 104 East Twenty-Sixth Street, a lovely brick house with a big yellow door (Herman insisted that we paint it yellow). In our first weeks there, Herman would sit on the stoop in his jacket and tie, smoking cigars. He seemed at home here, as the dry leaves scraped along the ground. This *was* home, really: his point of origin, the place where he must ultimately return.

We had no choice but to abandon Pittsfield, as the prospect of another winter in the country seemed beyond us; indeed, the last one had been arctic in its cruelty and protraction, with snow drifting against the doors, confining us for weeks on end. Icicles hung like prison bars in the windows, gleaming. The well froze in February, and the apples in our cellar dwindled. Our poorly stocked cupboards had to sustain us as best they could with canned vegetables and salted beef. Herman was of course used to hardtack from his seagoing days, so he didn't mind, shutting himself in the study, where he worked incessantly on what he called "a sequence of poems."

Poems!

I begged him to move to Boston, as my stepmother (after Father's death in 1861) would have welcomed us warmly—minus the meddling sisters Melville and *la* Melville *mère*. But H.M. never felt at home in Boston. He was a New Yorker at heart, and wished to die there. "It's a lovely place to expire," he said. "There is so little fuss. They simply add you to the heap of trash."

I agreed to return to New York as a way of liberating myself from the country, though I never let go of Boston—or the idea of

Boston. The prospect of better schools for the children also drew me to the city. Their education had run its course at Miss Williams's one-room shack in Pittsfield, where the children trudged daily through *McGuffey's Reader*—as Herman put it, that book only produced "McGuffey's morons." The boys, in particular, were lost in this dull and claustrophobic classroom. Malcolm played hooky, going off by himself into the woods for long walks, not unlike his father. Stannie was dutiful, almost to a fault, although he didn't do any work. On weekends he kept to himself in the south parlor, drawing cartoons or doing the puzzles in *Robert Merry's Museum* (even I had become addicted to that magazine, so I could not fault Stannie for his obsession).

Miss Williams was fine if your ambition was to keep a farm, but I dared to hope for more, even for the girls (Fanny, in particular, seemed bright as a new penny and worthy of cultivation). These were indeed the grandchildren of the chief justice of the supreme court of the Commonwealth of Massachusetts!

At first it looked as though Manhattan would improve Herman's mood. He cheered up at once, taking long walks in the afternoon, roaming galleries and museums, occasionally buying a cheap painting, a sketch, an etching. It was odd that a man whose eyes gave him so much difficulty wished to stare at pictures, but logic was never his strong point. This interest in art eluded me, though we visited the galleries together on weekends. In the evenings in our bedroom, Herman would rehearse the lectures he planned to give on the road, and I listened dutifully. This was, he said, his "new profession," that of lecturer, and he had lined up a fair number of engagements for the coming year—the lectures being on Italian painters, a subject he had researched on his travels. That he had no gift for public speaking was, from his viewpoint, a mild impediment.

Evert Duyckinck had argued that Herman's literary prospects would expand in the city, where he would rub shoulders with editors and critics. (Duyckinck himself was something of a gadfly and would attend the opening of an envelope if invited.) The remoteness of Pittsfield, he explained one evening over dinner, had put Herman at a distance from the engines of culture.

"You must make yourself relevant again," said Duyckinck.

"Is there any relevance?"

"The audience for your work has diminished of late."

"There was never an audience."

"You do yourself a disservice, Herman. I believe you had quite a following after *Typee*."

"It has been downhill since then, eh?"

"I like your stories very much."

"I'm no Hawthorne."

"In a sense, you improve upon him."

"In what sense?"

Poor Duyckinck. He could not get a leg up, and Herman seemed determined to shake off any attempt to encourage him. It did not surprise me that Evert lost interest in Herman's career.

The fact was that Herman despised literary fashion and would go his own way, "dollars be damned," as he liked to say. In any case, our financial situation had improved with the death of my father, and I kept a separate account in a Boston bank, on the advice of my brother Samuel. It was *my* money, after all, and I'd had about enough of H.M.'s profligate ways. I determined to see that we had sufficient funds to last through the end of our lives, having no wish to end up like Maria Melville, a tedious old shrew with fantasies about her "position" in society.

Of course Herman would have liked to support the family as a man of letters. But how? My father had encouraged him to return to stories like *Typee*. "A good seagoing yarn is what's required," he told my husband only a month before he died.

And now H.M. determined to write poetry!

He was a conventional poet, at best, as reviewers would later observe—the few who bothered to review his work.

Much to our chagrin, the sale of Arrowhead had not gone well, with our notice of sale posted in the *Berkshire County Eagle* like a badge of shame. Thank goodness for Allan, Herman's sensible younger brother, who bought the farm and thus preserved Herman's dignity—and the family name. Arrowhead would remain among the Melvilles, a house for anyone who needed a break from city life. In midsummer, we could still swim in Pontoosuc Lake or picnic in the shadow of Mount Greylock. Arrowhead would remain in our lives, a "touchstone," as H.M. called it.

All would be well, Herman assured us.

But all was never well. He had been in poor health for many years, and as he crossed the Rubicon into his forties, the problems multiplied. Headaches often left him in bed through much of the day. His back, which had not been good since he was thrown from a wagon near Pittsfield, worsened considerably. And he seemed prone to grippe, requiring frequent visits by a doctor.

And then there were his moods.

I had hoped that New York would cheer him, as it seemed difficult to be lonely in the midst of millions. But this proved illusory. H.M. remained very much alone, writing poetry in the mornings and wandering the byways of lower Manhattan in the afternoons, or sitting by himself on a bench overlooking the harbor. He dreamed of the sea, longing for another long voyage, though this was out of the question. No ship would add to its crew a man of ill temper who required constant medical attention.

The death of Nathaniel Hawthorne in the spring of 1864 pushed him into deeper spiritual waters. Mr. Hawthorne had been touring New Hampshire with his close friend, former president

Franklin Pierce, who had done much to promote the fortunes of his friends, securing him consulships abroad. Mr. Hawthorne died quite unexpectedly in his hotel room, just fifty-nine years of age.

The obituaries were somewhat excessive. Page after page celebrated the loss of a major American writer. The *Tribune* was typical: "Thus, one by one, the writers who have created for us an American literature, original and self-sustaining, are departing." Other writers were often mentioned as his associates in letters, including Longfellow, Whittier, and Sedgwick. But not a single article mentioned H.M. or referred to his friendship with the deceased.

"The great eraser has struck," said Herman. "I have vanished from the public mind."

Unusually for him, Herman scarcely left the house for weeks that spring after Hawthorne's death. He lay in bed most days until noon, unable to write, even to read. He had lately been less inclined to walk in the afternoons, as the garbage-removal crews had been on strike—a development that outraged Herman, who grew more imperious by the year. Trash mounded in the streets, raising an unholy stench that added to the reek of horse dung and bad sewage. New York had become, for me, a nightmare in every respect.

I began to think fondly of Arrowhead, recalling a place where in the spring whiffs of flowers and new grass came through the open windows on winds off the Berkshires peaks.

Mr. Lincoln's war only added to Herman's agitation and melancholy. He felt a sense of remoteness from the battlefront, deciding now he must write about this terrible conflict. He would compose "a sequence of poems that will tell the true story," he said.

But was there a "true" story? When he talked like this, he sounded more like a politician than an artist, tumbling into patriotic clichés. An artist never makes pronouncements; he makes art. But I kept these thoughts to myself, as such topics did not admit to easy discussion in our house. Opposition sent Herman into a rage these days, and I suffered most from each flare-up. There was no telling what he might do, how he might fling out, swiping me with the crude back of his hand.

Maria turned a blind eye to his eruptions. "You must not upset him," she would whisper.

Upset him! He was upsetting me!

As the war simmered, then boiled over, the idea of visiting the front consumed Herman, and nobody could argue that this was not done. Families regularly visited military hospitals and camps in Virginia, for instance, and there was every reason to attempt such a journey, as Colonel Henry Gansevoort, his cousin (with the Thirteenth New York Cavalry), was encamped in that state, in the town of Vienna—not so terribly far from Washington as the crow flies. Herman wrote to him, and a letter came by return of post, inviting him to visit. "I shall introduce you to General Grant," he said.

That was a bit of meat in the trap, was it not?

Thank God for Allan, once again. He volunteered to accompany Herman to Vienna. So they crossed the Potomac to Alexandria on a ferry, making their way on horseback to Fairfax, where they found the camp a few miles to the west of the village. A barricade of trunks cut from nearby pine forests had been erected, and the guard had been suspicious of these civilian visitors; but Herman showed him the letter from Colonel Gansevoort, and they were taken to Henry's tent. He was not there yet, so the Melville brothers introduced themselves to another officer, Charles Russell Lowell, the gallant nephew of James Russell Lowell, the poet from Boston who had belonged to my father's circle of eminent friends.

The threat of attack kept everyone alert, if not terrified. The guerrilla leader John Mosby and his men, all of them "irregular," as H.M. liked to say, hovered in the region, striking where and when they could. Materializing from nowhere, drawn from the local population, they attacked at night, cutting supply lines or disrupting transports. Herman thought one could write an interesting book about this young man, dashing in appearance, a brilliant tactician who treated captured prisoners well, especially if they were officers. He was known for quoting large passages of Byron by heart, and this endeared him to Herman. Journalists from the South called him the American Rob Roy—the patriot-warrior immortalized by Walter Scott (in the one book of his I could read without yawning). Mosby was a descendant of noble Scottish lineage, too: not unlike Herman, as H.M. himself liked to note.

Mosby was wildly popular among the genteel classes, a Southern legend. One night, while Herman was nearby, he swept into a wedding at a hotel near Leesburg—a daring appearance in the middle of a war! The Union Army had got wind of his possible manifestation, and they attempted to surprise and capture him. But the maneuver failed miserably. Not only did Mosby evade his would-be captors, but the Union suffered a number of casualties. Showing compassion, the owner of the hotel took special care of the injured men, letting them sleep in his rooms, feeding them, even cleaning their wounds. (A local doctor by necessity performed an emergency amputation in the hotel kitchen!)

H.M. arrived on the scene only a day later—with Colonel Lowell's patrol—to collect the dead and wounded from the hotel. It was the first time he had experienced war at first hand, or its consequences, and the ghastly scene left him shaken.

"So sad it was to see the poor young men," he wrote to me, "with limbs torn from their bodies, with hideous burns, with broken skulls patched together in a most haphazard fashion. I had no idea how to address or comfort them."

He and Allan pitched in, helping to pile the wounded into carts. They proceeded slowly over a rutted road, the injured men groaning. Several of them died en route to camp, one of them in Herman's arms.

"I will never complain about my life again," he wrote to me. "I have looked into the eyes of the Devil."

Henry Gansevoort arrived at last, taking H.M. and Allan into the surrounding country to visit Union encampments. It was at Culpeper near Lake Pelham that H.M. met U. S. Grant.

Even in the middle of war, the general entertained civilians in his tent. It surprised Herman that Grant was so unprotected, sitting at a makeshift desk with two or three aides beside him, chatting as he worked. The general offered cigars to his visitors, and they sat for half an hour in a circle, talking about the war and its progress. Herman brought up the campaign at Chattanooga, which had proved a turning point for the North. It was really a series of battles, following the tragic defeat of the Union Army at Chickamauga only a month before. Grant's men had opened a supply line to feed a famished contingent of men and horses, fighting off the Confederates at Wauhatchie. Major General George H. Thomas, fighting under the command of Grant, had issued commands from Grant that had been misunderstood (or willfully ignored). Thomas's men surged up Missionary Ridge, where they overwhelmed and destroyed the Army of Tennessee. This ended Southern control of that state, opening the door for Sherman's Atlanta campaign of 1864, which effectively ended the war.

In later years, Herman often recalled his conversation with Grant. He had tried to get the general to acknowledge his tactical brilliance at Missionary Ridge, but Grant had merely said, "It was all an accident, you see. I ordered them *not* to charge. They did so anyway. I never saw anything like it!"

This led to a discussion of the role that luck plays in life.

"Luck is everything," said Grant. "Or almost everything. I'm a man of very ordinary gifts, you see, but I persist, and I've thus far had astonishing luck."

Herman had not been so lucky in life, as he saw it.

Upon his return from the battle lines—his journal full of poetic fragments—H.M. worked in the evenings with a kind of intensity I had not seen in years as he assembled the poems of *Battle-Pieces,* which (to my astonishment) he persuaded the Harper brothers to publish. (They may have felt guilty about the fact that most copies of *Moby-Dick* had been burned in a warehouse fire not long after its publication, and they had not bothered to reprint in some years, letting the stock dwindle until only a few hundred remained.) It was, perhaps, their small gift to him, a gesture of reconciliation after years of rancor. In any case, they printed a mere handful of copies, which never sold and attracted few notices. Poetry, in Herman's case, became a way of life more than a living.

H.M. added a prose supplement to the poems, arguing for decent treatment of the South after the war. I didn't know why he bothered, as the gesture only alienated his core readership in the North. But he admired General Lee—failure always fired his imagination—and felt sorry for this sad, proud man undone in such a public way, a man of principle who came to Washington with hat in hand, pleading the case for his beaten Rebels. They were "not happy about their demise," as Lee explained to the U.S. Congress, but they nevertheless accepted defeat, wishing only due consideration of their position as freshly incorporated citizens.

That H.M. said nothing about slavery in this supplement surprised more than a few readers, but it was a subject he rarely broached. My father had of course been staunchly abolitionist, and I agreed with him. I could hardly bear the thought of millions of our fellow human beings in captivity like animals in a zoo. I had found myself engrossed by Mrs. Stowe's chilling novel about Uncle Tom, and I lived for days on end in its pages, in the world it summoned, so harrowing and vivid. As he would, Herman dismissed that eloquent novel as "popular sentimental rubbish." He had never actually been "for" slavery. It simply remained far from his daily concerns, something that lurked in the periphery of his vision.

Not unlike his friend Mr. Hawthorne, he believed resolutely in "evil." It was indeed this belief that led him, more and more, to rail against Mr. Emerson. "Waldo does not see it! He believes all will be well because we are good people at heart. Good people at heart!" This was "dangerous ignorance," he said, and it represented "the silly side of Rousseau that has somehow taken root in Concord."

Evil, he said, lay in those wagons of beautiful young men that he helped to load into ambulance carts in Virginia.

Herman grew increasingly petulant in the mid-sixties, when he had no real work. I don't think he wrote much poetry, though he sat diligently at his desk in our bedroom in the mornings. He seemed mostly to read, underscoring books as if he were about to sit for some examination. He kept voluminous notes, mumbling to himself or wiping his brow with a handkerchief. In the afternoons he set out for the Maze, which is how I thought of lower Manhattan. He staggered from street to cobbled street, standing on corners, sitting in parks in his sunglasses. Often he visited the Battery or Fulton Market. He loved the wharves, too, and liked to see the tall ships coming and going. Apart from Evert Duyckinck, he seemed without friends, and even Duyckinck avoided him.

In a pleasant if surprising turn, he decided that he *must* find employment, and the idea of working in the New York Custom House appealed. His grandfather had done similar work in Boston and Hawthorne had also worked in customs, as a weigher and gauger. This activity had been the subject of one of Mr. Hawthorne's better stories, as Herman pointed out. I confess, we breathed a little more easily when Herman got the appointment, thanks to the intervention of Johnny Hoadley, who had married Herman's sister Kate. In a way, Herman had already become a customs officer, wandering the docks by himself, noting what ships arrived or departed. Now he did so with official authority, prowling the Hudson every day but Sunday, inspecting cargoes and comparing ships' manifests against what actually lay in their holds.

He did an hour or two of paperwork each morning in a dismal office on West Street, sharing a desk with the port manager. But that gloomy chamber demoralized him, so he fled its airless confines, scooting along the embankment on foot. He might stop for a while to watch men unload coal in trundles from canal boats or stack bales of cotton from Southern steamers. There were any number of lumberyards, ironworks, and icehouses along the way, and several railway depots. The oyster market, at Tenth and Eleventh streets, also attracted him: it teemed with men who hoisted and filled containers, shifting millions of barrels each year. Herman was amazed by the commercial energies at work, with commodities, produce, and products of every sort being loaded or unloaded, shipped and sold. "Work," he said one evening over dinner in one of his pontificating moods, "consists of the removal of objects from one space to another."

"You're a philosopher," I replied.

What most interested him, of course, was the variety of ships that arrived from every part of the world—cargo and passenger ships, steamers, brigs and schooners, barks and cutters. They docked in serried fashion below Tenth Street, a forest of masts and thick smokestacks, bowsprits jutting over the piers, decks strewn with bleached nets and tackle, sails hung to dry, rigging of every kind, jackstays dangling. It all brought back a glorious era in my husband's life—his time as a green boy on packets or whalers, a lost adventurous dreamtime in the far islands of youth.

Herman's job was nonetheless a demanding one, as he supervised any number of inspectors. The landing of cargo, in general, concerned him, although one could measure and control only a small portion of this activity, as he liked to say. He would occasionally board a foreign steamer to examine the baggage or check passenger lists, though freight of any kind was mainly his concern, as tariffs were at issue. His gaze moved broadly over portside activities, looking for anomalies, chinks in this invisible fence erected by customs. It could be exciting, as ships often tried to hide munitions or contraband of one kind or another. "I'm on the lookout for brigands," H.M. would say, with a touch of melodrama.

At night, he left his life on the docks behind him, settling to his desk, where he worked on *Clarel*—which he referred to as "the longest poem in the history of humankind." I didn't dare disturb this activity, however pointless. He had earned the right to sit there at his desk in our bedroom for as long as he wished, a lamp flickering beside him, his cigar whitening to ash, retaining its fragile shape for a time, before crumbling into dust around him.

I realized, as I watched him working and thought about our long life together, that it was all dust in the end, of course.

Everything was.

*The report was this: that Bartleby had been a
subordinate clerk in the Dead Letter Office at
Washington, from which he had been suddenly
removed by a change in the administration. When I
think over this rumor, hardly can I express the
emotions which seize me. Dead letters! does it not
sound like dead men? Conceive a man by nature and
misfortune prone to a pallid hopelessness, can any
business seem more fitted to heighten it than that of
continually handling these dead letters, and assorting
them for the flames? For by the cart-load they are
annually burned. Sometimes from out the folded paper
the pale clerk takes a ring—the finger it was meant
for, perhaps, moulders in the grave; a bank-note sent
in swiftest charity—he whom it would relieve, nor eats
nor hungers any more; pardon for those who died
despairing; hope for those who died unhoping; good
tidings for those who died stifled by unrelieved
calamities. On errands of life, these letters speed to
death.*

Ah, Bartleby! Ah, humanity!

H.M., "Bartleby, the Scrivener"

DENIQUE COELUM

16.

"Heaven at last."

In Latin, it was the motto of the Melville clan, as H.M. knew. He had immersed himself of late in the history of his family, and their independence of mind was a deeply ingrained trait. King Edward I had demanded the fealty of all Scots landowners, gathering the names of no less than twelve Melvilles—from Fife and Stirling, Aberdeen and Peebles. He considered it of utmost importance to gain the allegiance of this eminent clan. Years later, Sir John Melville of Raith had been a favorite of King James V, and this led to the granting of a broad demesne in Fife, including an estate at Murdocairnie. But Sir John supported the Reformation and had conspired in the assassination of the powerful Roman bishop of St. Andrews, Cardinal Beaton. The king had him executed in 1548, although His Majesty wept at having to follow through with the hanging. He apparently loved John Melville, who had "shimmering hair like flax," according to one contemporary source, but the king adhered to the rule of law with an icy love that could be neither dismissed nor ignored.

A later Melville in Fife, Sir Robert, had been a beloved ambassador at the court of Queen Elizabeth I. Yet he could not restrain himself in the face of injustice, and he protested the murder of Mary, Queen of Scots, whom he had personally known and admired for her piety and shrewd intellect. The Virgin Queen had been shocked by this disloyalty, and she threatened him with imprisonment. "I cannot countermand my conscience," he had told her.

She sent him back to Scotland, which she claimed was "punishment enough."

Herman allied in his heart with these marvelous forebears, all men of independence and character, who went their own ways despite the hostility or indifference of those in power.

Through hard decades he had kept his eye on the horizon, moving forward at his own pace, losing step with his contemporaries. Most critics brushed him aside as an irrelevancy—a mad fellow who toppled off the path somehow; he was lost to most readers. But he had summoned a vision: not once but time and again. The novels lay on his shelf as evidence for the defense. To remind himself of his achievement, he occasionally plucked a volume from the shelf in his bedroom, scanning the thick, creamy pages with their dust of mites, finding passages as perfect as any in the language. If readers failed to see the glories of his work, so be it. He did not require their assent or confirmation.

He had traversed the globe, in reality and within his imagination, gone inside and out. He was a voyager, and he believed old men should continue their quest, find fresh passages. He would find his, he felt quite certain about this.

.   .   .

Evert Duyckinck introduced Herman to the busybody journalist and quondam poet E. C. Stedman in 1865. H.M. found something agreeable in the young man, with his hand-tailored English suits and broad-brimmed hats—a literary affectation. Stedman seemed to know everyone in the New York literary world. Indeed, he buzzed about Manhattan like a bee in midsummer, sipping from a hundred flowers a little bit of pollen, depositing this treasure where and when he would, creating alliances and honeycombs of interest. The golden nectar of fellowship gleamed in his presence.

For a solitary man like Herman, it was useful to know such a person.

Stedman reminded H.M. of Hawthorne, with his dark good looks and abundant hair, his towering frame. Sympathetic in many ways, he had read Herman's shelf of books with great care, culling bits and pieces, which he alluded to in various conversations. He came for tea on Sunday afternoons whenever he could, bringing news of the larger society of books and bookmen. Sometimes Duyckinck would join them, and they had a jolly time. Herman came alive in these moments, and he looked forward to them, as they formed a lifeline with his literary past and a possible link to the future as well.

One day Stedman mentioned his friend Walt Whitman, passing along to Herman a volume of poems called *Leaves of Grass*. These rambling, lush, brilliant verses—if they could indeed be called verses, as the poetry adhered to no obvious meter or rhyme—appealed to H.M. in ways that scandalized and thrilled him. How could Whitman write in such a frank, evocative manner? He found the quality of phrasing almost too good, too original: a slap on the cheek of every poet who had gone before him. It made Herman's own efforts at verse composition seem woefully conventional, even boring. A sequence called "Song of Myself" struck Herman as memorable if sprawling and lubricious. But the eternal spirit gleamed in these lines. Here was real embodiment: transcendentalism of a kind Emerson could only posit in the most fanciful ways.

H.M. admired the lines about twenty-eight young bathers, all hale and lusty young men seen by a woman from afar. These self-delighting fellows reminded him of the tribal boys he had found among the Typees and he had bathed among so long ago and far away:

> The beards of the young men glisten'd with wet, it ran from their
> > long hair,
> Little streams pass'd all over their bodies.
>
> An unseen hand also pass'd over their bodies,
> It descended tremblingly from their temples and ribs.
>
> The young men float on their backs, their white bellies bulge to the
> > sun, they do not ask who seizes fast to them,
> They do not know who puffs and declines with pendant and
> > bending arch.
> They do not think whom they souse with spray.

On Stedman's next visit, Herman thanked him for the book in the most generous terms. "I admired it greatly," he said. "In fact I do believe Whitman puts everyone else to shame."

"I shall arrange a meeting," Stedman said.

"What do you mean?"

"I have met our Mr. Whitman. He's a strange but interesting fellow."

"I should think so."

"Within a month, you shall meet him."

Herman did not say no.

Indeed, they met only two weeks later, drawn by Stedman to one of the poet's favorite haunts, a dark underground tavern on Broadway called Pfaff's, known for its ales in pewter flagons and an array of Rhine wines. Its owner, Charles Pfaff, an immensely fat German with a bristle of short white hair crowning a massive head, invariably stood at the bar like the captain of a ship. The adipose folds of his neck inflated, bulging over a stiff collar in pink folds like an overfed baby. His geniality drew a large crowd most days for lunch or dinner, and he remained open into the late hours for stragglers, who gathered at long tables to discuss cultural topics while eating chops and drinking.

Herman arrived late on the appointed afternoon, finding Stedman at a table in a corner of the vaulted chamber under a sconce. To Herman's relief, Evert Duyckinck was there, too, in his tweed suit, wearing a pince-nez, looking every bit the editor of the *Literary World*. Duyckinck hunched in conversation with a broad-backed fellow in a Norfolk jacket, white shirt, and pink scarf; this man— Herman assumed it must be Whitman—seemed roughly the same age as himself. His fine silver hair and beard were impressive, and the poet's eyes shone with intelligence and wit, winking like stars with a blue-gray sheen. His fleshy nose, though large, was hardly in disproportion to a generous face.

As he approached the table, H.M. sensed a dangerous quality in the poet, a sense of license and decay. His hands were those of a laborer: calloused and coarse, with nicotine-stained fingers. His smile revealed sharp yellow teeth, a few of them badly discolored, almost black. He had a harsh, booming laugh that bordered on the manic.

Whitman would, Herman supposed, have few boundaries. One could see that in the poetry, with its refusal to set limits. He opened himself to the world, and the world flowed through him. He was more conduit than keeper of a sacral flame.

"Ah, Melville," said Stedman, rising. "You found us!"

Duyckinck smiled blandly.

"This is Walter Whitman," Duyckinck said, gesturing.

Herman extended a hand to Whitman, who shook it without enthusiasm, though he smiled warmly enough.

Herman said, "I have indeed read your book, Mr. Whitman."

"It is many books, I suspect," Whitman said, "all hiding under one cover."

"*Leaves of Grass*. A good title."

Whitman sighed with pleasure. "I have so few readers. I'm happy to meet one of them."

"You have no fewer readers than I," said Herman, suppressing a chuckle.

"You have *no* readers," said Stedman, joking. But the remark brought only a frown to Herman's face. He remembered now why he generally avoided literary company.

Duyckinck shook his head, displeased by Stedman's foolishness.

"I'm sorry, Herman," said Stedman. "I can't resist a bit of a joke now and then."

"Some jokes," said Duyckinck, "are better than others."

"And the same can be said of books," said Herman.

He took a chair as Duyckinck waved to a barmaid, ordering four flagons of ale for the table.

"The ale is good here, and there are wines as well. Speak now or forever hold your peace."

"Ale is fine with me," said Herman.

He now wished he had not come. It was easier to meet some-one for the first time alone, and he could already feel Stedman's dampening effect on this encounter. At least Duyckinck offered a measure of safety, with his familiar face and genteel manners. A real conversation with the poet might have been possible under different circumstances, but that would not happen now. Once again, he would fail to connect with a spiritual kinsman.

"Mr. Melville is a poet, too," said Duyckinck. "An excellent poet, in fact—much better than the critics know."

"I must confess that I read an early novel or two of yours, Mr. Melville. Indeed, I reviewed them—I was working for the *Eagle,* then. I fear my reviews did not help your novels. It is a difficult business."

Herman could feel his earlobes sting. "It has been a while since I thought of myself as a novelist," he said.

"I've been instructed by Mr. Stedman—your advocate and friend—to read *all* your novels," Whitman said. "They have peculiar names."

"*Typee, Omoo, Mardi,*" said Stedman.

Whitman nodded. "I remember *Typee,*" he said. "Full of pretty cannibals, as I recall."

"You should try *Moby-Dick,*" said Herman, "if, indeed, you can find a copy. They are quite rare. There was a fire at the publishing house."

"My poems are always setting the publishers on fire," said Whitman.

Stedman intervened. "Herman's novel is about a white whale."

"A sperm whale," said Duyckinck.

"A lovely phrase," said Whitman, repeating it, with an emphasis on *sperm.*

Herman shifted the subject to a safer realm. "I believe you know Mr. Emerson quite well—"

"Not so well."

"But he wrote a fine comment on your book."

Whitman looked away, embarrassed. "He complimented my verse in a letter. I used it on the book, as a calling card. Very naughty of me."

Duyckinck nodded. "He was not happy about it, no?"

Whitman said, "We met face-to-face in Boston—some years later. He forgave me for my indiscretion, and suggested that I remove certain stanzas from my latest poems, what he called the 'indecent ones.' I refused, of course."

"I admire your indecency," said Stedman.

Herman smiled faintly. He liked these stanzas, too, but he would not say it aloud. One could not be too careful in public. It was bad enough to be seen in a well-known bar with Walt Whitman himself.

Duyckinck smiled as the waitress set a flagon of ale before each man. He had not enjoyed the drift of this conversation and seized the reins, offering a brief disquisition on what he called "literary trends" in the United States. Whitman apparently had no interest in these trends, and he sank into his flagon of ale, asking for a second round before the rest had taken more than a few sips.

Duyckinck had just published an edition of the poems of Philip Freneau, and he gave a lengthy disquisition on this poet, whom he referred to as "a neglected hero of American verse." Whitman yawned as the conversation moved in slow circles, with Duyckinck stirring the pot with the ladle of his monologue. He noted that Freneau, like Herman, had gone to sea at one point, and that he had lived in the West Indies.

"I have not lived in the West Indies," said Herman.

"Nor I," said Whitman. "We have this in common."

It was obvious that Herman Melville and Walt Whitman would not strike up a friendship, though they had shared many things, including the year of their birth and New York City, which each man called home. But Herman was a patrician by instinct and breeding, and Whitman was the son of a carpenter ("not unlike Jesus," he would say). Stedman had told the poet about Herman's distinguished lineage before his arrival, and the mere fact of this difference in backgrounds formed an invisible barrier over which neither man could easily climb. And they chose not to climb it, preferring instead to listen to Duyckinck's assessment of the literary scene and the neglected poetry of Freneau.

The monologue, at last, dribbled to a close.

"I look forward to further books of poetry by you," said H.M. to Whitman, after an hour or so, getting unsteadily to his feet after a second or third round of ale. "They are brave poems, yes. They are . . . *physical* poems, and they celebrate the affections. I applaud you."

Whitman stood to embrace him, kissing Herman on the lips, much to his distaste.

With that, H.M. staggered through the smoky room and disappeared.

In 1888, Herman felt a peculiar, undeniable urge to travel somewhere, *anywhere*, by sea. As he grew older, the pattern of life had its own complexity and interest for him; but it seemed important now to examine this pattern again—from outside, if possible. The sea was always otherwhere for him. It was a non-place, time out of time. It was a version of eternity.

For twenty years he had padded about the docks in lower Manhattan in sunglasses, a frock coat, and wool seaman's cap, boarding ships of every kind and origin, checking cargoes, meeting the crews, talking to officers and ordinary seamen who fetched tales of wondrous places, times, people. In the afternoons, in retirement from the Custom House, he would sit on a bench above the harbor at Battery Park, watching vessels come and go, their flags aloft and snapping, each of them a floating metropolis, a world unto itself. The smell of salty wind never lost its appeal for Herman, and he could recall morning watches aboard the *Acushnet*, the dazzling pitch and roll of the ship as he leaned over the prow and figurehead, with the blue-green swell and swish of waves below.

That was raw and tingling life, and he could imagine nothing better.

He envied his younger brother Tom, who had made a career of the sea, rising to the rank of captain (before taking over as governor of Sailors' Snug Harbor—a home for retired seamen). Once Tom had invited Herman along on a voyage, in the summer of 1860—nearly three decades in the past now. He could hardly have wished for better circumstances, with "a noble ship and a nobler Captain." They planned to circumnavigate the globe, rounding Cape Horn—that haunted place, with its brackish shoals, the sharp rocks like blades of bone. The voyage began in Boston Harbor, and they plied their way to San Francisco—a journey of a hundred days. From there, they had planned to proceed to Manila and beyond, chasing the sun as it set over the Pacific. Herman nursed a fond hope of seeing Hawaii again—it would be like reentering a dream.

The *Meteor* was a frisky and well-designed clipper, with the finest rigging and brightest brightwork Herman had ever seen. They sailed into a succulent morning air off Massachusetts, making straight for the Bermudas and beyond. Herman had leaned out to the flying-boom end in his summery clothes—recalling times when he had sailed into balmy seas in the South Pacific aboard the *Acushnet* or the *Lucy Ann* or, more recently, into azure Spanish waters aboard the *Egyptian*. Each passage had imprinted itself in memory. Now the *Meteor* caught a rash of trade winds that blew them into warm tropical waters. By the third week in June the Southern Cross rose in the night sky.

This counted among the happiest journeys of his life, with Tom in command, so wonderfully benign, eager for his brother's company. H.M. felt under no obligations of any kind—this was pure holiday. He lingered in his cabin for much of the day or stood beside his brother at the bridge, often assuming the role of able seaman, keeping a lookout. After dinner, in Tom's roomy aft quarters, they would play chess and drink brandy, smoking earthy Partagás cigars that Tom had acquired in Boston from a ship that had been in Cuba.

Tom was no literary man, but he listened sympathetically as Herman talked at length about books by writers he admired. Sometimes H.M. read aloud from Milton and Byron—he retained a fascination for *Childe Harold*—or tried out different translations of Homer's *Odyssey* on his brother, who rarely commented, although he found Pope's rhyming "somewhat too consistent"—a remark that H.M. treasured.

That Odysseus had failed to find Ithaca after so many years struck Tom as "a sign of weak navigational skills."

In early August the *Meteor* encountered "gales, with wet snow, rain, sleet, mist, fog, squalls, abominable head-winds," as Herman recorded in his journal. On August 8, he noted a view of the Cape just before sundown: "In a squall, the mist lifted & showed, within twelve or fifteen miles of the horrid sight of Cape Horn (the Cape proper)—a black, bare steep cliff, the face of it facing the South Pole—an invisible continent of ice and despair." They tacked to the southwest, skillfully, with Herman admiring his brother, a man of steady nerves under pressure. Steady nerves had never been part of Herman's makeup.

Every journey by sea thus far had yielded a book of some kind, and he required material, a fresh viewpoint. One only had to give it time, and things would occur—memorable things—as when Ray Walton, a handsome red-haired boy from Nantucket who had

caught Herman's eye, slipped from the main topsail only a day after
rounding the Cape. Falling, he struck his head on one of the spars
and landed, a dead man, nearly at Herman's feet. Ray's closest friend
aboard the *Meteor*, another boy from Nantucket called Ned,
crouched over the body of his friend and wailed.

Ned later told Herman that he had lost his best and only friend.
"His mother will go crazy," he said. "She did not want him to go to
sea. She was afraid something terrible would happen, and it has."

Herman wept, putting a hand on the boy's shoulder. He could
barely stand the pity of it.

Only a couple of hours later came the burial at sea. Tom read a
brief passage from the prayer book before half a dozen men tipped
the plank, allowing the body to slip from the poop into gray folding seas. Mists swirled, and within seconds Ray Walton of Nantucket was gone forever, dropping from the collective memory of
the crew within days. Only Ned continued to grieve for his friend;
he wandered the ship like a ghost for a month or so.

"Death is indeed the King of Terrors," wrote H.M. in his
journal.

He made a point of sitting with Ned in the evenings, talking to
him, letting the boy weep in his presence. The boy reminded him
of himself as a child of twelve, after the loss of his father. He had felt
impossibly sad, even desperate at times, but nobody had talked to
him. They turned to their affairs with cruel efficiency, relieved that
somebody else had died and not themselves.

Rarely a day passed for Herman aboard ship now without
thoughts of death. He had a feeling he might die in warm Pacific
seas—that would somehow be fitting, as John Troy was probably in
the vicinity, probably deceased. (Over the years he had written a
few letters to John, trying different addresses, but no response had
been forthcoming.) He dreamed one night that he was tipped overboard from the poop, with the sound of his brother's voice fading

as he fell. After swimming for a while in murky seas, he washed up on black rocks. Exhausted, he clambered onto a boulder-broken shore, where he sat amid goldenwrack and beach debris: driftwood, jawbones, gull feathers. Finding himself whole, he stumbled toward the distant hills, where he came upon a bamboo-and-thatch hut at the edge of the jungle. Inside was John Troy: he had somehow managed not to age. In fact, he looked younger than when Herman had last seen him. They embraced, in tears, and fell together onto a tapa mat on the floor of the hut.

Herman disliked such troubling dreams. They unsettled him for hours after waking, often ruining a whole morning. He lived too often in dreams and wished he could stay in the present, could allow the full weight of reality to press upon him, to buoy him. But this was hard to do, and he was weak. His mind drifted into fearful places.

The King of Terrors continued to haunt him throughout this journey. He felt weirdly disembodied at times, leaning over the taffrail, watching the swill of the wake, gulls swooping, with sails snapping behind his back. It seemed as though he were looking down at himself, a speck on the aft deck, a tiny integer in some complex universal equation. How had he come to such a juncture?

He had made a huge effort, writing books in a blaze of focused energy, an infernal bonfire that consumed his heart and mind. It had been harrowing and heroic, and yet he—or his work—had turned to ash before his own eyes. Now in middle age, aboard the *Meteor*, white hairs had begun to mingle with darker ones in his beard. His skin had become a sheet of parchment, written on by time, in profound lines. His brow was a stanza of grief. He could not stick with anything—could hardly listen to his brother as he mused about the trade winds, recalled earlier voyages, or plotted a course. Tom had never known their father, had never had the kind of intimate contact with their mother that Herman had suffered.

Indeed, Tom—whether or not he realized it—had been set free in the world, left to his own devices, and this had made things easier for him. He was a free man, able to imagine a life for himself beyond the encroaching legacies of Melvill or Gansevoort—these boundaries and lifelines that had guided and restrained H.M. for more than four decades.

Herman relished his free time aboard the *Meteor*, reading favorite authors, whose books he had stuffed into his trunk before embarkation. After a certain age, he decided, one preferred rereading to reading. He waded deeply into Chapman's Homer—which he lately considered superior to Pope's version. His *Odyssey*, in particular, had become a touchstone as he traveled the watery byways himself, at a loss to find home. He often thought of Odysseus weeping beside the shore, desperate for Penelope, longing to connect to his beloved son, to repossess his island kingdom. What H.M. needed was an Athena to plead with Zeus on his behalf, as she had done for Odysseus. A little supernatural aid would come in handy, he told himself.

Inspired by his reading, Herman wrote fragments of poems in his journal as the ship sailed northward along the coast of Peru, toward California, with a layover in Mexico. But this poetry felt unsatisfactory—shards of disassembled light. He fantasized about writing an epic of the Americas—a better poem than the one that Joel Barlow had done, his portentous *Columbiad*. Herman had recently gathered a volume of poems, the best of his recent work, and hoped that upon reaching San Francisco he might open a brown envelope and see, for the first time, this book in print. The prospect was a lure that drew him toward that western city.

But no such package awaited him in general delivery in San Francisco, only a brief note from Evert Duyckinck. "I'm afraid the market for poetry—at present—is much weaker than expected,"

Duyckinck wrote. "These are good poems—I have no doubt of this—but they have not sparked enough interest."

Not sparked enough interest: the phrase would haunt H.M. over the years to come.

The owners of the *Meteor* cut short the voyage, summoning the ship back to Boston, thus ending its round-the-world journey. For his part, Tom had grown used to such changes of plan; but Herman—in a fit of disgruntlement—decided to return to New York overland. He felt uneasy about wasting time, and planned to redouble his efforts to get his poems into print, convinced of their value. He would not allow the narrow-mindedness of a few editors to stymie him. It was, after all, not terribly expensive to publish a volume of poems—the typesetting costs were low, and the paper outlays hardly seemed insurmountable. If he must, he would pay for the book himself, counting on the reviews to draw interest to his verse.

He wrote to Duyckinck on his last night in California: "The Pacific journey is aborted, and I am coming home. I plan to write more poems en route, thus bolstering the current volume, and we shall find a publisher! Mark my words."

The last decades had been an uneasy affair, after the death of Malcolm in 1867. The Melvilles would, of course, never forget that awful day, preserved in the amber of memory. In grief, they had circled each other warily for years, although their agony formed a bond of sorts. They learned how not to disturb each other, running in separate grooves. In certain respects, H.M. grew milder in old age—less prone to bouts of temper, less miserable about the way his literary career had unfolded, or failed to unfold. He had come to feel at home in poetry, which was neatly removed from commercial expectations. Nobody expected any money from the endeavor, and the prospects for fame, as a poet, were slight. All one required was a handful of grateful readers, and H.M. could summon those among his circle of literary friends.

He was a man of routines, and poetry had afforded a channel, a creek bed into which he poured himself wholly. This was only possible because he had given up prose altogether. Fiction was more difficult for him, requiring a kind of sustained attention he could no longer summon. He could plausibly write poems after work: each poem was a discrete universe of feeling and thought. *Clarel*, his epic about the search for love and meaning in the Holy Land, had been a quiet obsession for several years, as he "adjusted" the stanzas most evenings after dinner, sitting at his heavy burled mahogany desk, sipping brandy and smoking cigars. As usual, he built towers of relevant books around him, reading treatises on Protestant theology or histories of the Levant. He immersed himself in Jewish folklore and once consulted a rabbi about a point of Hebrew etymology. He made notes about the archaeology of the region, its flora and fauna. Of course he kept other long poems beside him, for inspiration—marking up his personal copies of Scott's *Marmion* and Tennyson's *In Memoriam*. He lingered happily in the witty passages of Byron's *Don Juan*—a work so radically different from his own but no less inspiring.

Once finished, Herman submitted it to various publishers, who uniformly turned their backs on this ungainly epic. It was a bequest from Herman's dying uncle Peter in Albany that made it possible for him to issue the long poem privately in 1876—much to the consternation of Herman's daughter Bessie, who understood the precarious state of the family finances and resented the selfishness of her father's decision.

Bessie found him alone at the breakfast table with a newspaper spread before him.

"May we have a word, Father?"

He looked up dazedly from his paper. He felt sorry for poor Bessie, so crippled by arthritis that she could barely cross the room without the aid of a stick. "Only a single word, my dear?" he asked, unable to resist a facetious turn.

"I don't see why we should spend our money on this poetry of yours. Surely a regular publisher would do it."

"I have tried the regular publishers. They have found my work . . . irregular."

"Surely it's a *good* poem, and will find an appropriate outlet in due course."

"In due course?" H.M. rose from the table, red-faced. "I have spent many years on this project. *Many* years."

"But can we afford it?"

"I have no idea." He sighed, relaxing a bit. "What you must understand is that poetry has a small audience in this country." He was shocked by how white his daughter's hair had become. Her life had come to nothing.

"I don't mean to trouble you," she said.

"But you do, Bessie. You *mean* to trouble me."

"I am sorry, Father. I shall leave you in peace."

"Sorry is the right word," he said, and sat down again, leafing through his paper.

The news, as usual, was fraught with tension. A contentious presidential election was under way at the moment, pitting Rutherford B. Hayes (a former general in the Union Army from Ohio) against Samuel J. Tilden of New York—a man who had worked tirelessly to fight corruption in Tammany Hall. This was the sort of thing Bessie would never understand, as she read no papers and paid little attention whenever her father brought up political subjects. He listened for the tap of her stick to grow muffled in the hallway before he resumed reading where he had left off, shaking his head in despair.

.   .   .

H.M. never expected sales but he had hoped for strong reviews of *Clarel*. These had not come, however. The *New York Times* suggested without a trace of irony that it might have "been written in prose to better effect." The *Independent* referred to his poem as a "vast work in scope and ambition," although they found it "destitute of interest or metrical skill." Indeed, this particular reviewer considered it "more akin to prose than poetry." A critic for *Lippincott's* had not found "six lines of poetry" in the entire epic, adding another sting for good measure: "One has to wonder about the willingness of this author to commit such a work to print." A wit in the *Boston Gazette* had written: "Mr. Melville may be beside himself, but we are not beside him."

And these were the better reviews.

Herman withdrew further into his private world. He believed in the value of *Clarel*, into which he had poured his intelligence and most intimate feelings. It had not the wild freedom of *Leaves of Grass*, nor the momentum of anything Mr. Longfellow might put forth. It was hardly *Paradise Lost* or, for that matter, *In Memoriam*. Yet he had lived deeply in this poem, which amounted to a play of ideas, a fusion of thought and feeling. His thinking about God infused its strenuous stanzas; the various characters occupied positions he could himself occupy on various days, even at various hours. His frustrations in love had been sealed in those halting rough-hewn lines with their yearning. And he had inhabited brave and deeply painful moments of expression, as when he suggested openly that young Clarel sought an emotional, even a physical, connection with Vine, a character modeled closely on Hawthorne.

Duyckinck had once suggested that blank verse might have

been a better medium for his thoughts, pointing to *The Prelude*, Wordsworth's autobiographical epic, but that was foolishness. The restrictions of Herman's chosen form—a halting but rhymed tetrameter—were awkward in the way life itself was awkward. One had to live according to conventions, as these made life possible, mimicking the strictures of his daily routine in New York, this modestly comfortable prison of days wherein he worked and wrote.

Family life had brought few consolations, so he sought comfort or inspiration elsewhere, as when gazing at the minarets and towers of Jerusalem, but he found no solace there. The deserts of the Levant had offered only a mirror to his interior dryness, his desiccation of spirit. He had sought comfort in the affections and attentions of Nathaniel Hawthorne, yet no comfort had come—only pain and frustration. Not even the art and architecture of Rome and Florence had changed him in permanent ways, as he assumed they would.

He envied the Old Testament prophets and John the Baptist. God spoke to them directly, with an unmediated voice. But He had not spoken to Herman, not in unmistakable terms, though He had offered signs and wonders—many signs, many wonders. And H.M. felt increasingly grateful for these.

A decade of uncertainty had followed Malcolm's suicide, though routine work at the Custom House kept him afloat, if barely. He lived by, even worshipped, the clock, welcoming the hourly gong, the tick and tock of habit, the quiet call of duty to which he responded. He rose early most days, unable to sleep past six. He breakfasted quietly, reading a newspaper or two, then walked to the Custom House, where he did a bit of paperwork, patrolled the shoreline, stopped to chat with one or two acquaintances. He wandered home slowly, passing the Gansevoort Hotel on West Street. It pleased him to see his family name on display.

Once, in a fit of personal pride, he entered the hotel and stood at the front desk.

"May I help you, sir?" inquired a young man in a green jacket with brass buttons.

H.M. asked for tobacco papers, and he was duly served. After a moment, he said, offhandedly, "I am wondering, sir, about the name of this hotel."

"Gansevoort?"

Herman nodded.

"I have no idea," the clerk said. "It's an odd name, I think. They should change it."

A middle-aged man on a sofa nearby piped up. "Oh, I know the source. This hotel—and the nearby street bearing the name of Gansevoort—they are called after a rich family who in old times owned a great deal of property hereabouts."

This fellow had obviously never heard of the hero of Fort Stanwix. The name of Gansevoort had passed into history, with all of the usual distortions and simplifications—the noble Dutch appellation a pale elegy to what it signified.

Herman scribbled into his journal that night a Latin phrase that Hawthorne had called to his attention, and it always moved him: *sic transit gloria mundi.*

So passes away the glory of this world.

He began to think of Hawthorne again, his dear and long-dead friend. His death in 1864 had come as a shock. He died so unexpectedly, in the White Mountains of New Hampshire, at a hotel very close to where Herman and Lizzie had gone after their wedding. Herman had not seen Hawthorne since their parting in Liverpool, years before, but he always imagined that they would meet again, and it would be joyous, with tears and frank confessions. He had staggered around Manhattan after dark on the day he learned about his friend's death, resting for a while on a bench in Battery

Park, facing the harbor, with its view to infinity—the Milky Way like a gauzy scarf above him, a reminder of how insignificant all human fears and sad thoughts were in the vast scheme of the universe. The water folded upon itself, deeper than thought. It was May, however, and the apple blossoms in the park left a rich tang in the air. A soft breeze circled, enlarging the scent. H.M. took off a shoe and sock, letting his foot dangle in the cold grass. He pressed it hard against the ground, so wonderfully palpable. Here was the source of his strength, his life. He had no wish, like Emerson, to transcend anything. This was the only sphere where human love flourished, and it was sufficient. Even death changed nothing. He would forgo paradise for this, the good earth.

At home that night, in the early hours before dawn, he lit a lamp over his desk and reread a favorite but lesser story by Hawthorne, "Monsieur du Miroir." The opening sentence stuck in his head, as it seemed to apply to the author of the tale himself: "Than the gentleman above named, there is nobody, in the whole circle of my acquaintance, whom I have more attentively studied, yet of whom I have less real knowledge, beneath the surface which it pleases him to present."

That sentence had haunted H.M. since.

In the margins of the story, he had written in India ink: "He will pass to the dark realm of Nothingness, but will not find me there."

Retired from his job in the Custom House after nineteen years, with its comforting and self-obliterating routines, Herman wondered that his life had come to so little. "I go about my days in a dream," he wrote in his journal, "a sort of lazy, happy-go-lucky, good-for-nothing, loafing, old Lear." The quiet dullness of his days wore on him.

He was sixty-eight now, and had once again had to pay for the publication of his poems—a slender volume called *John Marr and Other Sailors*. The twenty-five copies—that was all he could afford— arrived in three packages, and they sat on his desk in neat piles, bound in delightful mauve-colored boards with gold lettering on the spines. He would send them with polite inscriptions to a few friends and relatives, who would say how glad they were to have this work in hand. If he were lucky, a few reviewers would offer words of notice.

He had become a version of the Maldive shark of his poem— the best single poem in this volume, as he knew. He recited it to himself, sitting in his favorite tavern on Pearl Street, moving his lips without sound:

> About the Shark, phlegmatical one,
> Pale sot of the Maldive sea,
> The sleek little pilot-fish, azure and slim,
> How alert in attendance be.
> From his saw-pit of mouth, from his charnel of maw,
> They have nothing of harm to dread,
> But liquidly glide on his ghastly flank
> Or before his Gorgonian head;
> Or lurk in the port of serrated teeth
> In white triple tiers of glittering gates,
> And there find a haven when peril's abroad,
> An asylum in jaws of the Fates!
> They are friends; and friendly they guide him to prey,
> Yet never partake of the treat—
> Eyes and brains to the dotard lethargic and dull,
> Pale ravener of horrible meat.

He wished he were *more* like this old shark, with a handful of acolytes. He had in fact become a lonelier shark than this idealized creature. Perhaps one day he would discover himself surrounded by pilot fish—a delicious thought. Yet this seemed unlikely in his present state, as he had such a limited readership. He might actually have trouble giving away these pristine copies of *John Marr,* and he could already hear Lizzie and Bessie as they whispered behind his back about "poor dear Father" and his sad literary pretensions.

Poor Father, indeed!

He had become a sorry sight to many in lower Manhattan, an old man wandering the maze of streets by himself, pausing in Fulton Market to leer at salacious postcards, nibbling at oyster bars, drinking pints of ale on Pearl Street. He was easily the oldest man in the tavern this afternoon, and this unsettled him. The young men—most of them sailors—laughed and joked, but he could not share their mirth. He was not part of the crowd, except nominally. Finishing a cigar, he walked outside. This was his place, after all: near the ocean, in Manhattan, his place of birth. This was his version of Ithaca, and he was Odysseus, home at last.

But the comforts of home eluded him.

He paused at the Coenties Slip, a manmade inlet and breakwater. He had written about the slip long ago, in *Redburn,* observing the grim-looking warehouses arranged along the docks, the red-brick warehouses with their rusty iron doors and shutters, the windows like missing teeth, and the gray-tiled roofs. Abandoned anchors, chain cables, and old rigging lay here and there beside the wharves on wooden pilings. As a young man he had admired the sea captains who strolled along these wharves, cigars lit, their faces burned by the sun; he tried hard to listen as they talked among themselves, referring to ports in Havana, Liverpool, Calcutta. They were the true gods of this world.

Some of these men still remembered him—nineteen years in the New York Custom House had guaranteed a place in their minds. They would nod politely as he passed, and he would return the nod.

In conversation, they quickly saw that H.M. knew their world as well as they did. (His knowledge of nautical instruments was extensive—indeed, he had recently acquired from a dealer in London a gimbaled brass compass and sextant, which perched on his writing desk, a reminder of his early years at sea.) He questioned them closely about the latest nautical instruments or asked questions about ports in Brazil and Peru, the Sandwich Islands, San Francisco. He was always eager to hear fresh tales. That he had been a strict inspector of foreign cargoes only added to his reputation on the wharves. He would have made an excellent captain, they often said—a man you could trust in brisk seas, with a storm approaching. Attention to detail of a certain kind could save your life in heavy weather.

Herman was relieved that money no longer posed an obstacle for him, a barrier he must leap and leap again. A number of Lizzie's elderly relatives had died in the past decade, and their bequests had made the Melvilles comfortable if not wealthy. H.M. could forget about earning money. If he so pleased, he could retreat into dreams of youth, memories of travel, so many brilliant passages.

Yet still he woke up in the early morning afraid, startled by the rapidly dissolving days.

Four score and ten, he thought.

That was the span of life, for a lucky man.

Time had turned his beard to frost and made him wobbly on his legs. Some days the thought of death actually comforted him, it being a kind of sleep, devoid of turmoil. Nobody asked much of the dead. Yet the idea of oblivion troubled him. He rarely made it through a day without changing his mind on the matter.

He could feel within him the unfathomable world of spirit, so many lives—past and future—that mingled in a single consciousness for a brief span of decades. He knew he would never die—that question had been settled for some years, since he had learned this truth in a cave near the Dead Sea. He could not die: he felt sure of that. It was simply not possible to kill the soul, which was a compound entity composed of layers, a deep well of being into which the self could drop its bucket, with a rich crash, and draw sustenance, a sweet, cool water.

He disliked most of the preachers he heard through Lizzie, who would drag him to services at the Church of All Souls. The Christian fear of sexuality generally upset him—Saint Paul had not helped in this regard, Herman would say. But he did not want to upset Lizzie, who attended these services with regularity and listened with a good deal of enthusiasm to the Reverend Mr. Theodore Williams, her latest clerical friend and confidant—a handsome but nervous young man with mousy blond hair, a thin mustache, and an Anglican collar. Williams spoke endlessly of right and wrong, and H.M. had amused himself considerably at his expense one afternoon at tea by quoting Emerson: "The only right is what is after my constitution; the only wrong what is against it."

He gave it to Waldo there. The Sage of Concord had once again picked a needle of truth from the proverbial haystack.

Lately he had followed Emerson and his protégé Thoreau to the East, reading in the Hindu scriptures, the Vedas and Upanishads, and much of this made sense to him, especially the idea of a God who lived within the human heart. There was abundance in this tradition, and it granted ease of being to those who could understand its truths. Herman considered the Hindu savant a kind of ideal, with his noble serenity and mindfulness. Hinduism put forward a more impersonal idea of God than that advocated by the Hebrew and Christian Scriptures. The human mind was illimitable, Herman thought. It was sublime in its depths and range. By contrast, the material world was illusory, and one should never put stock in goods acquired by cash.

The tribes of the Levant were desert people whose lives were obliterated by the sun; they would quite naturally bow before the

fire of a monolithic sky god. Herman much preferred the Indian
gods, with their many faces, hands, and feet. He had lately worked
his way through a German thinker, Schopenhauer, who had studied the teachings of Vedanta. "The Indian air surrounds us," he had
written, "the original thoughts of kindred spirits." He had wisely
sought a philosophy that combined ethics and metaphysics. H.M.
wanted his own philosophy to combine a larger view of the universe with a way of acting in the world.

Kindness is all, he said to himself.

But he had been unkind—at various times—to Lizzie and to his
children. He had not given his sisters their due. He had failed to listen, even failed to love. This was a bitter fact that he faced, with
deep remorse, wishing he had behaved otherwise.

A steamer made its way out to sea, into an easeful and opulent
sunset. And the hammered pink and gold of the water entranced
H.M., absorbing everything into its vast surround. He felt another
shift inside him, a log jolting to ash with a sudden and surprising
glow.

A year after Herman retired from the Custom House in 1885,
Stannie died in San Francisco, barely a man at thirty-five, a fellow
with less stability than a tumbleweed. He had been swept hither and
thither, trying his hand at various professions, dying in a state of
despair from a tubercular ailment that no doctor diagnosed to anyone's satisfaction. "Things look up, and I remain hopeful that something will come of my efforts at business," he had written to his
parents only a week before his death.

His efforts had never been sufficient, outstripped by his hopes
in every instance. He had gone to sea, like his father, tried dentistry
and surveying, sold lightning rods and feed for horses. In a land
where entrepreneurial vision was prized above all else, he had—like

most caught in that swirl—drowned in the fast-moving current. The age had gilded only a few, leaving many more to rust.

By 1888, only Bessie remained at home, barely able to walk or dress herself, as her arthritic hands and feet had grown less and less flexible. She had been a dutiful daughter, however—obedient to her father although quietly rebellious behind his back, affecting indifference to his poetry, never admitting to having read his novels (although he had seen *Mardi* on her bedside table). She limped about the house, using a Morocco cane with a Derby handle that had belonged to her grandfather Judge Shaw. She often wept in her room at night—her parents could hear the sobs, however muffled. In summer she spent time with her younger sister, Fanny, and her husband, Henry—a gifted entrepreneur. Bessie would hold Henry's success over her father's head, noting her brother-in-law's accomplishments, the luxuries of his house, and the "stunning sweetness" of his little girls, especially Eleanor, the oldest.

H.M. had also noticed Eleanor's sweetness. In fact, he doted on the little blond girl, who liked to sing. "Sing for your old grandpa," he would say to her.

It was, however, painful to him that most of her songs were hymns. He had grown to dislike hymns, as they reminded him of churchgoing, which increasingly struck him as a chore, a waste of time. Lizzie insisted that he should attend a number of services with her, and he often acquiesced these days. He no longer wished to fight her, especially over trivial matters.

They had settled, in their measure and style, on a kind of truce. She no longer felt afraid of him, and there was nothing to fear. He sought comfort in her mere presence, especially at night.

As Herman prepared to sink wholly out of sight as a writer— *John Marr and Other Sailors* would hardly revive his public face—an enthusiastic reader, an Englishman, raised a loud and thoroughly pleasant voice from the wings. "One must search the pages of the

Elizabethan dramatists to parallel the pages of *Moby-Dick*," the critic,
W. Clark Russell, wrote in a Chicago paper, sending the article to
H.M. in New York. He had previously dedicated *An Ocean
Tragedy*—one of his novels—to Herman, who only learned of this
dedication now. A few years earlier, Russell had written of *Moby-
Dick* in heartfelt terms in London's *Contemporary Review*. It was no
usual novel of the sea, he declared, but "a medley of noble impas-
sioned thoughts born of the deep, pervaded by a grotesque human
interest, owing to the contrast it suggests between the rough realities of the cabin and the forecastle, and the phantasms of men conversing in rich poetry, and strangely moving and acting in that dim
weather-worn Nantucket whaler."

Herman had never lost faith in *Moby-Dick* as a work of unusual
depths and cadences, a poem in prose. It had come as a gift to him
from a loud-voiced muse, and he had written it down as quickly as
his lame hand could manage, working late into the night at Arrowhead. It might take a hundred years for readers to find their way to
its pages, but they would arrive. He felt sure of that as he prepared
to go to sea again, for what he knew would be the last time.

Yes, he was going to sea again, taking a brief respite from winter by visiting Bermuda.

The winter of 1888 had been hideous, with snow billowing in
the streets and sharp winds cutting around the corners of buildings,
finding H.M. wherever he tried to shelter himself. He had been ill
from October onward, suffering from neuralgia, coughing and
wheezing, with frequent chills and fevers. His heart ached, quite literally: the dull pain began somewhere in the cage of his ribs and
radiated, pulsed into his shoulders, at times causing his hands to
seize. His legs grew weak, and he could not glide around Manhattan in the afternoons as usual. This hitch in his routine unsettled
him. He depended on these passages—through layers of ideas and

memories. It was in walking that he found the current of feeling that he identified as soul. He was not an individual in these moments but a communicant of profound energy that he guessed was similar to what Christians and Jews referred to as God. Yet it was not God. God was a crude attempt to humanize what could not fit into human terms, a catchall monosyllable that ill served its grandeur and strangeness.

He found a passage in the fourth chapter of the Bhagavad Gita that made sense in these terms: "You must understand what action is, what wrong action and inaction are as well. The true nature of action is profound, and difficult to fathom. He who can see inaction in the midst of action, and action in the midst of inaction, is wise and can act in the spirit of yoga."

H.M. liked what he considered "the spirit of yoga." The body acts, moving in time; but this is not necessarily the true self. The eternal self was indestructible, outside of time, extraterritorial.

He would take his copy of the Indian scriptures with him on his passage to Bermuda. It was a good companion for an old man on what, he knew, must be a final voyage.

The idea of Bermuda had taken him by surprise. This cluster of islands had been a place of fascination to him for many years, ever since in his youth he read William Strachey's account of being shipwrecked in that haunted, entrancing place, which he assumed had been the setting for Shakespeare's *Tempest*—the last great play by the Bard, which H.M. had recently reread with reverence. He treasured the words of Prospero, the magician, who spoke frankly to his daughter, Miranda, about his troubled mind in old age. On this cell, his island kingdom, he would take long walks—"To still my beating mind," as he put it.

Herman would still his own beating mind in Bermuda.

Now Lizzie said, without conviction, "I should go with you."

"No, dear," he said, "I must go alone."

He pitied his poor wife these days. The death of Stannie had fallen hard upon her, and she had become a loose strand of her former self. He tried to help her through this difficult time, but there was no comforting her. Grief is a lonely country, as he well knew.

"You are not well," Lizzie said.

"I must get away. I'll be fine."

"I'm not sure about travel by sea. It could be difficult."

Herman just smiled. "I'm well enough to visit the Bermudas. But I will never visit the Galápagos again—have no fear. I shall go no more a-whaling."

With trepidation, she bid him goodbye on a raw, clear morning in early March.

The *Orinoco* was a steamship of 1,800 tons owned by a company from Quebec, and H.M. eagerly inspected this impressive vessel, which could make the trip to Hamilton, the main port in Bermuda, in just sixty hours. It had every amenity: large light-filled cabins, well-appointed lounges, and a dining room with silver cutlery, china, linen tablecloths, and waiters in black ties. One could walk the wide decks or lounge in one of several bars or passenger salons among potted plants and capacious leather chairs. Herman had never experienced this degree of luxury aboard ship, and he thought of the contrast with the *Acushnet* and other vessels from his past. The *Meteor* had been comfortable, for a clipper. But this was another world, and the passengers were a civilized crowd, mainly New Yorkers who sought relief from the winter in the balm of Hamilton Harbor, where the temperature rarely dipped to bone-chilling levels.

There was a sunny aft salon where passengers could gather for a game of cards, drink and smoke, or read the newspapers, and it was there on the morning of the second day out that Herman first saw the boy.

He was a waiter.

A handsome boy in his late teens, he was tall and slender, with large hands.

His manner was breezy and fresh. His green–gold eyes—the eyes of a cat—caught Herman's gaze, and he grinned at the elderly gentleman with a grizzly beard and gruff manner.

"May I get you a drink, sir?" he asked.

"I would like that, yes," H.M. said. "A coffee?"

The boy nodded. He soon brought a cup of coffee in a white mug that bore the crest of the *Orinoco*.

"Have you been working aboard this ship for long?" Herman asked.

"Only a few months, sir."

The boy stood for some minutes conversing. In short order, Herman learned that his name was Alexander Swift, and that he was an orphan. He hoped one day to sing in public, and he had studied the piano, the flute, and the guitar at St. Patrick's, a well-known Catholic asylum for boys in Westchester.

Herman said, "I'm not terribly musical, I must say. But I do listen carefully. Every artist wants an audience."

Alexander promised to sing for H.M. one day, then excused himself—he had other passengers with demands. The burly, red-bearded barman watched him grimly, looking for missteps, and Herman could see that the boy felt under pressure.

He simply could not stop watching Alexander as he skipped about the room, waiting on others, pausing to chat, shaking his head in a most fetching way. And he was not alone: all eyes seemed to follow the boy on his rounds. His reedy voice had a high and piping quality. Yet he did not seem weak: not in the least. There was a steely aspect to the boy, perhaps the result of his testing years in an orphanage. That could not have been easy for him.

Captain Garvin stepped into the salon, looking noble in his

white uniform. He was a man of fifty or more, with a well-trimmed
beard and blue eyes. He summoned Alexander to his table, asking
him to sit beside him on a footstool. This was odd, H.M. thought.
A captain rarely socialized with an underling of this kind, a mere
waiter. But they seemed quite engaged in whatever it was that concerned them, and it surprised Herman that the boy had no fear of
his superior, who patted his knee at one point in the most avuncular fashion. The captain laughed at some remark, covering his mouth
to stifle the outburst. For his part, Alexander beamed.

Herman watched the barman, who grimaced as he rinsed
glasses in the sink. Nobody could doubt that he disliked what he
saw. This unconventional mingling of captain and waiter threatened
to upset the apple cart. It was important to maintain hierarchies
aboard a vessel, for any number of good reasons—and this was a
dangerous precedent. Captain Garvin was taking the orphan under
his wing in ways that breached the usual boundaries which kept officers and crew in their separate spheres.

In his cabin that night, smoking by gaslight, Herman thought
only of Alexander Swift. He was convinced he had somehow seen
the boy before, however unlikely that must be. He wrote in his
journal: "What a bright boy—all collateral light. Alexander is the
name. I seem to know him already. Could this be so?"

The next morning H.M. made his way to the salon after breakfast, moving along the starboard deck, nodding to other passengers,
including a well-dressed man in a silk top hat and patent-leather
gloves whom he had met over dinner the night before—a wealthy
merchant. The *Orinoco* was chuffing along at high speed, free of
coastal tides, perhaps a hundred miles or more from New York. The
air was fresh but hardly cutting, and the sun felt almost warm—a
rare day for early March in this part of the Atlantic. Intense light
scalloped the water around the ship—a silvery-blue light—while a

flock of seagulls followed them, eager to consume anything the kitchen staff tossed overboard into the curling wake.

H.M. made his way to the aft salon, where a handful of men smoked and chatted. He took up the same seat as the night before, a club chair of dark leather with brass buttons, ordering a cup of coffee from Alexander, who—much to Herman's delight—was at work this morning. The boy looked even brighter than before, his teeth white and straight, his hair part of the light that streamed into the room through tall windows and honeyed the oak floor. Recalling the way the captain had treated the boy, Herman invited him to sit for a moment. Alexander obliged, although he glanced awkwardly at the barman.

"I wonder if you actually *like* being at sea," H.M. said. It was the only thing he could think to say.

"I like it well enough, yes."

Herman nodded, too eagerly under the circumstances. "How old are you, if I may ask?"

"Eighteen."

This surprised Herman, who thought the boy no more than fifteen or sixteen.

"What do you prefer to do, apart from the music that you mentioned?"

"I read books, when I can."

"What kind of books?"

"Novels, or poetry."

"Poetry?"

"I like Mr. Longfellow very much, especially the one about Hiawatha."

Although Herman found the poem about Hiawatha an insufferable piece of doggerel, it pleased him that the boy liked poetry; he rarely encountered readers of verse among the young.

"I have written some poems," H.M. said, tentative.

"Oh, I'd like very much to read them, sir!"

"In which case, I will send you a book when I return to New York. I will sign it for you, if I may have your name and, of course, an address."

Herman felt embarrassed to ask for this, pulling a compact note-book from his breast pocket. He handed the boy a pencil and watched as the young man wrote his name, using his left hand, in a rather ornate style, with considerable flourish. His postal address was still St. Patrick's Orphanage for Boys in Westchester—a fact that sur-prised and saddened Herman. He had imagined that the boy lived in a boardinghouse in lower Manhattan, where he might visit him on his walks. They might sit together in the summer on a bench in Washington Square and read poems aloud.

After he finished his coffee, Herman returned to his cabin, where he sat back in his bunk and thought, for a while, about the case of his older cousin Guert Gansevoort, who in 1842 had been involved in a notorious mutiny aboard the *Somers*, a U.S. brig. The captain had sentenced three men to death by hanging—one of them a little fellow by the name of Elisha Small, who had cried out from the gallows: "God bless that flag!" Herman had been trying to write a ballad about this tragedy, but it had failed to cohere. Now, with Alexander Swift so presently in mind, he began to write, almost involuntarily. A story loomed in a hazy light, and yet Herman found the sentences following one upon the other quickly. This was a con-genial feeling he had almost forgotten, the sense of being borne aloft by a narrative. Now the name of a character floated into his head: William Budd. His story—in the roughest draft—began:

In the years before the advent of steamships, perhaps more fre-quently than nowadays, a walker along the docks of any port might have his attention caught by a group of mariners or merchant-sailors ashore on liberty. In certain instances they would flank, or, like a bodyguard, quite surround some superior figure of their own class, moving along with them like Aldebaran among the lesser lights of his constellation. That shimmering object was in this case a "Handsome Sailor." With no trace of pride about him, rather with the offhand unaffectedness of natural regality, he seemed to accept the spontaneous homage of his shipmates.

William Budd was the boy, this handsome sailor.

H.M. crossed out William. Billy made better sense here. Billy Budd, the handsome sailor.

Was this perhaps the boy who stepped out of a cave in the Holy Land?

He often thought he must have imagined that experience, had never actually left the camp that morning while others in his party slept. But he knew he had gone off by himself. He spoke about his adventure soon thereafter with a member of the party, although he never mentioned the shepherd boy or the cave. At times he woke to that voice, the soft lilt, a lovely echoing sound in the blue grotto of memory. It brought tears to his eyes, with its heartbreaking innocence—the idea of a boy on the brink of manhood, hovering between worlds, still buoyed by the brightness of childhood, unaware of the darkness on the other side.

When he had finished his initial bout of writing—he filled perhaps ten pages in his journal in a closely cropped hand—Herman poured himself a tumbler of whiskey to celebrate. It was midday, well before lunch, but he could use a drink now. Soon his head spun, and he lay back in his wide berth, feeling the slight roll of the ship—a gentle rocking motion that comforted him, easing him to sleep. When he woke, it was already dusk. He had missed lunch and dinner both, but he felt no hunger.

In haste, he made his way back to the aft salon, drawn there with a peculiar urgency.

He found Alexander Swift in open battle with the bartender. They spoke in harsh tones about some infraction on the boy's part.

H.M. took a chair nearby and listened, afraid for Alexander.

All ears and eyes were upon the two of them as they argued, standing behind the bar.

"Ain't got no right!" the bartender shouted. "This is a ship, fella. You do as you're told!"

Alexander glanced toward H.M. with a sheepish smile.

"Do you mock me, Swift? Is that so?"

"I do not mock anyone."

"What's that?"

Alexander replied in a clear voice, his vocal cords strained by the elevation in volume. His lips quivered, signaling fear, but he would not back down. "What I find amusing is not your business."

"Everything in this room is my business," said the bartender.

"I don't think so."

Herman realized the two of them had engaged upon a collision course. It would be impossible to stop them, and this could only conclude badly for the boy. The jaw of the bartender was tightly clenched, his face a blast of tomato-red. His red beard, too, was aflame.

"You're a scoundrel!" he cried. "The captain will hear about you, he will!"

"I will speak to the captain myself," Alexander said, without raising his voice, although everyone in the room heard him distinctly. He made sure of that.

The stocky bartender and the slim waiter stood face-to-face, only inches apart.

"The captain can't help you here, boy."

"The captain is my friend."

At this, the bartender drew back his hand, closing his fist into a white ball of fury. There was no doubt he would hit the boy hard. The tendons of his neck stood out like steel cables, and he sucked in a breath, coiling to spring.

But this boy had spent long enough in the predatory rough-and-tumble of an orphanage to understand the physical language of combat. Before his opponent could punch, he picked up a water glass and flung it brutally into the man's face. It shattered against his forehead, where a wound opened like a wide smile. A blood-bright curtain dropped, more ghastly in appearance than severity. But the barman was certainly hurt, and he fell to the floor in pain and shock, groaning. Another waiter hurried to press a cloth against the wound and call for a doctor.

H.M. suddenly recalled the name of Luther Fox, a young sailor he had heard about decades ago, in Hawaii. The poor fellow had lashed out with a knife, killing a shipmate—an impulsive gesture for which he hung.

As luck would have it, the captain stepped into the salon as if summoned by the squabble. At a glance he understood what had transpired, looking sadly at Alexander Swift.

It was as if the script had been written in advance, and there could be no alternate version.

Herman rose, unstable, unable to breathe, with his chest tight. What he needed badly was air, and he lurched toward the door, onto the deck. The sea reeled beneath the ship, tilting its vastness. H.M. looked toward the horizon—a pink-vermillion haze—but it could not be found, as the sea and sky had sealed it, a luminous glow as the *Orinoco* cut through blue-and-black water, pushing the crumpled sea ahead without pause, a low slush about the hull. He breathed deeply and could smell the bitter smoke from the stacks, with flakes of ash trailing, and he realized that he missed the old days of sailing, the ship almost willowy and hesitant, responsive to winds and weathers—not this hard, unthinking, mechanical drive toward a goal or destination, so typical of the age itself.

This was the new world, H.M. told himself. It was all push and compulsion. Scruple and indecision would be swept aside.

Herman held to the rail for balance, for dear life itself. His heart went out to Alexander, the handsome boy who would surely lose his job, his place in the world, perhaps even his liberty. It was a clear case of assault he had witnessed, however involuntary and provoked. The event brought to mind an earlier passage by sea, when as a green boy Herman had crossed the Atlantic and befriended Billy Hamilton, who had lashed out at Robert Jackson—an instinctive response to a lewd suggestion. The punch had toppled Jackson, but in those days one could get away with such a thing. Sailors often fought among themselves, usually out of the captain's sight. They were rarely punished, unless an officer was struck.

"Good sir," a voice came.

Alexander Swift glided toward him, himself a light source, his face aglow.

"My dear boy," said Herman, reaching a hand toward him.

The young man accepted the hand. He held it firmly.

"It wasn't your fault," H.M. said to him. "That man, the bartender . . ." He sputtered into silence.

Alexander spoke coolly: "I shall lose my job. I may even go to jail."

"Not that! I don't think so. You did nothing worth prosecution, dear boy. I will defend you!"

"Are you a lawyer?"

"No, but I have friends in New York who are lawyers. My brother will help you." He seemed to fumble for words. "I know a number of good people who will be glad to help."

"The captain has ordered me below. I'm to remain there for the duration of the passage. He says he will personally take me to the police station in Hamilton. I have assaulted a man."

"He should not do this!"

"Oh, but he is right. The captain is a fair man."

H.M. was startled by this easy acceptance of the captain's role in this matter. Alexander understood that Garvin must abide by the law, pushing away personal feelings. Nevertheless, this was not a simple case. There was rarely such a thing when a fight erupted between two men.

"Is the barman all right?"

With a bemused look, Alexander said, "He will not die. At least I don't think so."

"He bled like a pig."

"And the doctor will stitch him," the boy said. "That is why there is a ship's surgeon."

"You acted in self-defense. I shall testify to that end!"

"Your view is one view."

"But every view is single." Herman grew agitated as he spoke. "I won't let this stand!"

"You must not trouble yourself over me, sir."

"But I must. I will. Let me help you."

Alexander drew close to Herman, and they stood within inches, so close that Herman could smell the boy's breath. Quite unexpectedly, the young man—taller than Herman by an inch or two—kissed him on the forehead.

Hot tears filled the older man's eyes, and he trembled.

"I do appreciate your kindness," Alexander said. "It means a good deal."

"I intend to help."

"It's a good and well-intentioned thought, but there is nothing to be done."

He said that with a sad but sweet finality, as if Fate could not be gainsaid or countermanded.

Leaving Herman at the railing, he withdrew into the deepening twilight, which folded him into its shade.

Herman wept profusely. He could not explain the depth of his feeling for this peculiar and defiant boy, but he knew he wept not only for Alexander Swift but for John Troy and Toby Greene, for Eli Fly and Billy Hamilton, even for himself—the quaking boy who stood outside the bedroom of his dying father and felt a whole world of possibility slipping way from him. Yes, he wept for him as well.

Towards the end he sailed into an extraordinary
  mildness,
And anchored in his home and reached his wife
And rode within the harbour of her hand,
And went across each morning to an office
As though his occupation were another island.

W. H. Auden, "Herman Melville"

LIZZIE

17.

When he came home from the Bermudas, Herman was ablaze like coals in the grate that crumble upon themselves and break into fresh light. He was still old and ill—his skin like rice paper, his gait unstable—and I knew his heart would give out before long, as he paused on each step for several moments to breathe deeply, in evident pain. But he had accomplished something on this recent voyage. That was evident in his demeanor.

"There is a new tale, perhaps a short novel," he said, as he lay on the bed in his underwear and socks. He smoked a cigar consumed by its own whiteness, a fragile version of itself, its ashes still holding true to form, at least for a brief while to come—not unlike a man in old age.

I was impatient and, unlike myself, pressed for the details. It had been many years, even decades, since he had shown such urgency about his writing.

"It concerns a handsome sailor, Billy Budd by name. He strikes a man, kills him. It's as if he cannot help himself. But he is made to hang for this deed by a benevolent captain."

"Not so benevolent," I said.

H.M. sighed, as if I were a child who had failed to listen properly. "The captain loves Billy very much, and he regrets having to kill the young fellow in this way. Of course he has no choice."

"Of course," I said.

"Did Abraham have a choice, with Isaac?"

"Rather conveniently," I said, "God intervened."

"Not in this case. God does not interfere when there is a question of *human* justice."

He seemed innocent and self-delighting, a man I thought I had lost so long ago.

"But I shall need your help, Lizzie," he said.

I looked at him quizzically. This was an unusual request . . . from him. I had, of course, copied his manuscripts in the old days at Arrowhead. But I could hardly remember what that felt like, as time erodes such impressions.

"The manuscript is just fragments. I must somehow pull it together. If I can manage this, I shall go happily."

"Go where?"

"Hoboken," he said. "Isn't that where we all go when we die?"

He had, indeed, taken to visiting our daughter and grandchildren in New Jersey—mostly because he enjoyed the ferry ride. He could spend whole days crossing the Hudson, going back and forth, aimlessly. He insisted on calling it the Styx.

"If only my beloved mother had not held me by the heel when she dipped me into that water, I would be immortal," he said.

"You *are* immortal, Herman."

I said that only to tease him, but as I uttered the phrase I wondered if I had stumbled upon some truth. Lately a number of critics had rediscovered my husband's early books, and one or two had suggested that *The Whale* might well find an audience in years to come. It seemed entirely possible, though I still wished he had not included so much information about the whaling industry.

Most nights now, before sleeping, he asked me to read to him, as his eyes could not bear it. I would intone long passages from Homer, in Chapman's translation. "Chapman," he said, "is so luxurious." I had come to know the wanderings of Ulysses quite well in this version. As his hearing was also less than perfect, I found myself repeating everything twice or three times—not such a bad thing when it came to Homer.

In the mornings he worked on his story of the handsome sailor with a strange vengeance, right through the hot summer of 1889. He wrote in the cool of the bedroom above the front parlor, sitting in the red leather chair that had belonged to my father. His mahogany desk centered the room, heavily bearing up buckram and gilt volumes on four shelves. A shelf behind him was full of objects from his travels, such as an olive-wood cross with Hebrew lettering that he had brought back from the Holy Land years ago. There were prints and bronzes, and a favorite picture by Claude Lorrain. The desk itself he piled with books, many of them histories of the Napoleonic Wars—the period when his tale was set. He ransacked these tomes (never borrowed from a library but purchased at my expense from John Anderson, the pretentious bookseller on Nassau Street), scouring them without mercy, culling phrases, noting dates, or drawing lines under key passages.

He hovered over his ragged manuscript for hours at a time, holding the pages close to read them with a magnifying glass, aimlessly munching dates and figs kept in a small bag in the top left drawer. (Our little granddaughters—Eleanor and Fanny—adored these morsels, and would approach him gingerly whenever they came for a visit, hoping for a treat.) I tried my best to help him, pinning new paragraphs to the bottom of a page, making clean drafts

of difficult passages so he could see what he had done. It was sometimes impossible to know what he meant, and I didn't dare inquire
too closely, as questions tried his temper. Yet I could usually read
his intentions, silently correcting errors, smoothing sentences,
adding the occasional adjective or adverb. He was always pleased to
discover freshly recopied passages on the desk after breakfast.

"Oh Lizzie," he would say, "you *are* a miracle."

I had never been a miracle before, so this was a shift—a very
pleasing shift.

The most important thing at present was that, after two or three
lost decades, my husband had written a sublime piece of fiction. I
could not get the story from my head, and I knew—I knew this in
my bones—that Herman's life of writing had paid off. This was an
immortal tale, and I wished only for him to live to see the manuscript take its final shape.

Given his precarious health, he should not have set a foot in the
streets, but ritual prevailed. In the afternoons he left the house, taking a horse car down Broadway, as in the days when he went to the
Custom House. His uncertain steps still took him everywhere on
the island, often in the direction of Central Park. He would linger
in its rural byways, eating a bread roll with cheese by the lower
reservoir (where he liked the turtles—he said he wished to come
back after death as a turtle because they carried their home with
them in the water and could not easily be attacked because of their
hard shell). He might stop in the Sheep Meadow to watch the animals graze. Once in a while he made his way to Riverside Park,
going for "a walk in the country," as he put it.

It amazed me how far he ambled in his decrepitude. I got
"sightings" of Herman from friends in far-flung districts of the city.
Sometimes he arrived home impossibly late for dinner, rarely bothering to apologize or seeming to require further sustenance. I

assumed he had stopped for oysters or sausages at a tavern. Indeed, once I passed a bar on Broadway and saw my husband hammering away in his usual fashion at a crab, trying to break through the shell. (His manners always had appalled Bessie, who complained that her father had never lost the manners of the ship's mess hall.)

Now and then he would take Eleanor with him for a walk on Sunday afternoons. Once he took five-year-old Fanny, with her blond curls like corkscrews, for such an excursion, and it proved disastrous. I had worried when Herman failed to carry an umbrella, as thunderheads had pushed in from the west. The rain started about four, with zigzag lightning and lashing winds. He returned rather promptly—but alone! He stood in the front hall in his wet garments, wiping his forehead with a damp handkerchief. His hoary beard glistened, and he stooped to untie his shoes, breathing like a bull, gasping for air.

"Where is she?" I asked.

My son-in-law stepped into the hall from the parlor.

"Ah, Henry," said Herman, innocently. "How are you?"

"Where is Fanny?" Henry demanded. He had come to collect her in a cabriolet, which stood in the road. I could sense a panic in his voice.

"What do you say?" Herman wondered.

"My daughter!" Henry replied. "Why is she not with you?"

I felt sorry for H.M., as he grew quite agitated, moaning in a sad, low voice. He had somehow lost track of her.

Henry shouted now, "Where did you take her?"

"Madison Park," he said. "There is a bench under a big chestnut tree, with a shelter. She will not get terribly wet, I assure you."

Henry shook his head in disbelief and leaped off, slamming the door behind him.

He didn't find her, the poor, distraught fellow; but a nice young policeman appeared in due course with the little girl in tow. She was eating a piece of candy and seemed thoroughly at ease with the officer.

"Grandfather!" she cried, when she saw Herman.

He scooped her into his arms and kissed her wet curls. "I am so glad to see you, my girl!"

The policeman explained that the little girl had remembered where her grandfather lived, more or less. They had walked around for nearly an hour until she found the right house, with its yellow door and potted geraniums on the stoop.

"Ah, the yellow door!" said Herman. "She always liked that door. A cheerful portal."

Her father returned an hour or so later, much the worse for wear. I explained to him that all was well. Fanny had gone to sleep upstairs in Malcolm's bedroom, and her grandfather, too, had taken to his bed. Herman was quite unnerved by what had happened, and had no wish to confront Henry Thomas, who had a fierce side to him.

"He is lucky I am a patient man," my husband said before going to sleep that night.

As ever, he would frame a situation to his advantage.

This was not the only instance of his forgetfulness, but it was the most egregious and one he would not live down. But Herman had little time to fret about such things, as the end of life approached. Anyone could see that. He would suddenly go abstract, his eyes glazing over. When he was taken by one of his periodic spells, his eyes seemed actually to roll back into his head. Toward the end, Dr. Perkins became a frequent visitor in his long black coat, as did our dear friend Mr. Williams, the minister of All Souls.

Mr. Williams was a fine young man who offered prayers and consolation, and Herman took communion from him without hesitation, saying he had "never turned down a meal in his life."

Mr. Williams could not quite understand my husband's humor, which took a little getting used to, with its wryness.

H.M. had become sentimental lately—a surprising turn for him—and often wept over the daguerreotypes of Malcolm and Stannie that we kept on a table by the bed. Increasingly he wanted, even needed, to talk about the boys, remembering the golden days at Arrowhead. "Barney liked to pick berries," he would say of Malcolm, using the old nickname from childhood. He seemed able to recall conversations with his sons almost by rote, and this delighted us both.

He began, in fact, to speak of dear Malcolm more frequently, in softer tones, as if an old love had been refreshed, as if Malcolm were somehow alive and present in our lives. I did not understand this, but it gave me joy. I was not myself well—an arthritic condition had settled in my knees and hands, and I struggled to get through my days. But there was finally a sense that old wounds in our marriage, in our lives, had healed over. I could not begin to account for this turn, except to believe that God answers prayers.

For his part, Herman had to accommodate increasing quantities of debilitation during the last two years of his life, when his enlarged heart brought his long walks to a halt. He ventured out less and less into the city streets, and I noticed that he took each step deliberately as he climbed the staircase to bed, a little earlier each night. He often drew a blank stare at dinner—sucking a breath suddenly, the cords of his neck would tighten like steel cables.

"Are you all right?" I would ask.

He would insist all was well. He was just fine. It was only a digestive problem. "Do not fuss," he would say.

But on the twenty-seventh of September in 1891 he could not get out of bed. He lay there, grunting. Sweat formed on his brow like sickly dew. He asked for Dr. Perkins, who wore gold-rimmed spectacles on the end of his long, slender nose and whose shoulder blades stuck out like wings under his pale jacket.

"You must be sure to take your medicine," Dr. Perkins said, adopting a fatherly tone that hardly suited a man of his tender age— I guessed he was not quite thirty.

"Oh, I shall take anything you wish to give me, dear boy," H.M. said, touching his hand.

Herman had a soft spot for any young man, especially a gentle one.

On the afternoon of the twenty-eighth, Herman's chest pains grew dramatically worse, and I gave him a dose of amyl nitrate powders. It seemed to have little effect, however.

"The doctor should come again," he said, in a whisper.

Bessie sent for him, while I remained at Herman's side.

Soon enough, Dr. Perkins arrived with his medical bag and concerned look, taking up a chair by the bed. Fanny arrived later that day, kissing her father on his damp forehead. Bessie, as ever, hovered anxiously. Mr. Williams was there, too, standing at the foot of the bed, holding a prayer book.

Herman smiled to see us gather. "A death watch!" he cried, bemused by the number of onlookers.

"You are not so badly off," said the doctor, listening to my husband's heart. "It's still ticking."

I made further inquiries, but the doctor silenced me, putting a hand on my wrist.

"Your husband will feel better in the morning," Dr. Perkins said. "We should let him sleep."

It did look as though the crisis had passed, so Fanny and Bessie went to bed, and Dr. Perkins returned to his family.

At once I got into bed with Herman, who kissed me fondly on the forehead, as he had not done in many years. "You are a dear girl, Lizzie," he said. "I'm so glad, so very glad, that you married me. I was an unlikely suitor."

"An unlikely husband," I said. "My friends were surprised that I would marry you."

"I failed you miserably," he said.

"You did not."

"I did."

"All right, you did," I said.

"The story of Billy Budd, it's quite good, you see. I hope you may piece it together. I've left rather a hodgepodge."

"It's your best work," I told him. "A masterpiece. I feel quite sure of this."

He grunted, and I took this for approval.

"I could have used another few months," he said.

"And you will have them," I insisted.

But I didn't believe what I said. I could feel the force of life as it slipped away from him. He had entered into a dark passage, and it would take him away from me forever.

"I cannot die," he said.

"You won't."

"No, my body—it will die. One can hardly control nature, not in that aspect. One should never attempt such a thing! We may obey nature, that's all."

"I don't want you to leave me," I said.

He looked at me with complete love, and he said, "I'll be here, my Lizzie. I swear it."

I admired this certainty, which offered a degree of comfort. He had followed me to services at All Souls, now and then, and feigned a belief in the creed. And yet his faith was deeper, and so much stranger, than anything Mr. Williams would understand. I didn't myself understand it, but I knew he had a wonderful and wild faith in the operations of nature. He was not unhappy about the fate that loomed.

I fell asleep around midnight, waking half an hour later, and I knew at once that Herman was no longer present in the body.

"Herman!" I whispered loudly.

I kissed him on the lips, which had not turned cold, not yet. But no breath came, and he was not in pain.

He slept like a child, and I made no attempt to wake him.

And I knew in the bottom of my soul that he would live forever, as he said he would.

That was quite true, I told myself, with a growing sense of comfort in the midst of wild grief.

Herman Melville would live forever.

The most mighty of nature's laws is this, that out of Death she brings Life.

H.M., *Pierre*

ACKNOWLEDGMENTS

This is a novel, not a literary biography. In other words, I made up many things, shifted events to suit my narrative purposes, and invented dialogue, as well as certain letters and journal entries. Nevertheless, I have stuck to the essential facts of Melville's life and circumstances. So, for instance, if I say that Melville took a steamer to England in 1856, he will have done so. But there are places where a conventional biographer cannot go, and for this we have fiction.

Needless to say, I've drawn on countless books and articles on Melville in the course of writing this novel. Primary among them was *The Melville Log: A Documentary Life of Herman Melville, 1819–1891*, edited by Jay Leyda. This vast compendium in two volumes, published in 1951, brings together a wealth of source material, as does Hershel Parker's two-volume biography (1996, 2002). Nobody has assembled more raw data about Melville than Professor Parker in this monumental work. I have also made use of biographies and critical studies by a wide range of scholars, including Andrew Delbanco, Laurie Roberston-Lorant, and Elizabeth Hardwick. One of the classic books on Melville that I found especially useful was

Newton Arvin's *Herman Melville* (1950), among the first substantial studies to note the homoerotic aspects of this author. In thinking about the "gay" Melville I referred often to *Hawthorne and Melville: Writing a Relationship* (2008), edited by Jana L. Argersinger and Leland S. Person. I'm also grateful to James Creech for his excellent work on Melville's homoerotic side in *Closet Writing/Gay Reading: The Case of Melville's "Pierre"* (1993).

I wish to acknowledge that I seeded this text with words and phrases drawn from the writings of Melville himself. That was part of the fun of writing this novel. I should add that very little is known about Lizzie Melville, so I made her up.

As ever, I relied on a circle of friends to read and critique this work at various stages. In particular, I want to acknowledge the help of Gerald Howard, my editor, who first put the idea for this book into my head. His friendship and deep knowledge of the subject have been invaluable to me. I should also thank my longtime agent and friend, Geri Thoma. Charles Baker, George Cotkin, and Mark Dunphy have also been helpful, reading the manuscript in rough draft and offering suggestions that proved invaluable. I am grateful for their help.